P9-CIW-476

EX LIBRIS
Gladys Wingled

STRAY KAT WALTZ

Also by Karen Kijewski

KAT SCRATCH FEVER

HONKY TONK KAT

ALLEY KAT BLUES

WILD KAT

COPY KAT

KAT'S CRADLE

KATAPULT

KATWALK

STRAY KAT WALTZ

KAREN KIJEWSKI

G. P. PUTNAM'S SONS NEW YORK

G. P. Putnam's Sons
Publishers Since 1838
a member of
Penguin Putnam Inc.
200 Madison Avenue
New York, NY 10016

Published simultaneously in Canada

Library of Congress Cataloging-in-Publication Data

Kijewski, Karen.
Stray Kat waltz / Karen Kijewski.
p. cm.
ISBN 0-399-14368-8 (acid-free paper)
I. Title.
PS3561.I364S77 1998 97-46986 CIP
813'.54—dc21

Printed in the United States of America
1 3 5 7 9 10 8 6 4 2

This book is printed on acid-free paper. ♾

Book design by Ellen Cipriano

For my husband Tom

I've seen too many old movies not to know what it meant. You remember the ones . . .

The woman was young and beautiful but a little sad and wistful, bravely so. She was in the kitchen baking or doing the dishes when the doorbell rang. As she walked to the door she wiped her hands on her apron and brushed a curling tendril of hair off her forehead. Passing through the living room, her step faltered slightly, her eyes lingered on the ornate silver-framed photo of a man, young, handsome, and in uniform. A smile fleetingly crossed her lips, tugged at our hearts.

She opened the door to a man in uniform, older, reserved, serious, with his hat in his hands and sadness in his eyes.

I opened the door to Davis, Hank's partner.

"No. *Oh God,* no!"

"Katy, I'm so sorry."

"You're here to surprise me . . . for my birthday . . . or Valentine's Day . . . or . . ."

He held out his arms.

He was here because Hank was dead.

CHAPTER 1

Her eyes were large, smudged and bruised-looking in the way that frightens me. Her voice was soft, honeycombed with desperation. She had walked into my office without knocking, without invitation. And she was unwelcome.

"I'm sorry." I spoke politely, woodenly. "The office is closed."

"You must help me. You must. You're all I have."

"I'm sorry," I said. I was all I had too, and there wasn't much of me at the moment. Not enough to go around.

"My husband's going to kill me. The question is not maybe but when." The smudge around her eyes got deeper, more bruised and purple, like torn and crushed grapes.

"Go to the district attorney's office and get a restraining order. Go to the police. They are committed to stopping domestic violence; they will help you." Mechanical words.

"It won't work." The deadness in her voice threaded through the honeycomb of desperation. There was no light or life in the eyes ringed in bruised purple. "I can't run; I can't hide. He will find me no matter what I do."

"The police will help you."

Outside, sirens screamed. We listened in silence that she finally broke.

"No." A soft sigh that seemed to have neither beginning nor end trailed off into tomorrow and days after. "No, my husband is the police."

An image of Hank overwhelmed me. And then loss. I missed her next words, heard only the end.

"I have run before and he has always found me. He will kill me. Soon."

"I can't help you. Please go."

Her eyes held mine for a long time. "I'll be back." The words were quiet. The desperation was still there.

In the bathroom I splashed cold water on my face.

My eyes were large, smudged and bruised-looking in the way that frightens me.

I too was fighting for my life.

CHAPTER 2

The alley behind my midtown Sacramento office was empty, as it usually is in the evening. There are occasional parked cars, garbage cans, and *No Trespassing—This Means You!* signs, but no streetlights. A dog barked lethargically and then the barks drifted off into a bored whine. I thought I heard an owl and froze briefly in the fleeting moments of evening silence. Nothing. Several blocks away a car alarm went off. Business as usual. I unlocked my Bronco and climbed in.

It was a whisper, nothing more, a small sound easily ignored.

Always check the back seat.

Instant rewind. A heartbeat. I was almost out of the Bronco.

Take no chances.

A hairy well-muscled arm around my neck pulled me back and against the headrest into a choke hold.

Never let your guard down.

"I've got a gun. It would be a mistake to fight me." The voice was a harsh whisper, the breath hot on my cheek, the smell of aftershave in my nose. *The taste of fear in my mouth.* The cold metal of the gun, the barrel resting against my cheek.

Don't lose your head.

"Where is she?" The harsh whisper.

"Who?"

"Sara. I know you're hiding her."

"I don't know any Saras." *Stall for time. One person walking down the alley, a police car on patrol. Hey, I wasn't picky, a pimp or drug dealer was fine.* "Unless you mean my cousin in Maine? *That* Sara? Oh, and Sara Lee of course, I *love* her cakes. How about you? What's your favorite?"

"Fucking with me would be a big mistake." His voice was ugly, discordant. The pressure on my neck tightened. "Sara Bernard came to your office two days ago. I want to know where she is and you are going to tell me." He said it with a note of dark finality. Done deal. Dead PIs were nothing to him, *nothing,* his tone said—all in a day's work.

Sara Bernard, the one who said her husband was going to kill her? It had to be. "A woman came to my office two days ago but I don't know her name. I know nothing about her."

"You're going to tell me where she is."

"I don't know."

He laughed. Unpleasantly. "There's an easy way to do this and a hard way. Give me the car keys."

Have it out right there, the cops tell you. Don't let them take you someplace; it only gets worse. Fast.

"Hey, pal." *I exaggerated wildly on the pal part.* "There's a guy over there walking his dog. He can see the gun. Bad news. *Every*one's got a cell phone these days." My voice was easy, conversational.

The gun slipped away from my cheek, the pressure on my neck eased. I stabbed his forearm with the car key. Hard. Slammed against the door and rolled, hitting the ground with my shoulder. The first bullet ricocheted off the pavement next to me. That's when I scrabbled under the Bronco. And lost the car keys. Damn. Damn. *Damn!*

I was on my own.

There was no one walking a dog. I'd lied. The second shot slammed through my consciousness. Then another slam. The car door. The starter turned over, died. I scrambled, slithered frantically. If I stayed where I was would my body clear the muffler? Would I drag? Asphalt, gravel, broken glass, digging into my hands and chin; visions of me hooked onto the Bronco and dragging digging into my imagination. The starter again. My head and shoulders cleared the Bronco on the passenger side. I dug my elbows in. Hauled. Tucked my knees up. Rolled. The starter caught.

More gravel and glass in my face. Brake lights. The screech of tires. And then silence. I thanked my lucky stars that I hadn't gotten around to the tune-up that the Bronco was way overdue for. For once procrastination had paid off. Big time. The blood on my lip was salty, ugly-tasting. But I was alive, and I wasn't dragging.

The night was cold with bright sparkly stars. The promise of spring and the smell of winter woodsmoke were in the air. The daffodils had been up this morning, yellow and white and dancing in the soft breezes and lacy sunshine. Stars sparkled and then misted in the blood and pain and relief that drenched me. It was, I realized, the first time in days that I had felt anything but grief and the loss of Hank.

"You okay down there?" a gruff voice called out from the second story of the alley building in the midtown area that is both residential and business.

"Please call the police." I had to say it twice. The first time it came out whispery and hoarse. Bruised vocal cords and the residue of fear. Above me the window slammed shut.

I lay there staring at the stars trying to breathe right and wondering if everything on me still worked. I heard the sound of steps before I heard the voice.

"Don't you worry none. It's just me. I called the coppers and they're on the way over." A tall, impossibly skinny figure wobbled into my upside-down view. He was seventy-five, easy, with a blanket in one hand and a baseball bat in the other. "I thought of bringing you some coffee, brandy woulda been smarter yet, but I figured we was better off with Ole Trusty here." He swung the baseball bat expertly.

I grinned, then winced. Cut on my lip. "Thank you." I could hear the sirens now.

"You want I should drop this blanket on you?"

I thought about sitting up. Lying here was easy, but cold. Getting up was inevitable, but difficult, as I couldn't brace myself on hands, knees, or elbows. Everything was banged up and bruised, or cut and bloody. I made it to a sitting position, finally, and he dropped the blanket on my shoulders.

"Name's Harv. You?"

"Kat."

"Yeah? Reckon you just lost a couple of those nine lives. Heh heh." He grunted at his own joke.

I tried to smile but it was too hard. The sirens were very loud now. A black-and-white sailed around the corner and stopped ten or fifteen yards from us. Then another. I blinked stupidly in the lights. Harv waved the baseball bat at them and jumped up and down. Big night for him, I guess. He especially liked the run down the alley and the drawn guns. I was okay with it too. Good guys with guns are a lot more attractive than bad guys with guns.

"Gol dang, this is just like that TV show, *Nine-one-one*!" Harv started to sing a song about bad boys bad boys. The cops looked us over—the harmless and the pathetic—and put away their guns.

"You okay, miss? Jerry, better call an ambulance."

"No," I protested. Took me two tries again. Jeez. "I'll be all right."

He looked doubtful. "You don't look so great."

Arguing with that was pointless. "Can I get a hand up? Please."

He nodded, reached down, hands under my arms, picked me up effortlessly and planted me solidly on the ground. I didn't wobble all that much. He steadied me. He was not much taller than I but obviously worked out. The dark eyes and hair indicated an Asian heritage. His face was in semidarkness. "What happened?"

I told them, everything but Sara's last name.

"You get the plate on the vehicle, miss?" This was Jerry, the other cop, a nice guy but not, as my grandmother Alma would say, a firecracker in the brains department.

His partner, Sam, the one who had picked me up, closed his eyes briefly and shook his head. "It was her car, Jer."

"Oh, yeah."

I gave them the license plate number. "Do you know an officer with the last name of Bernard?"

"Jed Bernard, sure."

"A patrol officer?"

"They kick him upstairs, Sam? He a detective now?"

Sam nodded. In the glare from the patrol car lights his eyes were curious. "You know him?"

I shook my head. "Just heard his name somewhere. Just wondering. Does he work nights?"

"No. Not regularly, anyway." The curious in his eyes deepened.

"Hey, Kat, is this yours?" Harv walked out of the darkness into the lights of the patrol cars carrying a flattened shoulder bag with a broken buckle and muddy tire tread markings.

"Yes." I breathed out in relief. One less thing to worry about.

The cops finished writing up their report, then left me with Harv, who let me use his phone and wash my face. He made me coffee too, though I disappointed him by refusing to have a slug of brandy in it. So he had one for each of us. Three calls: to the locksmith, who does more work for me than I would wish; to Rafe—my friend who is a swell, and tough, guy with a Dirty Harry kind of attitude—so that he would watch my house until the locksmith got there; and to Charity, my best friend, to come get me. I was hurting pretty badly by then.

Charity didn't say a thing—not about my job, or my torn-up face and hands, or my stolen car—just scooted me out of Harv's apartment and into her 4Runner. Harv made me promise I'd come back and visit. I made him promise he'd leave his baseball bat in the corner. Which made him grin. And then I slept the forty minutes out to Charity's ranch.

I'd been having kind of a tough time lately.

Gol dang, as Harv would say.

CHAPTER 3

Dear Charity,
My boyfriend ran off with another girl. She got pregnant so he said he was going to marry her, but then he said it wasn't his, so I took him back. But he left again. He said he needed more fun, excitement and good times. Oh, and he took all my money so I couldn't make the rent or gas bill or anything which was pretty embarrassing! Now he wants to come back and I'm not sure what to do. When he's not drinking or doing drugs he can be a lot of fun. And he has a tattoo of a heart with my name in it! Cool, huh? Also I really love him! What should I do?
Up in the Air in San Antonio

"What do you think, Katy?" Charity is a nationally syndicated advice columnist; answering letters like this is her job.

"It's a fake, don't answer it."

"That's what I thought at first but two of my researchers called San Antonio and she checks out."

"I don't care. No one's that dumb. She doesn't have the wits God gave a turnip. Even people in soap operas have more sense."

"Do soap opera people have lives like that?"

"Yes and no. They screw around, lie and cheat and steal, but they seem to do it with a little more style and finesse. And fewer tattoos." I know these things because Alma, my grandmother, is a soapaholic who insists on filling me in on the plots of her favorite soaps. I reached out and tossed another log on the fire. "Let's ski for a little while."

Charity moaned.

"Just an hour?"

"Katy, I'm tuckered out, we skied all morning. Okay, listen, let's open a bottle of wine first, and get some of those yummy crackers. Cheese too. Tomorrow—I promise!—I'll ski all day if you want to."

I opened a bottle of wine and tossed her a glass and a box of crackers. Then I pulled on my ski stuff. Charity has a not-to-be-believed cabin at Tahoe—you can step right out the door and cross-country. So I was. When I ski I can forget; I can stop thinking. Freedom.

It was dark by the time I got back and the cabin overflowed with welcoming smells: the log fire, roast chicken, and a gazillion-calorie chocolate decadence dessert. After dinner, but before chocolate decadence, she made me listen.

"Okay, here's my answer:

> "Dear San Antonio,
> You are not up in the air, you are out in the ozone. Your boyfriend cheated on you, stole from you, and told you you weren't enough for him. Remember show-and-tell? The whole idea is to learn, not repeat our mistakes.
> Charity

"Does that seem too tough, Kat?"

"No. Put something in about tattoos too."

Charity giggled and poured herself another glass of wine.

"Do you think it was Jed?" I asked.

She frowned at me. "How the hell would I know? I've never even met anyone from San Antonio. You can call him Jed if you want but I'm betting Out in the Ozone would fall for someone with a name like Jim Boy or Shorty. Jed sounds too wholesome."

"Not him, the guy who attacked me. Sara Bernard's husband's name was Jed."

"Oh sure, that's logical. Do you have any facts to support your theory, or is it just a wild guess?"

"You think the woman's visit and the attack on me two days later was a coincidence?"

"I don't know, Katy. What does it matter? You've decided to take some time off from work—this should convince you that your decision was the right one. Have a gooey." She held out the dessert plate.

It wasn't distraction enough. "He tried to kill me. Have you ever thought about what it would be like to be dragged underneath a car?"

"Katy, don't."

"Have you?"

She shook her head.

But I had; I'd thought about it a lot lately.

When I picked up my office messages there was one from a woman who identified herself as the person who had spoken with me in my office several days ago. Her name, she said, was Sara. Would I please please please call her back. She was too afraid to come again to my office, she was too afraid to leave a longer message, she was too afraid to do almost anything. Please please please . . . She had repeated that over and over, as if it were a prayer, and she sounded as though she too had thought about being dragged behind a car. At top speed.

I didn't call her back.

Ohmagod, Katy, listen to this one:

> "Dear Charity,
>
> My husband cheated his company out of thousands of dollars. He was in a position to make a decision that favored the client, not his company, and he did. The client then wrote him a check for more than he makes in a year. He has been very happy lately, but of course he doesn't know I know this. I was raised never ever to cheat or lie, and am just sick at heart. What am I to do?
>
> Torn in Tulsa

"It breaks my heart to hear stories like this, it really does. No matter what she decides, she won't be happy. She can't be. She has to choose between her principles and her husband and she can't have both. Not to mention that her husband isn't what she thought he was, and now, if she's honest, she knows he never will be."

Was that what happened to Sara? I wondered. Did she have to make that choice? I thought this, I wondered this before I could catch myself.

But I didn't call.

I skied. And I thought about Hank. Always. All the time. Sometimes I cried but the tears in my eyes and on my face hurt in the cold and wind. So I cried inside instead. I was used to that.

"People fight so hard not to see the truth. It's sad, don't you think?" Charity's voice was wistful, plaintive.

Sad? Maybe, but it was a protection too. In my dreams Hank was still alive and I was happy. It was hard to fall asleep, to stay there in my dreams. I skied every day until I was ready to drop from fatigue. A glass or two of wine and then . . . dreams.

Sara called again. Twice. I decided not to pick up my messages for a while. The police called too. And Harv. One day there were twelve hang-ups on my machine. I skied. And tried to dream. I went snowshoeing, though I'd never been before. At first I laughed at my awkward motions on the snow surface and then I cried at the lonely pattern my snowshoes made across the pure white drifts. One pair of snowshoes. One set of tracks.

The tears froze on my cheeks.

And Sara called.

The dreams stopped.

I was alone.

CHAPTER 4

It had all been about sex, she realized now, sex and the unfulfilled fantasies they had flung heedlessly into the waiting expectant emptiness of the other. In the still of early mornings the light had been a cool breaking gold that shivered and shimmered in the moments before it collapsed into the brightness and day that followed.

Then his hands would slide across her skin so softly that at first it was part of her dream, the edges between dream and reality a blur. She liked to stay there as long as she could, half awake and aware with endless possibilities. Finally she would glance at him through hooded eyes and he would smile at her, desire in his eyes, in his hands and mouth.

Sometimes he would awaken her by blowing across her face, the softness of a breath passing over her cheek, caressing her eyelids, dying in the soft swirl of her hair. She would fancy she heard her name or endearments in that exhalation and then she would forget everything, his fingers straying over her body.

She never used to sleep naked. He had taught her that too, taught her to desire his touch every moment, awake or sleeping, until finally she was restless, achy, and unhappy without him. Often they would make love without a word, without a sound even. She imagined it was like being with a stranger—there was nothing to say with words, only with your body.

Whenever they could both get away from work they would meet at the house, taking their clothes off the minute the door closed behind them, dropping them on the floor, and making love wherever they were when the last piece of clothing came off.

It was an insatiable hunger. How much sex did it take to fill up the emptiness in you? She had asked him that once and he had laughed and told her it didn't matter, they had forever. She had laughed too. That was when forever had seemed a wonderful unending good thing. Like sex.

Like the way he covered her face with kisses and then let them trail across her breasts and body. Feather-light kisses that drove her wild, made her want to open her body up to his completely. He was gentle like that until she was almost crazy with her need for him. She didn't want gentle then, she wanted hard and hot. Fast.

His hands would cup the roundness of her buttocks and pull her on him, pull her into his control. She surrendered, lost all sense of time and space then. Nothing existed but the hot wildness that was sex. He could wait for a long time and she would come again and again. Fast at first and hard and then slower, she on top, pacing herself, playing until the urgency was there again and she flung herself against him with abandon and relentlessness.

Then she would tumble off, pretend she was too tired to continue, would lie there on her belly, her body naked except for the fine sheen of sweat, her pulse racing still. And his hands would float over her body; he would kiss her back and neck and buttocks with little kisses and nibble with bites that didn't hurt, just made her shiver with desire.

His hands would shift her body. His fingers and tongue would be in her, teasing at first, then slipping, sliding. Until she was crazy with desire again and his control would be almost gone too; then they would come together, disappearing in each other, becoming separate again only after the sex had worn off.

Even sated, the desire was always there, a small worm gnawing gnawing. Even later . . . when she started wondering about things. It was always there, an addiction, a drug that she couldn't leave behind or do without, not even when her mind said it might be time, it might be better.

Suppose no one ever made her feel that way again? Or knew to be gentle and rough at the same time? That was an unbearable thought. Sometimes she felt like she was dying, drowning in him and in desire and ecstasy. Only it didn't feel like dying, it felt so good she couldn't stop.

And she would call him. "Lunch?" she would say.

"Lunch," he would answer.

"Twelve?"

"One."

"The usual place," she would say.

"Yes," he would agree, and hang up.

Sitting at her desk, she was devoid of all feeling but anticipation and desire. Empty, waiting for him. The sexual craving was a physical sensation in the lump in her throat, in the aching of her thighs, in the place below her belly. Her eyes always on the clock. Ten-fifteen. Ten-seventeen. Eleven twenty-two. Time dragged on, desire making her heavy and light at the same time.

Later, she caught herself sometimes reaching for the phone, starting to dial the familiar number.

"Lunch?" she wanted to say.

"Lunch," he would answer.

She wanted him still. Even now.

Lunch . . .

CHAPTER 5

The doorknob turned slowly, silently, the door opening with almost no noise. Framed in the opening was the woman who had come to my office, the woman I took to be Sara Bernard.

Her face was white and still. One hand covered her mouth, the other arm was held out stiffly in front of her, palm facing me—like a traffic guard. "Oh my God," she whispered. "Please don't. Please, *please* don't."

I lowered the gun. I didn't say hello; I didn't ask her in. Her eyes stayed with the gun, compelled, riveted. I waited her out, the gun in my hand, my arm hanging loosely at my side.

"Why?" she whispered. "You don't have to. Not with me. *Me!*" She dragged her eyes off the gun and looked at me. She was trembling and there was fear in her eyes, eyes that were ringed in black and purple. Not makeup, bruises—black eyes, the best I'd seen in a long time. "Why?" Her voice was a little stronger; her eyes, fascinated, slipped down again to the gun.

"This is private property, which you were entering without permission, surreptitiously and suspiciously. People with legitimate business call ahead; they also knock on the door."

"But I did call. Over and *over*." Her tone was aggrieved, wounded, badly used. It was the tone of one who had been abused many times before and expected to be again. "You never answer the phone and you never return my calls even though I beg you to. Oh, I *do* wish you'd put that gun away. Could you? Just let me talk to you this once, explain things—then I promise I'll leave you alone if you want me to."

I acceded to the inevitable. "Come in, close the door behind you." I indicated a chair and perched on the desk facing her. Although I holstered the gun in the clip-on holster at my belt there was nothing friendly or welcoming about my attitude. I wanted her out of here. Fast. In one week I had been in my office less than an hour. I had come here to get my gun, nothing more. I am not a big believer in coincidence.

"Were you watching my office?"

"Oh no, of course not. I would never do anything like that. I *abhor* sneaky people."

I stared her down.

She dropped her eyes. "Okay. Well I was, sort of. I wasn't here all the time or anything, just kind of drove by whenever I had the chance—sometimes I'd watch for a little while, just hoping and hoping to catch you. I wasn't being sneaky, it's just— Oh God, Kat, I'm so desperate!"

"Why didn't you knock?"

She frowned. "I don't know. I should have done that, you're right. I think I'm so used to slipping around, to tiptoeing and being quiet and invisible that I've forgotten how to behave. I'm so sorry. I didn't mean to scare you or anything, that was the last thing on my mind, honest." She held up her hand like a Girl Scout. Not that I've ever seen a Girl Scout with two black eyes.

"You have ten minutes," I said coldly.

Her mouth dropped open and she stared blankly at me for a long moment, then spoke in a sudden burst. "I-told-Jed-I-wanted-a-divorce. A-month-ago. I-asked-him-to-move-out." She strung her words up fast, high and wild like birds lined out on a telephone wire. Black birds. The ominous variety.

"Slow down." I spoke a little more gently.

"He refused." She was hugging herself and shaking.

"Refused what?"

"Everything. He said he didn't want a divorce and he wasn't going to move out. He said he didn't want me to move out either and that he wasn't going to let me. I asked him why he'd been following me. At first I had thought I was crazy, that it was just my mind playing tricks on me, but I kept seeing him. Everywhere. Outside the building at work, or in the car behind me, or the parking lot at the supermarket. I just knew. He can't have always been watching me, I mean he has a job, but it sure seemed like it."

"What did you do then?"

"When?" She looked confused.

"When he refused to move out or consider a divorce."

"Oh. Well, I moved out anyway. But not right then, I didn't dare with him watching and everything. I got a girlfriend to come with me and help. Mostly I just took clothes and a few personal things. And I went to a lawyer too, I told her to file for divorce."

"And?"

She looked at me steadily. "And the shit hit the fan."

"How did you get the black eyes?"

Her eyes dropped. In shame? "Jed."

"How long has he been hitting you?"

"Not-long-really." She ran the words together again, beads on a string. "Six months. Maybe a little longer. He's always sorry afterwards and he says it'll never happen again. At first I believed him. He never really hurts me, just pushes me around. Bumps and bruises, that's all. I know that this will sound funny but I'm not afraid of him physically. I don't think he'd ever really hurt me."

I kept my expression blank. It didn't sound funny, it sounded stupid. It sounded like what a million other women had said before they landed in the hospital or morgue.

Her earnest expression was belied by the black eyes. "He won't hurt me; it's just that someday, when he realizes I really won't come back, he'll kill me."

Killing wasn't hurting? The distinction was too subtle for me.

Her voice was calm. She had stopped shaking and hugging herself. "And he'll do it in a way that makes it look like an accident or suicide. He'll kill me and he'll get away with it. Because he's a cop he knows about all kinds of things that you and I don't, wouldn't even think of or imagine."

"You need a restraining order." I tried to be patient, though it was the second time I'd said this. Not to mention the obvious thing to do. "The cops take the situation much more seriously when there is a restraining order."

"The cops." She stared at me in amazement and then laughed. Not a nice laugh, one with a high sharp edge. "I don't have a chance with the cops.

Suppose *he* shows up? Then what?" She shook her head emphatically. "I can't work within the system, it's stacked against me. My only chance is to fight it my own way, to fight it with someone like you, someone outside the system who-believes-in-me." She rushed the words together, filling up the pauses so I couldn't respond without interrupting. "My lawyer mentioned your name, you know. She said you were the best. She said if anyone could help me, you could."

"Who's your lawyer?"

"Jill Gilbert."

I nodded. Jill is an excellent lawyer and a friend of mine.

"I can't help you, Sara, I'm sorry."

"Yes you can, you can. Please, you didn't even think about it. Don't just say no. Can't you at least think it over, maybe talk to Jill?"

I stood, walked to the window and looked out. Spring was coming to midtown. Tulips, snowbells, and daffodils, framed in new green and dirt, were scattered about, welcome harbingers. The piles of fall's dead leaves, winter's broken branches and debris were mostly gone. Birds were running amok with joyous trills, songs, and slapdash chirpiness. Squirrels and dogs were a little goofy. Spring has always been my favorite time of year. I turned to face Sara, who was biting her lip and fidgeting in her seat.

"The man I loved and was going to marry was killed two weeks ago. I can't help you, Sara, I can't even help myself."

She stared at me, a portrait of despair—black eyes and a bleak soul peeking out of them. The silence in the room lengthened into a long, dark ribbon.

She broke it with a non sequitur. "What happened to your face? It's all bruised and cut up." She was whispering again, her face still and unreadable.

"Someone stole my car the other night, then tried to run me over when I wouldn't tell him what he wanted to know."

"What did he want to know?"

"He asked about Sara Bernard. He wanted to know where you were."

"Oh my God." She covered her mouth with both hands, then lowered them slightly to murmur, "What happened to your boyfriend?"

"He was killed on the job. He was a cop, like your husband."

She closed her eyes and squinched them up tightly like a child who refuses to see the bogeyman. When she opened them the fear was gone. They were clear, almost luminous. "Don't you see? We're in this together. I was with a cop, so were you. And now we're not. He'll see it as a betrayal, a betrayal by both of us. Now he'll hate you too."

"I didn't leave Hank, he was killed." I stated the blindingly obvious.

"It doesn't matter. He associates you with me now. That's a betrayal too. And he'll kill you. He'll kill you the same way he'll kill me. It will look like an accident. Or suicide. He almost succeeded the other night, didn't he? No one would have tied him to it. It would have looked like a street crime, a carjacking gone bad. Oh Kat, he's so good. He would have gotten away with it. You don't want to die like that. I *know* you don't. It would be horrible, meaningless. Stupid."

"I'm not with you." I stated it simply, sticking with the factual and shrugging off the rest of what she had said.

"I know that. You know that. But he doesn't. He's seen me come here. He thinks you are working for me. And that's all that matters—you can't reason with an irrational person, you know. There is nothing you or I could say that would change what he thinks. We're in this together, we really are. I'm sorry, I didn't mean to get you involved this way."

There was, I thought, just the smallest edge of triumph in her voice. She had meant to get me involved; she didn't care how.

"Your ten minutes are up," I said politely and started for the door.

"You're going to help me, aren't you?" She bounced up out of her chair like a jack-in-the-box with an overtight spring and large black eyes.

"No. I'm not. Good luck." I opened the door.

She slammed it shut. Her eyes were hard now, a mean yellow with black rims. Her mouth was in a thin, tight-lipped line.

"Bravo." I almost smiled.

Her eyebrows whipped up like surprised and hyper little exclamation points. "Huh?"

"I'm glad to see there's still some fight in you. I was beginning to think you were just into playing the victim."

"If I didn't need you, I could hate you." She snarled the words at me, trying to make them hard-edged and hurtful.

"You know everything you heard about me, Sara?" I made my voice patient, gentle.

She frowned, knotting her forehead up in a puzzled way as though I kept throwing her off base. "Yes . . ." The *s* dragged out into a sibilant question mark.

"That I can leap tall buildings in a single bound, see through the hearts and souls of men and grind out the evil there as simply as squashing a bug under my heel? Alas." I shook my head. "Not true." I rested my right hand on the gun at my hip. "That I'm a two-gun Sally who can shoot a blackguard's eyes out at a hundred paces, drill the evil out of a man's heart, or trim his macho down to size? Not true. That I can make bad boys walk the straight and narrow and good girls go to heaven? Not true."

"You're making fun of me." There were tears in her eyes. Spunky was gone and the Suffering One was back.

"No, I'm not. I'm trying to tell you something. The job description of a private investigator is reasonably specific. I am not a bodyguard, a caretaker, a people fixer, or a psychiatric problem solver."

"I know all that. Don't be stupid." She shook her head impatiently.

I laughed at her.

"What's so funny?"

" 'Don't be stupid'? You have practically no common sense, fewer manners, and so far no charm. And you want me to work for you? How many times do I have to throw you out?" Suddenly I felt very tired. "Enough." I spoke wearily. "I'm calling the cops. They get paid to do this kind of thing; I don't." I backed away from the door and reached for the phone.

She pounced, moving with a silent and deadly certainty like a fully focused killer animal on *Wild Kingdom.* And tried to knock my hand away from the phone.

So now we knew that I was better at playing chicken than she was. Adults, I reminded myself sternly, didn't play chicken, they handled things in a mature manner. And then I thought that maybe I was too tired, too sad, and too beat-up to do that.

"Get your paws off me. Get out of my office. Get out of my life. Put it into high gear and scram." I wanted to go back to Tahoe and ski until I dropped, until my mind stopped thinking about what could and should have been.

"I don't want you to be Superwoman. Here's all I want . . ."

"Are you deaf?" I asked in amazement. At least she had retracted her claws and taken her mitts off me.

She ignored my question. *Surprise.* "I want you to follow Jed, to document what he's doing. It has to be someone like you, someone independent, not me or a friend of mine. That kind of knowledge and documentation will scare him off, will make him stop. He doesn't want to get caught, to lose his job or go to jail. He doesn't want people to talk about him, snicker behind his back, or think he's a loser who beats on his wife. As long as he thinks he can do this and get away with it, he will. The minute I can prove all this, the minute I'm in a position to use it against him—it will stop. Until then—"

She shivered. "Until then he thinks he's invincible. He thinks he can get away with anything. And he can. He has. He thinks he can get away with murder. Until now, until you and your help." The pleading note was back in her voice.

"Jill will give you the name of someone else."

She shook her head, the black-rimmed eyes a little wild now. And blurred with tears. "You're the best, she said."

"Don't let the door hit you on the way out." Subtlety had long since deserted me.

She brushed the tears away. "You still don't get it, do you? It's not just me, remember that. It's you too. He tried to kill you too. You think this is not going to happen again? You're wrong."

As exit lines go it wasn't great, but it wasn't bad.

CHAPTER 6

We saw it on the news, just like everyone else. Two women were pulled from the American River. One was bundled into warm clothes, wrapped in blankets, and tucked in an ambulance, the other was zipped into a body bag and stowed in the coroner's van. Their names were not released, pending notification of the dead woman's family. As they announced this in a pious TV news pseudo-caring way, the camera zoomed in on the woman being helped into the ambulance. Wet hair clung to her skull and face, dark strands pasted against the blue-white of her skin and large frightened eyes ringed in black.

I gasped.

"Every year," the pious news voice droned on, "dozens of people drown in the American River. In the spring runoff the river is fast and unpredictable. Currents are strong and the water level is high enough to hide deadly rocks, trees, and branches. Do not," the news voice scolded with a strong note of admonishment, "go swimming, diving, boating, or rafting. Do not walk too close to the river. The often placid and peaceful surface hides deadly danger."

"Katy?"

Charity stood next to me with a bowl of cookie dough in her hands and a concerned look on her face. She has definitely bought into the Betty Crocker concept of love—*Nothing says lovin' like something from the oven*–type stuff—and is a fervent believer in the theory that home-baked goodies make you feel better.

"That was Sara Bernard." I answered the unspoken question.

"The woman they pulled out of the river?"

"Yes."

Charity plunked the cookie bowl down on the coffee table in front of us and we both stared at the TV. A newsperson was going on and on about fake fat globules and how we would soon be able to eat whatever we wanted and stay skinny, followed by another newsperson reporting a human interest story involving a cat, a duck, and a rabbit. I wrenched my eyes away from the screen. Sports was next; the news was over.

"Quit eating cookie dough, Katy, you'll make yourself sick."

I stared stupidly at the spoon in my hand. Oops. No chance these cookies were made with fake fat globules either.

Was it an accident, or murder and attempted murder?

I waited for an hour and a half—time enough to eat six chocolate chip nut cookies—before calling my office and picking up the one message: "This is Sara. We didn't get too close to the bank. It wasn't an accident. We were pushed."

It took me three calls to find her. She was out of the emergency room, her condition serious but stable, and yes, she could see visitors on the approved list, what was my name?

No "please." I *know* Miss Manners and I are not the only ones who deplore the lack of courtesy in this country, so where are the rest of you? "Kat Colorado," I said, with just the hint of a formal rebuke.

"You're on the list," she stated without interest, and hung up, unmannered and unrebuked.

I strolled by Sara's room at ten the next morning, tossed a quick sideways glance in that direction and kept moving. There were at least four people in there, probably a couple more I couldn't see tucked out of sight in a corner, and all of them seemed to be distraught and crying. It was a *Feet don't fail me now* kind of situation. Bad hospital coffee suddenly seemed very appealing.

Half an hour later the crowd had thinned to two but tears and tissues were still very much in evidence. What the heck. I decided to cruise the gift shop downstairs—you never know what you'll find. At five past eleven I tried again, wondering how many times I could do this without starting to look suspicious, although all the nurses I saw were either overworked or indifferent.

The room was empty.

The bedcovers were turned back, and a magazine rested facedown on the bed. A candy wrapper and several *Get Well Soon!* cards lay next to the magazine. The room was filled with flowers that had been bred for beauty and durability, not fragrance. The bathroom door opened and Sara shuffled out.

"Oh"—she looked at me dispassionately—"it's you."

She slopped along in slippers, barely lifting her feet, one hand bunching the inadequate hospital gown together in back. Her bare arms and legs were covered with bruises and there were fresh scratches on her face and hands. Her eyes, still ringed in black, had gone completely opaque and dead.

It took her forever to climb into bed and arrange her gown and the covers. Her eyes drifted around the room, finally sliding to a sullen stop on me. I wondered what kind of drugs they had her on. I hoped it was drugs. Really hoped.

"Are you all right, Sara?"

"My friend is dead."

"I'm sorry."

"Because of me."

"You don't know that."

"I wish I didn't, but I do."

"What happened?"

"I told you. Someone pushed us."

"One person, or more than one?"

"One."

"Who was it?"

She hesitated and then blurted out her reply with a clarity too strong for the hesitation. "Jed, my husband." The last was spoken with bitterness and hatred. "I guess he wasn't kidding when he said 'till death do us part.' I just didn't realize the death was going to be mine."

"You saw him then?"

"No. He came up behind us."

"And . . ."

"And he pushed us. The bank was slippery and steep there and very close to the path—the flood had washed out a lot of the riverbank all along that stretch. He didn't have to push far. A couple of good shoves and we were over the edge. Lorraine didn't have a chance. She's not a swimmer.

"Oh God, I can still see pictures of her in my mind—slow motion—trying to grab on to the bank. But it was so steep. And the bank was just dirt and mud and it broke away in her hands. She managed to grab a tree root sticking out but it wasn't strong enough; it just broke away in her hands.

"She looked at it like she couldn't believe what had happened and then she looked at me. She didn't even look scared, she just looked like she understood everything, like she knew she was dead; she knew she didn't have a chance.

"It happened so very fast. God. I tried to reach her, to grab on to her. I can swim, you see, and I thought maybe I could save her. If I could grab her . . . if I could get us to some rocks or a log or a stronger root sticking out of the bank . . . But I couldn't. I couldn't do any of that. I couldn't reach her. Or grab her. Or save her. I watched as the water pulled her under and she disappeared. She didn't even make a sound. One minute she was there and the next minute she was gone."

Sara spoke in a flat slow monotone, as though the story had been rehearsed, or recited many times already. And as though she was on drugs. Carts rattled in the halls—lunch, I assumed, as it was eleven-thirty. Sara took no notice.

"I grabbed on to a branch of a tree that had been uprooted and washed downriver. I was stuck there. The current wrapped me around the tree and there was no way I could move. I thought I was dead too, Kat. The water was so cold I could feel my arms and legs going numb. When I got too cold and numb to hold on, the river would take me, I knew that. That's what would have happened too, except that somehow the tree dislodged and was swept downriver. We caught in a bend and ran aground. I managed to drag myself along the tree and out onto the bank. I was lucky. I didn't have much more time, the water was so cold. Someone on the trail saw me and got help. It was all luck. Mine, not Lorraine's."

"Lunchtime!" A white-clad hospital worker spoke in that false-cheerful voice that is so common in addressing the sick or the old. *As if age or accident robbed you of your intelligence and maturity.* "My my, doesn't this look yummy!" We looked. Bleech. *Or your common sense.*

It didn't look yummy, it looked disgusting, like something under a log or in a Martha Stewart nightmare. All white, all blah: creamed chicken on rice with cauliflower, tapioca for dessert, and milk on the side. *Bon appétit!* I averted my eyes. Sara pushed it away without another glance.

"You see, Kat? An accident. Just like I said. An accident. No one would ever think it was murder."

"You can identify the man who pushed you in? You saw Jed?"

She shook her head. "No, I told you, he came up behind us. I never even had a chance. Lorraine started to turn around. She saw, I could see that by the look on her face, the surprise and fear. But of course that doesn't matter now. She's dead—you know what they say about dead men telling tales . . ."

"Then you don't know it was Jed." It was a statement, not a question.

"Of course I do." Her voice was scornful. "Who else would it be?"

"You don't have any proof?" I revised my question.

She nodded. "It smelled like him."

"Smelled like him? Sara, you're a person, not a basset hound. And people have a very limited sense of smell."

She made an impatient gesture. "People smell different, you know they do. And their clothes do too. And it felt like his hands."

I let that one go. "Jed pushed you and Lorraine into the river? Two able-bodied women against one man—however strong . . . How was that possible?"

She shook her head. Puzzled? Rueful? "I thought and thought about it—it doesn't seem as though it should happen, does it? But he caught us off guard. We were so surprised. You just flat-out don't believe anyone would push you into the river. You don't believe it, you don't expect it, you're not prepared."

"At some point it was clear." I stated the obvious.

She nodded. "It was too late."

"Too late? If you'd dropped to the ground, held on to his legs, if—"

"Yes, I know. It just happened so fast, Kat. Maybe we could have done that but we didn't, we got caught in the momentum and went over."

I tried a different tack. "I know you are sure this is Jed, I know he has threatened you, but that is not the same thing as proof. You understand that, don't you?"

"Oh yes, of course. But Kat, he spoke to me too. I heard his voice. He said: 'This is for you, Sara. So long.' "

I thought about that. And about memory and drugs and hatred. "What did the police say when you told them?"

"The police?" Her voice faltered.

"You didn't tell them? Sara, for *gods*sakes."

"Of course I didn't tell the police. Jed *is* the police. It wouldn't help me, it would make it worse." Tears filled her eyes and spilled over in pathetic trails down her face.

"Someone else could have seen all this go down, could have seen Jed. It doesn't have to be your word against his."

"If someone saw, why haven't they come forward? No, there was no one. The trail all along the river was deserted."

"Why, if you feared for your safety, would you be out on a deserted trail?"

"It was daylight. I was with Lorraine—you know, safety in numbers. I thought it was all right, I really did."

"If you didn't say anything about Jed, what did you say?"

"That we got too close to the edge, that Lorraine slipped and I tried to save her but couldn't and we slid down the bank."

"This was murder, Sara, and you're calling it an accident?"

She stared at me, her face as white as her lunch.

Not just murder, murder at the hands of a police officer.

"Oh Sara, oh you poor poor *poor* little thing, how *are* you?" A large vision in pink and blue and tears advanced on us with open arms.

Sara gave me an imploring and pitiful look.

I left.

In the background Sara made a squeaky sound.

I walked out of the hospital, walked away from all of it. For good. That's what I told myself.

But that was before Sara tried to commit suicide.

CHAPTER 7

The police called the next day. They'd found the Bronco. When I asked if I could come pick it up, they laughed. I went out to the Rancho Cordova wrecking yard anyway.

There I picked my way through cars in varying stages of dismantlement, through stacks of car parts and hubcaps with rusted bolts and lug nuts in them, and on out to the back. I wouldn't have recognized or identified the Bronco without directions. I didn't laugh.

The car was stripped. Not just the radio and accessories. Everything. The wheels were gone, as were the seats, doors, floor mats, gearshift knob, steering wheel, fenders, interior upholstery paneling, and transmission. It was a skeleton picked clean by scavengers. I stood there with tears in my eyes. It wasn't just the loss of the Bronco but the sense of shifting, of quicksand. Things were sliding away from me—Hank, the future we had planned, even the Bronco—and I couldn't hold on, couldn't stop the slide.

The sunshine was warm on my face, it was almost eighty degrees, the sky clear blue with fluffy innocent clouds. Two small birds darted in and out of the rusted chassis of a pickup truck where they were building a nest. Beginnings were often improbable. And endings.

The Bronco was a total loss. I kicked a hubcap on the way out, sending the rusted lug nuts flying, briefly airborne metal Cheerios against the bright blue of the sky. Sadness and anger.

Was Jed Bernard responsible for this? The thought of him was starting to piss me off. Big time.

I dropped in on Jill Gilbert when I got back to town, even got lucky and caught her. "I thought you liked me. What did I do to deserve this?" My voice was melancholy, a long plaintive note running through it.

Jill laughed and waved me to a chair. "Sara Bernard?" Her voice was happy, lilting. I'd sounded like that once—it seemed far away now but I remembered. And I noticed that she figured my question out immediately.

She sighed. "Situations like this are so difficult. So volatile. Let me fill you in on the background. Sara has given me permission to do so. I am assuming you know something about the situation an abused woman is in?"

"Yes. Take it from the top though, don't take my understanding for granted."

"All right. Many people assume that victims are on the bottom rungs of the ladder, at the lowest end of the socioeconomic scale. Not true. Spousal abuse cuts through all the lines: economic, educational, professional, racial, age. I think, though, that women in the lower socioeconomic levels are more in evidence. They turn to hot lines, safe houses, and public assistance because they have nowhere else to go. Women with resources, with jobs, cars, credit cards, with family and money, are obviously in a much better position, though still very much at risk.

"Sara came to me a month ago and asked me to start divorce proceedings. She told me that she had moved out of the home she and her husband own and share, or had shared, when he refused to do so. At that point she stated that she had removed her personal things and a few items of furniture, that she had taken half the money in their various accounts, that she had been careful to do all this as secretly as possible, both out of fear for her safety and to conceal all information about her whereabouts. She told me she feared for her life."

"Does Sara work?" It is as easy to find someone at work as it is at home. Sometimes easier.

"Yes. She is a computer programmer for the state, but is currently on leave. She felt she was too vulnerable and visible a target there, as well as a danger to her fellow workers. At present she works temporary, short-term, and consulting jobs here in the Sacramento area as well as in the San Francisco Bay Area. She hopes in this way to maintain a low personal and professional profile and keep her whereabouts unknown while still continuing to support herself."

"Family and friends?"

"She has told very few people where she lives or what she is doing now. *I* don't know. I have only a voice mail number and a post office box."

"Is she an emotionally stable person?"

Slight hesitation. "I believe so."

I was silent, waiting for Jill to explain the hesitation.

"Sara Bernard is a very capable and intelligent professional woman. I believe her to be emotionally stable but it is clear that stress, fear, and uncertainty are taking a toll on her. This is neither unexpected nor surprising."

No. If true, it was not. "And you believe her version of things, and that this is not a move in a complex game of power or divorce or ugliness?" And we, Jill and I, pawns on the game board?

"That never occurred to me, Kat, and I am pretty hard-nosed and cynical."

Yes. She was.

"In my experience this is not the kind of story a woman makes up."

"She should go to the district attorney's office for a restraining order. And to the police when he stalks or harasses her. That is what I told her."

"Yes. I told her the same thing. And I imagine she gave us both the same answer. That it would do no good, that Jed was the police and so on. I have argued with her about it but to no avail."

"Sara is in the hospital. Did you know that?"

A long silence. Jill was afraid to ask, I thought, and I didn't blame her. I answered her unspoken question.

"She and a friend were walking along the American River trail. A man pushed them into the river and the friend drowned. Sara survived and was found by a passerby. She did not see her assailant, but based on smell and one line he spoke to her, she identifies him as Jed. She did not tell the police any of this."

Jill's face was utterly devoid of color or expression. "This is *not* good," she said finally in what I took to be a colossal understatement.

"No," I agreed, in the same wildly understated way. "And it argues considerable intellectual misjudgment, emotional instability, and insufficient moral and ethical . . ." I ran out of big words. ". . . grit."

"It does." Jill nodded. "Or great fear."

That was the other possibility.

"Sara wanted somebody, well, wanted you, to be working for her, to be an unbiased witness to her experience, to document that experience and, she hoped, to scare Jed off."

"Me." I spoke it as a dull, lackluster word.

"Yes." Jill looked puzzled. "You're perfect, Kat. You have an excellent reputation in this town and an estimable and unquestioned relationship with the community, the legal profession, and law enforcement. People know you're good, careful, thorough, and fair. If it's a question of money, I can assure you that her resources are sufficient."

I walked over to the window and looked out. Jill's office was downtown and considerably more high-rent than my midtown office address. Fewer trees. No daffodils. And I couldn't hear the lyrical spring songs of birds through the double-paned windows, although the clouds were still big improbable marshmallow puffs of white against a cerulean blue.

"Hank was killed not long ago, Jill. I'm having a tough time; I'm not in a position to help anyone."

"Katy, I'm so sorry." Jill stood next to me, her hand resting lightly on my arm. We don't see each other often but we've known each other a long time, long enough so that words don't always have to be spoken.

"I think you are in a position to help, Kat, to help yourself and someone else. Work can be healing. Please think about it."

I went back to Tahoe that night. Skiing, not work. I skied hard every day, falling asleep the moment I went to bed, then waking at one or two, unable to sleep again until dawn. I still wasn't dreaming. Hank seemed farther and farther away from me. White snow and loneliness. The snow, I knew, would be gone soon, the skiing over. It was spring in the Central Valley; soon winter would leave the mountains.

Fear and loneliness.

Was that what Sara felt?

CHAPTER 8

She could remember the exact moment when she had first understood it all, that first glimpse she had caught of herself in the mirror. She had looked so young, a face pure in its whiteness and stillness, devoid of everything but fear. How long, she wondered as she felt the fear choke her, had it been going on? How long had he been following her and she so unaware?

She pretended then—that was the start of it, she was always pretending now, that she didn't see him, that he didn't scare her—and pulled another dress off the rack, holding it up, looking at herself in the mirror. Her eyes were large and vacant as she stared blindly at the dress. By turning her body slightly she could see his reflection. He was just outside the boutique, hands shoved into his pockets as he stared raptly at the mannequin, then frowned thoughtfully. The outfit perhaps, an improbable combination of fabrics and colors, or the mannequin, who had no face, no hands, no feet. His eyes slid smoothly over it and then over Sara.

The dress almost slipped from her hand. She forced herself to look away, to hang the garment on the rack. She fought the fear that had started as a hard knot in her belly and now made her feel like throwing up. When she looked out the window he was gone. Later she glanced around, easily, nonchalantly, as she walked down the sidewalk and to the car. She was mistaken, she told herself, upset, overwrought even, that was it.

She no longer lied to herself; she no longer told herself that. Not now—not the part about being mistaken, anyway. Upset, yes. And afraid. She hadn't been afraid to confront him, not at first. She had spoken boldly, angrily.

"I saw you at the supermarket; you were following me."

"No." He smiled at her, his eyes kind and crinkling up at the corners the way that used to make her feel weak-kneed, happy and in love. "I don't even cook, why would I be at the supermarket?"

"Not for food," she said, "to follow me." Her voice sounded stupid and confused.

"Why would I follow you?" His voice, calm and patient, calm and reasoned, which was the way *she* wanted to sound. "I trust you, Sara." The smile started to disappear and his face got hard. He didn't look like her husband anymore; he looked like a cop. "Is there any reason I shouldn't?"

"No. No, of course not." She shook her head hard and fast. Too hard, too fast. Her voice sounded defensive. How did he do that, get *her* on the defensive? She felt the despair rise inside her. He always did that: he made her feel wrong and look bad when she was right and he was the one who was wrong. Other people believed him, not her. Sometimes, if she wasn't careful, she even started believing him too. Oh God.

"Why do you do that? You always turn it around. *You* were following me. And I asked you a question. Answer me. *Now*." She had hoped it would sound firm, decisive, but it didn't; it sounded petulant.

"Let's not talk about it anymore." His hands on her upper arms were too hard, unyielding. She thought there would be bruises. He looked down at her and smiled, pulled her in to him though she tried to pull away. His eyes were as uncompromising as his hands. When she struggled, he let go.

"Let's go out to dinner, someplace nice that you like."

"No. I hate it when you do this. Good cop, bad cop. Do you think I don't notice?"

"I'm not playing good cop, bad cop; I'm not playing cop at all. I'm your husband."

Yes, she thought bitterly, her husband. And that was the problem. She couldn't just ditch him like a bad date or a bad dream.

It wasn't just the supermarket, of course. There was the time in the gym. He had come in with another guy—a cop, it had to be, all his friends were cops. They were wearing workout clothes and acted surprised to see her. Oh right, like she was dumb enough to fall for that. The surprise had lasted in Jed's friend's eyes and then it had changed to something else, appraisal at first and then interest, desire.

She was seeing that more and more these days, she thought with satisfaction. He had looked away, finally, but only because she was Jed's wife, not because he wanted to. She had smiled a little, in pleasure and because it made her feel so good, but then she wished she hadn't because Jed had turned around and caught her. And the pleasure had turned to fear and become a wash of acid sitting in her stomach and eating away at her from the inside.

She had looked in the mirror that day—it was hard not to, there were mirrors all over the gym—and she liked what she saw. She almost always did now. Tight spandex on a slim body that was increasingly muscled; straight hair, medium brown with blond streaks, pulled off her face into a twistie; a prettiness that needed no makeup or jewelry to showcase it. She would have to stop wearing so many dark colors, especially black. It had made her feel better, more like background, when she was heavy, but she didn't need that now. Part of her, a big part really, wanted to be noticed.

She smiled at herself, willing the fear to go away, and moved to another machine. She wouldn't, she absolutely wouldn't let this mess up her schedule. She watched in the mirror as the muscles in her arms and legs tightened, bulged. Her body was beautiful, she could say that now, though she remembered when there had been no tight muscles and lots of bulges.

Beware the sins of pride and vanity. Her mother's voice, always yelling at her. Maybe that was why she had hidden behind a layer of fat for so long. It wasn't vain to be proud of how you looked, especially after you worked so hard for it, was it? No, she wouldn't believe that, just like she wouldn't let Jed scare her or change her schedule.

She moved on to another machine but the easiness was lost now. She was looking around all the time. Afraid. She left after that, hating herself a little bit. Just for now, she thought, just until things settled down with Jed. Just until she had her life back. She promised herself this, she really did. *Cross my heart and hope to die, stick a needle in my eye.*

The supermarket, the gym, the post office, the mall—he had followed her into all those places. How much worse could it get? She had asked that before he started being so physically threatening. After that, after the threats, she had stopped asking.

Because then she knew.

She knew it would get worse and worse. She hoped it wouldn't but she believed it would, and she wondered how long she could stand it. How long before someone cracked?

Before she did?

CHAPTER 9

Jill's message was terse and to the point: "Please call me. Sara Bernard tried to kill herself last night."

Somewhere the balance had tipped. I recognized that as I picked up the message. No longer could I push Sara out of my mind. She needed me, perhaps I needed her; the distraction really, not her. Nor did I need the sadness of another young life going down. The image of Lorraine pulled under flooding river water haunted me. A drowning—sometimes Lorraine, sometimes Sara, sometimes me—was as close as I got to dreaming these days. Nights really. Nights and nightmares.

"What happened?" My question to Jill.

"She tried to overdose on pills. A friend became concerned when she dropped by last night and Sara wouldn't answer. She broke in, became even more concerned, and called an ambulance."

"Sara's in the hospital again?"

"She's home now, with a nurse."

"Tell her I'm on the job."

A long sighing breath. "Thank you, Katy."

"I'll need some names, addresses, and numbers."

She gave them to me.

. . .

Jed Bernard came out to the front desk of the Sacramento Police Department on 8th and I to greet me. "Hey." His comment was informal and friendly, his smile welcoming and his handshake strong. Batting a thousand so far. "Kat Colorado? Jed Bernard. It's a pleasure to meet you. Come on back here where we can talk." The officer at the desk buzzed the locked security door, Jed held it open for me. "On up here and to your left."

We entered a small room with a table, three chairs, and bleak to stark ambiance.

"Interrogation room?" I asked.

He grinned, indicated one chair for me and took another for himself. "We call them interviews now. Cops have been a little slow on the PC angle but we're trying to catch up."

I was trying to catch my breath. Drop-dead gorgeous is the term that would occur to the average female (and I included myself in that category). *Jeez.* Mentally I smacked myself on the head. I hate it when my brain stops working independently and drops on down to cliché function. I realized I'd been thinking of Jed as repulsive and ugly, a fairy tale kind of bad guy. Instead: a gorgeous dirty-blond stud muffin.

"Thanks for seeing me."

"You kidding? Anytime. I love my wife and I'm very concerned about her. I'm pleased she's got help." He reached back to a hip pocket and pulled out his wallet.

I watched the muscles pull in his thighs, shoulders, and arms. Jed either worked out or played a lot of sports; he had certainly made the most of his genes. He wrote a phone number and address on the back of a card. I took the standard-issue police department business card he was handing me, then looked the question at him.

"My home address and number. Call me anytime, here or at home."

He was open and forthcoming. Of course, I could have gotten the same information from Jill. I had, in fact.

"You say you're worried about your wife, detective."

"Jed. Yeah, I am. Big time."

"Specifically?"

He shrugged helplessly, hunched his shoulders a little. His eyes were brown and expressive. His mustache partially covered his upper lip but his mouth was full and sensual. A slight smile tugged at the corners of his mouth.

"Jeez, Kat. Where to start? There's so much." He sighed. "She's told you, I'm sure, that I'm the bad guy. Hell, she told everyone else, why not you?" He sounded not just bitter but angry. "In this story she tells, I am emotionally abusive—an all-American shithead of a guy—and I physically push her around, slap her around, or beat her up." With slumped shoulders he looked tired and beat up now too. "Choose your version, take your pick, she tells it different ways different times."

"Do you?"

"No." He looked me straight in the eye, never faltered or wavered. He was either telling the truth or one damn good liar. Of course, that was exactly my evaluation of Sara. So there you go: The detective business is not an open-and-shut thing.

"Because of this, the 'alleged abuse,' she wants a divorce, has left me, refuses to inform me, or *any*body as far as I can tell, where she is or what she is doing. I have no idea where she's working or even *if* she's working. She's on leave from her state job. They're very hostile to me when I call, won't tell me anything, so I guess they bought into her story."

"Most people would."

"Yeah." His voice was dry. "You're right. I would too if it weren't about me. Honest to God, Kat, I don't know where all this is coming from, that's one reason I'm so worried. Maybe she needs medical help, maybe something's screwing with her mind. Hell, I don't know what it is but it scares me. She changed slowly over a matter of months—I've tried to remember how long now but I can't. Five? Six? Something like that. She went from being the woman I knew and loved to a woman I don't know, can't understand, can't even reach."

He dropped a hand palm down on the interview table. Numerous obscenities were scrawled and carved there: *LIFE SUCKS. FUCK THE SYSTEM. UP YOURS.* Edifying, uplifting, and colorful stuff like that.

"I couldn't get her to a doctor. I couldn't get her to a shrink. Or our minister. Finally I couldn't even get her to come home. It's like my world is spinning apart and I don't have a clue." His voice broke. "I even went to the police chaplain. He told me that sometimes people externalize the violence or uncertainty and unhappiness they feel within them and put it on someone else. If that's what it is, she must be very unhappy. And suppose she stops putting the violence onto someone else, onto me, and turns it on herself? I'm worried. Shit, I'm *really* worried."

Unconsciously his fingers traced the deep grooves that formed the letters to *LIFE SUCKS.* And gave me a lopsided grin. "Hey, this is different, huh, a cop spilling his guts in the interview room?"

Yes. Or maybe it wasn't so different. Lately cops had popped up as bad guys a little too often.

"I even wondered if Sara was having an affair. I thought that could explain pretty much everything. You know, the emotional distance, the jumpiness and fear. Maybe even the need to make me look like the bad guy instead of her. It would almost be a relief to know that. At least it would be something real, something concrete, something I could deal with." He smacked his palm on the table with each "something." I sympathized. I often wish life were concrete, simple, and straightforward.

"These stories, yours and Sara's, are very different. What would you, as a police officer, do in a case where the stories of two witnesses were so dissimilar?"

"I'd ask the questions over and over again. If you're not telling the truth the stories are going to add up a little different here and there. There will be changes, discrepancies, inconsistencies. Ask me anything you want, Kat. Ask me as often as you like."

Good answer, still batting a thousand. "Did you ever follow Sara, Jed?"

He made a little frowning gesture and nodded, his eyes open, clear. "I did, yes, I was worried about her and wanted to see if I could figure out what was going on. I thought if she was off her usual routine it might tell me something. Maybe I could figure out what was messing things up and help her.

"I thought if she was having an affair, well . . ." His mouth tightened and his eyes got hard. "Well, then I'd know that too, then we would deal with that. I was pretty open about it, Kat. I mean I didn't tell Sara I was following her because if she was hiding something—out of fear or lack of understanding—then I needed to know that to help her, but I talked to everyone else. To her mother and sister, to her friends, to people at work, back when they would still talk to me," he added wryly.

"Did you find out anything?"

"No. I didn't."

"No affair?"

"If she's having an affair, she's covering her tracks well."

"Everything else was business as usual?"

"Except that she seemed very nervous, jumpy, even scared. None of that is like her."

"Couldn't that be just because she felt she was being followed? And her family and friends questioned?"

He nodded. "It could, yeah. But then we're right back to where we started, which is why I was following her in the first place: Why the change? What's going on?"

"Are you following her now?"

"No. I don't know where she is or what she's doing."

"Have you ever physically harmed your wife?"

"No. I wouldn't do that. Ever. I've grabbed her by the shoulders or arms in an attempt to get her to listen to me, but that's all."

"You have never hit her, slapped her, thrown her, shaken her?"

"No. Does she say all that?" A spark of anger.

"She says that when you realize she won't come back, you'll kill her."

The anger died. He looked stunned, shaken. "Kill her. *Kill* her? I don't understand how she could think like that. You don't keep something you love by killing it."

Something. It.

"Love is not something that can be forced, I know that. There was a movie a while back about a man, a doctor, who amputated the arms and legs of the woman he loved to make her dependent on him, to make her love him because she had no choice. Sara was fascinated by that. I thought it was sick, I wanted to leave in the middle of the film."

"What kind of movies do you like?"

"When they're about love? I'm a romantic. I like the old ones best, *An Affair to Remember* or *The African Queen.* Even *Ghost.* In those movies you're not trying to force someone to love you, you're loving them for who they are, knowing all the time they are free to go. Isn't that what love is all about?" His voice was strong and sincere as he leaned forward in his chair, elbows on his knees.

"Hey Kat, you okay?"

I wasn't, no. A tidal sense of loss had swept over me leaving me gasping for breath, almost drowning.

"Can I get you a glass of water, a cup of coffee?" His voice was gentle, solicitous. If he was telling the truth, why had Sara left? Hank wasn't given the choice Sara was. And neither was I. The loss engulfed me.

"Kat?" He put his hand lightly on my knee.

I shook my head. "Nothing to drink, thank you." And took a deep breath. Two. "Is there any other reason that would explain why Sara is acting the way she is?"

"None that I know of."

"A death in the family, the breakup of a friendship, a financial setback? Perhaps she was victimized in some way?"

"No. If anything like that has happened, it's news to me."

"Other problems between the two of you?"

"No." He started to say something and stopped.

"Jed?"

"Nothing." His voice was adamant.

"Sara was almost killed. She and a friend fell into a river. The friend died."

"I heard about that. Not from Sara, of course." His voice was sad. "From people who saw it on TV and recognized her. I was hoping she'd come to me, for comfort, for . . ." He put his head in his hands.

"Sara says they didn't slip; they didn't fall; they were pushed. By you."

His head was still in his hands. *Dammit,* I'd timed that one badly.

He sat up, his face solid, composed, blank—like just hardened concrete. "I didn't hear that. And I would have if she'd said anything."

Score one for Sara.

"She didn't make that statement to the authorities, she made it to me. And to her lawyer," I amended, deciding I didn't want to be the only acknowledged recipient of that information.

" The day it happened?" Face like concrete, voice like gravel.

"Yes."

"I was working."

"There are others who can back you up? Who were with you?"

"What time of day?" His eyes met mine aggressively.

"You were with someone all day?"

Now his eyes hardened and narrowed. Naturally he saw what I was doing. Undoubtedly it was what he did a good part of the time.

"I was at my desk from eight to ten in the morning and later in the afternoon, say four to five-thirty. I had lunch at a Mexican restaurant, ran into another detective and joined her. Around twelve or twelve-fifteen, I guess. The rest of the day I was in the field."

"Talking to people?"

He thought back. "Trying to. I kept missing, leaving messages that weren't answered, hitting out-of-date phone numbers and addresses. Like a dog chasing its tail, that's what my day was."

"Okay, thanks."

He wouldn't ask and I didn't tell him, though he could find out easily enough. Two-thirty. And he wasn't covered; he could have done it. He looked at me but couldn't read it on my face. I can't do concrete, but I can do blank. The silence stretched out. We were both using it; we were both comfortable in it.

Jed broke first. "Hang on, Kat." He walked out of the interview room leaving the door open. A minute, tops, and he was back with another cop. I stood. This one was short, balding, and nondescript in shirtsleeves and a gun. "This is my partner, Tony Kily." Jed closed the door and we all sat down.

"Tony's a good friend, not just my partner. He knows things haven't been so great for me at home." Jed switched his attention from me to Tony. "Kat Colorado is a private investigator retained by my wife. I'm not sure what Sara wants to find out but I've got nothing to hide. Nothing. As a favor to me, Tony, I hope you'll answer any questions Ms. Colorado might have. Now and in the future." He broke off abruptly and stood. "I'll be around when you guys are finished." The door clicked shut behind him.

"Son of a gun." Tony's left eye twitched in a nervous tic. "He's the last guy I'da thought of. The *last*."

CHAPTER 10

He's a stand-up guy." Tony spoke as though that was indisputable, right up there with the Ten Commandments and the Bill of Rights. Hah. I thought of all the stalkers, serial killers, and mass murderers of whom nice things had been said.

"So he's a nice guy and a good neighbor, only kinda quiet—a guy who keeps pretty much to himself?"

Tony grinned; he got it: "The description of a guy who's about to run amok, huh? Maybe climb a tower in Texas and take out a dozen people? No, that's not how I'd describe Jed. Good thing too, right?" A quick grin. When he smiled he went from plain and nondescript to a liveliness and warmth that pulled you right in.

"Jed's a very outgoing guy, a guy who's in love with life. He likes his job, his wife and family, all the things he does in his spare time. And if something comes up that he doesn't like, he changes it or leaves it behind. He's not a complainer or whiner; he fixes things or moves on."

All very attractive qualities, I had to admit.

"What did Sara tell you?" He spoke casually.

"That her husband physically abused her so she moved out, that he is now stalking her, and that she believes he will kill her when he understands she is not coming back."

Tony listened to that thoughtfully, as though he were running a tape through his mind a couple of times, a couple of loops. "I like Sara a lot and I think I know her reasonably well. That sounds like her too, pretty much."

"Sounds like her or the truth?"

He shrugged. "Truth is relative, isn't it?"

"Jeez, Tony, if I wanted philosophy I'd go to the library. Instead, I'm at a police station where I was hoping we could talk facts—concrete, solid, provable stuff."

He chuckled. "Sara has a flair for the dramatic. She likes things a little bigger than life. Or rather, she changes things around so they seem a little bigger than life. Drama. Theater. I never really think of her as an actress, more as someone who would fiddle with the sets, change the actors' lines and costumes, rearrange things. Or—remember the old Punch and Judy shows, all those little puppets dancing on the ends of strings? Like that."

"Okay." I took a deep breath. "Meanwhile back at the truth. There's Sara's version and Jed's version—if I can just drag you away from the philosophical for a moment?"

"Yeah, sure." That ready smile again. "Jed's a what-you-see-is-what-you-get kind of guy. Sara is more subtle, more hidden, more of an unknown. Sara's hard to get to know, elusive; Jed's just the opposite. Jed's straightforward.

"He's a cop because he likes nailing bad guys, getting them off the street and into the slammer; he likes helping people; he likes doing the right thing. He's a good cop, liked and respected in the department as well as on the street. He tell you what he does in his spare time?"

I shook my head, making the assumption that Tony wasn't talking about Jed stalking his wife. Not that he had told me that either.

"He coaches a bunch of kids in basketball. Tough kids, street kids, the kind of kids we'll be booking into our jails tomorrow if a guy like Jed doesn't make a difference today. He also takes a weekend off every month or so and helps build houses for families who couldn't get into the housing market except for sweat equity and community assistance. He makes time for family stuff, he's always got a remodel or a project going at home, and time to go to church and get involved there. Job, community, family, church; it's all real important to him."

"Does that make Sara a liar, Tony?"

"Not necessarily. She just sees things differently."

"Bruises and black eyes look the same to most of us."

"She said *Jed* hit her?"

"Yes."

He shook his head, not in contradiction but in disbelief. "I don't get it, I really don't. I've never seen anything like that, never seen him even speak sharply to his wife, never seen him involved in any rough stuff on the job. And you do see it with some guys. A job like this can bring it out. I've never seen it in Jed. I still don't. I guess I wouldn't believe something like that until I had to. I don't believe that Jed Bernard would beat his wife."

"Or threaten her life?"

"No. I really don't believe that. If that's the way Sara's talking—I don't know, she needs help or something."

"That's me, I'm the help."

"Yeah. Good luck." He stood. "You know where to find me if you need me. I got to get back to work." He had come in friendly, open; he left closed up, angry. The door clicked shut on his heels.

And I wondered, not for the first time, what else I could do with my life. When the bottom falls out of your world there's a certain freedom, a scary freedom: freedom born out of a shattered future, sadness and recklessness. What had Janis Joplin sang/cried/belted out in "Me and Bobby McGee"—that freedom was nothing left to lose? I wasn't quite there yet.

Was Sara?

Or Jed?

What did freedom mean to them?

The door clicked open and Jed walked in looking like a guy who was tense, maybe unhappy, trying to appear relaxed and totally at ease. He placed a piece of paper on the table in front of me.

"Names, addresses, and phone numbers of our friends, family, minister, anyone I could think of who might help. You're free to talk to everyone. If there's anything else I can do, let me know. My hope is that this will get cleared up as soon as possible, that we can just go back to—"

He broke off, looked away from me, looked down. You can't go back, you can only go forward. And forward is unknown. Jed understood that as well as I did.

"Hey!" A note of alarm in my voice. "Eeewww!" I grabbed at the cuff of Jed's long-sleeved button-down shirt, unbuttoned it and pushed it away from his arm. "A big bug, a spider, something." I shuddered. "I hate spiders."

He turned his arm over, shook it, then shook the sleeve down. "You sure? I don't see anything."

"I'm sure." I shivered at the thought of a spider trotting around under my clothes and on my skin.

Jed laughed at me. "Scaredy Kat?" His voice was light, teasing.

I tossed the hair out of my eyes and tried to look nonchalant. "Well, yeah, but only with spiders."

He rested a hand briefly on my shoulder. "C'mon, I'll walk you out."

Out into the sunshine and tumble of the downtown lunch hour and a scramble of people: attorneys, judges, jurors, police, and in-trouble scum. Out and into my thoughts.

I had lied twice: I like spiders and I hadn't seen a thing that was spidery on Jed. I had also learned that he had a hairy, well-muscled forearm. Like the guy who strong-armed me in the Bronco. I sighed. Like a lot of guys. We're not talking DNA ID certainty in hairy arms.

Just a start.

I liked Jed too. He seemed like a good guy and a good cop. Like Hank. It was hard to keep an overlay of Hank from sliding onto everything.

Sergeant Friday would never have gone for that kind of reasoning. *"Just the facts, ma'am."*

If a cop goes bad at work, it's society's problem; if he goes ugly at home, it's personal. Not exactly. Not anymore, with the new law which states that anyone convicted of spousal abuse loses the right to carry a gun. If you're a police officer or in the military, that's your job. Just the facts.

There was a lot at stake here, more than was coming out. A lot more. Good detective work, huh? I just didn't know what it was or where to find it.

Yet.

CHAPTER 11

It's hard to follow someone. To do it right you need at least four guys, four cars. Or more. One on the subject, one in the car ready to pick them up the minute they move, another couple ready to trail, to use for trade-off and backup. North, south, east, west. This is assuming you don't want to be seen.

And he didn't.

There was only one of him though, so sometimes he was more obvious, more open than he would have liked. Still, he was good. It was part of the training, part of the job. Of course, this was personal, not something he could ask for help on, or even talk about. Not even something that most people would understand. Sometimes even he didn't understand. That was the hell of it.

She thought he didn't know where she lived now. That kind of thing made him smile at her ignorance and naïveté. At her complacency. So far she'd done all the right things, he'd give her that, done a good job as far as she'd gone. She'd moved out when he wasn't around, hadn't left anything behind to tip him off as to her whereabouts. She'd taken half the money in their joint accounts but hadn't written any checks or used their joint credit cards for anything so there was no possibility of tracing her that way. No canceled deposit checks on an apartment or a payment to a friend she was staying with. No charges to a local market or ATM withdrawals that would give him a neighborhood or starting place.

Either she hadn't told people where she was or she'd sworn them to silence. That in itself was unusual. Most people were too trusting of their friends, believed too much in their ability to keep a secret. And it was a rare person who could keep a secret. Most times you came at someone sideways, you could get what you were after. He'd seen a lot of people who'd told. It was funny—they made up their minds to something else: that the person wasn't dangerous, that the two people should work it out, even that they didn't want the responsibility. He never could understand that—that a friend couldn't take the responsibility of keeping his mouth shut when someone's life was in danger.

She hadn't made those mistakes though. He was guessing very few people knew where she was, or how to get in touch with her. And the ones who did wouldn't talk. Her mother and sister hadn't looked convinced when he said he was worried, that he thought she was losing it and that her safety was at issue. They hadn't looked convinced when he said he loved her, that he wanted only the best for her.

Oh, they'd been polite, barely, but closemouthed; they'd shooed him off pretty damn quick. Not so fast that he hadn't looked around though. And seen nothing. None of her clothes or things, no cosmetics or toiletries he recognized in the bathroom. No messages for her jotted down on the memo pad. No mail forwarded to her in the mailbox—he'd swung by one day and checked. So he knew she probably wasn't there.

Same thing at work. Nothing. What was different was they weren't even polite. They were cold and hostile, told him to leave immediately. He'd had to work to respond formally and politely, to keep the anger inside. That was the last thing he wanted anyone to see, his anger.

He'd gotten the forwarding address from the post office. They were used to it—it wasn't all that unusual, requests from law enforcement. A lot of people who try to cover their tracks are on the run from the cops. It was a mail drop, one of those mailbox places that try to sound like a business address.

He tried the obvious first: waiting before work, at lunchtime, after work. People don't realize how much you have to change, that you can't do the obvious, the predictable. You've got to completely alter the mold, break the pattern. You've got to stay alert in everything you do in every minute of every day.

Pay dirt at twelve-forty on the second day. He was in his car eating a sandwich, drinking a Coke, reading a newspaper—just a guy eating lunch and relaxing.

He didn't recognize the car she was driving. She'd left her own car behind in the garage. Cars were way too easy to recognize, to trace—she'd known that. He smiled to himself and jotted the license plate number down. He'd recognized her immediately, though she'd gone to a lot of trouble to change her looks. Her hair was blond now, not brown with blond streaks, and shorter, just below her ears, a smooth shiny cap of light bouncing in the sunshine. Her clothes were bright, much brighter than she usually wore. A red suit with yellow blouse and accessories. He'd never seen her wear red before. Or yellow. They looked good on her.

And they were tight. He frowned. All right, not tight exactly, but fitted. They showed her figure and they made you want to see more, that was for sure. The frown deepened.

She didn't look around at all. A quick glance before she crossed the street, that was it. She thought of herself as different, protected. New clothes, new hair color, and she was across town. Her walk was the same though, jaunty, swinging, easy. Recognizable even at a distance. Her posture too. You have to change everything, the way you walk, hold yourself, talk, the way you tip your head to one side or move your hands animatedly when talking. And she hadn't.

He wrapped the rest of his sandwich in paper and stuck it back in the bag. Finished his Coke. Waited.

It wasn't long. Less than five minutes. She hadn't looked around that time either. Just got in the car and drove off. He had to follow her pretty closely. Too easy to lose her otherwise. But she hadn't noticed. She wasn't looking around; she wasn't paying attention. She felt safe. Another mistake. He followed her to the downtown area where she parked in a high-rise lot, exited on foot and walked to an office building less than a block away.

Heads turned when she walked by. He noticed it and he knew she did too. He had to push the anger down again. Later. There was a time and a place for everything.

He'd gone back to work then. One of the things he prided himself on was focus, his ability to concentrate totally on something, blocking out everything else. It was one of the things that made him so good. He'd been back that afternoon at four-thirty, picked her up again at five twenty. Followed her to a little restaurant with great fish tacos and take-out, then to a new apartment complex. He watched where she parked, the entrance she took; he caught a glimpse of her on the outside second-floor walkway before she turned a corner and disappeared, her briefcase under her arm, tacos in a bag in her hand.

She thought he didn't know where she lived but she was wrong. He smiled to himself. Piece of cake. All in a day's work.

Teddy was on him the minute he got to the gym. No dad, mother on booze, crank, and welfare. He understood.

"Jed! Hey man, you're late. You're never late."

He cuffed the boy affectionately on the shoulder. "Got hung up at work. Stuff happens." He wouldn't let the kids swear on the court so he was careful to watch his language as well. Every kid was different but they were all desperate for a good example. He tried to give it to them.

"What kind of stuff?"

"Police stuff. If I tell you, I gotta kill you." He winked. "I'll be right out, two minutes to change. Tell the team I said to warm up." As long as he was around, didn't even have to be right there, they were okay. If he couldn't show they fell apart, didn't practice, picked on each other, left early looking for any kind of trouble that was available.

By the time he got to the court they were all at practice, shooting baskets, passing, dribbling. God, he loved the squeak of shoes on the hardwood floor, the sound of voices and balls bouncing around, the smell of sweat. He loved everything about basketball. When he stopped growing at five eleven it had been a big disappointment. It had ended a dream, a hope that he could go pro.

"Hi Jed."

"How's it going, Ginny?" He gave her elbow a friendly squeeze, careful—always—not to get physical with the kids, especially the girls.

"I been practicing my jump shots. Wait till you see, I'm getting *go-o-o-od*."

"Atta girl."

He smiled at her, watched her beam with pride and pleasure. Just to be noticed was something for these kids. And here, on the courts, was one of the few places they did anything they could be praised for.

He blew the whistle.

CHAPTER 12

Davis?"

"Hey, Katy, how are you?"

I thought of the *LIFE SUCKS* carved into the interview table at the police station. "Not so great." It was an understatement and Davis knew it.

"I'm sorry, Katy." He and Hank had been partners for years. His loss was different but was, I knew, as great as mine.

"How are you and Maggie?"

"The same."

We sat in silence for a minute because the same wasn't the same anymore. And would never be again.

"Have you guys found out anything yet?"

"Not yet." His voice was gentle. The first forty-eight hours are critical in a homicide case. The odds of solving it go down astronomically after that.

"Nothing?"

"Nothing."

"You still have no idea whether it had anything to do with what he was working on?"

"No. It could have been a case; it could have been a drive-by; it could have been someone with a grudge and a gun. And maybe the grudge was against Hank, maybe against cops, maybe against the world. We don't know."

"I'm coming down, Davis." I'd stash Sara away in a safe place and leave town. "There's got to be something I can do."

"Katy." Davis's voice was gentle. "We'll find out. Hank was a cop; we're cops; we won't ever stop looking. You don't know Vegas; you have no authority here. Leave it to us."

"I don't need no stinking badge." I tried to sound tough, like the guy in *The Treasure of the Sierra Madre,* but I didn't; my voice cracked.

"Katy, honey." His voice didn't sound so great either. "We're doing everything that can be done. You know that."

"I know that." I did. I just couldn't stand it.

"Give us a little more time."

I clenched my teeth. It seemed that time was all I had these days.

"You're too close to it too, way too close."

Yes and no, I thought. There was power in obsession, another thing Davis knew as well as I.

"We'll never let it go, Katy. Never. And we'll get there. Anytime you want to come down, stay with us, do it. You don't have to plan—just get on a plane, call us from the airport. We always love to see you. And Maggie could use help with the new baby. Josie's a six-week-old handful."

"Thanks, Davis. I don't think I can right now."

My voice broke again. I couldn't separate Hank from them, from all the good times we'd had together, the dinners, the barbecues by the pool, the ease of loving friends and laughter. It was better, for now, for me to do things that Hank hadn't been so much a part of, or that I'd always done alone.

"How's Mars?" My voice almost under control. Mars is Hank's black Lab. Another thing I couldn't cope with yet, so he was staying with Davis and Maggie.

"He's doing good, loves the baby and is very protective of her. He makes us all laugh, the worried expression he gets when she cries."

I almost smiled.

"Take care of yourself, Katy. I'll call the end of the week just to check in."

"Okay, and remember . . ."

"I know." He chuckled. "You don't need no stinking badge."

He said it much better, and badder, than I did. I almost smiled again.

There were a lot of loose ends that needed to be picked up, loose ends that I couldn't cope with either, not yet. The funeral had almost ruined me. The memories still did. Mars, Hank's cars, his serene old-style adobe house with the Indian rugs, the simple furniture, the hand-thrown pottery—it was all mine now. Outside in the courtyard of the house the fountain that splashed and played in the once lush square of green and flowers had been turned off. Already the water had turned green with algae amid the litter of dead leaves.

The music there was gone, the life dead.

Like Hank.

It had been so difficult for me to let Hank in, to trust that he would always be there . . .

The receiver in my hand whined at me. I stared at it in blank noncomprehension and then hung up. You can't hang up on parts of your life; you can't easily walk away from what you have lost. Hank smiled at me from the ornate silver-framed photograph on my desk. I tried to smile back but I couldn't.

Not yet.

I jumped when the phone rang, my heart racing wildly. And had to wait three more rings until my mind got the rest of me under control.

"Kat, it's Sara. I got your message. Have you found out something? Did you talk to anyone? Where are you? What's going on?" She bounced around topics like a butterfly on speed. "What have you done? I can't wait to hear! Tell me, *tell* me."

"I want to talk to you. Let's meet somewhere."

"Okay. I'll come to your office."

"No."

"You come over here then."

"You said he was good, Sara."

"Yes?" Her voice was hesitant, the excitement gone.

"Those are both ways that he can locate you—easily, in fact. Meeting someplace else would be a much better idea, someplace you don't usually go, in a part of town you don't frequent. That goes for him too. And cops or anyone else who might recognize you." Belatedly I'd decided that I'd better spell it all out. "Take nothing for granted. Absolutely nothing."

"Oh. Okay."

Hiding was new to her, a skill to be learned.

"Where, Kat? I don't know what to suggest."

"Do you ever go to the zoo?"

"No. I have only the vaguest idea where it is."

"William Land Park. Twenty minutes. Stay in your car in the front parking lot. I'll find you."

"All right." The butterfly was gone. Her voice was subdued now. "See you soon."

The Sacramento Zoo is a small one, as is the parking lot, and I found Sara quickly and easily. She saw me approaching and got out of the car when I waved at her to do so.

"Hi, Sara. You look different. Very pretty."

She smiled at me and swung her short, shiny blond hair. "You said to change, so I did. I look really different, huh? I never used to wear clothes like this either." She looked trim and professional in fitted beige slacks with a navy jacket, gold shoes and accessories. "Where are we going now?"

"To the zoo."

"Really? Okay. Why?"

I bought two tickets, keeping her at my side and in my sight, then gave her a gentle shove through the turnstile and relinquished our tickets.

"I like bears. Do they have bears here? And giraffes. Do we need a map or anything? Or just wing it?"

"Let's sit here for a minute." I pointed at the bench seating in the entry and shop area.

"Okay. Why?"

"I thought we'd watch for Jed. There's only one entrance here."

"Oh." Her subdued voice again. "Oh yes, I see. Good idea." She tossed herself on a bench and I seated myself beside her.

"I did a good job, huh?" The hair flip again.

"At what?" A quick glance and a smile. There was very little zoo traffic on a cloudy midweek midafternoon and I was able to monitor the turnstiles easily.

"At changing my looks."

"No."

She snatched a breath in. "No? *No?*" And sounded pissed off.

The sun pushed its way through the clouds and fell on us. Warm, wonderful still, not the solid blanket of unrelenting 105-degree scorch and bake that it would be soon.

"You did a wonderful job of choosing a look that is very becoming, stylish, even eye-catching, but you do not look different. You look like the same person, only prettier, brighter. Even happier?" I made it a question and threw her another quick glance.

"Yes." Her voice was a little startled, surprised, as though the idea that she could be happier—or happy at all?—was an unexpected one. "I am, I am much happier. I feel safe and free."

"I'm glad. But please remember that it is a matter of degree. You are safer, freer, not safe or free." Relative concepts, I thought wryly, and wondered if I was starting to sound like Jed's partner, Tony.

"The way I changed my looks, that was a matter of degree too, wasn't it?"

"Yes."

"How would you do it, do a really good job of it, I mean?"

"You had straight hair before. Either go really short, or curly, or wear a wig. Wear clothes that disguise your size and shape. Wear styles and colors that you don't usually wear." I shrugged. "Not necessarily flattering. The more nondescript you make yourself, the better. You want to look like unremarkable wallpaper, not showcase art."

She wrinkled her nose. "Oh *God,* I don't want to do that. It's exactly what I *don't* want to do. Or be."

I smiled at her tone.

"I've never felt pretty. Now I've lost weight and everything . . ."

"You want to show off."

"Yes." She seemed to hesitate over the words "show off."

"And good for you. Just remember it's not a change. It won't keep you unrecognized or safe. Not in the case of someone who's looking and paying close attention. I think we can safely assume that Jed will be doing just that."

"Yes." Her voice now was not only subdued, it was glum.

"A few more minutes and we'll head for the giraffes. Tell me about your job now, Sara."

"Are there giraffes here?"

"I don't know."

She giggled. "There's something about giraffes that I love. They look so long-legged, cute and goofy, vulnerable even, but then you watch them move and it's really something. They can run very fast, you know. And those long necks? They evolved so that giraffes could feed on leaves and branches that other grazing animals couldn't reach. So they're not cute and goofy at all, they're very specialized."

I smiled at Sara. Her voice was as jumpy and nervous as her babbling words. "Let's walk, shall we?" I stood and she followed suit.

"Did you know that lots of zoos now exist, at least partially, to protect species that man has almost driven into extinction? We've either hunted them down for their furs, feathers, skins, hooves, and tusks or destroyed their natural habitats so they can't survive on their own. Isn't that *awful*!" There was genuine distress in her voice.

"It's very frightening to feel that you are the hunted, isn't it, Sara?"

Sara burst into tears. The flamingos standing delicately and placidly pink on one foot in the lovely water lily–studded pond took no notice of us. A little boy in shorts, T-shirt, and ice cream walked by pulling at his mother's hand as he turned to stare at us. "Look Mommy, the pretty lady is crying. Does she have an owee?"

Sara gazed at me, making no attempt to check the tears. "Is that it, Kat?"

No, I thought but wisely did not say. *You have a target, a bull's-eye pinned to your chest.*

Sara gripped my hand, hers cold and damp in the warmth of mine. "I feel frightened almost all the time now, Kat."

"Fear is good. Fear is a survival technique. What we need to do now is stop the situation creating the fear as soon as possible."

She nodded, let go of my hand, and began to fish about in her bag for a tissue. I changed my mind about my original line of questioning—about jobs and details—and decided to follow the fear.

"The pictures I get of Jed from speaking with him and his partner, Tony, and from speaking to you are very different. I don't doubt you, but I do find it curious."

"Yes. He's very good. I told you." She spoke simply, taking no pride in being right.

I waited for the explanation I hoped was coming and watched the flamingos stretch and preen. The underside of their wings was black; I hadn't realized that before. Where was the survival, the evolutionary value in that? I wondered. Or in their pink color? Such a large splash of pink seemed improbable, even in a tropical country. I started to drift over to the sign to see where they were from. Sara trotted docilely along with me. The West Indies, Asia, and Africa. Hmmmm. They got around.

"How did he seem to you, Kat? Like a nice all-American heart-as-big-as-outdoors and good-as-gold guy?"

"Pretty much. He was very open too; he did not act as though he had anything to hide."

"But he denied following me. And that's a lie. So right there you know you're dealing with someone who's not telling the truth. He lies with his words and he lies with his actions. He pretends, he makes you think he's a different kind of person from who he really is. He's a liar, a dirty rotten liar. He's a Iago—a two-faced manipulator who was someone different to everyone, who was lying, deceitful, and exploitive."

"He didn't lie."

"He didn't lie?" Her voice was a hollow, disbelieving singsong.

"No."

"He didn't deny following me?"

"No."

She stared at me, her mouth open in an O of disbelief. Somewhere behind us a lion roared, and then again. Sara was oblivious, lost in the jungle of her thoughts.

"That son of a *bitch*!"

The bitterness distorted her words, made them harsh and ugly. And her face. The beauty, the radiance, was gone. Even the fear.

It was hatred and ugliness unadorned and unmasked.

CHAPTER 13

"What did he say?"

The tone was lighter, almost conversational. The ugliness was gone, a moment in time—like a road sign at high speed on a freeway, passed and left behind.

"That he was following you out of concern. That you were acting so differently that he thought something might be wrong."

"Something?" Her voice was scornful. "What?"

"That you might be emotionally upset—"

"*See!* He's trying to make me sound unbalanced."

Her voice was hysterical. She *did* sound unbalanced. I headed for the lions.

"He was also worried, even afraid, that you might be having an affair."

She snorted. "I *wish*."

"Are you?" My voice was neutral: no judgment, no condemnation. Just information. Just background. *Just the facts, ma'am.*

"No, of *course* not."

There was a long pause. We were strolling past emus and ibex but Sara accorded them no interest, not even a passing glance.

"Sometimes I wish I were though." A wistful longing in her voice now. "I wish I could be with someone who wanted me, who cared about me. Who didn't scare me."

"You will. This will be over."

"Ye-e-e-ess." Disbelief heavy in that word.

"Was Jed like that once?"

"Oh yes." She smiled and looked almost happy. I waved at the antelope as we ambled by. They didn't wave back. Or even look up. "I remember it really well, it just doesn't seem that he is the same person now that he was back then. I don't believe in that old Jed now. This Jed, the one he is today, has changed, maybe destroyed that Jed entirely, the Jed I married."

"Tell me about the Jed you married."

"I imagine he was very like the one you're seeing now, the one a lot of people who know him and us will describe." Her face was open, her expression candid. "You feel he's a really nice guy, all-American, like I said. A Boy Scout. The small-town kid you grew up next to. He's hard-working, reliable, would do anything for a friend. You know . . . honest, loyal, true-blue, walks little old ladies across the street, all that Boy Scout kind of crap." She waved away the rest of it with a shooing motion that was almost an obscenity.

"He's caring, affectionate. He's smart, really smart—he was good at school and is good at his job. He's ambitious too, he wants to go places. He's not daring though." She frowned. "I don't mean he's not brave in his work. He is. How do I explain it . . . He doesn't like the unknown, he doesn't like to take risks or be adventurous. He likes things to be predictable. You know—get married, have two point four kids, get promotions, go to church, do community work, all of that. He likes doing the same thing day after day, year after year. He doesn't find it boring."

"And you do?"

"Oh yes. For me that kind of thing is a living hell. I like things to be different, exciting! And I don't mean—" She scrunched her nose and mouth up into a funny face. "I don't mean going to Yellowstone one year and Yosemite the next. Or getting the house painted a different color."

We stopped and gazed at the hippos, rhinos, and elephants. They looked large, placid, and peaceful. Of course, so did Jed.

"Sometimes I think that's why he's so angry at me now, why he'd rather kill me than . . . than let me change. He doesn't want to change, you see. It upsets him. So of course he doesn't want me to either. He wants me to stay the same with him. He wants us to live happily ever after just like we were before. And I can't do that. So he'd rather kill me than lose me. But that's not right." Her voice was tentative as she looked the question at me.

"No. That's not right," I agreed.

Not right, not understandable, not moral or legal.

"When did you start seeing the Jed you now know?"

"Huh?"

"When did the man you married change?"

"I don't know." She shook her head in genuine puzzlement. "That seems like such an obvious and easy question, not just to ask but to answer. And I can't. It was so gradual, I almost didn't notice it happening. Only one day you wake up and you realize that things have changed. We've been married for three years. The first year Jed was the man I knew, the man I married. I think maybe it was sometime in the second year. Maybe. But it's only been extreme in the last six months."

"Extreme?"

She looked at me quickly. "Threats and physical violence."

"Is there anyone else who noticed these changes?"

"I don't think so. He was careful to hide things, to act the way he always did in public, to put up a good front. My family and friends knew because I told them. And because they saw the bruises." The last was angry.

"His friends?"

"Oh *right*." She snorted. "Like he would show that to them. Puh-*leeze*. They think he's the greatest thing since sliced bread. Look at them, Kat, they sleep all the time."

We stared at the sleeping lions, watched a tail flicker, a whisker twitch.

"They look like big harmless pussy cats, don't they?"

"At this distance," I replied dryly. I am not the kind of person who thinks wild animals make fun pets or should be cuddled up to. Respected, yes.

"Jed's like that."

I lost her on the last segue. "He sleeps all the time?"

"No-o-o-oo. Of course not. He looks harmless but he's not."

I was tired of hearing about Jed. "Where are you working now, Sara?"

"Temporary stuff. Wherever I get a job. Right now a downtown bank. I have a lot of experience as a programmer and over the years I've established a bunch of contacts in the computer field. Now I'm taking on short jobs, a month or so—for obvious reasons I don't want to be in one place too long. Consulting projects, mainly. It's fine for now, the work is reasonably interesting and I'm always on the move. I feel a lot safer this way too. Jed doesn't know where I am or where I work."

"Are you working with people you know?"

"Do they eat people, Kat? Do you think they're vicious?"

"I think vicious is a human characteristic. Animals kill for food and attack when threatened."

"They're not hateful the way people are?"

"Why would someone who had degrees in zoology be doing my job?"

She gazed at me blankly.

I sighed. "I think most animal behaviors are instinctual, not emotional, and that they are directly related to survival. Which brings us back to why you hired me. To survive, remember? Would you like to answer a few more questions now?"

"All right." She said it meekly and cast her eyes down but I thought I caught a flicker of humor there. "No. I'm not working with people I've known for any length of time. Just this job and that's been three weeks. I'm very careful not to tell them where I live or anything much about myself. I keep to myself and do my work."

"Other friends?"

"I haven't stayed in touch. I feel badly about it but I don't know what else to do. The world is full of blabbermouths, I found that out the hard way," she added sadly.

Yes. It's a plus in my job of course, but not in general.

"And your family?"

"I talk to them, I trust them, but we haven't visited much. I know you're right and that it would be way too easy for Jed to follow them to get to me or watch their houses for when I showed up. I feel so lonely, so isolated. I hate it, I really do."

I nodded.

"And I feel as though I shouldn't, really shouldn't make new friends—" She broke off and stared at the lions, blinking back tears. "Look what happened to Lorraine. How can I ever forgive myself for that? How could I possibly expose anyone to that risk?" A tear slid down her cheek.

"You did not kill her, Sara."

"No, but she died because of me, there's no getting around that."

There wasn't, no. "You did everything you could to save her."

"It wasn't enough; there's no getting around that either."

I was ready to go back to the eating habits and temperaments of lions. No kidding.

"Anyway—" She kind of hiccuped and snuffled. "It's not just that. I'm afraid to make new friends because I don't know who I can trust anymore. One person can make you distrustful of everyone else. Isn't that awful?"

I didn't answer that. I wasn't really in a philosophical mood.

"You'd be better off leaving town—"

She made a face at me, like a child's face when she's told to go to bed. "Maybe. But I'm not going to so don't even bother."

I shrugged, getting more philosophical by the moment. *Que será, será,* I guess. "Do you and your husband have a will?"

I got the open-mouth O again before a hand quickly covered it over. "Oh . . . my . . . God . . ." She pushed the horrified sounds through her fingers.

I took that for a yes. "You do then."

"Yes. If anything happens to me, he gets everything. Oh my God, Kat, he could murder me dead and get all my money."

Murder me dead? Somewhere a grammar teacher rolled over in her grave.

"Is there a lot of money?"

"I don't know what you think of as a lot, but yeah, to me it is. For a while we were both working long hours and overtime. We made a bundle and invested it all. I bet there's about sixty thousand now. And we each have a life insurance policy for another hundred and fifty thousand. And the house and cars and bank accounts. Still, it's tough to believe that someone would be killed just for money, isn't it?"

Back to philosophy. Or naïveté. "People lose their lives all the time for much less." For nothing. For ten dollars at a 7-Eleven holdup. "Would Jed kill you for money?"

She thought it over. "I honestly don't think he would. And it's not that he doesn't care about money, he does. But he doesn't think it's the most important thing, and he's willing to work for it. In fact, he's kind of puritanical that way. He thinks you enjoy things more if you work for them."

"Do you?"

"No." Big happy grin. She held out one hand palm up and then the other. "Try me. Go ahead—throw money at me." And then frowned. "That was another thing Jed didn't like about me, my willingness to do things the easy way. I mean, sometimes you can't but if you can, why the heck not? He didn't even like it when I bought lottery tickets. *Jeez,* what a spoilsport."

I had to keep reminding myself that the issues here were life and death. Listening to Sara made it sound like a squabble between children, a squabble that should be settled with a rock/paper/scissors game.

But there was Lorraine and the drowning. Bruises and cuts, threats and fears. And the unknown, which was open-ended.

"Do you ever go to your house now, Sara?"

"No." Her face grew still and fearful.

"But you still have a key?"

"Yes."

"Do I have your permission to go into the house?"

Fear written on her face in capital letters. "Do I have to go with you?" she whispered.

"No."

She nodded her assent. The fear stayed in place. "Be careful." The whisper again.

"C'mon, let's go see the bears." I was hoping her spirits would perk up at the sight of more carnivores. Hmmmm. Or do bears eat nuts and berries? Never mind, they were fierce. I was getting the idea that one of the things that Sara needed was more positive role models. Lions and tigers and bears.

Hey, it was a start.

CHAPTER 14

She was careful to dress appropriately. No, that wasn't quite it. Effect. She was dressing for effect, as though she was staging something. Dress, makeup, attitude, it all counted.

At work she was quiet and mousy. Wallpaper you don't notice, she dressed that way now. God knows that was easy. All she had to do was walk to the closet and choose from the stacks of clothes she'd worn before she lost weight. Twenty-five pounds made a big difference. Twenty-five pounds and working out. Her clothes from before hung on her, shapeless, blah. She had to laugh when she caught sight of herself in the mirror. She could hardly remember the person she had been before. God knows she hardly ever wanted to, needed to.

The days went quickly. One of the things about fear, about danger, is that you learn to live in the moment. You have to. If you forget, if you let down your guard or daydream, then POW!—right in the kisser. If you were lucky it was just cuts, bumps, and bruises. If you were unlucky, you were dead.

She smiled at herself in the mirror and fingered the tube of lush, red lipstick. Her number wasn't coming up, not for a long time. She had plenty more to do. *Plenty*. Love was another thing that made you live in the present. That made her smile too. Funny. Love and death both did that. One a beginning and one an ending. She opened the lipstick, looked at it with longing, then put it down and brushed on a colorless lip gloss. Tonight she would wear the red lipstick.

She blew herself a kiss in the mirror, then picked up a drab sweater and a brown bag. It was fortunate that she loved the challenge of what she did, that the days went by quickly, evenly, easily.

Walking out into the spring sunshine she let the smile slip from her lips. The masquerade had begun. It was like a dance, an elaborate dance. But she knew the steps well.

The smile in the mirror was bright red, the eyes sparkled, enhanced by color and makeup. *Clothes make the man*. It was probably an advertising slogan, she thought in disgust—she hated being manipulated—but it was accurate. The browns and beiges she had worn earlier today lay in a puddle at her feet where she had let them drop, then stepped out of them, kicking free.

She wished it was as easy as that, kicking away everything in the past that held her back, everything brown and ugly.

The orange and red she wore tonight glowed. The saleswoman had shown her how to put those colors together. Well, she smiled at herself again and smoothed another layer of lipstick on—not because she needed to, but for fun, for red red fun. The *old* her wouldn't have had the courage. The new one was figuring it out. She picked up the brown crocodile leather bag and headed for the door. She had a two-hundred-dollar bag from Nordstrom. Imagine! And she smiled again. She was smiling a lot more these days.

In the car she looked at the map before driving off, the address an unfamiliar one. It didn't matter. She knew the city well, could find things easily, quickly. It was a church tonight, a seven o'clock meeting. She thought of nothing as she drove over, her mind empty of all but the streets and turns and directions. She paid attention to what was in front of her but not in back. If there was someone following her, she thought idly, she wouldn't know it, but there wasn't. She didn't have to look back to make sure. She was secure. All was right in her world. When she pulled into the church parking lot there was a place right up front near the door and in the light. She smiled. Wouldn't you just know it?

There was a hum of voices in the room, a hum that broke when she walked in. It picked up again, after a moment, but not as strongly as before. She looked around for the one familiar face here, found it and nodded. A short introduction and then she was on. She was It.

"Hi, my name is Steffie. I have a last name, as of course you do, but I understand one of your rules here is to use first names only and I respect that."

She paused and smiled at everyone, fourteen or fifteen anxious and curious faces. She tried to make eye contact with everyone, tried to make each person feel as though she was speaking to her alone. Mostly anxious. All women. Women she recognized because she had been one of them. Most were quite overweight, although one or two were way too thin, almost anorexic. Their clothes were mostly uninteresting and unflattering. Her eyes lingered on a putrid floral number in fuchsia, hot pink, and turquoise. Yipes. She let her smile broaden to include everyone in the room. Most tried to smile back but for a few it was too much. She remembered that feeling too.

"I know you want to hear my story. I hope you don't mind if I show you a few things first."

Show-and-tell. When he told her, she had laughed out loud—it seemed that stupid. But she agreed to try it and he was right, it worked. It made them believe her instantly and it made them believe in her, that she was one of them. Later she would make them see that they could become her.

She held up the photograph. No one said anything. No one seemed very interested. "This is me ten months ago." They gasped then, they always did. She had had that snapshot blown up to fifteen by twenty and mounted on posterboard. It was black and white and grainy. She loved the black-and-white effect, especially now, next to her in red and orange and smiles. After the gasp a murmur ran around the room and then the questions started.

"How much weight did you lose?"

"Forty-two pounds." She only admitted that at times like this. Never to friends, sometimes not even to herself—then she said twenty-five. She couldn't stand to admit that it had gotten as out of hand as all that. Except here. Except for this.

"How long did it take you?"

"Six months."

"Dieting?"

"Eating sensibly. I didn't diet, I changed my lifestyle. I chose to eat different foods, to exercise, to change the pictures and opinions I held of myself."

Absolute silence.

She knew what they were doing, every single one of them. They were hating themselves in every way they could think of. For being too fat or too thin, for being unhappy, for taking it out on their families, for trying and failing over and over. They were even hating themselves for hating themselves. She knew this with total certainty because she was one of them and she had been there.

"I know what you are thinking," she said, and then she told them. And there was another absolute silence, this one torn by the sound of a woman crying, softly at first and then louder as though something had broken inside her and she couldn't stop, couldn't do anything but cry. Steffie walked over, knelt beside her, put her arms around her and held on, hoping she wouldn't break up completely. Sometimes they did.

This one didn't though. Steffie stood, handed her tissues from a nearby box. Others were crying as well. Steffie walked back to the front of the room.

"Do you know why we cry? Sometimes because we're hurt, or lonely, or sad. Sometimes because we're afraid. And sometimes . . ." She paused and looked around the room. "Sometimes we cry because although we have been hurt very badly, we see a way to leave that hurting behind us, and even more importantly, we see hope in front of us. We . . . see . . . a . . . new . . . beginning."

She looked around. There wasn't a dry eye in the place. "Look!" She kicked her red high-heeled pumps off and raised her voice dramatically. "This is how *I* used to look." She reached into the shopping bag at her feet and pulled out a huge brown skirt and jacket, pulled them on over the clothes she was wearing, slipped her feet into shapeless brown loafers. She gave them a moment to assimilate it, to process it. Then she let her hold go, stepped out of those things and back into her red pumps. Like Cinderella.

"Clothes are something we choose. Our clothing is a reflection of our inner selves. This is *very* obvious. You know this, of *course* you do. But . . . did . . . you . . . know that how we look is also something we choose?"

A murmur in the group. Some frowns. They didn't like that. It was easier to be a victim. She understood. She was on their side. She was one of them.

"I know." She smiled warmly, sympathetically. "It doesn't feel like that. It feels like we're trapped by our genes, our busy schedules, our budgets, even our beliefs. At least that's how I felt. But you know what I discovered? All of that is just for now, *not* forever."

The frowns were gone. She had them again. She picked up the loafers and brown suit, wadded them up and tossed them into the shopping bag. "You may leave the past behind you anytime you choose." She turned and kicked the bag, did a little two-step and pirouette. "*And* you may dance into the future. I will tell you how." She inclined her head in appreciation as they burst into applause.

"The first thing I will tell you is that you have already started to change. You would not be here tonight if that were not so. You are already on the path. Congratulations." She raised her hands in the air and clapped in warm appreciation of them. Everyone smiled this time.

"The second thing I will tell you is that you are working with others. You have chosen to meet and talk about things together, to love and support each other, and that is a very good thing. We are social beings, we humans, and we need the help and support of each other.

"Whatever our issues are—weight gain or loss, self-esteem, abuse in childhood—we need reliable and expert information. About food, exercise, positive mental attitude, maybe therapy, and about how all of these things can work together in your favor to realize the new healthy you that right now is still just a picture in your mind or a dream in your heart.

"There are many good groups to join. Your doctor can help, so can a nutritionist and a personal trainer and a therapist."

She looked around. The light had gone out of many of the eyes trained on her. "But perhaps even now you are thinking what I used to think when people said that to me. *Ha ha.* It wasn't real laughter of course. I belong to an HMO and my doctor never had any time for me. A nutritionist, a personal trainer, a therapist? How could I afford that? Hey, back then I figured I might just as well wish for a trip to the moon where I would weigh hardly anything anyway."

They laughed and nodded.

"No!" She pounded her fist on the table. "That is not help, it is a cruel hoax. I will tell you the help you need *and* where to get it."

They leaned forward, all of them, on the edge of their seats. They were hers, all hers. She savored it for a moment before she began to speak again.

CHAPTER 15

Strangely, the house felt almost unlived in. The furniture, the jackets hanging on a coat tree, even the cereal bowl and spoon in the sink did nothing to change that. I slipped the door shut and headed for the alarm pad.

I came primed with a line and a story but if Jed had changed the alarm code I was going to have to move quickly or talk fast. Maybe both. The code worked and I let my breath out in a happy whoosh. I don't know why I think holding my breath will help.

Actually I was holding my breath about a lot of things. That Jed was as busy as the taped message at his office made him sound, that he wasn't in the habit of popping by home during the day, that the neighbors weren't the nosy kind who, even now, were watching and dialing. I picked up the pace. If I got busted, at least I wanted a little information.

Quick cruise. Everything was picked up and neat, even dusted. No evidence of everyday life in the living room. No books or magazines open, not even a *TV Guide.* No sweatshirt tossed on a chair or sneakers under the coffee table. The kitchen, except for what looked like breakfast dishes, was also impeccable. Guy food in the refrigerator: beer, soda, juice, pickles, TV dinners, that kind of thing. Nothing moldy or yucky. Unlike my refrigerator. I caught my breath again—it had been Hank who shopped, cooked, stocked the fridge, Hank who— I wrenched my mind back, blinked away the tears.

Back to the front hall and coat closet where I yanked out Sara's raincoat and winter coat and piled them on the back of the couch. God knows why—it was spring in the Valley, winter was history and so, almost, were the rains. It was part of my story: *Sara needed some things, was afraid to come here by herself, or even with me, afraid because of Jed.* As stories go, it was only so-so but serviceable, I hoped. What I really hoped was that I wouldn't have to use it.

I took the carpeted stairs to the second floor at a run. Yuck. Whatever would possess someone to indulge in that particular shade of pale green? No accounting for tastes. Upstairs: master bedroom and two smaller bedrooms, one doing duty as an office, the other as an exercise room. In the bedroom the bed was neatly made, clothes put away, nothing seemed out of order. I zipped through two chests of drawers, one half emptied of Sara's things (or half filled with a girlfriend's things—a girlfriend with really crummy taste), one filled with neatly folded guy stuff. Then on to the nightstand.

A box of tissues, a well-thumbed Clancy novel, a pad of paper and a pen. Nothing written on the pad. Rats. Inside the only drawer was a Bible, a clip for an automatic handgun, and a box of condoms. Ribbed. Well, well. In a reflective and philosophical moment I could make a lot of that.

I didn't find anything in the closet but clothes. Predictable but disappointing. I grabbed a few blouses and sweaters at random and stuffed them into the tote I was carrying, added the small jewelry box on the dresser and headed for the bathroom. There I started tossing in cosmetics, perfume, feminine toiletries. Uh-oh. Suppose Jed did have a girlfriend? Oops. From snooping to a felony just like that. I crossed my fingers and finished tossing.

By now I pretty much had my heart set on the office. It was looking like that was Last Chance in the Interesting Possibilities Ahead Department. And there I was on really shaky ground.

"Why could I be in the office?" I had asked Sara.

She shrugged, a bit carelessly and callously, I thought. "Dunno, it's all his stuff, not mine."

"Work with me here, Sara." Okay, it came out a little tart. "Income tax records, your birth certificate, health records, what?"

"Dunno. He does the taxes and I kept my stuff somewhere else."

Dunno. I might have to fall back on that. I started pulling open file drawers and flipping through stuff. Very neat, very organized. Very predictable. Nothing out of line that I could see. No nefarious plans, damning memos, or how-to books like *21 Ways to Kill Your Soon-to-Be-Ex-Wife Without Getting Caught, Stalking in Your Spare Time,* or *Slap Her Silly and Get Away With It!* Nothing like that. Not that that wasn't being a little overly hopeful and optimistic on my part.

His office seemed more personal, more lived in, a short stack of bills on the desk, the beginning of a to-do list. Interesting stuff like—pick up bathroom hardware, fix sprinkler, call Mom, flea collar. Flea collar? There was a *dog* here? I could feel the hair on the back of my neck stand up. I love dogs but I don't like to meet them for the first time while I'm ransacking their houses. And why the hell hadn't Sara said something about the damn dog? Hah, watch my vocabulary deteriorate in a stressful situation like this. I thought back quickly. Had I seen a dog door into the house? I was almost sure I hadn't. Damn damn damn. Almost is okay with a Peke maybe, but not a rottweiler.

I flipped through Jed's appointment calendar. Either he led a really dull life or he was leaving the juicy stuff out. I saw nothing about Sara; she was as absent there as she was from this house. I stared at the framed wedding photo that stood on the desk. At least I assumed it was a wedding photo. Jed was in a dark suit smiling at the camera with a hand floating on his arm and flowers all around. His bride was gone, had been ripped away leaving only her hand behind. I shivered. It seemed like a violent, ugly thing to do. Had it been Jed or Sara? I wondered.

No other photographs. Lots of trophies. Basketball, softball, bowling. Nothing else that was very personal or endearing. Jeez. I could learn more by reading a job application. I scooped up my tote bag, bolted down the stairs, latched onto the coats, and made for the door.

Oops.

I headed for the front-room window to see if the coast looked clear. Which it did. There was a kid on a skateboard but he was a teenager with a cap on backwards and an attitude way too superior to notice the likes of me. I was out the door in a flash, zooming down the driveway and starting to get that home free and happy as a lark feeling when I remembered the alarm. Damn and blast.

And went back in to reset it. Holding my breath.

Snooping is such fun.

What is this?"

"My alibi."

Sara was picking through my tote bag looking confused. "Huh? I don't get it."

"Is that all your stuff?"

"Yes, of course. Stuff that I don't care about, that's why I left it behind. What do you mean, alibi?"

"If Jed walked in on me snooping through the house, I needed a reason to be there. Picking up some things for you was the reason."

"Oh." She shivered.

"Did you and Jed use condoms, Sara?"

"What?"

"There were condoms in the nightstand. Was that a method of birth control that you used?"

Sara had flushed a deep red. "No, no we didn't. Is that—that son of a bitch!—is he having an affair *already*?"

I shrugged. "No idea. Maybe it's just the Boy Scout in him getting prepared. Anyway, why do you care?" I was definitely curious, even surprised at her response. I thought she would have welcomed a focus of interest other than herself.

She bit her lip. "I don't. Really. I guess I was just surprised. You caught me off guard. I mean we *are* still married and all. You know."

But I didn't. I waited to see if she would say more. But she didn't, not for a long time. Just stood there and bit her lip and furrowed her brow, her mind sailing along, a Frisbee on a downwind course. When she turned her eyes on me finally, they were dark, opaque. Her voice was flat. "Did you find out anything?"

"Nothing important."

"What are you going to do now?"

"Wait until you call me."

"Oh."

Sara's instructions were to call me if she felt she was being watched or followed. I would show up. And then we would have me following Jed following Sara.

I sighed. Like the Three Stooges. Only two of us were armed. I sighed again. Then registered a flicker of fear.

"Do you have a gun, Sara?"

"No. Do you think I should?"

"Probably not. Do you know how to use one?"

She shook her head.

"*Definitely* not. Why didn't you tell me about the dog?"

"What dog?"

"Did you and Jed have a dog?"

"No. Does he have one now?"

"I'm not sure."

"Condoms, a dog . . ." Sara shook her head and looked mystified, even dismayed. Or maybe as though she had expected things to continue as predictably as she had left them, had forgotten that the future is unwritten, uncharted. "What else, Kat?"

"I don't know." I was trying for patience there. "It doesn't matter to me, nor should it to you. The only thing that matters is your safety. Actually, the sooner Jed gets a new life, the better off you are."

"Why don't you know?" Her voice was shrill. "Isn't that what this is all about? You've got to find out everything about Jed. *Every*thing." She was jabbing a finger in the air at me with each syllable, her face hot and flushed again, her eyes glittering and unpleasant.

"That's not what this is all about. Calm down."

She started to shriek at me.

Bad move telling her to calm down. Being sensible and reasoned naturally infuriates people who are about to totally lose it. I waited for the shrieks to subside. Soon, I thought; it's not that much fun to shriek at someone staring out a window and ignoring you. I was thankful she didn't have a gun. Knife? Mace? Hmmmm . . . maybe check that out later. The shrieks trailed off into a whimper. I waited for that too to end. Then spoke into the silence.

"Why don't we just write that off to nerves and fear. For future reference though, I don't like being yelled at. Do it again and you can color me gone." I turned away from the window and looked at her. "You hired me to document your charges of harassment, threats, intimidation, and stalking. Not to dig up dirt on your husband. You want that, you hire someone else. Are we clear on this?"

She nodded.

"Say it."

"Yes." She pushed the word out as if with tremendous effort. "But if you do find out things about Jed, you'll tell me, won't you? If you just happen to, I mean. Not that that's your job. I understand. Just, you know, if you do."

"No." I didn't like the mess this was becoming. And I had always refused to have anything to do with divorce cases. Which this wasn't supposed to be.

"But—"

"Why did you attempt suicide, Sara?"

Her face went from flushed to pale just like that.

"Wha-a-at do you mean?" She stammered.

"Just that. Why?"

"I felt so helpless, so afraid. I know this sounds stupid but it seemed like that was the only way I could control things. I guess that's the kind of thing that makes sense to a frightened and lonely person. Don't you think?" Her voice begged me to understand.

"I don't know. I've never been that frightened or lonely. So frightened that you would kill yourself to end the fear?"

She nodded. "And I didn't want him to have the satisfaction of knowing how frightened I was, of seeing it. The counselor told me that it was not an unknown reaction in a situation like mine."

"You are seeing a counselor?"

The nod again, a single short hard jerk. She seemed to be measuring me with her eyes. "I'm sorry. I didn't mean to yell at you. The more information I have, the more I feel in control, that's all. Doesn't it seem reasonable, sensible, when you look at it that way?" she asked reasonably and sensibly.

Oh sure, you bet, only I remembered the shrieks. And the suicide.

"I'm trying to be like the giraffe and adapt to my situation. Evolve and survive." She gave me a sweet, winning little smile. "We never did see the giraffes, did we? Too bad. Want to go again?"

"I want you to call these people and tell them to talk to me." I'd typed up the list of names that Jed had given to me, friends and associates of both of them.

"About what?"

"About anything. Isn't that all right?"

"Oh. Well. Yes, of course."

She neither looked nor sounded like she really meant it but it was good enough for me.

"And Jed?"

"I'll keep an eye on him."

She didn't seem real excited about that either. I guess it looked better in the movies with Sam Spade and Philip Marlowe.

In black and white.

There's a comfort in that.

CHAPTER 16

S*we-e-eet dreams of yo-o-ou.*

Patsy Cline's voice ran through his mind, threaded and woven into images of her. He could remember the softness, silkiness of her skin, the sweetness of her breath, the exotic smell of the perfume she wore at night.

She lay in his arms, sleepy, drifting off. His fingers played across the naked silkiness of her back, pulled gently through her hair, caressed her wherever he touched. She stirred slightly in his arms, shifted so that he could reach her, touch more than her back. His fingers slid across her belly and he felt her shiver, tremble under his touch. The languid sleepiness in her limbs was almost gone, she was awake and alert though her eyes were closed. Why? he wondered. To fantasize? To substitute a different life, a different story, to make up another lover?

She would never tell him, would say only that she liked the darkness, the total concentration on him and his touch. She threw away her self, she said, and slid into his being, into the circle of his arms, into the totality of his touch.

His fingers played across her belly, getting closer and closer, teasing, approaching, retreating, making her stiffen and beg with her body for him to keep going—*Don't stop don't stop don't stop,* she cried out sometimes when they were making love. *Do that.* He loved it when she spoke, when she cried out. *Touch me there more more more.* And he did and then his hand would slide away, would slip somewhere else, and she would moan, in her desire for him both to touch her there and to go back to touching her in the last place.

He traveled over her body with his hands, his kisses, his tongue until she was wet, slippery and wild, until her words were sobbing, inarticulate cries, animal sounds, and she shoved him to the mattress, pinned him there with hands and knees, pushed herself on him and him deep in her. He loved that moment, touching the center of her. Until then he was under control, watching himself, pacing himself, careful not ever to finish early, to leave her behind.

He could tell by her rhythm; sometimes he would wait longer. Faster, wilder, she would arch her back propping herself with her hands on his chest. She would throw back her head, her throat arced, white and beautiful, and the cries would start, the cries of excitement, desire, and then of satisfaction, completion. Totality as she fell on his chest, sobbing softly sometimes, sliding in next to him, her fingers threaded through the hair on his chest.

Sometimes he let her sleep then. Sometimes he would start again, the gentle caresses that slipped about, taking her imperceptibly from satisfaction back into wanting, into desire. She protested then, sometimes, pushing him away and saying that she needed sleep, that it was a workday, that . . . It was easy though, easy to make her forget.

Sweet dreams.

He loved the sound of her cries.

Later he could take the same things and make them different. The cries, the arc in her throat as she leaned back. He thought of her crying out in fear, he imagined the feel of his hands around her neck. So slender, slippery with sweat—not in anticipation but in fear. In terror. He could feel his fingers tighten, his thumbs on her windpipe, her body rigid with terror. Nothing of desire.

She would beg him then too, beg him for breath, for an end to the terror. Beg him for life. He could hear his laugh, hear his enjoyment.

He loved it when she cried out, when she begged.

Her arms and legs would thrash, would flail about, would push against him. But that was nothing. He could pin her body down easily. She was strong but she was no match for him. Nor for his desire. He hated to think of her pretty face ruined. The death grimace, the bulging tongue, the purple color. No, he hated to think of that.

There were many ways. He was trained, after all. Trained to defend himself. But defense is easily turned around into offense. He could press her carotid artery, press her into unconsciousness or death, smother her with a pillow, snap her neck.

Snap her neck. He liked that. It seemed simple, clean. It was the way you put small animals out of their misery. He liked that too, the idea of putting something out of its misery. Whose was the misery though, his or hers? Or both? Who was the animal? And the victim?

Or drowning. Sitting with someone in a hot tub, warm soft water caressing you. A glass of wine in your hand. Stars. Dark silky blackness above. And then the water, warm, welcoming. Dark silky blackness below. And all around. And then nothing. Flatline. Peace.

Sweet dreams.

There were two ways for terror to end. And desire.

There were dreams and nightmares.

CHAPTER 17

"You understand that, ordinarily, this would never happen?" He was very earnest, eager, and determined that I grasp the simple point he was making for the third time.

I stifled a yawn. "I understand."

"Anything told to a member of the clergy is imparted in the strictest confidence, a confidence that should not and cannot be violated."

I sighed inwardly. Fourth time. "I understand."

"Jed has asked me to make an exception here. I respect this request although I am not entirely comfortable with it. Well—please go ahead."

"What is your impression of the relationship between Jed and Sara?"

He shook his head sadly. "Sara is an impetuous, foolhardy young woman, I'm afraid."

I stopped my eyes from widening and stifled a snort. Barely. He sounded like a pompous, stuffy old codger but I was willing to put dollars to doughnuts that he wasn't out of his twenties.

"Really? In what way?" I spoke only after I had my voice and responses under strict control.

"Marriage is a holy contract entered into by two people. The husband is the breadwinner, the center around which the family radiates. The wife is his helpmate, his support in life. Her duty is to God, husband, and children. Instead we see that Sara was preoccupied with career, self-aggrandizement and fulfillment, with the shallow, hollow things that young women of our age are increasingly losing themselves and their spiritual ways and values to."

He took a deep breath and puffed out his cheeks, the perfect picture of mindless bombast and empty rhetoric. I stared in admiration. He smiled condescendingly at me. "Ah, you seem to understand. You seem not to be one of those unfortunate young women so obsessed with career and their own path."

Appearances can be deceiving. It was a tenet I never forgot in my job. My eyes wandered about his office briefly. A dark room with dark walls, almost drawn curtains, and pictures of Jesus suffering. And suffering. And suffering. I looked around again. Yup, just suffering. Not healing, or reaching out to children, speaking with his disciples or working miracles. Just suffering. A lot of blood too. I caught myself. No point in taking this too far.

"It is God's way," he intoned pompously. "Women of Sara's age should be having babies, taking care of their husband's and children's needs, doing church work and other good works. I'm sure you agree, Miss Colorado?" He smiled benignly at me.

I smiled right back, no slouch in the benign department. "There is a time and a place for everything, Mr. Jolson." Or the misdirection department. "And Jed? What was his feeling?"

"He allowed his wife a little too much rein." Jolson spoke with an edge of regret. "Better to curb that from the beginning, to set the training firmly in motion." *Too much rein. Curb. Training*. Was this a marriage or a circus act? I thought of the animals we had seen at the zoo trapped forever in a life they had not chosen and which was not natural to them. A zoo, a circus, or a prison?

"Jed loved his wife very much, he allowed her a great deal of freedom. Too much, I am afraid. Too often husbands and parents alike mistake the granting of freedoms for the expression of love."

"Are you aware of Sara's allegations that her husband physically abused her?"

"Discipline and structure are necessary things."

"You condone a man beating his wife?"

"Each man is master in his own home."

So that was a yes. I stared at him. He smiled in complacent satisfaction; he believed that his work and church embodied the teachings of Jesus. And it made me sick to my stomach. There were millions like him. Okay, that made me even sicker. Jolson was still smiling, the reflection evidently a pleasure to him.

"And you must ask yourself, miss, what it was that Sara had done to provoke her dear husband to such a reaction."

"There is no legal justification for spousal abuse. You may not beat the tar out of people just to set them straight."

Jolson arched an eyebrow at me and permitted himself a superior and self-satisfied smile. Looking down from moral high ground, I suppose. Inwardly I shook myself. Why did I do this—allow myself to be drawn into any kind of debate with this lizard?

"Did Sara ever come in for counseling, either alone or with Jed?"

"Regrettably not. I have hope for them though, as I know Jed does. We pray together. I pray for them."

My flesh was starting to crawl. Soon it would leave, with or without me. Understandable.

I stood. "Thank you for your time."

"You're welcome, my dear." He was doing his smarmy avuncular routine, even though he was younger than I. "Please come back again. Our doors are always open for the lost and straying little lamb." He came around the desk and patted my elbow. Earnestly. I could smell his cheap cologne. "*Always.*" He patted me again.

I withdrew my elbow. "We would not be a good match, your church and I."

"We would be happy to see you. Irregardless."

"There's no such word."

It punched a hole in his avuncular demeanor. I smiled as I walked out.

"I'll pray for you," he called after me.

A lizard praying for me. What a concept. The outside door hissed shut behind me.

So that was the religious element in Jed's life. I wondered what the other formative influences had been.

Mike Cavett answered on the second ring. "Yeah." His voice was brusque and businesslike. "Oh sure." He brightened up when I told him who I was. "Jed told me you might call. C'mon over. I'll make time to help a friend like Jed any day. You know where I am?"

He gave me an address in West Sacramento where he was a plant manager, packing and shipping materials, something like that. I was forty minutes away and I told him so.

"Be here all day." He laughed heartily. "See you when you get here."

West Sac is pretty industrial, although the Port of Sacramento is also there. This could make it exotic and exciting but it doesn't, even though efforts have been made in that direction. Years ago the main highway went through West Sac. Trucks, lots of trucks. And sleazy motels, diners, and hookers. Many of the trucks were gone, but the rest of it was still there. Especially the hookers. They had the look of those to whom life has not been kind and hope is just a word.

I pulled into the parking lot of a beautifully landscaped industrial park, still in Charity's 4Runner as I hadn't coped with the loss of the Bronco. Loss? Demolition was more like it.

Mike came out to the front office to meet me, a short husky man, balding with hair neatly combed over the top of his head, a firm handshake, and a ready smile. He shooed me on back to his office and plied me with coffee and doughnuts. I acquiesced because it was easier than fighting, apparently the only other alternative.

"The coffee is only so-so but the doughnuts are great. Here, have another one." He added a fluffy glazed number to the heartily sprinkled gooey chocolate one already on a napkin in front of me. Jeez. I'd been there less than two minutes and already I was outnumbered. I took a sip of coffee that turned out to be terrible, not so-so, and lukewarm to boot.

"How can I help you, Kat?"

"How well do you know Jed?"

"Shucks, we go back twenty-five or more years now, to the fourth grade. We were best friends then and pretty much have been ever since. Jed's a hell of a guy."

"Do you see each other a lot now?"

"Not as much as we used to but yeah, we do. We go out for pizza and a couple of beers. Used to go over to each other's place, barbecue, visit. These days that's pretty much changed, what with Sara and all."

"What's going on?"

"More like what's not going on." He said it glumly.

"Okay." Kat, the ever agreeable one. "What's not going on?"

"Damned if I know. One day everything seems all hunky-dory, the next Sara's getting skinny and anxious, Jed's getting concerned and upset and the whole thing seems to be going to hell in a hand basket."

"Upset—like angry?"

"No, more like worried, concerned. He loves Sara, wants her to be happy, wants things to work out for both of them."

"Both of them together?"

"Well, yeah, that's first choice, but apart if it comes to it. To be honest I don't think Jed's got a clue. Guys don't a lot of the time." He said that in a little burst of candor that was maybe, I couldn't quite decide, a bit disingenuous. "We think everything's okay and then WHAM!—it blows up on us. Maybe women know these things are coming but we sure don't. Jed was worried at first that Sara was sick, she started losing weight and all, but it turned out that she wanted to, was trying to. Me, I thought she looked fine but I like to see a little squeeze on a gal."

"What was it that was coming? Or going on?" I struggled to get back to something that resembled a factual statement.

"Damned if I know. After it turned out that Sara was losing weight on purpose I think Jed kinda wondered if maybe she was having an affair. A sudden change in looks, in personality—it could be."

He shrugged philosophically. He was, I thought, the kind of man who would have affairs, who would say that he kept them separate and that they were not a threat to his marriage or family.

"Was it?"

"I don't know. If it was, Jed never said. Fact is, he said the opposite."

"Was Jed having an affair?"

Don't take anything for granted. Get everything on record. Ask all the questions you can think of. This is the kind of thing that investigation is built on.

"If he was, he played it close. I honestly believe he wasn't and I never heard anything. Anyway, he's a one-woman man, always has been. Never played the field, dated a lot of girls, or screwed around. Just one gal. If it broke up it'd take him a while to get over it and then he'd find someone else, start up another relationship."

"And Sara? Would she have an affair?"

He shook his head. "I sure as hell can't see it."

"So what was the problem?"

"Damned if I know."

"Sara alleges that Jed has beaten her and wants to kill her because she's left him."

"What!" Mike came out of his chair like a bottle rocket. "That's the biggest load of crap—pardon my French—that I ever heard. Jed wouldn't hit a woman, Jed wouldn't hit a goddamn dog!"

I reviewed in silence all the men I had come across who treated their guns and dogs better than their women. Hmmmm. Quick add-on in that mental review: Bibles too. So it was going to take a little more than that to convince me.

"I've known Jed all my life. He treated his mother with respect, his teachers, my mother, any woman he met. His father taught him to be a man and his mama taught him to act like a gentleman. I've never known him to treat Sara, or any woman, with anything but respect and consideration." He paced around the office. One of my doughnuts hit the floor on a sharp turn and sudden hand gesture.

"This is not something that comes out of the fucking clear blue sky, you know." He picked up the pace, passed his desk again, slammed a fist down. "A guy doesn't just get up one day and say, *What the hell, I think I'll slap my wife around.*" He shook his head. "Sounds to me like Sara's out to make trouble, out to get him. *Damn* it all! I hate to hear that, I really do."

There was a tap on the door and a woman poked a face with a shy look on it around the corner. "Mr. Cavett—"

"Yeah." He spoke brusquely and waved the shy face away. Obediently it disappeared. "Look." He wheeled and faced me. "I don't mean to give you the bum's rush but I got work to do."

"I understand." I stood. Uh-oh. I'd forgotten the doughnut. And stepped on it. It was the gooey chocolate one too so I knew it was not going to be pretty. I decided not to look. "Thanks for your time." I held out my hand.

He shook hands with me as though I were a snake. Guilt by association, I guess. Spiders, zoos, lizards, snakes, I couldn't seem to get away from the animal kingdom these days. Mike Cavett seated himself and snarled at some papers. I let myself—and a chunk of chocolate doughnut on the bottom of my shoe—out, squeezed past the shy-faced assistant and headed for the parking lot.

The oh so reverent Mr. Jolson wanted me to come back. The pissed-off Mr. Cavett didn't. I wasn't exactly batting a thousand.

Time to try basketball.

Maybe a slam dunk?

And to lose the doughnut.

CHAPTER 18

They all acted differently when they arrived; everyone has an individual way of handling things. Still, there were certain common denominators. Fear was one. And excitement. And determination—sometimes with a little levity, sometimes harsh and grim. It was understandable, certainly. They weren't small things, the reasons that brought them here. And he was as serious, as committed as they.

Sometimes he watched them come in, walking up the sculptured cobblestone path, admiring the flowers, the lush shrubs and overhanging trees. It was a verdant paradise and it put everyone at ease. Or he watched them in the sitting room. The mirrors there were windows, one-way glass into an adjoining office. He got a very clear impression of people, watching when they thought they were alone. Open, unguarded. Sometimes even unmannered.

But always he greeted them, he did his best to make them feel welcome, happy, and at ease. It was, after all, their health, their life. And their dime, he thought wryly. He had come into this a dedicated, idealistic professional, naive and unrealistic as well. But that was some time ago. He glanced quickly into a mirror, straightened his tie, then took the back way from his office to the sitting room.

The young woman there sat at the piano, hands resting lightly on keys that hardly anyone touched or played. What a shame, he often reflected. He loved to hear the joyous sounds of Chopin and Mozart, the sober dignified strains of Bach and Beethoven, the wildness, the gaiety of Offenbach and Strauss.

She turned as he entered and looked at him with a quizzical expression. Her eyes were beautiful, deep. When he was younger he had set great store by first impressions—evaluations, he called them then. He did so no longer. It was a conceit of youth, he thought, the notion that you could take the measure of a man in the sweep of the eyes and senses, in a single calculation.

"Welcome, Ms. Jansen. I am Dr. Saunders."

She slid gracefully away from the piano and held out a hand, the fingers long, slim, cool. Her eyes were calm. She was, he thought, an extraordinarily self-possessed young woman.

And yet she was here.

He tried to think back to the forms, the applications, but no specifics popped up. Not on this one. He looked into her eyes again. In a sudden startling moment of clarity he realized that she was the kind of woman they burned as a witch in the Middle Ages. Those eyes spoke of depths, of knowledge, of the unknown. He imagined—no, he was sure—that those eyes got her into trouble.

"Shall we sit over here?" He gestured toward a seating arrangement—a love seat, two chairs, and a small table. On his way there he pressed an inconspicuously placed buzzer. And he noticed that she noticed. She settled herself into the love seat and he took a chair. Lily entered, dressed as a maid today, and smiled, a warm gesture that included them both. "How may I help?"

"Tea for me, please," Saunders said. "Ms. Jansen, tea, coffee, lemonade?"

"Lemonade."

"And refreshments," he added before he turned back to the young woman. The door clicked shut behind Lily as he spoke. "Please tell me why you are here. No fancy talk or medical jargon, just your own words."

"Because I am deeply unhappy." She spoke with a calmness, a serenity that belied her words. "Because I do not know how to change that." She leaned forward slightly. "Have you ever known such a feeling?"

"Yes." It was a simple question and he answered it simply.

"Will you tell me?" she asked.

"It was after Vietnam. I killed men for no reason or for reasons I did not believe in. Not just men but women, children, whole families. When I came home I could not see the value in life. I could not find beauty or meaning in anything."

"What did you do?"

"I listened to music."

"Music?" She wrinkled her nose in puzzlement.

"Mozart, Mendelssohn, Beethoven, Wagner. Later Strauss, Chopin, Haydn. It was a long walk back but for me music was the first step."

"I see."

They sat in a companionable silence. He could hear the birds outside, the music and harmonies of nature; he could read nothing in her eyes. She would allow it or not, he thought; it would be her choice, not his. Then a tap on the door and Lily entered with a tea tray. She moved quickly, easily, and without intruding on the silence in the room. Or the quiet places of the heart. He looked at the little cucumber sandwiches and was pleased. His grandmother had also made those for him. It was thoughts and memories of her that had led him back too, that had pulled him away from the horror and meaninglessness.

"It is a death of the soul, is it not?" She broke the silence after Lily left.

He pondered her words, pushed them through his mind first one way and then another. "I think not. If the soul were dead, chances are we would not think of it as such. We would not mourn and we would not be lost. It is a hardening perhaps, or a loss of touch and understanding. If it were dead, we would be empty; there would be no hope. Perhaps death would be more attractive than life."

"I tried to commit suicide. Did you ever do so?"

"No. Because I was so proficient at killing, I knew I would succeed. I knew I would not make that choice until I was past all hope."

She nodded. "That is why I am here. I still have hope, sometimes at least. And the suicide attempt frightened me. If I ever do that again I also believe I will not fail. Do you think you can help me?"

"Except in prison, I have never met anyone beyond help and hope. And if I cannot help I will find someone who can."

She smiled. Her eyes became open for the first time and he saw the light in them. The beauty. The depth.

The hope.

She sipped lemonade and he had another cucumber sandwich. The birds were loud, joyous in their spring songs. He thought about first steps.

CHAPTER 19

By watching the exit to the employee lot I picked up Jed after work. A bright red Ranger is not exactly inconspicuous. I followed him at a discreet distance figuring he was more likely than the average guy to pick up on a tail. Undoubtedly he wasn't expecting one—who is, after all?—and there was an element of safety in that.

Sara didn't know what his schedule was now. Basketball two evenings a week, she thought. And bowling. She didn't know when; she didn't know the rest of it, if any. So we were on an open agenda, Jed and I.

Or I was on a wild-goose chase.

I wore sunglasses. My shoulder-length hair was piled on top of my head under a baseball cap which I had jammed down around my ears. Add hot-pink hoop earrings and matching lipstick and I didn't look like me at all. Certainly not on a first, second, or third glance.

First stop was a sports store. They were BIG ON BOWLING. I knew this because of the sign in the window. Well hey, why not? Nothing like a new bowling ball to perk up a guy's spirits. And game. I wondered if Jed was in this for fun or competition. I've seen some pretty cutthroat bowlers in my day, not the kind of person I'd want to meet in a dark alley.

I scrunched down in my seat as Jed came out, apparently oblivious of his surroundings. He looked like he was whistling and he carried a bag. I scrunched a little more. Have I mentioned recently how hard my job is on posture?

We sat in the parking lot for a while after Jed exited the sports store, Jed talking on a cell phone, me scrunching. Wriggling a lot too, since scrunching is bad news not only for your posture but for your back as well.

Finally, dying of heat and boredom, I turned on the car, cranked up the a/c, and fiddled with the radio until I found a country station playing oldies. The songs were all about sorrow and lost love—jeez, I was practically in tears by the time we took off. "Satin Sheets to Lie On, Satin Pillows to Cry On," "Dreamin' My Dreams of You," "Please Help Me, I'm Fallin'," "He Stopped Loving Her Today." That one was a chilling tear-jerker about a man who could only leave a lost love behind in death. Which is what no one wanted to see happen here, I thought.

I hoped. Or maybe no one except Jed, he was the wild card. Jed's brake lights flashed and I pulled out into the parking lot, moving on out to the perimeter. And tried to think of a happy George Jones song. I couldn't. Word was George had beaten on Tammy Wynette too, Tammy our "Stand By Your Man" gal and his wife at the time. I pulled out into traffic behind Jed.

One stop on his way home. For pizza. Which reminded me how long it had been since I had eaten. Regular mealtimes, that's another thing my job worked against. There's nothing like the thought of pizza to make you feel really hungry too. Desperate even. I tried singing "Stand By Your Pizza" to the tune of "Stand By Your Man" but it didn't help. Didn't sound that great either. Some songs just don't hold up in translation.

When I was reasonably certain that Jed was heading home I dropped way back, let him lose me. Obvious only takes you so far, especially with a cop. Fifteen minutes later I cycled past the house. Bingo. His car was in the drive and the porch light was on.

God, I bet there are a million country songs about porch lights on and broken hearts, lonely lovers, lost souls, or (d) all of the above, in the house. I started to hum "Porch Light's On, Nobody's Home," and parked down the block. No scrunching this time. I got out a map, ostentatiously spread it out on the steering wheel. *See,* that gesture said, *I'm just an innocent lost bystander*. I dug out the cell phone for effect too, pulled out the antenna, held it up to my ear. *See, not to worry, I'm calling for directions now*.

I had a fifteen-minute wait during which time I tried to remember to move my mouth occasionally. Talking was the point of being on the phone after all. Bingo again. A white Corolla pulled into the driveway and parked cozily next to Jed's Ranger. The inside light went on and I watched a woman comb and fluff her hair and then apply lipstick.

Fluffing and glossing? Pizza? Just a shot in the dark but I was guessing this wasn't business. I watched the woman get out of the car, shake back her hair, and, not walk—glide? slip? float?—something like that, up to the front door.

Short wait. Jed opened right up and she floated on in. It was too dark to see her features, even her hair color, although I thought it might be blond, but she had the moves down. Just another guess, but I was betting they didn't meet at church.

I wrote down her license number as I drove past. Wistfully. It was definitely one of those if-only-I-were-a-fly-on-the-wall moments. Once around the corner I picked up the cell phone and dialed.

Jed and his companion weren't the only things on my mind. Pizza was too. Mushrooms, peppers, olives, tomatoes, pineapple, artichoke hearts. Yum.

And tonight was not the night to check out his love life.

CHAPTER 20

He thought about names for the children sometimes. He liked the simple old-fashioned ones like Mary, Jack, Trudy, Steven, and Anne. Sara liked the new ones, the trendy ones that the schools were already filled with: Jason, Jon—but not spelled properly with an *h*—Jessica, Jolene. They could compromise though, he knew they could, Jessica Anne or Trudy Jolene, they were both pretty. Anyway, a name was just a name.

The important thing was the child, a little bit of him and her but all the same someone totally different. Like snowflakes. He marveled at that, at the wonder of a new life. He thought of little fingers curling around his, of breath so soft and sweet and gentle that even when you held the baby, Jessica Anne, to your face, your heart, you could hardly see or feel the little breath, the small sturdy heartbeat of life.

But you could hear them. That was another marvel, how loud those little ones could be. They were impossible to overlook or forget, not that he would. He wanted a big family, lots of children. Jessica Anne and Steven, Trudy, Jack, Robert. Sara would call him Robbie or Rob, he thought. Well, that was all right. A roomful of children—happy faces around the breakfast table, the dinner table. Happy voices in the backyard and the driveway.

He had plans already for a wonderful playhouse. It had a ladder up and a slide down, doors and windows, a trapdoor, and an elevated walkway to a swing set. There were so many things he wanted to build, so many ways to show his love. They would play games. Everything. Softball, basketball, croquet, and miniature golf. He had a glass hoop already in the driveway but he would put another one, a smaller one, in too. Later there would be track and swimming and Little League.

For all of his kids, he thought. He didn't hold with separate activities for children. He wanted his daughters to have strong, healthy bodies, to be competitive and aggressive; he wanted his sons to know how to cook and wash their clothes, to be thoughtful and considerate. There was no reason, he thought, to keep on making the same kinds of mistakes generation after generation.

Their house would be too small with a big family. He could always add on, build out into the yard, but that would cut into the kids' outside play space. Maybe it would be better to look for a bigger place, more room in the house and the yard both. He wanted the children to have pets too. If they could move out a little he would get acreage, get the kids a horse.

He would do everything he could. He saw what happened, every day he saw it over and over—what happened when kids didn't have things to do, good things, constructive things. They turned to gangs and drugs and running in the streets. The boys got bad, the girls got pregnant. He didn't blame them. Kids are raw energy and it needs to go someplace. Like water, it will forge its own channel if you don't give it one.

He would give them plenty of things to do. There were games to play and books to read and music and art. He wanted his kids to have an appreciation of all kinds of things. And they would go hiking and camping—learn about the outdoors. He would take them to Yellowstone, Yosemite, and the Grand Canyon. To museums and art galleries. And to church. He would share with them everything he loved and valued, he would show them the beauties and wonders of the world.

Money would be a problem. He knew this, he was realistic. You can't raise kids on love alone. And how far does a cop's salary go? Not far at all, not these days. Still, there were a lot of ways to stretch things. You could be creative, you could make things happen. He was willing to work hard. He believed that where there was a will there was a way. What you wanted to do and worked for, you could accomplish.

What he most wanted was to hear the sounds of children's voices in his home:

"Daddy, can we play?"

"Can you help me, Daddy?"
"Will you read me a book?"
"Tell me a story, please."
"Can we go for a walk?"
"I'm hungry. What's for dinner?"
"Daddy, I love you. I love you, Daddy."

CHAPTER 21

The phone blasted into my consciousness, shaking me suddenly awake and immediately into fear. It had been this way ever since Hank's death. Now I feared for everything I held dear, for Alma, Lindy—my adopted "niece," and Charity. The unexpected was disaster, was the end. I was shaking as I picked up the phone.

"Kat, is that you? Oh my God, the most awful thing has happened."

"Who is this?" I couldn't clear my head. All I knew was that it wasn't Alma, Lindy, or Charity. It wasn't someone dear.

"Sara. Sara Bernard." Her voice was outraged, angry that I didn't recognize her.

"What's the matter, Sara?"

"Please come over. Please. I'm so upset. I can't be alone and right now there's no one else to call. I'm too afraid to leave. I—"

"What happened?"

"He called. He said he was going to kill me. He said he was just waiting for the right time. He said that I should be very, very frightened, that I should say my prayers and goodbyes. Oh God, oh God—" She started sobbing. There was nothing put on about her distress, her hysteria.

"Where are you?"

"In my apartment."

"Give me the address." I wrote it down. "I'll be there in half an hour. Don't answer the phone, don't answer the door. If anything, *any*thing, makes you suspicious, dial nine-one-one. You don't have to give your name. Say that someone is breaking in, that your husband has threatened to kill you. Do not open the door to anyone who says that he or she is a cop without verifying it. Got it?"

"Yes."

"I'm on my way."

I'd been dreaming of Hank, I thought. Hank. And then I was torn away.

Sara opened the door the moment I knocked. No hesitation, no voice asking me who I was. Death wish or slow learner? Take your pick.

"For crying out loud, Sara, I *told* you not to open the door without verifying who it was. You understand how dangerous this is. Why are you acting like this?"

She burst into tears. "But I was expecting you. I knew you were coming. And I have this." She pointed a gun at me.

I dropped. Like a stone. "Put it away. *Now!*" My cold, hard, do-as-I-tell-you voice coming from behind the couch where I had rolled.

She put it on the table looking frightened, I thought. I only hoped she was as frightened as I had been. I scrambled to my feet standing between Sara and the gun.

"I'm going to go through this slowly and carefully, Sara Bernard. Pay attention."

Frightened eyes fixed on me.

"Guns are not for scaring people, making a point, or looking cool. Guns exist for one reason and one reason only. To kill. If you point a gun at a person it should be for one reason—you plan to kill them. And you must assume that they will retaliate in kind. They will try to kill you. This is not a game or a bluff. This is life and death."

Dark frightened eyes in a white face. Two spots of color high on her cheeks. Blond hair tousled in a sexy just-got-out-of-bed look.

"If you *ever* point a gun at me again, I not only won't work for you, I won't even talk to you. That's assuming I don't kill you."

"You're joking." Her voice cracked.

"No. I never joke about guns." *Or killing.*

"I'm sorry, I really am."

She sounded sorry, she looked sorry. But not sorry enough. "Is it loaded?"

"Yes."

"Have you ever shot it?"

"No."

"Or any gun?"

"No."

"Why did you get it?"

"For self-protection. That's the *only* reason I would *ever* use it."

"Against Jed?"

"Yes, of course."

"But you pointed it at me."

"I told you I was sorry." Aggrieved, almost whiny.

"If I had been Jed, do you know what would have happened?"

"I would have shot him in self-defense. Just shot to wound him, not kill or anything."

I shut my eyes briefly. What is *wrong* with this country that we don't have gun control? Instead we give weapons to gangbanger children and—I stared at Sara shyly smiling at me, pleased with herself and her answer—nitwits.

"That is *not* what would have happened. Not even close. If Jed wanted to kill you, you'd be dead. By your own weapon. He would have disarmed you in a heartbeat. He could disarm you, could take complete control of the situation because you would have hesitated. You are not prepared to kill. Your goal is not, cannot ever be to wound, to slow down, to temporarily stop someone who is threatening you. There is no assurance that you can accomplish that. Death—killing—is your only guarantee."

The mouth in the small white face moved but no sound came out.

"You are no match for Jed, for his physical conditioning, training, and cop survival instincts. Unless you catch him asleep or off guard you will not kill him, or anyone with that level of training. He will kill you. This is not a guess on my part, this is a certainty. You are not going to scare him, you will barely faze him. He may reason with you, he may laugh at you, he will certainly kill you if he chooses."

Her mouth flopped open, finally made a noise that became words. "I really think that you are underestimating me."

"No."

"I could have stood up to him. I could have killed him. *If* I *had* to."

"There is only one way you could have killed him, Sara, and that is if you had emptied your gun through the closed door into his body. That would probably catch him off guard. Of course, you might kill someone else, an innocent, or Jed might kill you shooting back. And you would *certainly* face a murder charge."

"Not in self-defense," she whispered.

"If you shoot a man through a closed and locked door without calling nine-one-one, without any evidence of attempted assault or break-in, without an overt threat on his part, without a restraining order and a documented record of assaults and violence, you would—without question—be facing a murder charge."

Sara dropped, fell into a chair as though someone had thrown a forty-pound sack of flour at her.

"Fortunately you're one of the few people I know who would look good in orange. Well, you'll need a bright lipstick to get over that washed-out look."

"Orange?" she whispered again.

"Jail jumpsuit orange," I said cheerfully. "Hey, don't bother with a manicure either; I hear the handcuffs and shackles are tough on your nails."

Sara burst into tears.

I watched without sympathy, without compassion. When she slowed down to a snuffle I held out my hand. "Give me your gun."

She shook her head.

I dropped my hand.

"But I understand your point and I won't ever make those mistakes again, I promise."

I already had a lot of empty promises and hopes on file. Now I had one more. Great news.

"I'm going to make myself a cup of hot chocolate. Do you want one?"

A child's illusion: a cup of cocoa, a bedtime story, and all was well in the world. If you could believe. It was tough but I tried; only I chose the bedtime story. "When did you get the threatening call?"

"It was almost two, I think."

"What did he say?"

"I *told* you." She sounded annoyed with me.

"Tell me again."

And she told me again. The same story.

"He identified himself?"

"No."

"You recognized his voice then?"

"Well, no, he'd disguised it. It didn't sound like him at all really, but of course I knew who it was. I knew it was Jed."

"How?"

"Who else would it be?"

"People, women especially, get threatening or obscene phone calls all the time. Sometimes from people they know, sometimes from absolute strangers." I explained the obvious.

"It wasn't a stranger, it was him. I know that."

"Can you prove it?"

She glanced at me. Her hands, I noticed, were at her sides and were clenched into fists. "Don't you see what he's doing, Kat? It's just like what happened to Lorraine and me, or to you in your car. We know it's him but we can't prove it. If we can't prove it, we can't stop it. And he'll keep on doing it until he gets me. He'll get me, he'll kill me, and he'll go free." She walked from the stove to the cupboard. "That's his plan, that's always been his plan. Here." She handed me a mug.

Cocoa with marshmallows.

Marshmallows?

I was starting to feel like one myself.

I checked the front door to be sure it was dead-bolted, then walked the one-bedroom apartment. For a small place it had a lot of lights, was lit up like a Christmas tree, to be exact. I left one on in the bedroom and one in the living room, then settled down on the couch with my cocoa and Sara, the phone within reach.

"What's his number?"

"Whose?" She looked a little worried.

"Jed's."

"Why?"

"Spit it out." And I punched numbers as she spoke.

A sleepy male voice answered with something in the hello/grunt/groan department in his intonation.

I made my voice a little high, a little squealy and fast. "Jimmy, where the hell are you? You promised, you *promised* to pick me up and here I had to catch a ride home from work and now you—"

"This isn't Jimmy, you've got the wrong number."

"You're not Jimmy?" I did confused. "Well, who are you and why are you at Jimmy's?"

"I'm Jed. There's no Jimmy here. You've got the wrong number."

"Is this—" I rattled out a number that was two digits off.

"No!"

I held the phone away from my ear just in time, just missed the slam.

"Well?" Sara's voice was accusing.

"It was Jed. He's home and he sounded sleepy—well, first he sounded sleepy and then he sounded annoyed."

"That doesn't prove anything."

"No," I agreed. "Just something to consider." I took a sip of cocoa, the marshmallows leaving a fluffy white mustache on my upper lip.

"Don't go yet," she begged. "He still might come over. Want more cocoa?" She bounced up. "I can make it in a minute. In *seconds*."

"No, thank you." I wiped off my mustache. "Sara, tell me what attracted you to Jed. Why did you marry him?"

She dumped a packet of cocoa into her cup, filled it with hot water and stirred. Thoughtfully. Then picked up the bag of marshmallows. In slow motion.

"Seriously?"

"Yes."

"One word: sex."

I kept my face expressionless but it was an effort—it was the last thing I expected to hear.

"I was always kind of a plain Jane, a little overweight, no sense of dress or style. I never had a lot of boys around me. I never dated a lot or had much experience with men. I wasn't a virgin when I met Jed but I sure didn't understand the big deal about sex. I found it uninteresting, even boring. And messy." She wrinkled her nose and smiled.

Yes. Like divorce and death. I thought most of life was both interesting and messy.

"And then I met Jed. You know the fairy tale about Snow White?"

I nodded.

"I understood it then in a different way, as a metaphor. A young woman is sleeping. And cold. Living but in a deathlike state. And then she is awakened by a kiss from a man. She comes alive, she wakes up to the pleasures of the flesh. Well, that's how it was with me and Jed. Before I met him I was half aware, half asleep, half dead. And then . . . Jed. Remember in *The Wizard of Oz* when the movie suddenly goes from black and white to color?"

I nodded again.

"When Dorothy steps out of her house and into Oz, the world becomes color. That's exactly how I felt when I met Jed. I left Kansas and went to the Emerald City.

"My mother used to sing a song, something about how are you going to get them back on the farm after they've seen Par-eee. I think it was after the war, I don't know if it was World War One or Two, but all the soldiers, boys, who had gone overseas and seen war and Paris and came back—why would they want to come back to the farm, to Kansas?

"I guess that's true of a lot of things, isn't it, Kat? You can't go back. Not in time, or knowledge, or expectations. You can only go on."

Or get stuck. As I was now, unable to leave Hank and our love, our life behind. He was gone, it was over, and I was stuck. Like Jed?

"Jed and I were married for three years and except for the end, I've never been happier. I don't know if I'll ever be that happy again. The sex was wonderful, was everything, every day was Paris and Oz. And then things started to go bad. It started with me losing weight. Truthfully, I think that he liked me better before, he liked it that no one noticed me but him. I didn't do it to be noticed, though I do enjoy that; I did it to feel better about myself. But of course I was noticed, even at work where I got a promotion, and especially by men. It made Jed crazy."

"Crazy?" Talk about a word that's used way too loosely.

"He went nuts. I saw a side of him that I'd never seen or even suspected before. He turned out to be a very controlling person, Kat. He wanted to know where I was, who I was with, what I was doing. And he wanted me to be with him. All the time. And I do mean *all* the time. And then you know what I found out? Well, not found out, but finally admitted to myself."

I shook my head, my role in this conversation apparently a well-defined, limited, and silent one.

"That everything he did was one *huge* yawn. I mean *seriously* boring."

I tried to think of seriously boring stuff, which is tricky because it's so individual. "Like watching TV all the time?" My definition of seriously boring.

She shrugged. "Oh no, he was too active to do much of that. He coached kids at basketball, played in a bowling league, worked in a community organization that helped older and poor people renovate or build their homes, did church volunteer work. Oh God, the list was endless."

"It doesn't sound boring to me."

"Maybe not for *older* people." Silence while we stared at each other. I am thirty-three to her twenty-seven. "Kat, I'm young, I'm pretty, I wanted to have *fun*. I wanted to dance and party and play and travel. And I'm ambitious at work. I want to *go* somewhere, *be* someone, be successful and make money. I want a life and I'm not interested in the do-gooder, charity junk that Jed is."

Silence while, I assumed, she thought that one through a little more fully.

"That sounds pretty bad, I know, and I don't mean it to. I admire people who give of their time, energy, and money to good causes. I do that too. But it's not my whole life. With Jed, I felt that it was. He defined himself by doing things for other people, both at work and after work. And he wanted me to do that too. But that's him, not me. It didn't work for me.

"Jed doesn't like to lose, you know. That makes him a good cop, a good coach, a hard worker—but it doesn't necessarily make a good marriage. Marriage is built on compromise, on being willing to lose or bend sometimes. And—well, you get the drift, I don't have to fill you in on every crummy little detail of our marriage." She slurped up the last of her cocoa and the final marshmallow, sagging back into her chair, looking and sounding very tired.

"I stayed longer than I should have." In her face merely tired had been layered over by exhaustion. "It was the sex. It was always magic. I still think about it, I still want him. I wish I could have that and nothing else." She laughed. "I sound like a guy, huh? Just sex and no relationship." She sighed. "Lovely messy sex and no messy relationship." She shook herself. "I can't have it though, I know that."

"Now what, Sara?" I asked the question gently.

"I'm off to Paris. No more Kansas for me." She smiled. "And I don't mean Paris, Texas. But you knew that."

I smiled back. "I knew that. Get me a pillow and blanket. I'll spend the night on your couch."

"You don't have to. I'm okay now. I'll be fine. Thank you for coming though—I really wasn't fine before."

"You're welcome. And the gun—"

"I know." She sounded impatient.

"Take a gun course if you decide to keep it. Know how to handle it and use it; know exactly what to expect."

"Yeah." She waved me off.

"Jeez." I made a face. "You can lead a horse to Paris but you can't make it—"

She laughed. "Okay, I promise. Thanks again for your help."

Forty minutes later I dropped into bed, just missing the sunrise.

My dream about Hank stayed gone.

CHAPTER 22

I woke up in less than an hour. Something was wrong but I couldn't figure it out; something besides the fact that I'd had forty-five minutes' sleep, I mean. Sara? I was supposed to be somewhere? Jed? Bingo—two out of three. I crawled out of bed. Good thing I'd just taken my shoes off and climbed under the comforter, not into the sheets.

I pulled on my shoes, washed my face and combed my hair. Big help—I looked like something the cat dragged in, no question. I put myself in gear—low was the best I could manage—and headed for the door, grabbing a large canvas bag with a bunch of rolled and banded newspapers in it. And a clipboard, a snoop's—or criminal's—favorite prop. No one notices or questions someone with a clipboard. That's the theory, anyway.

On my way. Back to the streets to FIGHT CRIME, that was me. And back to Jed's. I smiled in satisfaction as I paused at the intersection closest to Jed's house. The Corolla was there, cuddled up and cozy next to the Ranger. I went around the block, then parked on a corner where I could see everything. Assuming—a tough assumption—I could stay awake. Seven-fifteen. A.M. I propped my elbows up on the steering wheel and my chin in my hands. Too uncomfortable to doze off was the theory here. I left the engine running and got the phone out. Just what a paper carrier, waiting for a call and an address confirmation, would do. I hoped.

Twenty minutes. Not bad. I put the car in gear.

Jed walked her to the door but not outside. He didn't look very dressed to me. Barefoot and bare-chested in sweatpants and a sleepy expression; that was Jed. The woman was dressed haphazardly with mussed hair and no makeup. She was a young attractive blonde and she walked slowly and unsteadily. No fluffing or glossing this time. She looked tired, disoriented, and very happy. Okay, forget happy, try smug and sexually satisfied.

Jeez, was Jed *that* good? He ought to write a how-to book in his spare moments, clean up big time on all the guys who didn't know how to put smiles on their girlfriends' or wives' faces. The blonde got into the Corolla and started up—although it took her two tries—backed out in the street and headed toward the intersection where I was lurking. I waited until she was almost there, then pulled up to the stop sign, yielded to her right-of-way, then took off behind her. Just like a little duckling toddling after mama.

Once we hit traffic, I dropped behind a little. Not too far though. Little white cars are a dime a dozen and I couldn't afford to take my eyes off her or give her too much lead. Home turned out to be a neatly kept little house in the Natomas area. I dropped her off in her driveway, sailing along without even a sideways look—tempting though it was. Ten minutes later and I was back. Nonchalant as all git-out. I pulled up in front of her house in the now almost deserted block and double-parked, grabbed a paper and my clipboard and ran up to her entryway.

I dropped a paper on the porch, read the name on the box and made tracks.

Smooth, simple, sweet. Twenty seconds later and I'm in the 4Runner laying down rubber, almost breathing easy. The metaphor was a toss-up: baseball or basketball? Home run or slam dunk? Slam dunk, I decided. The home run was still to come. I thought about S. Medlar, the name on the mailbox. Susan, Sally, Stephanie, or Sheila? Or maybe Sam, Scott, Sean, or Stan? Had I followed Ms. S. Medlar or was S. her husband or roommate? I yawned.

Bedtime.

Again.

I wondered if anyone would bother to look at the newspaper, would notice that it was dated sometime last week. Oh well. I checked the phone book when I got home: three Medlars, only one at the right address. I punched out the number and yawned again. A woman answered.

"Hello, we are doing a community survey to determine if more schools, fire and police protection are needed. Would you mind answering just a few questions?"

"Oh. All right. Just a few though."

"Adults in the home?"

"Just me. Well, one."

"School-age children?"

"None."

"Would you characterize your employment as professional or nonprofessional?"

"Non, I guess. I'm a student but I work as a waitress."

"Really?" I dropped the bland, interviewer voice and went for the chatty "girlfriend" approach. "I mean, I was just thinking that maybe that's something I would like to try. Where do you work if you don't mind my asking? Not," I added hastily, "that this is in the survey or anything, just me."

"I don't mind." She sounded very sweet. "I work at Chevy's down by the river."

"Is it better to work days or evenings?"

"Evenings, but you might have to work day shifts first. Pay your dues, you know."

"Thanks. Thanks a million! Oh, one last question." Back to formal. "Have you been satisfied with the police and fire protection in your area?"

"Yes. *Ab*solutely. *Especially* police."

And she giggled.

I did too, but not until I hung up.

I slept most of the day and then I called Charity.

"Why can't we just go out for fun?" she asked me in her I'm-being-reasonable-but-don't-push-it voice.

"Work first, fun second," I explained patiently.

"Why do you need me? I'll meet you when you're done."

"You're the bait." Still patient.

"Bait?"

"I'm trying to hook a big one and you're the bait."

"Me? Bait?" She started to laugh.

I had her. Speaking of hooking. "Meet me at seven." I said it complacently. "Dress for the part. But don't overdo it," I added hastily. I'd seen what could happen when Charity got carried away.

I'd called ahead so I knew what time Stevie—I hadn't guessed her name right—came on. And I knew she worked tonight on the outside deck. I picked her out visually the minute we went outside, and headed for an empty table in the section she was working. There were a lot of empties; it was midweek, a little chilly outside and definitely slow.

The deck was attractive, lit with outside lamps and candles. Below us we could see the river and throngs of spoiled ducks waiting for the chips they hoped we would throw. One of the millions of examples of man mucking up Mother Nature's plan, I reflected glumly. Charity picked up a basket of chips on an empty table and tossed them to the ducks, watching happily as they tore into a hideous feeding frenzy.

"Good evening, I'm Stevie, may I help you?" She glanced at me, then looked at Charity. "Oh . . . my . . . God, don't *tell* me. It's you, *isn't* it? It's *really* you, Dear Charity in person!"

Charity inclined her head modestly and I got glum about the excesses of fame and fortune, even though that was precisely why I'd brought Charity along. I'd noticed that lately almost anything could make me glum. Even little stuff. Before, when I had Hank, the little stuff didn't really touch me. Now—I looked at the ducks again. The chips were all gone and they swam docilely, companionably, angelically around.

"Kat?"

"Hmmmm?"

"What do you want to drink?"

"Oh. Margarita. Top shelf on the rocks. No salt."

Stevie smiled perfunctorily at me, then turned back to Charity.

"Anything else?" She spoke as to a spiritual authority.

Oh well, why not? I thought, moving from glum to cynical just like that. If we're going to make TV and movie stars, rap singers and ballplayers our heroes, might as well make advice columnists spiritual authorities. And Charity had my vote over the likes of Dennis Rodman, Howard Stern, or Tupac Shakur any day. Although I did like Candice Bergen, Oprah, Matt Williams, and Larry Bird. I forced myself back into the present—chips, ducks, margaritas and all.

"What you do—is it difficult?" Stevie asked Charity.

"Oh yes, but it's wonderful. I love it. Things aren't that busy for you, are they? Come sit with us and talk."

After you bring me my margarita, I said, but inside and silently.

"Oh—could I? Oh, oh, oh, that would be *wonder*ful. I'll see if one of the other girls can cover for me." She went flying off, dancing on air, excited by life.

"Katy?" Charity's voice seemed to come from a long way off. I looked into eyes full of questions. "You came here with Hank, didn't you?"

I nodded.

Stevie danced back.

With two margaritas and a Coke for her. Chips too, and salsa and guacamole. "All set." She slid into a chair. "I've always wanted to do what you do," she said. To Charity, of course, not to me. Not that I was eager to bring up what I do.

"Are you involved in anything else besides this?" I inquired politely.

"Oh yes. I'm a student, an English major. I want to be a writer. There's room for one more great American novel, isn't there?" Her tone was mocking but her eyes were anxious. She picked up a chip, looked at it in a puzzled way, tossed it over the ledge to the ducks.

I didn't look but I could hear a wild flapping and splashing. An unhappy squawk. A boat roared by drowning everything out.

"I think it would be fascinating to do what you do."

Stevie was talking to Charity, not me. I sipped my margarita and ate a chip. The ducks were quiet. I was too. I waited for Stevie to spill her guts to Charity. It amazes me, but it happens all the time.

"Why do most people write you?"

Charity looked at me trying to figure out what answer I wanted. "Love." She guessed right.

Stevie sucked in a breath.

"Is that what you write about?" I inquired.

"Some." She nodded. "I think it is the hardest thing in life though."

I looked at her hand and she shook her head. "I'm not married. I have a boyfriend. Well, I guess he's my boyfriend. The sex is wonderful, is the greatest ever." She blurted it out and then blushed. "I'm sure I'm the only girl he sees but—" Desire and fear were naked on her face. "What do you think, is it love?"

"What do you do together?" Charity asked as I thought about what Mike told me, that Jed didn't run around, that he liked to have a relationship with one woman at a time.

Stevie blushed. "Well, mostly we just hang out at his place and stuff." She bit her lip. "Mostly we just have sex. Sometimes I want more but I know he's busy and he's just getting over a divorce and all. And mostly . . ." She sounded miserable. "Mostly I don't want to lose what we have."

"Is he over his wife?"

"I guess." She shrugged. "He never talks about it."

There was a long silence, so I amused myself by making up a Dear Charity letter while I waited for the junior detective to coax more out of Stevie. Role reversal.

> Dear Charity,
> My boyfriend—well, I *think* he's my boyfriend—hardly ever calls and when he does all we ever do is sleep together. The sex is great, but gee—shouldn't there be more?
> Hopelessly in Love

> Dear Hopeless,
> Well, duh.
> Charity

I glanced at Charity. Of course, she would never be abrupt and cold like that. Instead she smiled at Stevie with her life-is-tough-but-you-can-do-it! expression and patted her hand.

"What kind of a person is he?"

"Very intense. Caring. He makes you feel like the center of his life." She still sounded miserable. "While you're there, I mean. And then sometimes he won't call for a while. I try to give him space and stuff but it's hard. I wish . . ." Her voice drifted off and we all thought about what she wished. "I hope he cares, I'm just not sure."

"Does he see his wife?" Charity, junior detective at work, asked.

"I don't think he sees her. I don't even know what she looks like—there are no pictures of her around or anything. Sometimes I think he's not over her, I just get a feeling, I don't know how to explain it. And once, when we were making love, he started calling me all these sweet funny names and things, only he never does that, and when I spoke back to him he looked at me all weird, startled maybe, and then he stopped. Maybe he forgot who I was, maybe he was making love to her even though I was the one there. Oh God, Charity, what am I going to *do*?"

"Perhaps you should step back a little, not become too involved. Live your life and give him a chance to figure things out."

"Yeah." Her voice was listless, almost dead. We all knew it was too late, she was too involved.

"It's the sex, the sex is so good. I can't just walk away."

"Love is more than sex." I stated the wildly obvious.

Stevie looked at me with pity. "Maybe you've never had sex this good, maybe you don't know."

"Is sex without love and companionship enough?" Charity asked hastily before I could do something rash and stupid, like pop her one.

Stevie's face was tight and pinched. "Maybe not forever but for now."

She was lying but we didn't say anything. She knew.

"He's not over his wife, is he?" she asked.

He'll kill me before he lets me go.

"He won't let me have any say about anything; our relationship is only what he wants it to be," she said.

He's very controlling. And he likes to win.

"Stevie, break's over." A waitress tapped her on the shoulder as she walked by.

"Oh God, Charity, what am I going to do? *What?*"

"Maybe you should stop seeing him for a while. Wait until things are settled in his life and he can offer you a relationship that is good for both of you."

"I can't." Her hands twisted in her lap. The youth and prettiness had drained from her face and I got a sudden image of what she would look like when she was old. "I can't," she whispered. "I can't."

She walked away from our table with a slow, dragging step like an elderly person. Or someone sick or hurt.

"What does he look like, Kat?"

"Jed? *Very* nice-looking. Clean-cut. It doesn't surprise you that he's a jock and a cop."

"Sexy?"

"Not obviously so."

"No clue?"

"No clue," I agreed.

Not about the sex, the stalking, the need to control, the desire to win, the willingness to murder. "Bad guys don't necessarily look like bad guys," a DA once told me. "A haircut and a new suit and they sit there in court with a shy scared look in their big baby blues, and all you can think of is that they look like the kid next door and no way like a cold-blooded killer. We lose cases on that; juries can't make the leap—they believe what they think they see, not what they hear. Listen to the evidence. Don't go by looks. Ever."

It was difficult to remember with someone like Jed. A cop, a coach, a community and church volunteer; it was easy to believe that what you see is what you get.

And of course good-looking bad guys use this.

So do good-looking PIs.

"Katy?"

Charity was eating guacamole and looking a question at me.

"Let's go." I answered the unspoken query. I had gotten what I'd come for.

The ducks were quiet, the deck was filling up. We threaded our way out through people, drinks, and good cheer.

"There are too many women like Stevie," Charity remarked sadly. "Not facing the truth, not choosing what's good for them."

"Asking to be victims."

"It doesn't always come to that."

But often it did.

CHAPTER 23

"Kat." The message was frantic. "Call me *right* away. Lorraine's funeral is today. I can't go alone. I just can't. You have to come. Call me, *call* me."

I called.

Sara almost sobbed in relief. "Oh, I'm so glad it's you. You'll go with me, won't you? Please! Say you will."

"Yes."

I gritted my teeth when I said it. Funerals are not fun; Lorraine was not someone I knew. It's part of the job, I reminded myself. "Why is it so late?"

"Late? Oh. The coroner didn't release the body for a while, something yucky like that. I didn't exactly ask for the details. It's at noon. I'll meet you at your office at eleven-thirty, okay? Lordy, I don't think I have anything in black. Not in my size now, I mean. What am I going to do?" She sounded distressed.

"I'm sure anything is fine, Sara. It's your presence, your support of the family, that matters." I reviewed the outfits I'd seen her in lately. "Not the red and yellow though."

"Of course not." She sounded scornful. "I hardly even know her family, for crying out loud. I don't even know why—" Her voice was petulant and annoyed now.

"Why what?" I asked, keeping my voice neutral.

"Why I'm even *going*."

"You told me that Lorraine was killed because of you."

"Yes, *I* know that but *they* don't. Maybe they would understand if I didn't go? The memories *are* very traumatic, you know." Her voice was hopeful now, the voice of someone who sees a possible out.

I said nothing. Discretion and valor and all that.

"Kat, hey, what do you think?"

"I think you should go." I also thought she was acting like a jerk. Was she that unhappy? Or afraid?

"Oh. All right. I'll see you at eleven-thirty then."

"Did you send flowers, Sara?"

"Flowers? Oh. I never even thought about it. Do you suppose I should? Maybe it's too late now. What do you—"

I hung up. I had reached my limit.

The service was held in a chapel at a Catholic church. It was small, serene, and quiet, with lots of light coming in through lovely stained-glass windows. There were flowers everywhere. The coffin was closed.

We sat in the back, Sara demure in an elegant chocolate-brown outfit and clutching a hanky. Only the hat and veil were missing. She sniffed and dabbed at her eyes as I watched people enter and seat themselves. It was sad to see so many young people; Lorraine had died before her time. I watched as Jed walked down the center aisle and seated himself in the middle of the chapel. Was he paying his respects or playing it balls to the wall?

"Kat, did you *see* who just sat down?" Sara hissed at me. "My God, talk about *nerve*, talk about—"

"Hush."

"But—"

I shushed her again. This was neither the time nor the place.

The service was touching, loving and appreciative of Lorraine in life, and somber regarding her early and unexpected death. Along the chapel walls the depictions of the stations of the cross were a constant reminder of pain, suffering, sacrifice, and death. Grim. Maybe it's easier if you believe in heaven.

Next to me Sara was restless and wiggly. Jed sat still and composed, impassive as marble and staring straight ahead. I admired his composure. And wondered how well he knew Lorraine, or if he knew her at all. At the end a young woman with long black hair and a pure, sweet, and innocent voice sang "Amazing Grace." People wept.

Sara was distraught, but not with grief. "We have to get out of here, Kat. We *have* to. Jed. Who knows what he'll do. I can't bear being so close to him. I'm afraid. Don't you see, I'm so afraid that—"

She babbled like this under her breath and I couldn't shush her. We left at the earliest possible moment, Sara looking behind us constantly, a nervous jittery wreck.

No one else left. No one followed us. Jed was nowhere in sight. Sara was a basket case.

I tried to think of any expression of grief, loss, or regret for Lorraine on Sara's part.

But I couldn't.

Nerves? Fear?

Sara was draped over the couch at her apartment looking pathetic. She had stopped babbling, seemed washed out, washed up, and exhausted. There had been no question of going to the cemetery or back to Lorraine's family's house. I was trying to think of a good way to say what needed to be said.

Only there wasn't one. Luckily Sara beat me to the punch.

"How long is this going to go on, Kat?"

"What?"

"Living in fear. Jed. All of it. I can't stand it. I really can't."

"I don't know."

"But you have *some* idea? I mean you've talked to people, to Jed and his friends, to the minister. When will you have enough on Jed to stop this?"

"Enough? Sara, I have nothing."

She stared at me. "What do you mean? Of *course* you do."

"Theories, allegations. We can't prove anything. We can't tie anything to Jed."

"Lorraine's murder. The attack on you. The threatening phone calls to me. The way he followed me around. There's all of that."

"We can't prove it's Jed. There's nothing until we can prove it."

"Nothing?"

"Nothing."

She began to cry, whimpering at first, and then sobbing.

I parked some distance from the Ranger. I thought it would be fun to be a surprise. Okay, fun was an exaggeration on my part. Surprise wasn't. The car matched. The license plate number matched. Still, I watched from the back and side for a moment just to be sure. It was Jed. He was wearing warm dark clothes and drinking coffee. He was armed. Not that that was a big surprise, most off-duty cops are. If he was having fun he hid it well.

I stood out of sight on the driver's side of the truck and rapped my keys against the window. Hard. Loud. He came out of his seat like a rocket, spilling coffee, scrambling for his gun, tumbling out of the truck still not fully assembled.

"Hey, Jed, how's it going?" My voice was friendly, everyday. "Didn't startle you, did I? Sorry," I lied cheerfully.

He straightened up, tried to put the gun away without me noticing, tried to toss a smile on his face. One out of three, not impressive.

"A gun?" I shot an eyebrow up in inquiry. "You here on police work?"

"I'm not at liberty to say." He spoke stiffly. The gun was holstered. The smile attempt had been put to bed.

"Why are you here?"

"I told you, I'm not at liberty to say."

"All right." I was affable and sweet, a nice combination I think. "Naturally every police officer *and* department would welcome a call from a concerned citizen who found an armed man in a residential—make that *deserted* residential—parking area. A department would be happy"—I exaggerated here a bit—"to confirm that an officer was out in the field and on duty in a particular area." I smiled sweetly, winningly, and pulled a cell phone out of my pocket.

Jed squirmed like a kid with a lizard in his pocket who's just discovered the hole in the pocket, the loose lizard. I smiled and dialed.

"Hey, hold it, let's not be too hasty here." Jed put his hand—read paw—over mine, effectively interrupting the dialing process.

I waited with a happy, expectant look on my face. After thirty seconds

I let happy droop and started tapping my toe. Syncopated rhythm. I wonder if I should consider amateur theater? I seemed to have a knack for this. After a minute, no smile at all, I started the redial process.

The paw again. Sheesh. Real theater wasn't this mindlessly repetitive. Not to mention boring.

"It's not police work." Jed said it hard, mean, nasty. Like a cop. Like a cop with the intent to intimidate and shut up a citizen.

"What is it then?" Shutting me up is a long-term process, a virtually unattainable goal.

"None of your goddamn business."

"Okay, fair enough. What is my business is the fact that an armed man is lurking in an unlit residential parking area. My business, community business, and now, police business." I let a self-righteous note creep in there. Nails on a chalkboard—that irritating.

"Don't meddle in what doesn't concern you." He spoke through clenched teeth. I could see a muscle jumping in his cheek.

"It does concern me."

The muscle jumped steadily. He was tempted to push me away, to push me around, I could tell. Only we both knew I wasn't Lorraine.

"Nice service today, didn't you think?"

He stared. The muscle jumped. Jeez, I really dislike it when people don't pick up their end of the conversation. "Did you know Lorraine?"

"Yes."

"Well?"

"Not well. Enough to be saddened at the news of her death and to pay my respects."

"Kind of an unusual accident, don't you think?"

He shrugged. "In my job you see unusual every day. This was foolish, stupid and preventable. The riverbank all along there was unstable. People had been warned, told to stay off. No one thinks it will happen to them. We see it all the time."

"Yet it was Lorraine who died, not Sara."

"What was it Einstein said: 'God plays dice with the universe'? And since it's God you got to figure the dice are loaded. He has His way, we have ours."

"It was a roll of dice that took out Lorraine?"

"So to speak."

Dice and God. Nice, easy, unquestionable answer. Pat though. A little too pat, in fact.

"Let's send out for pizza. What do you want?"

"Huh?"

"I'm starving. It's cold; it's going to be a long night, so let's split a pizza." I poised my phone in the ready position. New gadget, I admit it, and as with any new gadget, it's tough being moderate.

"What do you want on your half? I think I'll go veggie on mine. Skip the tomatoes though, they're cardboard this time of year. Hurry up on your half." I started dialing again. "If you don't make up your mind, I'm ordering Canadian bacon and pineapple, which, coincidentally, just happens to be my second choice. Wanna Coke? Coffee doesn't really go with pizza."

A car pulled through the parking lot briefly raking us with lights.

"Hi. . . . Yes. I'd like to order a pizza. Delivery. A parking lot on— That's right, a parking lot. . . . What? Oh. No. I don't have any coupons. Wait a minute. Jed, do you have any coupons? No? No coupons. . . . Sure. I know it's unusual but no big deal—"

The paw again. A disconnect.

"You're starting to piss me off, Jed. *Big* time. Do you have *any* idea how tough it is to talk someone into delivering a pizza to a parking lot? Now I have to start all over. Just for that you can pay. Give me my phone."

"What's your problem, Kat?"

I started laughing. "Problem? *I'm* the one with the problem? Give me a break. You're the problem, I'm your headache. And I'm here until you go away. Which is precisely why I was ordering a pizza, I figured it could be a while. You got any candy or gum?"

"I want you out of here."

He slammed my phone down on the roof of the Ranger. I winced—*damn* it all, that was an expensive phone—and quickly stuck it in my pocket.

"You mind your own business, you leave me alone. You don't, you'll be sorry. *Very* sorry. Got it?"

"Yeah, you're threatening me."

"Warning you."

"Sara is my business."

"Sara is none of your goddamn business. She is my life, my wife, my business. If I choose to sit in the parking lot of her apartment building and watch over my wife, it is not your concern."

I smiled. Well, well. "Nice, Jed."

He stared at me, a lot of muscles jumping now.

"In your previous statement to me you denied knowing where Sara was or making any attempt to find out. You also denied following her. *Oops*, my mistake, the legal term for that would be stalking."

"Fuck you." He got in the Ranger and slammed the door.

I got ready to jump on top of a nearby car just in case he decided to play bumper tag. He resisted the temptation, slamming the truck in gear and peeling across the parking lot laying rubber with abandon.

I reached into my pocket and retrieved the cassette recorder, turned it off. Now there's another gadget I love.

CHAPTER 24

I called Sara as I walked over to her apartment. Having told her about shooting bad guys through the door, I wasn't about to walk over there unannounced. My confidence in her ability to distinguish good guys from bad guys wasn't that great.

Sara opened the door the merest wedge and hauled me in. I felt like a character in a body snatchers' movie—one minute you're there, the next you're not. No gun in sight this time, so that was good news.

"What happened? Was it him? Where is he? What's going on? Do you think—"

"What's the fastest pizza place, Sara?" Sad, huh? I was sacrificing quality for speed.

"Pizza?" She sounded outraged. "Who *cares*! What about Jed?"

"You had dinner, right?"

"Yes."

"I didn't. Or lunch. And then you called and here I am. Now back to pizza."

"Kat—"

"First pizza, then Twenty Questions."

So she ordered me a pizza, but honestly?—she wasn't that good a sport about it. Then she offered me a glass of wine, trying to make up, I bet.

"No thank you, the night's not over yet. Okay: it was Jed. We had a little chat. He admitted he knew you lived in this complex. And I have it all on tape."

"Yes!" She sounded excited, even euphoric.

"This is not good news, Sara." I seemed to be explaining the obvious a lot lately.

"It is *too*. It means we have something on him. Finally we have proof."

"It also means he knows where you live."

"Oh." Her face fell as that sank in.

"Get ready to move."

"Oh Kat, I can't. I'm so tired of this, so tired of running and—"

"Do you want me to paint a picture of the alternative?"

Bleak eyes in a bleak face. "No." The knock on her door startled her, panicked her.

"Oh." Her hand flew to her mouth. "Is it him?"

"Let's hope it's the pizza." My stomach growled. I peeked through the peephole at a baseball cap looking down, asked who it was. A fresh-faced pimply youth popped up his head and answered. Pizza. I was in luck. I made a serious dent in the pizza but Sara just played with her slice.

"I'll be okay tonight, won't I, Kat? He won't come back the same night?"

"People do it all the time. It's impossible to guess. If you're screwy enough to be a stalker, you're too screwy to predict. For tonight at least you need to go someplace else. To a friend's or relative's. Even if Jed knows all the places you might go there is safety in numbers. Or a hotel, that would be best."

"I'll go to my sister's."

"Pack some things. I'll follow you over there."

"I feel like this is never going to end."

"It will." I spoke grimly. "It will."

Sara's sister welcomed us but she was annoyed. She did not really want us there and she certainly did not want anything to do with Jed. Not that I blamed her. Situations like this are tough on the whole family. She was older than Sara and looked the way I imagined Sara had looked before—a little overweight, neatly dressed and made up, no zip. She didn't smile.

Her name was Joy. Go figure.

"Aunt Sara AuntSara Auntsaraauntsaraauntsara!"

Two little girls, about five and seven I guessed, came pounding in and immediately pounced on Sara.

"Hi, we're so glad you're here!"

"How long are you staying?"

"Do you want a cookie?"

"Come see our room. We changed it all around."

They dragged Sara off and I turned to Joy, hoping she would offer me a cookie. The pizza hadn't really done the trick. Joy just stared at me, out of smiles, out of good cheer, out of cookies, I guess. I'm a philosophical person, I moved on.

"Please tell me what you know about Jed."

"Jed?"

"Yes."

Yet another blank stare.

What was the problem here? Was this a tough question? Brain surgery, putting a man on Mars, balancing the national budget?

She sighed. "Jed. Yes. Come on, let's go into the kitchen and I'll make tea. Don't mind me, I'm just really tired. The last thing I needed was *this*."

"Sara's not doing it on purpose." Bad news, I was back to pointing out the obvious again.

She looked startled, then a little embarrassed.

"Actually, it was I who suggested that she not stay at her apartment. I don't think she's safe there."

Joy frowned. "Is this *really* serious?"

Oh, for crying out loud. Didn't she read the paper? "Do you have a chance to read the paper or listen to the news?" I inquired politely. "You know: 'Man Blows Away Estranged Wife and Three Kids.' 'Woman Killed, Husband to Blame.' 'Man Shoots Wife and Self in Jealous Rage.' 'Pregnant Woman Stabbed 22 Times by Husband.' That kind of thing."

"Oh."

"It's really serious. Women are dying every day at the hands of their husbands and boyfriends. Sara's doing everything she can not to become one of them."

"Oh."

She filled a kettle with water and placed it carefully on a burner. The set of her shoulders was stubborn and angry; she did not look as though she wanted to believe what I had said.

I decided to go back to Jed. "Is it that you can't believe your brother-in-law is capable of that?" My eyes got stuck on a huge glass cookie jar filled to the brim with Oreos, my favorite junk cookie in the whole world. I wrenched my gaze away, tried not to drool. The usual professional stuff.

"I really can't." She spoke easily, matter-of-factly. "I *really* truly can't. I've always liked Jed. He's a nice guy, very straightforward, very what-you-see-is-what-you-get, and now my sister tells me he wants to *kill* her." She shook her head. "I want to believe my sister . . . well, of course I believe Sara but . . ." She shook her head in evident disbelief. The teakettle whistled and she snapped to attention. My eyes drifted back to the Oreo jar before I could get them under control.

"Can you tell me more about Jed?" I asked, trying to leave it as open-ended as possible.

"What's to say? I told you, he's a nice guy. He's always friendly and helpful. He gets along with everyone. He comes to the family get-togethers, helps with the food, plays with the kids, he even changes diapers and loads up the dishwasher. I mean he's a *nice* guy. I've never seen him have too many beers or get mean or anything."

"Have you ever seen him angry?"

"Yeah. Maybe once or twice, but nothing that wasn't reasonable."

"What?" I wondered what she thought was reasonable.

"At a kid who busted his windshield out. They were just goofing off, didn't mean to do it, but it was still stupid and careless."

"Have you ever seen Jed become violent?"

"Never seen it, can't even imagine it." She fiddled with the teapot for a moment, then poured for both of us. "Sometimes I wonder if maybe Sara doesn't have a screw loose." She glanced at me quickly, then looked away. "I shouldn't be talking like this, should I, my own sister and all?"

She stood and drifted around the kitchen. "You want an apple or something?" she asked vaguely.

"No thanks. Oreos would be nice though," I added in an encouraging tone, my spirits rising.

She plopped herself down at the table. "Sara's always been . . . I don't know, sort of dreamy and different, I guess. She lived in her head a lot as a child."

"Don't many children do that?"

"Well, I don't know. I guess some do."

"Does she still do that?"

"I don't know. Sometimes I wonder, I surely do."

"Has Sara ever been known for lying?"

"Lying? No, not really I guess, just making things up."

I kept the frustration off my face and out of my voice but it was an effort. "What is the difference between making things up and lying?"

She took a sip of tea and thought it over. "I don't know. One is just kind of like making things up and the other—well, lying is mean, don't you think?"

"Jed was in the parking lot tonight watching for Sara. She didn't make that up."

"Well, he cares about her. We all know that, so it's not really a surprise, is it?"

"People who care about others don't spy on them."

She shrugged it off. "He's a cop, he's overprotective, that's just the way it is." *Case closed,* her voice said.

I gave up and went back to dreamy. "Is Sara still dreamy?"

"Sometimes. Course I think that's just because she has too much time on her hands. She's got no kids and a husband who thinks she's something special and helps out all over the place." There was a definite note of jealousy and envy there. "She needs a baby, that's what she needs."

I ignored that. Again, it was hard. "Sara's a successful professional in the computer field. That doesn't seem very dreamy to me."

"Just my opinion," she said a bit smugly and looked ostentatiously at the kitchen clock. "*My,* but it's late."

Sara and the kids trooped back in again. Sara looked a lot happier and more relaxed. "Mom, can Aunt Sara sleep with us? She can have my bed and we'll sleep together. Okay? Pleeze pleeze pleeze!"

"Thanks for everything, Kat." Sara's soft voice.

"You're welcome."

"What do I do now? Is it okay to go to work?"

"It would be better to start a new job. Better to change everything you can—work, housing, car. Assume he knows all of this."

"So I make another huge effort to hide everything and then he'll just find out again, won't he?"

"Probably. Do it anyway. We're buying time until we can stop this."

Prime time, not dead time.

She gave me a troubled look.

"Aunt Sara, tuck us in, okay? And will you read us a story?"

The kids and Sara walked me to the door and waved at me. I drove around the neighborhood for a while looking for Jed. Nothing. Then drove past his house. Two can play his game. There was a light on downstairs but no car in the driveway. I didn't hang around.

Oreos were calling my name.

And bed.

CHAPTER 25

She would have left that very night—she was so fed up—but she couldn't make it happen, not without everything getting upset. And there was her commitment tomorrow evening but then, oh then she was gone. She stretched out in the twin bed and imagined herself surrounded by pampering, indulgence, even luxury.

It had taken a long time for the anger to subside. She had made herself stop thinking, emptied her mind and listened to the quiet, even breathing of her nieces. She loved them dearly. And hoped they wouldn't grow up to be like their mother, her sister Joy. She hoped they would love life, savor it, laugh and smile and always have fun as they did now. Finally, lulled by the gentle rhythm of their breathing, she had gone to sleep.

In the morning Joy had acted as though it were the worst inconvenience in the world to help Sara. It was difficult to ask. "Please . . . you know I can't go to the apartment by myself."

"Why not?"

Her mouth was stubborn, set. She had been so much worse, so much more awful, Sara thought, since Sara had lost weight, gone blond and pretty. Hateful, that's what Joy was. But Sara couldn't say this now, could barely afford to feel it.

"Jed has threatened to kill me. Threatened and tried," she explained patiently. "Do you want me to die, Joy?" She didn't, couldn't say this in front of the children. She would never do that.

Joy made an unsympathetic sound. "You're exaggerating. You always do. You think you're so important. No one else has problems. Oh *no,* just little Miss Important."

"That's not true, Joy, of course it's not. You have problems, everyone does. I know this as well as you. And my problems are no more important than anyone else's." She let her voice tremble here. "If you don't want to help me stay safe—well, stay alive, really—just say so. I won't ask you again. I'll try to find someone else who can help. Someone who doesn't think that helping me stay alive is such a bother in their life." She let a bitter note creep in, turned away as though she didn't want her sister to see the tears.

"You're not going to die."

Oh God, Joy was so stupidly stubborn, so mindlessly obstinate. It made Sara crazy.

"Don't you think that's what Lorraine thought?" she asked in a careful, gentle voice.

"Lorraine has nothing to do with this."

"She got killed—even though I was the target, not Lorraine, not really."

"There you go again, dramatizing things, making them up. Why don't you just go to Hollywood? Maybe they'll make a movie out of your life." It was spoken cruelly.

Sara stared at her sister. She was glad she'd hugged her nieces this morning and told them she loved them. Just in case. It took a huge effort to control the anger, hatred, and resentment she felt for her sister. "Goodbye, Joy." She spoke carefully.

"Where are you going?" Joy's cross voice, the only one she ever heard these days.

"To a phone booth. I'll call Bob. Maybe if I wait for a while he'll be able to get away from work and help me."

It was a low, sneaky thing to do and they both knew it, not something Sara would have done if she hadn't been desperate. No, not just desperate, fighting for her life. Bob was her brother-in-law, Joy's husband, as kind and giving as Joy was mean and selfish. And he would be very angry with Joy.

"Bitch!" Joy spat it out.

Sara picked up her purse and walked to the door. She didn't make it—she knew she wouldn't—before Joy stopped her. Sara could see the hatred and struggle in Joy's eyes.

"Do you want me to die?" she asked again. "Do you?"

At the apartment Sara got everything she needed: a suitcase and garment bag with clothes and toiletries, credit cards and money. Even books to read. She didn't know yet when she would come back. Or if she could.

She called Bob later. "Joy won't listen to me," she said. "Please tell her I'm so sorry to be such a bother and a nuisance. I never wanted to be a trouble to her, I really didn't, it's just that I can't help Jed and what he does. I really can't." She let the tears fill her voice then.

Bob was beside himself. He took off work, took her out to lunch to a really nice place. And he gave her money and made her promise not to tell Joy. Prettily she gave him the promise. Later it made her smile.

She would have left then too except for the meeting. It was important, she knew, but oh, she wanted to be gone, to be far away and out of reach, to be another person. She wanted that a lot these days.

Good evening."

She smiled at the women in the group. Most of them smiled back, though tentatively, perhaps fearfully. There were almost twenty-five women that night, quiet in their seats, passive, almost inert. She smiled at them again, beautiful in her rich blue suit, navy pumps and bag, brightly colored scarf, and gold jewelry. She had dressed very carefully, thoughtfully.

"Thank you for inviting me here tonight. My name is Stephanie Ann."

She paused, as she always did.

"I am one of you."

Some of them gasped. Some of them stared and shook their heads slightly. Some nodded in quiet understanding.

"My husband beat me. I thought I deserved it: because I wasn't good enough and smart enough, because I didn't work hard enough or fast enough. Because—" She broke off. "Tell me," she asked gently. "What are the reasons?"

They looked at her in silence, silence that lasted a long time. Outside a car backfired and a siren wailed its way across town. And still the silence.

"Because you asked for it." A woman in back spoke in a low voice, a voice that found the words familiar.

Stephanie nodded.

"Because you drove him to it," another volunteered, secure too in the familiarity.

Stephanie nodded again.

"Because he loved you and was doing it for you."

Many were nodding now. And then the chorus started.

"Because dinner wasn't ready on time."

"And the kids were too noisy."

"And you talked back."

"And he never wanted to hit you but you made him."

"If you'd only acted right . . ."

". . . it *never* would have happened."

The torrent of words poured out, jumbled and jangled, bumped into everything in the room. Bumped into everyone's consciousness and then the words drifted off into a self-conscious embarrassed silence.

And Stephanie spoke. "And all that, all those words and reasons are bullshit. The man who said them was and is a coward and a bully. That's what men who hit women and children are. Not just hit." She paused and looked around, continued after a moment. "We know, don't we? It's not just hitting."

No delay this time.

"Punching and slapping."

"Broken bones, burns, hospital visits and lies."

"Forced sex."

"No self-respect."

"And fear. *Always* fear."

She could hear crying. There were tears in her eyes too, she was not ashamed of them. "Men who act this way are not just cowards and bullies, they are breaking the law. *Everything* we just said, and much *much* more, is against the law. We cannot change them but we can change the situation. And we can change ourselves."

"It's hard." The woman's voice made it sound hopeless.

"It's been going on so long. How can we change?" More hopelessness.

"He'll never let me go."

"He said he'd kill me if I tried." Frightened voices.

"And the children . . ."

"It's hopeless."

"Being here is the first step on the path of change. Congratulations." Stephanie smiled.

"It's easy to say," a sad-looking woman said, "but it seems impossible."

Sounds, murmurs of agreement chased around the room.

"No," Stephanie said. "No, it's not. It's possible because I have done it and I am one of you. And I will tell you how you too may do it."

The silence in the room was complete.

"All right," a woman challenged. "All right then, tell us."

And it was silent again.

Until she spoke, until she told them.

CHAPTER 26

He had to watch at a distance that day. It was important not to get caught. Not again, not so soon.

She left in the morning, late, after the children had gone to school, left with her sister and returned to the apartment. They hadn't stayed there long, half an hour perhaps, and left again. Sara had a suitcase, a new one he didn't recognize, and a garment bag. How far, he wondered, was she going this time? And how long? He wondered about patterns. About beginnings and endings and the in-betweens that stretched out for the longest time. Like now.

The car was closed, close, and he longed for fresh air. To be outside and moving around. To kick ass. He took a sip of coffee that had been cold long ago and was rank to his taste now, tried to stretch, to ease his cramped muscles. The worst thing about a stakeout was the boredom, the waiting that dragged on interminably and then could end in a heartbeat, in a rush of adrenaline and action and smooth, fast moves that had to be played out just so.

After the apartment she had gone to work. No excitement. No adrenaline. Sara had left in her car, Joy in hers. He was in the police car, the radio crackling softly. He didn't stay, he too had work to do, but he'd swung by frequently, he'd kept an eye on the situation.

He was not about to lose her now.

She walked out to lunch. He didn't bother to follow but was back again in the afternoon—early, just in case, but it was five-fifteen before she moved.

Before they moved.

One stop at a sandwich shop. Four minutes. She was dressed beautifully, better than for work, differently than when she had gone to work, or to lunch. Evening plans, he thought with interest. Something going on for sure. What a beautiful woman she was. Why hadn't he seen it before? Oh, he had in a small way. She had always been attractive to him, beautiful even, but he never thought of her as beautiful to others.

Neither had she, he realized. Maybe that was a lot of it. Then she had lost weight, gone blond, started wearing bright colors. And everyone could see it. He saw the way people looked at her in the street, the way his buddy had looked at her in the gym. She had changed and so had her world.

He started the car and put it in gear, eased it out into traffic, followed her to a mall, spent an hour or more there, and then back into traffic. Rush hour over, he had no trouble keeping her in view. It didn't matter. She wasn't really watching. She looked around sometimes but not carefully, not consistently. She wouldn't pick him up, not that way, not unless he made a mistake.

And he wasn't planning to.

Just before seven they headed out of town a bit. She seemed unsure of where she was going, speeding up, then slowing down to read street names, turning at the last minute, sometimes backtracking. He stayed behind, kept her in sight, followed her sometimes by feel. Gut feel. It pleased him that he had that, that he could rely on that.

It was dark by the time she parked in the parking lot of a small community center. There were others there already, a dozen or so. Several more arrived as he watched Sara park. Not from the lot but from across the street, parked under a large tree and away from the streetlights. The houses around him were dark in front. It was not a neighborhood that cared or noticed, he thought.

He got out his sandwich and a Coke. It would be a while. More tedious hours ticking by minute by minute. Food helped. And the radio. After the sandwich he had an apple and some cookies. It amazed him what people would say on the radio, on talk shows. Didn't they realize that someone would recognize their lives, their voices? He couldn't imagine being that desperate, that out of control.

A guy talked about losing his job, said it was like losing his manhood. *Jeez.* He winced. It made him uncomfortable just to hear that. And then a woman—she sounded very young to him—talked about losing her boyfriend and losing hope. He felt sorry for her but he thought she would get over it. She would get older and realize there were other men, other loves, that hope wasn't a onetime thing.

God, *he* was getting older cramped up like this in a car hour after hour. He stretched as best he could but it wasn't enough, it never was. Soon, he thought. It had been over two hours. He wondered what the hell she was doing.

A woman came out of the building, got into a car and drove off. He sat up, turned off the radio—alert, wide awake instantly. More women came out, some leaving together, some on their own. Nothing for a while, almost ten minutes. Then they started to straggle out again, first in ones and twos and then in a group of four or five. He didn't see her; no one went near her car. He drummed his fingers on the steering wheel, the same rhythm over and over. His body was taut, his concentration focused. Soon.

Action. Lights. Shoot.

The exodus stopped. Nothing. His fingers still drummed but he had lost the easy, snappy rhythm. Twenty minutes later he watched the lights in the community center go out one by one. A man slouched out the front door and over to a panel truck. The engine fired, caught, coughed up a funnel of exhaust as the truck pulled away. Her car was in the lot still. The only one.

He pounded the steering wheel. Furious. Waited another twenty minutes to be sure. He'd been had. He thought back to a slim woman in a long coat, a raincoat, that completely covered her clothes. She had left with another woman; he had given them a quick look, no more. He pounded the wheel again. And again. And swore under his breath. Started the car, wrenched it viciously out into the street and took off, tires squealing, rubber burning.

He didn't look for, and didn't see, the woman watching him watch her.

CHAPTER 27

I answered the phone with my mouth full of cookies. Oops. How many times had Alma told me as a child not to talk with my mouth full? More than I could count, that's for sure.

"May I speak with Kat, please?"

"Speaking."

"It doesn't sound like you." Sara's voice was hard and suspicious. I hadn't heard that voice before.

I swallowed the last bite of cookie. "Sorry, my mouth was full."

"What are you eating?"

"Oreos." I sloshed some tea down after the Oreos, looked at the bag longingly.

"My God, Kat, it's nine in the morning. Isn't that a little early to be eating cookies?"

I bristled. Her voice was a teeny bit judgmental. Guess how much I like that? I mean, it's not as though I was drinking Wild Turkey out of the bottle or pounding shots of Gold. Or stuffing down a triple-layer double chocolate whammy cake with nuts and whipped cream. With my bare hands. I'd gotten the regular size bag of Oreos too, not the super-duper will-feed-a-small-regiment size.

"What can I do for you, Sara?" I asked in a cold voice.

"Oh, I just thought I'd check in and let you know what's happening. I know you were worried about me last night."

Yeah? That was last night. *Before* the snide Oreo remark this morning. Now I could care less. Professional, huh? So I bit back that remark.

"I went back to the apartment early this morning to pick up some stuff, enough to get me through for a while if need be."

"Alone?" I eyed the Oreo bag with longing.

"No. Joy went with me." Her voice was funny.

"What's the matter?"

"I don't understand the way she's acting. She says she believes me, but then when I need her help, she acts as though it's a total imposition. She seems almost mad. At *me*. Why not at Jed? Why not tell *him* off?"

I thought about how to answer. I had seen it before. "People don't like their sense of things, of reality, scrambled up. Even though you're the one who is victimized by the situation, not causing it, you're in front of them, available, and they take it out on you. Sometimes people refuse to believe you, or say they do but then they ignore you or the situation completely. No one likes their world to tip." Change is difficult, denial is easy. Duh.

"Well, I think it's pretty crappy." She spoke with an edge of bitterness.

"It is, you're right. Are you close to your sister? Is she usually supportive?"

"Yeah, there's that." Glum. "No, she isn't. She always thinks that I have a better deal than she does and is mad at me because of it."

"People don't change just because you're in trouble and need them."

She made a funny little sound, sad maybe.

"Where are you, Sara?"

"In the lobby at work. I'll be here most of the day. After work I'm going over to a friend's for a bit and then away for the weekend."

"Where?"

"Oh, anywhere. Just to get away. Thanks again for last night."

"You're welcome. The bill is in the mail. Where?" I don't like vague in situations like this.

"Where what?"

"Where are you going for the weekend? And why are we playing games?"

"You told me not to tell, Kat." Her voice was huffy, annoyed and aggrieved.

"That's *other* people," I explained patiently. "You can't always trust the people you think you can. So, since you can't know, it's better to say nothing. I am not them." Hello again to the obvious. "You hired me because I am trustworthy. It is my job to know where you are and what is going on." Maybe I'd adapt a new motto: *Go with the obvious.* Or: *If it's obvious, it's working.* Hmmm. Have to play with that a bit.

"Listen, thanks for your concern but I'll be fine." Her voice speeded up. "Everything's okay for this weekend, *really*. Don't worry about a thing. Hey, gotta run, late for work and stuff. Talk to you soon. Bye." The ninety-mile-an-hour words screeched to a halt and smashed into the phone click as the line went dead.

I was pissed.

I get really annoyed when people hire me and then make it tough—or almost impossible—for me to do my job. Or maybe I still had a bad attitude because of the Oreos? That could happen too. I ate another cookie, put more water on for tea, and thought about it. Four cookies and a cup of tea later I had decided.

Picking up Sara and following her wasn't so tough—I knew her routine, after all. It was doing that and watching out for Jed that was a challenge. I like to invest my job with dignity, so naturally I find these Three Stooges–type scenes very annoying. What was even more annoying was that in this case Jed wasn't exactly a Stooge. Slapstick and slapdash wouldn't get me to first base here.

I sighed and thought wistfully of the high-tech homing devices where you smack a transmitter on the car you're following and pick it up on the receiver in your vehicle. I was picking up a couple of those babies, you bet, the minute I had a couple jillion spare dollars.

As it turned out, it wasn't that tough. Jed was focused on Sara, so I focused on him. The tunnel vision concept. Not to mention the obvious at work here again. *Obvious works.* Hey, maybe that was it. T-shirts, mugs, notepads. Sounded good to me. I dropped back half a block as Jed eased up on speed. I'd make a killing with that stuff, then sell out to a beer or a potato chip company. Hah. Set for life.

The hollow feeling in my stomach. *What life?* Hank was gone. I took a corner too fast and speeded up, focusing on Jed's taillights. *What life?* If this kept up I was going to have to bang out a corner of Jed's taillight. The poverty-stricken investigator's homing device. Of course, Jed might recognize that one, cops have been doing it since the Dark Ages. I mean, where do you think I learned it? *What life?* Oreos would be a help, I thought. Any port in a storm.

Sara parked in the parking lot of the community center, Jed parked on the street in front of a dark residence. Out of sight, out of mind was what he was shooting for. I wondered if Sara would pick him up in the police vehicle. Maybe just in the Ranger. I made a mental note to check on that as I zipped around the block and cruised the neighborhood, killed fifteen minutes and then headed back for the community center. I parked in a secluded place in the lot—one street lurker in the neighborhood was enough, I figured—and sauntered on into the center.

The ambiance was concrete block and bulletin board but the colors were cheerful and there were plants and bright, happy children's drawings scattered around. I couldn't see anyone but I could hear a voice. A voice that sounded a lot like Sara. I took off in that direction. The door to a smallish meeting room was open and I could easily see the backs of the listeners and hear a voice. Sara. And that was all I could see unless I wanted to risk being seen by her. Which I didn't. I propped myself against the wall just outside the open door.

Another someone was now giving a brief introduction, the kind that is long on verbiage and gush and short on content. I shifted my position against the wall. A spatter of clapping at the end of the intro and on to the main event.

"Thank you for inviting me here tonight. My name is Stephanie Ann," Sara said.

Stephanie Ann?

"I am one of you."

Silence broken by murmurs.

"My husband beat me."

Well, I'll be damned.

"I thought I deserved it because . . ."

A woman walked out the door, did a double take when she saw me, then advanced in my direction. *Rats!*

"You may go in. It doesn't matter if you're late," she whispered.

I shook my head, trying to look shy and abashed, basically a stretch—big stretch—for me. "No, I can't. I'm not ready," I whispered back in a stammering kind of way. "May I please just stand here?" Lost the stammer, went for desperate on that one. "Or maybe I'll leave, I'll—" Then went for frightened.

"No, *no*!" she whispered soothingly, and patted my arm. "You just do what*ever* is comfortable for you. And thank you for coming." Big soothing smile and she left.

So I lurked outside. I was used to that; it was pretty comfortable for me. And listened. And could hardly believe my ears. I wished I'd brought my tape recorder. You just never know.

There you go: *Right back to obvious again.*

I stayed for the whole presentation, scooted out as the applause started at the end. I hated to skip the question period but people get restless then and getting caught once was enough for me. I slipped out a side door and back into the car, then scrunched up and out of sight. It was dark, I was sneaky, and I'd turned off the interior car light. If Jed saw me he was better than I thought.

A fifteen-minute wait. Not bad, not bad at all.

I caught it easily but I was watching. I thought it odd that Sara had parked in an unnecessarily visible and conspicuous spot, a spot very easy for someone to keep an eye on, so I wasn't surprised to see a slim blond woman in a long trench coat slip out the door in a group of people. Sara. She and another woman broke off and headed for a minivan. In the flurry of activity in the parking lot, I started up my car and pulled out. The minivan was in front of me, another car in back. We left in an orderly procession. And I glanced at Jed, dark and stolid, as we drove off.

Zip zip zip. Twenty minutes tops and Sara (aka Stephanie) had been dropped off, picked up another car, and was speeding on the freeway like there was no tomorrow. Or California Highway Patrol. With me right behind her. I-80 West to San Francisco—a weekend away in the City. What fun. Past Davis, Vacaville, Fairfield, Suisun, then west on Highway 12 to Napa. Oops, forget the weekend in the City. Not that she was necessarily going to Napa. It was also the road to Calistoga, Sonoma, Santa Rosa, and dozens more small towns and cities scattered throughout the Napa Valley, along the Russian River, and on over to Highway 1, the winding road along the coast.

It was tempting to bag it right then. I had a good idea where she was going. It was late, I was tired, I'd had no dinner—was this turning into an ugly pattern or what?—and most important, I wasn't hired to follow Sara, I was hired to believe her.

Of course I hadn't known about Stephanie then. Things are hardly ever simple in my business. They might start out looking that way but it rarely lasts. So I stayed with Sara/Stephanie. If this surveillance routine kept up I was going to have to punch out one of Sara's taillights too. One minute a model citizen, the next a vandal. Tsk tsk.

The road to Napa is dark and winding, a canyon road making its way through foothills before dumping you into the lush and gorgeous Napa Valley. Flat, green, luxuriant with trees and flowers—you can walk in any direction and trip over a vineyard, fall into a winery. It's a small paradise of cultivated and natural beauty, quaint old towns, monasteries and ranches, and—unfortunately—the moneyed "elegance" of nouveau. Motels, spas, resort hotels, cutsie-pie stores. Something for everyone. And the more money you had, the better off you were.

I yawned, stared at the road, the unblemished taillights in front of me. I was going to start stocking my car with food. No kidding. Jeez. What I wouldn't give for a sandwich right now. Or an apple. Even half a stale candy bar stuck to the seat. And that's desperate.

The road straightened out and gave us choices. Stay on 12 and go to Sonoma, turn north on 29 and head for Napa. And Napa it was. But not for long. Didn't even slow down, just zoomed right past: Hello and goodbye. We passed the Napa State Hospital and I wondered if it was still in use. A beautiful and gracious old building on lovely grounds, it had housed the state's insane asylum. That's what we said back then, before we were politically correct. As children we had been terrified, and then terrified others in turn, with the threat: Be good or you'll go to Napa. We had no clear picture of what that meant but we knew it was bad. Being trapped is horrible, I thought, whether it's in your mind or outside. Or, in Sara's case, in a bad marriage. Now, grown up and sensible, Napa meant one thing: wine. Very good wine.

I yawned again, tried to pay attention to the road. Next was Yountville. And another wonderful old building, this one the Veterans Hospital. The sign was still there. Good news. It frightens me how the California of my childhood and my heart is disappearing. After Yountville we went through the tunnel of trees—which you can't really see at night but I can never forget—and into St. Helena. There was a *wonderful* drugstore here once with the greatest sandwiches—way too much bacon, cheese, tomato, and mayo—and unbelievable ice cream sodas and shakes. Now it's been turned into a ghastly pretentious little restaurant, the kind where they sneer at you if you ask for mayo. *Aioli,* they say in a scornful voice, *aioli*!

Oh God, I'm starting to sound like an old geezer. *Remember then . . . back in the good old days.* Back when it was simpler and safer, not pretentious or expensive. Back before all those people from the East Coast, with no love of our land or values, descended on us like a plague of locusts. Back then, back when. There are not a lot of fourth- and fifth-generation Californians, but we remember. And we're sad, even bitter.

I yanked myself out of the past. It was possible that we were heading for Clear Lake but I didn't think so. My money was on Calistoga. For years it has been a health spa and small resort town, abundant with natural hot springs and mineral waters. Also mud packs, steam wraps, and herbal treatments. It still seems kind of quaint and old-fashioned, a one-pony town off a two-lane road. Farther away, harder to get to than Napa, it has been harder to change, tougher to destroy.

When Sara pulled off onto the main street of Calistoga I followed her, then turned off onto a side street almost immediately. We were the only cars on the road—Calistoga rolls up the sidewalks early—and to say that I was obvious is to indulge in wild understatement. I zoomed around the block, just making it back in time to pick up Sara's vanishing taillights. I cut my headlights and followed, mentally rehearsing what I would say to the cops when they stopped me.

But Sara/Stephanie called it a night before the cops moved in. Climbing out of the car, she stretched and then moved quickly through a side gate and into the lush grounds of a small estate. The gate latched behind her; her figure blurred in the dim light and was gone.

The Sunflower Health Spa and Clinic was written in wrought iron and arched above the formal main gate and driveway. I lingered for fifteen minutes but saw nothing but the moonlight dancing in tree branches and the light breeze, heard nothing but the rustle of leaves, the crickets, and the far-off rush of water.

Home was two hours away. I started back.

With plenty to think about.

CHAPTER 28

He looked incredibly handsome in the tux. I'd only seen him in one a few times before. He smiled at me, close and far away at the same time, held out his hand. I held out mine too but there was so much distance between us. So far away and we couldn't bridge it.

My outstretched arm was covered in white silk and lace. Seed pearls danced down the sleeve and tiny buttons marched up to the elbow. *White silk and lace? Seed pearls?* I frowned and looked at my dress, at the full-length billowing white wedding gown. Behind me a train dragged. I touched my hair. A veil was piled on top of my head. And flowers.

But this wasn't right. We'd agreed that our wedding would be very simple. Hank would wear a suit and I a short dress. Flowers, friends, champagne, that would be it. Instead we looked like tarted-up dolls, Barbie and Ken at their wedding. I needed to talk to Hank. He would know, we would figure it out. I tried to walk over to him but it was so difficult, like walking in quicksand or glue.

Frosting?

The solid white-sugar swamp stretched all around me. We were wedding dolls, decorations stuck on a wedding cake. I stumbled, fell to my knees. The frosting and the dress made it so difficult. I looked across at Hank. I needed him. He reached out to me again and smiled. A bright red suddenly stained the starched whiteness of his shirt and he crumpled.

Hank! I fought through the sugar glue, tearing the skirt and train of the dress. *Hank!* When I reached him his eyes were closed and his face as white as the frosting. I knew he was dead. CPR. I put my lips to his but he was so cold. The frosting pulled him away from me, swallowing him up and leaving nothing but the slick white icing of the cake.

And me in a torn and somehow bloodied wedding dress.

I woke up, my heart pounding and tears in my eyes, turned on the lamp to dispel the haunting image of Hank's dead white face. Ranger, my dog, stirred on the rug next to the bed. The cats stretched and yawned and moved over to sit next to me, to lick my hand. They were used to me crying in the night.

I wasn't.

I never would be.

I didn't call, just went over. Surprise works, surprise plays. Surprise is fun. Not that I knew she was back. Even money either way. Vacation meant she was gone all weekend. Work? Probably back. I didn't see her car but that didn't mean much considering the way she was playing musical cars. I did see a vehicle that looked a lot like Jed's unmarked police vehicle.

See. Surprise is fun. I rest my case.

I took the steps to Sara's second-floor apartment two at a time, zipped down the corridor—all in a hurry and a fluster for a good time. The door to her apartment was the same old same old. Nothing remarkable there. I gently turned the knob. *Whoops,* there it was. And pushed the door in. Hard enough to open, not hard enough to bang.

Red-handed. Smoking gun. Crumbs on his face.

"Hi!" I said in my most insouciant and cheerful voice. "How's it going?"

A drawer slammed. He winced, his hand caught in the slam. Then: "What the fuck!"

I almost yawned. I mean, talk about being boring and predictable. I am seriously rooting for witty dialogue to make a gigantic and sudden comeback.

"Hi, Jed."

"What the fuck you doing here?"

Once again I rest my case. And moved on. "I find it difficult to believe that you have written permission to be in Sara's apartment, but what the hell, surprise me." I held out my hand.

"What's it to you?" Very belligerent. And he didn't surprise me. Shucks.

I went hard and formal, the way cops do when they're reading you your rights. *Not* that *I* would know from personal experience. "I have been hired by Ms. Bernard to look after a number of things for her. Including supervising her property, rental or otherwise, in her absence." Not technically true of course but so what, I was on much firmer ground than he was. "If you do not have written permission, you do not belong here. Not only are you trespassing, you are breaking and entering with intent to commit burglary." I indicated a pile of material on the coffee table and another on the desk.

"God!" I smacked my forehead gently with an open hand. "Nothing I hate more than seeing the city's finest, one of our boys and girls in blue, go bad. You guys still wear blue, don't you?" I asked on a lighter, more conversational note as I kicked the door behind me shut and crossed the room in the general direction of the telephone.

"Start talking. No weather, no chitchat, no 'How's about those Kings?' Focus on why I shouldn't call the cops and report this." My hand was inches away from the phone, my adrenaline racing, my nerve in gear.

"Nobody bothers about the Kings anymore. Talk about a loser team."

I picked up the phone.

"*Hey*, just kidding. Lighten up, will you?"

I shrugged, the jury still out on that one. "Burglary isn't one of my main topics of humor, Jed. I wouldn't have thought it was one of yours either."

"Well, no, of course it's not, but this is not burglary. Sara and I are married. Community property? Ever heard of that? I am not stealing, I am looking for information I need to do our taxes."

I snorted. A stupid lie like that was hardly worth a direct rebuttal.

"Oh really?" I asked in my sweet, thoughtful voice—okay, my imitation of sweet and thoughtful. "So when I look through these piles of stuff, that is what I'll find, financial records needed for compiling a tax return?"

He flushed. "Yes, basically."

I walked over to the coffee table and flipped through the top four or five items. "Odd how they're all dated this year, isn't it, considering that you would be working on last year's return?"

The flush deepened. "I might have pulled a few things I don't need in my haste. It happens." He shrugged, going for devil-may-care. Didn't make it.

"Yeah," I said. "Right." I did a better job on sarcastic than he did on devil-may-care. Way better. "You have a key to the apartment then, since you claim that you did not break in?"

Silence. I use that tactic myself. Why admit something damning when you can shut up and hope it blows over? Trouble is, it hardly ever works. As it didn't here.

"You're way out of line on this one, Jed. It's not just your marriage that's at stake, it's your job. Get your act together. Fast. Now scram."

And he did, hands in the air and trying to look innocent. I had him by the short hairs and he knew it.

I sat down and looked through the things that Jed had set aside. Most of it meant nothing to me, nor could I understand what significance it had had for Jed. Still, better safe than sorry is a useful maxim. I made copies of the whole batch on Sara's copier. Then I snooped around a bit myself, made some copies of other stuff. I wouldn't have broken in, but as long as I was here . . . I sighed. Was I starting to sound like Jed or what?

Bad sign.

Time to go.

I put everything back on Sara's desk making no attempt to put it away. How? Where? I was clueless as to organization here. Sara would know that someone had been through her stuff but that wasn't necessarily bad. It's always good to know what's going on, a reminder to stay alert and on guard. I could tell her what had happened but I wasn't going to, not yet. Too much seemed to be going on that I knew nothing about. This was one way to find out.

I didn't like what Jed was doing at all. And guess what else I didn't like. Sara/Stephanie. I wondered if there were any more of them out there.

We sat on the terrace drinking lemonade.

By now I was beginning to feel that I was in the middle of some kind of arty, experimental film that was disconnected, incoherent, and nonsensical—in a sad and scary way. Nightmares, burglary, lemonade—you make sense out of it.

"Jessie, you watch it, honey, that's slippery. You don't want another bang on your knee, do you?"

The child ignored her mother, slid off the edge of the pool, hit the water with a splash and a shriek of delight. She couldn't have been more than four but she was as at home in the water as she was on the ground. Two other children were also in the pool but they were older, seven and eight perhaps.

"I swear, I don't know what we did without the pool. It sure beats TV and the VCR. You ever see *The Little Mermaid, The Hunchback of Notre Dame,* or *The Lion King*?" I shook my head. "I've probably seen them about a million times, which is a million times minus one too many."

"Cindy—" I began.

"People with kids do not get out enough and that is the long and short and God's truth of it. Do you have kids?"

"No. I—"

"Have fun while it lasts." She glanced up as a howl emanated from the pool. "Twenty years of your life gone just like that. You know, I always wanted to be a park ranger. Sit on top of a lookout tower with binoculars and watch for wildfires. And look where I ended up. How did that happen?"

She's right, I thought, she doesn't get out enough. "I don't know. Can you—"

"You want more lemonade?"

"No thank you. I was hoping—"

"Course that's probably a pipe dream. You think so?"

I was lost. Lemonade? What happened? Being a ranger? What?

"Now you read about rangers with guns and people problems. Whatever happened to nature and peacefulness? You think they have rangers up in lookout towers these days?"

"Jed," I said.

"What?"

"I'm here to talk about Jed."

She grinned at me. "Oh, sure. I don't get to talk to grown-ups much. I'm starting to rattle on like the kids. Sorry. What did you want to know?

He said for sure to go on and tell you whatever. How about how he used to pull the wings off flies?"

"Did he?"

"No-o-o. Sometimes I just make stuff up. It's less boring that way."

"Just tell me about Jed. What kind of a guy is he? And, *please,* don't make anything up."

She winked at me. "Jed is big-time boring to talk about, he is such a nice guy. You know how brothers and sisters fight?" She waved in the direction of the pool where a shouting match was in progress. The *Do too, Do not, Do too, Do not* kind. "Well, I won't say we never did—who would believe that?—but he was really a great older brother. He took care of me a lot, watched out for me, was always kind. He answered my questions, never let big kids pick on me, even let me tag along sometimes." She smiled at me. "What more could a little kid ask for?"

"Kids change. They grow up and become adults."

"Sure. But I don't think he did, not in the essentials anyway. He's still a really nice guy, very responsible and caring. Loyal too, especially to things like his job and his family."

"And his wife?"

"Sara? I like her. She seems like a really nice girl but quiet. I was surprised when Jed married her. He always liked the lively, outgoing types. He likes smart too though, and she sure is that. All that computer stuff? She's a whiz. You know what else surprised me?"

I shook my head.

"Jed's always loved kids. I told you how good he was with me. He always wanted a big family. We all figured the minute he got married and settled in there would be a baby. Lots of babies. But here they've been married for three years and nothing. No talk about it even. I've never asked, I mean, it's none of my business, but I was surprised. He's always coming over here to visit and play with my kids. Always.

"You know, come to think of it, I'm not even sure that Sara wants a family. I know she loves her work. I don't know if she'd want to take a break and have a baby. Children are a big responsibility. And Jed's old-fashioned. If they had children he'd really prefer it if she stayed home and took care of them. I never could see that happening with Sara."

"What about Jed and Sara's relationship?"

"They always seemed to get along really well, no fights or anything.

Jed was crazy about her. I kind of wondered if they had something special going, you know what I mean? It was the way they looked at each other."

"Something special?"

"In bed. And now they're separated. I don't know why, I don't have a clue. I never noticed anything wrong and Jed won't talk about it."

"Do you see Sara at all now?"

"No."

"And Jed, does he seem different?"

She stared off into the distance, over the kids and into the horizon, for a long time before answering. "Yeah, he does, in some ways."

"What ways?"

"Well . . . he's not as easygoing or talkative."

Suddenly neither was she. "Does he talk about Sara at all?"

"Some. Well, a lot actually. I think he should just let it go. He thinks about her all the time. He's almost . . . almost obsessed with it. Sometimes I worry. I think maybe he might have gone off the deep end with this one." Her pretty face got tight, closed. "I don't want to talk about this anymore. He's my brother and I love him."

Sara had loved him once too.

CHAPTER 29

I was starting to wonder when I hadn't heard from Sara by Monday afternoon. Not nice thoughts either. More like Grim Reaper stuff. By two-thirty there was a change. Sara's phone was answered by a hollow, unplugged, couldn't-care-less voice that announced that this number was either disconnected or not in service at this time.

Instant tracks.

Half an hour—speeding, tires squealing—and I was at the apartment complex. I didn't see any car I recognized as one she had driven but I didn't stop to look carefully; I took the steps up to her apartment two at a time. The door was wide open—I could see it from down the hall—and there seemed to be a fair amount of activity and noise. The bad feeling started in my stomach. No cops or EMTs though. So that was good. I took the rest of the hall at a run.

"So I says to her, you don' wanna see me, why'dya ask me over, huh? You don' think time is money, huh? Well, lemme tell you—"

I didn't think time was money either, not with him, a guy who leaned on an upright vacuum yakking. Time, I thought, was something he killed, spent, or wasted. About twenty-five, with lank, dingy hair pulled back into a ponytail, squinchy eyes, blotchy complexion, dirty jeans, and shirttails that weren't tucked in and probably never had been, he looked at me with mild interest. Not the what-can-I-do-for-you? kind, the hey-one-more-reason-not-to-work kind. His buddy was more of the same but older and with a good-sized potbelly. They stared at me. Well, one stared, one squinted.

"I'm looking for the woman who used to live here."

"Yeah."

"She moved out?"

"Yeah."

"When?"

"This morning."

"Do you know where she went?"

"Naw. I left my crystal ball in my other pair of pants." That was Squinty. Potbelly guffawed in appreciation while Squinty smirked.

Talk about dim bulbs. "She was supposed to leave me a note. I'll just look around."

"No skin off my butt." Squinty gave me a smarmy look.

Both of them slouched and watched as I peeked around. It was back to basics in Partially Furnished Apartment Land. Clothing, personal items, computer. Gone. Food, phone, and papers? Gone. The apartment had never looked much like Sara; there was nothing left of her here now.

"She owe you money?"

I looked at Squinty. Money and on the run; that was about as far as his thinking could take it. Not, I reflected, that one out of two was bad.

"She had a nice car. Go for that," Squinty advised.

"What was it?" I asked.

"What's it worth to you?" Squinty held out a hand. Potbelly grunted in appreciation again.

I looked at the callused, dirty hand with nails that had either been gnawed down to the quick or hacked off with a blunt instrument.

"Ten, man, that's what it's worth." Potbelly almost drooled in anticipation.

I said nothing.

Squinty ran his eyes over my jeans and sneakers, over the hard look on my face. "Five," he said. "Five'll do it." He belched.

Silently I counted to ten. "You guys ever watch David Letterman?"

"Yeah." They assented but looked puzzled.

"You'd be perfect, I swear."

"Huh?"

"You'll knock 'em dead, wow 'em. Stupid Pet Tricks, it's *you.* Absolutely definitive." I nodded sagely and started out the door. They stood there doing stupid—talk about proving my point—mouths agape and slack. Those four-syllable words, they're tricky all right.

I took the stairs two at a time and headed out to the rental office. The woman there was very nice but didn't know much more than I did.

"Someone pushed an envelope through the slot with her apartment key and a note saying that she was giving the place up. She didn't give a reason and it wasn't signed. Course she was prepaid through the end of the month, so it wasn't a problem or anything. I hope everything's all right—she seemed like such a nice person, like someone who was going to stay for a while."

"Did she leave a forwarding address?"

"No. Nothing. Nothing at all. I went up to see the apartment, which was fine, very clean and nice, and then I sent the maintenance crew up."

"Slug and Bug," I muttered, only slightly under my breath.

She grinned. "Yeah, aren't they something? I'd fire them in a minute if I could find someone better."

"Thanks for your help."

"Sure. Good luck to you. I hope you find your friend."

I would, I was grimly certain of that. But in one piece, one alive and well piece? That was another question. My next stop was the downtown office building where Sara worked. I struck out there:

0 for 2.

I called the people on the list I'd compiled from the names Sara and Jed had given me. Nothing. I called Joy, who hadn't heard, didn't know, and apparently, didn't care.

Strike three. I was out.

That's not all I was. I was pissed too.

CHAPTER 30

Her motions were hurried, jittery. Fear had done that, had cut back on her efficiency, her economy of motion. Now she lived a life where she was always looking over her shoulder. This was a lesson to her, she thought. Before this she had stopped the looking. Tried to forget the fear and to tell herself that she was safe, that he didn't know where she was or how to find her.

She had been wrong about both those things.

She hung her clothes in two garment bags, tossed underwear, shoes, and small things in the suitcases. The laptop computer went into its carrying case, the rest she flung into boxes. Packing was a luxury she had neither the time nor the inclination for.

Inadvertently she caught sight of herself in the mirror. So pale and washed out, the fear back in her eyes again. The smile, the color, the excitement? Just a memory. It had faded into the past quickly, and now seemed far away and out of reach in the future. Like a dream, transparent and fuzzy around the edges. She pinched her cheeks. It heightened the color but the deadness was in her eyes still. Deadness, flatness.

A noise outside in the hall. She froze, held her breath, listened. A man coughed, footsteps receded. Seven A.M. People were going to work. She unlocked the door and looked. Nothing. It took her four trips to load everything in the car. It was a wonder, she thought, that she hadn't tripped, always looking over her shoulder, always looking around. One more stop to drop the key off at the office and she was done with this place. Good.

How long could she do this, she wondered—move, start over, try to forget—before she got too tired to run? Before her resources were exhausted and she ran out of jobs and places? And the will. Oh God, it wore you down so much, the constant hiding and fear, the possibility of being found out, the danger. Wore you down to a thin little thread and then one day maybe you just snapped. BOOM. And it was over.

Or . . .

She imagined the knock on the door, the men standing there when she opened it. Would they be in uniform or plainclothes? She sketched it out in her mind, their faces strong, solemn, sad. Her face. She stepped back and looked at herself. First vulnerable and bewildered, and then comprehension, understanding just dawning. Fear and sadness and loss. The rest she would hide. She smiled.

"Mrs. Bernard? Sara Bernard?"

"Yes."

And they would pull out their badges, give their names and rank. Her tears would start then. That would be easy, she thought. Loss, fear, happiness—it can all make you cry. She would stand there and the tears would roll unchecked down her cheeks. They would reach out to touch her hand, cup her elbow for support.

"May we come in?" they would ask. "Shall we sit down. Can we get you a glass of water?"

"What is it? Why are you here? My husband—"

"There's been an accident. I'm sorry. I'm afraid we have bad news."

"He's been hurt?"

They would look at her in silence, their faces masks of pity and sorrow and relief, relief that someone wasn't talking to *their* wives.

"He was killed. I'm sorry."

"Tell me," she would whisper. "What happened? How? When?"

"A drive-by shooting . . ."

"A routine traffic stop. Things went bad . . ."

"A domestic quarrel. Jed got the guy but he had a knife. Hidden."

"His vest?" she would ask. "The bulletproof vest? He was wearing it."

"The guy got Jed in the throat," the officer answered. And she saw the red smile of blood curve across Jed's throat. And the air leave his body. And the life.

And she smiled too.

She would be a widow then, with a pension and a little bit of security. The house, everything would be hers. Not that that part mattered. Nothing mattered except never looking over her shoulder again, or feeling the grip of fear at a footstep behind her, a sudden noise in the night.

It could be an accident too, she thought. Easily. Anyone could get killed on the freeway. Look at all the people who did, who died every day. Maybe he would be going to work and a car would change lanes suddenly, carelessly. A big rig would swerve, brake, go out of control and jackknife or roll. A car would be smashed. Luckily there would be only one person in it. The driver. Jed.

A tomato truck, she thought. Two trailers of tomatoes loaded to the top. Jed would die with the sweet, overpowering smell of tomato juice in his consciousness, the fruit smashed and squashed all around him hiding the blood, washing it away.

Or a gasoline truck. His car would go up in a fiery, horrible explosion. It would make the news. Everyone would gasp in horror and anguish. Everyone except Jed, who would be a crispy critter.

And Sara, who would be smiling.

Or self-defense. In a way, that was her very favorite. She wanted to see the flush of fear in his eyes, even if it was only for a second, when he realized that she really would kill him. That he had threatened her and tried to kill her one too many times—that it was over now, all of it, the stalking, the threats, the fear that she lived with every day and every night. It was over with the pressure of a finger, the pull of a trigger. It was done, it was really truly over, she was free. She had freed herself, as she knew she could.

They would write about that in the paper too, she supposed, though she wished it could be avoided. The publicity, the talk, the speculation. She shivered. God, she hated that, all the people who had no lives and nothing better to do, who lived through the pain and feelings of others, who fed on them.

Maybe killed on duty was better. So much sympathy, so dignified and straightforward. But it wasn't fair. He had made her suffer, made her live in fear. He should die that way—in fear and suffering, not with dignity and heroism.

The tomato truck and the blood-red of the tomatoes—she liked that. Or the fire. The leaping, cleansing flames of death and hell.

She sighed out loud and looked around. It was difficult to imagine fire and dying and hell on this beautiful spring day. Seventy-five degrees and clear blue skies with birds singing as though each moment were a new beginning. She wished it were. What would life be without memories, without a past? Impossible, she supposed. But life without fear? That was possible, that would be wonderful.

She looked over her shoulder again. For the last time here. And got into the car. It was a new one. She had turned the previous one back into the rental company and gone to another company for yet another car. Now she had to find another job, another place to stay.

She was getting good at running and hiding and fear. She looked over her shoulder again as she pulled out into traffic.

She was getting good but she hated it.

CHAPTER 31

The tinted glass dish was filled with glass marbles; the bulbs in the dish flowered profusely in shades of pink and purple and white. I gazed over them at Jill, who was frowning.

"No leads?" she asked.

I shrugged. "I'll turn up something but everything obvious has been shut down. She cleaned out her apartment this morning, left without a forwarding address. The office manager at her job informed me that she completed her assignment last Friday. They asked her to stay on for another work assignment but she declined. The car she was driving was a rental and it was turned in Sunday evening. If she has another rental I can track it down but it's a long boring job and, frankly, one that doesn't interest me much."

"I'd like you to find Sara, Kat."

"Really? Why? In my experience clients who don't want to be found are not particularly desirable." I tossed a copy of my hours and expenses on Jill's desk. "The money you advanced me is gone. No money and no client. Gee, Jill, how would you make that call?"

"Couldn't you cut her a little slack? Please."

I thought of the several faces of Sara, the middle-of-the-night calls, the fight with Jed and charmers like Joy. "I have. Several times in fact."

"I'll advance you more money and guarantee payment. This is Sara's specific directive, I know she wants you on the job. Let's assume she's just very upset about Jed and not thinking entirely clearly. I'm sure that when she calms down she'll call in. Give her a couple of days, Kat, she's probably very frightened. Desperate even."

And deceitful, I added silently. But I agreed to the couple more days. Curiosity, not compassion, was the operative concept.

In that spirit I decided to go out and look for trouble, stir up some if I couldn't find any. And why not? What did I have to lose?

What do you mean, who knows Sara better than anybody?"

I hadn't thought it was a tough question but I tried again. "Who is her closest friend, the one she would be most likely to talk to?"

"Well, me, of course. I can't believe you're even bothering to ask that." Joy's tone indicated both surprise and outrage. Joy might act like she despised Sara and do everything she could to alienate her sister, but she either believed—or needed to believe—that they were best buddies. I bit my tongue and revised my question.

"Of course," I corrected smoothly. "Sorry I didn't make myself clear. I meant when Sara was young, when the age difference between you would have meant that you were running with different kids."

"Oh." Mollified. "That would be Alicia Schuman. She lives around here still but I don't know if they are close now."

"Is her name still Schuman?"

"I think so. She's married but has a business in her own name. She's a financial planner or consultant or something."

"How long have Sara and Alicia known each other?"

"Since the second grade. They were practically inseparable in grade school. Later on they ran around a lot together too but in a larger group of kids."

"What's Alicia like?"

"She's uh . . . she's okay."

I wished I could see Joy's face. This was the problem with phone interviews. "Okay?" I put a puzzled spin on the word.

"Yeah. She and Sara were good together. Alicia was kind of impulsive, a little wild even, and Sara was pretty shy and in . . . in . . . What's that mental word, the turned-in one?"

"Introverted?" I made a stab at translation.

"Yes. Anyway, it was a good balance and all. Alicia brought Sara out and Sara calmed Alicia down a bit. They're both into the same thing now too, this career-woman, high-achievement stuff." She sounded a little defensive. "Not that they would talk to me about it, *I'm* just a housewife."

I ignored that. If she hadn't figured out that everyone makes a contribution in their own way and is valuable because of it, it wasn't my job to enlighten her. *Also, ask me if I cared.*

"*I'm* not important like all you *working* girls."

Oops, now I was in there too, included in the scorn and dismissal. I tried to dodge that bullet. I thought homemakers worked very hard. The only thing I had against Joy was her attitude in general and her stinginess with Oreos.

"You've been a big help, Joy. Thanks a bunch." I made it light and breezy.

"Why are you asking all this, anyway? This is old stuff, history. How could it be important?"

"It isn't really, just background." Speaking of breezy. "Thanks again, Joy. Bye. Gotta run." I tossed all that out in a flash and hung up before she could think of something else I didn't want to talk about.

Hung up and dialed again.

Alicia was available, accessible, and thoughtful. She was also worried—and I didn't even tell her the really bad stuff—and pushed for time.

"I'm running. I'm having a dinner party tonight and I'm taking the afternoon off. Do you want to come over to the house while I cook? We can talk then. Boy, I can't believe this. I was the one who got into trouble, not Sara. Half an hour, okay? I've got to pick up some things. Grab a pencil, here come the directions."

Alicia opened the door wrapped in an industrial-sized apron and a smile. There was flour on her cheek, something slimy that I couldn't identify on her hair, and all of her not covered by the apron was splashed and spattered.

"Come in!" She waved a slotted spoon at me and a bit of something landed on my nose. "Oops—watch out for me, I'm dangerous in the kitchen. Let's go on back. I've got stuff on the stove."

I followed her at what I hoped was a guarded and safe distance.

"Sit here." She pointed at a stool tucked up to the kitchen island. "I'll get you some iced tea."

"Would you like help? I'll be glad to—"

"Oh no." She plunked a glass of tea in front of me. "I take up a whole kitchen when I cook. Just talk." She dumped a bunch of mushrooms and peppers on a cutting board and started chopping.

"Joy told me you and Sara were best friends when you were younger."

She nodded but didn't look up. The cutting board bounced on the counter.

"Are you still close?"

"We're still friends certainly, I wouldn't say we're close, at least not as close. We get together on occasion, three or four times a year maybe, but our lives are very different now."

"How would you describe Sara?"

She looked at me curiously. "I guess I don't understand why you're asking that. I thought you were working for Sara, trying to keep her safe." Her eyes were large and brown and they were fixed on me.

"Safe not just from Jed but from herself. Right now I don't know where she is. No one does, she's on the run. From Jed, her family, her lawyer, and me."

"On the run?"

"She moved out of the apartment, rented a car, and for all intents and purposes, vanished. My guess is that she's still in the area but I don't know where. Which is okay if no one can find her, but if Jed does before I do . . ." I let that sentence drift off.

"I see." The knife flashed through green stuff.

"In order to guess where she might be or what Jed might do I need to know Sara as well as possible. It is unlikely that either Jed or his friends will tell me anything helpful, if I were willing to risk going to them, which I am not. So it all comes back to Sara."

Alicia gazed at me for a moment—beautiful dark brown eyes—then resumed the wild chopping. A mushroom escaped, rolled over to me, tried to hide behind my iced tea. I rolled it back.

"When we were children we were very different. I was impetuous, impulsive, temperamental. Sara was sweet, thoughtful, considerate, and quiet. It seems odd that two such different children could be friends, but we were. We were inseparable. Over the years we seemed to balance each other out. I became less temperamental and more thoughtful, Sara much more outgoing and . . . well, not excitable and enthusiastic, but willing to try new things, to experiment and even, occasionally, be a little wild. She was fun. I mean, she always was but more so over the years. That's why I was so surprised when she married Jed."

"Why?" She lost me on that last one.

Alicia dumped her chopped vegetables into a colander and reached for a bag of large yellow onions and a head of garlic.

"You've met Jed, right?"

"Right, but I don't know him well."

"Well, he's more like the old Sara; I really think he would have made a better husband for *her*." She cut the outer skins of the onions and peeled them off with a gleaming evil-looking paring knife.

"What do you mean?"

"Jed's a really nice guy and I like him a lot." She frowned. "Well, I don't like him if he's annoying or threatening Sara, I wouldn't like that in anyone, but I mean aside from that, which I didn't know about until now and just judging from what I knew before—oh God, you know what I mean, right?"

"Yes."

"Okay. Well, he's like the old Sara, very dependable, responsible, and thoughtful. He's good at his job and he's a nice guy but he's not exciting. Not spur-of-the-moment. He likes to plan and organize and he likes to follow that plan pretty much to the letter. He likes other people to do that too. He'll play games, softball, or badminton, but not just hang out and goof off. He's outgoing but not spontaneous and playful. Do you see?"

I nodded.

"Well, Sara used to be like that but I don't really think of her that way anymore. I figured she'd marry someone more like her now than her then, that's all. Jed is very attractive though." She started chopping onions. "*Very* attractive. I wouldn't be surprised if sex was a pretty big part of their relationship. They had a way of looking at each other, touching each other."

Something boiled on the stove and Alicia turned it down, clunked the lid back on.

"Did you ever see him, or know him to be abusive—physically or emotionally?"

"Jed? Not Jed."

"Yes, that's what Sara says, that he hit her and threatened her life."

"He *hit* her, *threatened* her life?" Her voice was sad, her face streaked with tears. "Dumb jerk. Slimeball." She rubbed the back of her hand across her eyes. "Could you grab me a towel. These onions. Whew."

"Would Sara come to you if she needed help, needed a place to stay?"

"Sure. Well, maybe not in a situation like this, with Jed and all. This is one of the first places he'd look if he was looking for her."

"Where then?"

"In Sacramento?"

I'd start here. "Yes."

She wiped her eyes with the towel and started on the garlic. "Gee, I should have gotten more garlic. Roasted garlic is one of my favorite appetizers."

I waited patiently, watching my ice cubes melt.

"Someplace that Jed wouldn't know about?" Alicia asked.

"Yes. Or perhaps someplace so secure he couldn't get to her."

Alicia started chopping garlic. Idly, I wondered what kind of place that would be. And security. People can get to the President and Secret Service guys are as thick as fleas on him.

Alicia got down a huge skillet, poured olive oil in it and put it on a burner on a high flame. Her forehead was creased with a frown, her brown eyes clouded. She tossed a small piece of onion in the pan, waited for it to sizzle, then dumped the rest in. Stirred and frowned. "Would you hand me that pot holder, please?" She transferred her frown to me and pointed.

I handed the pot holder over.

"Oh!" The frown melted away. The onions and garlic sizzled. "Of *course*." She smiled at me.

I smiled back.

"Cousin Annie's."

"Sara has a cousin here in town?"

"No. Cousin Annie's is a bed-and-breakfast. Sara worked her way through college by being the housekeeper there. She cleaned the rooms, did cooking, and watched the desk in the evenings while she studied. She was always embarrassed about it though so she never told anyone."

I wrinkled my nose, puzzled. Alicia dumped the mushrooms and peppers in the skillet.

"She thought it sounded menial and horrible, cleaning rooms and all.

Her family was working poor, really decent, respectable, nice people but I think there were times when Sara's mother cleaned houses or did ironing or something. Sara was ashamed of that—when her mother did it and when she did it. It's silly, I know, but that's how she felt. Shoot, we knew girls who slept their way through college—sold it, I mean. That's something to be ashamed of, not cleaning houses."

Alicia turned the burner off, went rooting through the refrigerator, emerged with her hands full.

"Anyway, that's how she felt so she never ever told anyone what she did. She has a kind of secretive side to her, you know?"

No kidding. I was getting to know that side of her quite well.

"I think I'm probably the only person she ever told. We used to know everything about each other." She tossed a slab of meat on the cutting board and began pounding it. "And Belinda."

"Belinda?" I queried.

"Belinda Smythe. She owns Cousin Annie's and is like a mother to Sara. If Sara needed help or understanding or sympathy, she would go to Belinda. Belle would do anything for Sara. Anything."

"And Jed?"

"He's met Belinda, of course. He thinks she's a distant cousin or something but he doesn't really know anything about her, or that they are as close as they are. He would never know to find her there. Never in a million years."

"Where is Cousin Annie's?"

"In midtown. On G Street, I think."

"Thanks, Alicia."

"Are you going there?"

"Yes."

"Belle won't tell you anything, you know." She whomped the slab of meat a few times for emphasis. "Not a word. She's as closemouthed as they come." *Whomp.*

"All right."

"But you're still going?"

I nodded. I was almost there.

"Do people change with something like this, Kat?" she asked abruptly.

"Like what?"

"I don't know. Sara and Jed."

"Perhaps. Or perhaps it was always there with nothing to bring it out."

"Sara's changed."

"How?"

"I don't know. She just has, she's different. It started a while ago, I think. I just don't remember when."

"Or why?"

"No, I don't know that either. The days when we told each other everything are over. My guess is that now she never tells *any*body everything."

"Not even Jed when things were good?"

"Not even Jed. He likes to be in charge, to control everything. He's a good cop but not always the best person to talk to." She started slicing the whomped meat, knife flashing in and out of the red flesh.

I waited for more but there wasn't any. Just a good luck wish and a small smile.

Not luck, I thought, investigative work.

CHAPTER 32

Belinda was the last thing I expected. She looked a bit like the way I imagine the Old Woman Who Lived in a Shoe looks. Small round body, wispy white hair, rimless glasses. Her bright blue eyes twinkled, she had apple-red cheeks and a sweet smile right out of a fairy tale—I am not making this up, I swear.

"Hullo, hullo!"

The door jingled as I entered and she bustled out wiping her hands on her apron (blue gingham with lace ruffles—I am *still* not making this up!) in response. She smiled and bounced around as she greeted me. I smiled back. How could I help it?

"Welcome to Sacramento. I am Belinda. Do make yourself at home. How long will you be with us? Oh, I'm so pleased that we still have a garden room available."

"I am not here for a room." I felt a little guilty.

"Oh. Well then, how may I help you?" She folded her hands and gazed placidly at me.

"I am looking for Sara Bernard."

Nothing in her expression, face, or posture changed, yet everything was different.

"We have no guest here by the name of Sara Bernard." Her voice was pleasant but businesslike, no longer welcoming.

"Not a guest—" I began to explain, though of course she needed no explanation.

"I'm baking a cake." She gave me a perfunctory smile. "*Just* that crucial stage. I know you'll understand." She was backing up very quickly for a little round person, her hand suddenly on the bottom half of a Dutch door leading into the kitchen, her figure starting to slide out of view.

"Did Sara tell you Jed is trying to kill her?"

Her expression changed in a small, almost undefinable way.

"She hired me to help. Please tell her Kat came by." I turned and walked out, the bell jingling cheerily again. I had almost reached the car when I heard her voice.

"Yoo-hoo, oh yoo-hoo, miss. I think we might have a room for you after all. Won't you please come back?"

Belinda was waving at me from the front porch. I was a little disappointed to see that she didn't have a hanky in her hand. I retraced my steps and followed her now silent form back into the kitchen where—you won't believe this but that sweet little old lady had lied!—there was absolutely no sign of a cake in progress.

There *was* a somewhat sullen-looking Sara.

"How did you find me?"

"I'm an investigator, remember. This is what investigators do."

"Maybe Jed followed you."

"He didn't follow me." I was biting my tongue and watching my patience. Both efforts were starting to fail me.

Belinda made a noise that sounded like *cluck cluck* and bustled around producing tea and a plate of cookies in a remarkably short period of time. The homemade cookie kind, not the Oreo kind. I smiled my thanks and ate one.

"How about firing me?" That was my opening conversational gambit.

"What?" Sara gasped.

"You're not telling me anything; you're not happy to see me. Why not fire me?" I had another cookie, definitely starting to enjoy myself. The tea was good too. "I don't like jobs like this. In fact, I may even quit."

Sara sputtered.

Belinda smiled. "I like you." She spoke softly. "Have some more cookies, won't you?"

So I did. It was almost dinnertime, but frankly, after watching Alicia chop and whomp, I wasn't much into meat and vegetables. And let's face it, it's tough to find a time when you can't fit in a cookie.

As I munched I watched Sara who was still sputtering. Belinda smiled placidly.

I was starting to wonder what I could do next that didn't involve Sara. Belinda pushed the cookie dish next to me. Besides eating cookies, I mean. Okay, one more and that was it. Memories crowded in on me. Hank. Tears. The sputtering next to me stopped.

"I'm sorry."

The words were simple and she sounded sincere. It was a start.

"I shouldn't have done that, I know, left without telling you and all. Nothing was really planned. You knew I was going away for the weekend, I told you that. It was then that I decided I just couldn't go back to a place where Jed could find me. I didn't know where to go or what to do, so I came here. I knew Belinda would help me."

I looked at Belinda who was nodding and smiling. Forget the Old Woman in the Shoe. She was always kind of busy and harried-looking now that I think about it. Cinderella's fairy godmother, that was it. I half-way expected her to wave a wand, but she didn't. Cookies were her thing apparently.

"It's hard to think straight when you're frightened, Kat. I didn't mean to be difficult, I really didn't. When you're on the run all you think about is staying one step ahead of the danger. You don't really have time or energy for anything more, I guess. I won't do that again. Please don't be mad at me. Or quit. Please."

"All right. If it happens again though, I'm gone."

"I understand. It won't."

"What are your plans now?"

"I'll stay here for a few days until I can figure something out. My mind's not working real well right now. When I figure it out, I'll call you, I promise. If I leave for any reason, Belle—Belinda—will know where I am. And she knows it's okay to tell you everything. All right?"

"All right. Are you planning to work?"

She nodded. "I really need the money. I know of a two-week job that's perfect and I'll probably take that. Keep moving, that's my only plan for now. At least we're piling up evidence against Jed." She gave me a wistful, almost wry smile. "I've been telling myself that it will be over, that pretty soon you'll have enough on him, enough so that he, and everyone else, will have to admit what's going on. That's true, isn't it?"

"Yes. We have more than enough now for a restraining order, which is what you need."

She shook her head. "You know how I feel. A restraining order still leaves me open to an 'accident' like the one that killed Lorraine. I just can't live like that, Kat. I need enough against him so that he can never threaten or harm me because everyone will know. Then I'll be safe. It's a good plan, I think."

I said nothing. It was a plan and even a dumb plan was better than no plan. "What do you want me to do in the meantime, Sara?"

"I don't know. Maybe see if you can keep an eye on Jed, see what he's up to? Can you do that?"

I nodded, still working on the dumb-plan-is-better-than-no-plan theory. "I can give it a shot."

She smiled, a thin, feeble little smile, not a smile with gumption or git-up-and-go in it. It was a smile that fit the beat-up and running-scared woman, not the I-did-it-and-you-can-too professional woman or the sly woman who had slipped off to Calistoga. But Sara didn't know that I knew about those women.

I would keep my eye on Jed; I would also keep my eye on them. Maybe there were others. It could get busy, I thought.

"Do you have a car now?"

"Yes. I turned the last one in and rented another."

"What is it?"

"A dark blue Ford Escort. Why?"

"How will I know if Jed's following you if I don't know what you're driving? Chances are that I won't be close enough to see you." I spoke patiently.

"Oh. Yes, sure. I see."

"What's the license plate number?"

She rummaged through her purse and pulled out a key with a paper tag on it. I jotted down the information that was on the tag.

"Where do you park?"

She pointed vaguely. "In back. Belle has a little parking area there for guests."

I nodded. "I may swing by to check on you. *Don't shoot!*"

"No, no." She smiled wanly again. "I learned my lesson, I promise."

Belinda looked puzzled and alarmed both. Good. I liked people who weren't trigger-happy fools. When I stood to leave Belinda accompanied me, talking in a whisper as soon as we were out of earshot.

"She's so stressed and unhappy. My goodness! I have never seen her like this before. Please don't judge her too harshly, she's a very sweet, calm person usually. Everybody just loves her, I can't understand what's happening here. Jed always seemed like a perfectly nice young man. Of course he's the kind who likes to have his own way and we *all* know *that* can spell trouble." She said this darkly.

I watched her closely, still half expecting a magic wand to wave. Nothing. No pumpkin coach or rats for footmen either. Back to the earlier theory of fairy tale as metaphor. Cinderella. Servant to princess—every girl's dream one time or another. Had it been Sara's? Was it still? And of course a princess required a prince. And a kingdom? I rather suspected that Sara had her eye on both. I wasn't sure about her taste in princes yet.

I was pretty certain of her motto: *The end justifies the means.*

It was not a motto I respected.

CHAPTER 33

The little red light was blinking steadily when I got home. Two messages. Both were business, call forwards from the office. Jed's voice first, the tone light, easy, and friendly. "Kat, my apologies for our disagreement. May I buy you lunch and express myself in person?"

I listened to it twice. Perfect, I thought, didn't give a thing away. "Disagreement" was very low-key, a better choice of word than altercation or fight, both of which were more accurate. Disagreement was almost friendly, the way people are about sports, movies, or where to eat. It was a message that admitted nothing, was virtually useless as evidence but accomplished its goal, the extension of a friendly olive branch. It was also a message, I was sure, that had been carefully planned and rehearsed. Atta boy, Jed.

The second call was from Tony Kily who invited me to a basketball game. Jeez, if this kept up my dance card was going to be full in no time at all. Was I popular or what?

Or what. Definitely. Tony had been friendly up to the point when I had started questioning Jed's actions and motives, then—bang—his interest in my conversation and company had evaporated. Two seconds later I was watching him disappear. He was married so I didn't think it was a date—not that I thought for a moment that pushy, nosy women were his type. So that pretty much left the obvious, which was right where I'd started: Jed had put him up to it.

Hah, I liked it. And I thought it was way too coincidental. Jed had lost sight of Sara the night she caught a ride at the community center. I was the closest thing to Sara.

Bingo.

I called Tony.

"Yeah. Detective Kily."

"Hi. Kat Colorado."

"Yeah?"

Wow. Talk about excitable, that Tony was something. "Returning your call, detective." I muted my excitement too.

"Oh yeah. Yeah. Thanks. Look. I was thinking about our conversation the other day. Sorry if I got a little abrupt at the end there. Jed's my partner, best friend—you know how it goes."

"Yeah." I took a conversational page from Kily's book.

"Okay. Well, I didn't mean anything by it, that's for sure. Wouldn't want you to think that."

"Course not," I lied.

"Yeah. Well, maybe you heard some bum things about Jed. I wanted to show you another side. If you're still interested, I mean."

I allowed as how I was. I was still playing a little hard to get though, didn't want him to think I was a pushover after all.

"So howsabout a basketball game? Jed's a coach. Kids. I thought you might like to go to a game."

"Okay. When?"

"Tonight."

I agreed to that too. And said I'd meet him there in twenty minutes. On the way I had dinner, a diet Dr Pepper, and the small bag of cookies Belinda had pressed into my hand as she walked me to the car. My eating habits have never been that good and since Hank's death all my—well, really his—good resolutions bit the dust. It was difficult for me to focus on eating well; I was still trying to care about living.

I pulled open the gym door and the smell of sweat, rubber, and maybe desperation and hope hit me in the face like a wet sock. I had to push myself into it, make myself breathe. It wasn't a good smell. Voices were loud, balls hit the floor and shoes squeaked and pounded. The court was brightly lit and the players stood out in stark relief.

Everyone seemed to be on the court. No uniforms, just mismatched gym shorts, exercise clothes, or cut-off sweats. Balls were everywhere. Kids were warming up on the court or stretching on the sidelines. Boys and girls both. There was a lot of pushing and shoving but all of it seemed like good-natured camaraderie and the focus seemed pretty solidly on practice. There were kids dribbling up and down the court and taking turns at free throws. A runaway ball bounced in my direction and I bounced it back, got a hollered thank-you. I didn't see Jed.

I scanned the bleachers and a guy stood. Tony. He held up a hand, half wave, half salute, and I started in his direction. Already I was used to the smell. It was hot and the noise level was high. I was getting used to that too. I climbed the bleachers, sat next to Tony.

"Thanks for coming. I appreciate it."

"You're welcome. I'm glad to be here."

He nodded. "It's something special Jed does. If more of us did this, the world would be a different place."

The formation on the court changed, the kids bunching up on one end. Jed was in the middle of the bunch, I could see him now. I couldn't hear what he was saying but the kids were listening up. A few shouts, laughter, then they spread out over the court and started playing.

"Jed insisted that the teams be coed from the beginning. He said this wasn't just about basketball, it was about life. He hates the way boys relate to girls on the street, all that macho bullshit. He felt that one way to stop it was to make them work together, play together as equals and teammates. Any kid cops a different attitude, he's benched immediately."

A boy broke off, streaked down the court, passed the ball to a female teammate who made the basket. High fives, shoulder pounds. The girl was grinning ear to ear.

"That's why I find this talk about Jed harassing, threatening, or hurting Sara so damn hard to believe, Kat. Jed's not that kind of guy, he's really not. He doesn't talk the talk; he doesn't walk the walk. Look what he's doing with these kids, for crying out loud."

Tony's face was twisted with emotion. Odd, I mused. If I hadn't known better I would have said that the emotion was both powerful and negative, not positive. A skirmish broke out on the basketball court. I missed the beginning, musing on Tony and emotion, but the end involved a lot of shoving, posturing, and raised voices. A basketball slammed on the floor and then into a student's body. Voices slammed too. I thought I saw a fist. Tony was tense beside me, seemed to be having a tough time staying in his seat.

But this was Jed's game. And Jed was handling it. He never raised his voice. Instead the shouts muffled, then quieted. When the squabble was over three kids were benched, the rest subdued.

"That's the way he does it."

I looked at Tony, his face squinched up and sincere. "He never raises his voice or yells at the kids and he doesn't let them yell either. He says yelling doesn't solve anything, talking does. He says there's enough yelling on the streets and not enough talking anywhere. He says—"

I heard the squeak of shoes and the *punk punk* of the ball in motion, turned to see the flash of young limbs and smiles. Shouts now in fun, in encouragement. So much energy and so easy for it to get lost or unfocused or on the downhill and negative slide. The straight and narrow—tough to locate, hard to keep track of.

"He says use your brains, not your guts. You're gonna run out of guts and you're never gonna run out of brains. He says tough doesn't count. There's always someone tougher and meaner. What counts is liking yourself and what you do. What counts is respect. What counts is values."

I looked at Tony. His face was warped with emotion, his voice was tough-guy cop.

"You think many people talk about values to these kids? Nah. Most of these kids don't know shit. Or their values are screwed, like cool clothes, rap music, tough talk. Values are not like Nikes. That's what Jed says. The styles don't come and go. Values are here forever, they are things that count. You think these kids have even heard of the Golden Rule? Not too damn many of them and that's for sure.

"Well, Jed talks about that, all that. He takes kids to church with him. He gets them into projects like community cleanups or car washes to raise money for a good cause. And this is maybe the first time these kids have thought of helping someone else out, have had that satisfaction. Most of the time they are just focused on staying alive and together in the hard-knocks world of theirs. He makes their world a bigger place, a better place, a place with hope."

All I could hear now was Tony. The kids—the noise and the game—had been pushed into the background by the harsh insistence of his voice, the hammering of his points, one after another, into my consciousness.

"He says . . . He shows . . . He tells them what to do. Does Jed live what he says? Do what he preaches?" I asked.

"Yeah." Tony's voice was a little hostile. "Yeah, he does. Why would you doubt it?"

Look at that, a cop going naive on me. There was a new twist. "Talk is cheap, Tony, cheap and easy. You telling me you never heard of a cop busting people for the same laws he's broken, or a parent or teacher saying, *Do as I say, not as I do*, a preacher condemning sins of the flesh that he indulges in?" I took a deep breath. I had to watch myself here, I could really get going on this one, especially the holier-than-thou preacher angle. Jimmy Swaggart, Jim and Tammy Faye Bakker. Oops, see what I mean?

"I'm not telling you that." Tony's voice was definitely hostile now. "Shit happens. I see a lot of it. I'm telling you that Jed is not part of shit happening. I'd think you could see that for yourself."

"Okay."

So we watched basketball. Happy, healthy kids and our hero in the war against shit happening. I sighed to myself and wondered if it was too late to do something about my cynical attitude. Probably. I was a lot less cynical before— with Hank—but now . . .

The kids played ball for two hours and then they sat around and talked for a while. Finally Jed rounded everyone up and herded them on out. School night, school hours.

Tony stood and stretched. "He takes a bunch of kids home." His voice dared me to contradict him but I didn't. "They live in tough neighborhoods and there're no buses or anything this time of night, so he takes them home."

"Lighten up, Tony."

He stared at me, his jaw working. "What are you talking about?"

"Put yourself in my shoes. You're trying to find out something and you're starting out with an open mind. You talk to a guy and he's got one idea and only one idea. And he tries to ram that idea down your throat. What would *you* think?"

He just stared at me, his jaw working even harder.

"I got your point. You didn't even have to ram it. Not only did I get it,

I appreciate it. And I agree with you that it takes a special kind of person to do things like this. But that's still only one side of Jed and a person has a lot of sides. You say you believe in your friend. Well, act like it and quit being afraid of what I'll find out. Nobody's perfect but good people stand up pretty well to close scrutiny."

"Hey, Kat."

I turned and smiled. "Hey, Jed."

"Didn't expect to see you here."

"Tony talked me into it and I'm glad he did, I really enjoyed myself. And I'm impressed with what you're doing for these kids."

"Aw . . ." He dismissed that with a wave. "They're good kids, real good. They just needed to be pointed in the right direction. We all need that I guess." He winked at me. "You going to take me up on lunch?"

"You bet."

"That's great. I'll call you, huh? I don't dare make an appointment without my calendar. C'mon, you want to walk out with us? I gotta run some kids home."

And walk we did. Three adults and a bunch of kids, the latter trying to figure out who I was and where I fit in. With Jed? Tony? But weren't they married? Nobody enlightened them.

There are answers in life but they don't come easy. They knew that already, of course.

And so did we.

CHAPTER 34

God, she loved doing this. She felt more alive at these times than any other. She smiled to herself. Except for sex. Nothing really compared to that. In sex every cell in your body was alive and focused. In this too, almost. The comparison alone was such a rush.

It's not that she put these people down. She wouldn't do that. She didn't feel it, not at all. She was just so glad that she wasn't one of them. Every time she looked at them she knew that she had been there and that she never would be again. It was such a powerful feeling. Not just a feeling and not just power limited to yourself. Power.

She wondered if that was what preachers felt. *I have been there and I have sinned, but now, now I am saved and I will show you the way*. Power. It made her feel special too, knowing that she'd pulled herself up like that, made something of herself. Sometimes people who were special looked special, but sometimes they didn't. Look at Hitler. He was an ugly, funny-looking little man and the ugliness of his outside couldn't even begin to compare to the darkness, the bestiality of his inside. Yet he had made people think of him as special and treat him that way. Power.

She was special though. She knew that. And she wasn't ugly inside. She smiled and looked at herself in the mirror. Or outside. She smoothed her hands down her arms, over her flat belly, down her slim hips and thighs.

Yellow was the color of sunshine, of light and gold and hope. Yellow was happiness. Her dress was a bright yellow tube, slim and tight. Her jacket, also slim and tight, was collarless and turquoise. The scarf knotted casually around her neck was bright in yellows, blues, greens, and reds. She looked like a bright, beautiful bird, she thought, a parrot in a tropical jungle. A macaw, is that what they were called?

Now, when she walked into a room, everyone looked at her. She loved that, oh, she loved it so much. Beauty was power too, just as intelligence was. Or darkness and evil. Power was a neutral energy force, amoral. It could be used either to build or to destroy. That's why it was so seductive, so exciting. Building was a rush but so was destruction. She smoothed her hands over her hips again and thought about the demolition derbies she had loved as a child. Cars smashing into each other until, finally, there were only a few left.

She glanced at the clock, pulled the door open a little bit. Soon. She was ready—gleaming yellow and a ray of sunshine. And power. She was ready. She heard the crowd sounds die down into murmurs and then into silence. The introduction followed. And the applause. And it was time.

She heard the murmurs through the applause as she stepped out and walked across the room. She loved it, every minute of it.

"Thank you for coming here tonight. My name is Suzanna. It was not long ago that I sat where you are sitting. I was one of you."

There were no gasps tonight, just stunned silence. They did not believe her. She was so bright and beautiful. So shining. Powerful. They did not believe her.

But they watched. And listened.

Watched as she stepped out of high-heeled pumps and slipped off her jacket, unwound the scarf, climbed into the ugly brown clothes she took from the bag beside the podium. Watched as she slipped her feet into the solid, sensible, thick-soled shoes.

Watched as she went from Beauty to Beast.

"I keep these clothes," she said. "I will never throw them out. They remind me of where I was and where I am now. They tell me what I have done and what I can do."

When Suzanna stepped out of her drab, dreary clothes it was like seeing a phoenix step from the ashes.

They believed her. Then, they believed her.

"I was a prisoner and now I am free. I loved many things. I still do. And yet many of these things were bad for me. It was very difficult for me to even see this, never mind admit it." She smiled gently and looked around the room with a loving glance that included all of them, made them feel warm. And positive, the beginning of power.

"Some of the things we love are good for us in moderation; some are bad. When we love things, use them well and positively, when *we* are in control, then they are good. When *they* are in control, they are addictions. That is the only difference."

They sat, these women, with bemused expressions on their faces and something out of control within them.

"How do we stay in control?" she asked. And got no response. They had come for answers, not questions. They did not want the burden of understanding on them; they were willing to be told, to follow, to give her the power. And she was willing to take that power.

They listened.

In thrall.

They had hoped for, longed for an easy answer and there it was. The Sunflower Health Spa and Clinic. Not just a place for the rich and famous but for them. Their insurance would pay. Not far away in L.A. or Texas or New York but here, close by in Calistoga.

It was the answer to a dream come true and they were ready for it. Only one person left early. The rest clustered about Suzanna, a ray of sunshine, a beam of light and hope in her yellow dress.

CHAPTER 35

I left early, nauseated and awed both. Sara/Stephanie/Suzanna was gifted and charismatic. She could go right from here to the motivational circuit—television, national tours, the works. Shoot, I was practically ready to check into the Sunflower Health Spa and Clinic myself. I didn't have any addictions but so what? That's how good she was.

Her clothing was perfect. The whole setup was a classic Before and After, including all the cheats we're used to. You know, the After has not only lost weight, she's gotten her hair styled, is wearing makeup, and is happy, smiling, and spirited. The Before, of course, is not only overweight but the photo looks like a mug shot, only worse. Bleak eyes, ugly complexion, raggedy hair? All there. Black and white too. The After is in color.

Sara did the same thing, stepping from yesterday's shapeless overweight brown back into today's yellow and brilliance. It was primal, powerful, with the simplicity and impact of a fairy tale. *Once upon a time . . . and then she lived happily ever after*. And now Sara was willing to wave her wand and her magic over everyone else. They crowded around her when she finished, eager to hear more about the clinic, eager to sign up. Eager for the magic to begin.

I was the only one who left.

In the car I pulled off the baggy jeans, sweatshirts, and sweatpants. The layered look. I wore jeans, sweatpants over them, then another pair of jeans. Ditto the top half. It added, I figure, an easy forty pounds. That was topped off with a blah but convincing wig, heavy pancake makeup, and large tinted glasses. I don't know who or what I looked like but it wasn't me.

It took longer to get the makeup off than the clothes and wig but still not that long. Five minutes and I was myself again. People were starting to trickle out. I could hear their eager voices; I could see the excitement in the way they walked and gestured. As the parking lot emptied out I moved the car to a street space where I could easily see and pass, I hoped, for just another parked car.

Sara, walking with the woman who had introduced her this evening, was the last to exit. They got into different cars, the other woman taking off immediately. Sara sat for a long time, her hands on the steering wheel, her head leaning back against the seat, her eyes closed.

I wondered what was going through her mind. And if the power had gone to her head.

She did not go to Calistoga as I halfway expected she would. I followed her to Cousin Annie's, stayed there until almost all the lights went out forty-five minutes later, then drove by Jed's. The Ranger was there, the Corolla wasn't.

Everyone was safely tucked in. Everyone but me.

In the morning I started making calls. Informal inquiry is what we call it in my business. The Sunflower Health Spa and Clinic didn't have instant recognition like the Betty Ford Clinic (of course, what clinic does?), but it was known, at least in California. I didn't bother to take my inquiries out of state. Yet. I did try to pinpoint the clinic's approach, which was hard. Generalities are always easier to come by than specifics.

I finally called T.J. Barnes whom I've known forever, so long that I can't remember how we met. Occasionally I do a job for him—a teenage runaway, say—but mostly we confer and exchange information on a more informal basis. Bullshit is what T.J. calls it.

"What do you need?" T.J. asked me after the how-you-doing? and what's-happening? stuff.

"The Sunflower Health Spa and Clinic, have you heard of it?"

"Sure. It's fairly well known, I'd say. For years it was an old-fashioned spa. They used to be a dime a dozen in the Calistoga area. You know—natural hot springs, pools, mud packs, mineral waters, vegetable juices, all that kind of thing. Sunflower was one of the oldest, quite an elegant spa in its day. Over the years it declined. Poor management, neglect—things got real run-down and the place started to go south. Still, it was a beautiful location, lovely grounds, springs, lots of acreage.

"About eight years ago, the place sold. The cost was mostly in the land, not the facility, it was that run-down. I figured they'd open a bed-and-breakfast or something like that, but they didn't. They fixed up the place, restored it to its original beauty and elegance. The emphasis was on the baths, the spa, and health and beauty treatments."

I sat at my desk and listened and doodled, watching a robin eat berries outside my window. There was a definite wobble in his walk. The birds act like little drunks sometimes when the berries are fermenting, but I thought that was later in the summer. He flew unsteadily and wobbily out of sight and my doodles expanded.

"So it's all physical treatment, health and beauty therapies and conditioning?"

"*Interesting* you should ask that."

He did his imitation of a maniacal laugh which went on forever and ended in a high-pitched giggle. I keep telling him he'd be a voice natural in horror films.

"In the last few years"—his voice was back to normal, he sounded bored and sane now—"there have been some changes. I understand the clinic has expanded greatly and that they're now treating emotional, primarily addictive, disorders."

"And their reputation?"

"Everything I hear is good. They're new, it'll take them a while to get established, but apparently they've enjoyed a fair amount of success. Of course, in this particular field things are growing and changing constantly, as you can imagine. I wouldn't hesitate to recommend it on the basis of the information I have."

T.J. might goof off and laugh maniacally but in his work he's pretty conservative and cautious.

"A lot of it is the setting. It's very peaceful there, beautiful and serene and off the beaten path. I understand they have little cottages set down in the middle of exquisite gardens. Flowers, vegetables, even a small vineyard. That in combination with the hot springs, mineral baths, et cetera provides a background of beauty and physical therapy that is tough to match, never mind beat."

"Expensive?"

"I'm sure it is if you're on your own dime, but these days who is? Most people have insurance and a lot of the companies and health plans are lightening up and taking a more preventive approach. Obviously it's a hell of a lot easier to get someone off drugs and alcohol now than to pay for a liver transplant or chronic hepatitis down the line."

"Most of their work is insurance?"

"Probably. Most of *every*one's work these days is insurance. I understand their approach is very flexible so that most people and insurance programs can probably work with it. What's up, kid? This work, or are you a secret chocolate addict who's currently roaming the streets smashing your way into See's candy stores, ATMs, and Seven-Elevens in search of the next fix?"

"The former." I finished up a particularly ghastly doodle and thought about chocolate, wondered what the odds were that someone would drop by and offer me a Mars bar. Not good, was my guess. Not worth betting on. Rats.

"Yeah? Tell me about it."

"Later."

"Aw, c'mon."

"There you go, T.J., trying to live vicariously again."

He laughed. "Buy me lunch when it's over then."

"You're on."

After we hung up I walked out to a little corner market not far from my office and bought a diet Dr Pepper and a Mars bar. Did you know that the "diet" in the soft drink counteracts the calories in the candy bar? That's what I tell myself, anyway.

Delusion and the deluded.

Did Sara fit in there somewhere, in delusion and the deluded? Or Jed? This was one of the least straightforward cases I'd had in a while.

Oh, on the surface it was okay, simple enough: Woman fears estranged husband and seeks help of investigator. Simple, huh?

Well, yes and no when it turns out that the woman is secretive and is leading a professional life that no one in her circle seems to know about. Nor does she tell the investigator she hires. This is not lying exactly but it does raise some troublesome questions in the "truth, the whole truth, and nothing but the truth" department. And interesting issues—like unspoken ulterior motives.

On the other hand she was a victim of spousal abuse. It was natural, perhaps protective and positive, that her behavior become secretive and guarded. Her safety, perhaps her life, depended on such precautions. Blah blah blah. I had two choices: confront her or watch. I decided on the latter. I was beginning to have more and more unanswered questions about Sara.

I paid for my soda and Mars bar. They had sandwiches here too, and fruit and juices. None of it appealed. Junk. Quick fix. That's what appealed. I thought of the women I had seen at the groups Sara Charisma led. Desperate, unhappy, their hearts and souls hungry. Junk and quick fix looks good then, looks even better than the long road of hard work and effort needed to change. Junk thought, quick-fix drugs and answers—we turn to them all the time. I went back for a sandwich and an apple. It made me feel better about everything. *Quick fix.*

And the husband? He was a barrel of fun too. Cold-blooded and ruthless killer, or World's Best Guy and Heroic Fighter in the Battle of Shit Happens? Take your pick.

Both were attractive options. Both had vocal proponents and supportive evidence. Both were visible, or at least could be guessed at in the man himself.

On the way back to the office a homeless person hit me up for money so I gave him the sandwich. He looked surprised but he took it. Two for the price of one. Virtuously I bought a wholesome sandwich and then, virtuously, I gave it to someone who needed it more (conveniently leaving me free to eat junk).

Delusion.

I ate my candy bar and drank my soda and ran around like a trapped rat in the confines of my mind.

CHAPTER 36

She daydreamed about him. She daydreamed all the time, had even as a small child. She had daydreamed her way through high school and through college, through boring jobs and parties and the blues. Sometimes daydreams were to get by, to survive; sometimes to escape; sometimes they were to light up your life in rainbows, colored lights, and razzle-dazzle.

The trouble with daydreams—and this was a big drawback, she was the first to admit it—was that reality often paled in comparison. Reality was dull, was black and white and gray next to rainbows and razzle-dazzle.

He wasn't though. And their life together wasn't. It was Technicolor and fireworks. It was the Big Bang. She never had to fight, to make herself leave the daydream to come to him.

The traffic was sparse. It was early still. She had left town way before commuters were on the road, before some of them were even up. She loved the early mornings, loved the sense of freshness and newness and the way the birds sang each morning as though the world were brand-new, the world and the sunrise, and they couldn't wait to herald it, to let everyone know of the beauties and glories that were in store for them. She loved the way the colors of dawn leaked and slid out into the inkiness of the night, turning it gray and then blue and bright in an explosion of color.

She stretched and opened her window, the morning air cold and shivery on her face. It would be seventy or seventy-five today but it was sixty now. Things were warming up. She smiled to herself as she closed the window. *Things were warming up*.

She would stop for breakfast soon. There was a great little café she liked. Everyone stopped there, truckers, businesspeople, moms after dropping off their kids. And people like her, people who were passing through with dreams and ideas, plans and hopes. She stretched again in her seat, slowed down as she approached the small town. There was a parking place out front. She swallowed hard, her mouth watering. She was hungry now.

He came out to meet her, his arms open, his smile loving and welcoming. There were people around and so their greeting was formal, controlled. He took her hand, he touched her elbow. The excitement whipped through her, something wild, unrestrained and elemental. For a moment there was electricity, not blood, in her veins. It coursed through her, and through him, she could feel it when they touched.

She had never known this before with anyone. With Jed it had just been physical. With Walker her being was engaged, her soul, her mind, and her heart. She did not devalue the physical—the electricity ran through her again—but it was just one thing, was just part of the whole. She knew that now. Sometimes she felt closest to him when they were miles apart. Something would shift in her somewhere, in her mind and consciousness, and she would know he was thinking of her. She could feel his love then as it came into her. And she could reach out to him in the same way. She knew he could feel her.

"How are you?" His hand still held hers.

She smiled at him. "Well. Thank you."

"I missed you." He let her fingers slip away, let his hand rest gently in the small of her back. "You had a good trip?"

"Yes. I saw the dawn."

"I thought of you this morning early."

She laughed, startling a shy-looking woman who passed them in the lane that wound from the iron gates and the arch that spelled "Sunflower," through the exquisite rose gardens and herb beds, and back to the small Victorian house he used as his home.

"As if you were up." Her voice was mocking, affectionate.

"For a moment I was up, and I thought of you. Have you eaten?"

"Yes."

"Tea?"

"Please."

"My morning is open. We have business to catch up with, I know."

Business. The electric current ran through her again. *Business?* This business of love and sex and connection, yes. "Yes," she agreed, her voice as matter-of-fact and understated as his. "The roses are beautiful, the colors of dawn and sunset." The colors of love, the colors of all the letters of the alphabet and of possibility. The colors of today and tomorrow.

They climbed the steps to the porch, walked past the swing where they often sat in the evening drinking iced tea or cool white wine. He opened the door and followed her in. They stood apart in the hall, not touching but connected everywhere. The current hummed in her ears.

"I'll make you tea. Where will you sit?"

"In the little sitting room. The morning room." That sounded as Victorian as the house. She floated up the stairs in a dreamy way, a fugue state, found her rocker and settled in. Her whole being was open, expectant. She gazed at the climbing roses on the trellis outside the window. Later, when it was warmer, she would open the window, inhale their fragrance. Gently she rocked.

"Well?" He set down a tray, served her tea without cream or sugar.

"Eight. Ten maybe, or twelve, but eight that I am sure of. More every day. And I have three meetings next week." She spoke with simple pride.

"After that?" He smiled affectionately and stirred sugar and lemon into his tea.

"Another month or six weeks here and then I'll be on the road. Every day I make new contacts. The invitations and proposals come in faster than I can schedule them."

"I was right."

"Yes."

"You are a natural for this."

"Yes." It was as easy as breathing to her, as simple, as fulfilling. "The new facility?"

"Almost ready. A few more months, I believe. I hope we aren't rushing this." A frown creased his forehead.

"No." Her voice was serene and confident. "No, I can do this. Soon I will find someone else as well, train her. I am looking, but it has to be the right person. Anyway, for now I can handle it. I can do anything." She felt like that now, she really did. He had given her that confidence; now she would give it back to him. She leaned forward and smoothed away the worry lines on his face. The electricity again.

"The woman?"

"The private investigator?"

"Yes."

"It is working out well. She knows nothing but what I tell her. She is very nice, very trusting. And she is on my side, she will be a good witness."

"Be careful."

"Oh yes."

He smiled, visibly relaxed.

"But what is there to hide? That is the beauty of it. A health spa, a clinic treating addictions, gardens of paradise!" She laughed joyously. "It is all so wonderful, so beautiful. Walker, we are doing such good work. Don't ever forget that."

"No, I don't."

"Is this what you thought it would be like when you were in medical school?"

"What?" She puzzled him now, as she often did.

"Helping people, changing their lives, making them feel better and freer?"

"No." He smiled in understanding, or at her naïveté, or at the odd questions she asked—she couldn't tell. "Medical school in many ways is negative. The emphasis is on disease, not health. For many years I was focused on fighting disease. Fighting, attacking, combating—these are words we use often in medicine. Words of warfare."

"And now you run a clinic, a *health* clinic. Sunflower, the name is so perfect."

"Why?" She was off on another poetic tangent again. He was amused and charmed by it, both.

"Sunflowers turn their faces to follow the path of the sun, the light and life. Isn't the symbolism lovely?"

"Lovely," he agreed. He put down his teacup and reached for her. "Lovely."

Her feet were on the stool between them. He picked up a delicate small foot and eased the high-heeled shoe off. His fingers caressed and teased her toes. The toenails were painted a dark, deep red. Sexy. His hands slid up her legs, caressed her calves, her thighs, slipped into the warmth between her legs.

She shivered as he stood and held his arms open for her, dissolved into them. Trance state, fugue state. She let go of the power, let it slip from her. She had never done that until him. He met her in the same place, she knew.

"Walker," she whispered, barely breathed his name.

"Sara, my love." The syllables caressed her, fell around her in tones of love like the colors of dawn.

In the bedroom they took their clothes off. Not wildly, frantically as she had with Jed, always hurrying, desperate to catch the feeling, trap the passion. Not that at all. Softly, gently, secure in the knowledge that it was there, it was theirs. They had only to reach out and pluck it like a ripe peach, sink their teeth into it, taste of the fruit.

The humming in her ears increased, the electricity in her body. She was on fire. His hands slipped over her nakedness and hers over his. She knew every inch of him, every curve and hardness, and yet it was new each time. Time and space came together differently and something else was created. She slipped out of the self that was hers alone and into the being that was theirs.

The humming increased and then became the music of the spheres. And the rainbow danced.

CHAPTER 37

It was getting more and more difficult for him to go to work, to keep all the commitments in his life. He felt like his center was gone. He hadn't realized how important she was to him. He hadn't realized she was his center, his touchstone. *Sara*, he thought despairingly, *Sara, I need you.*

At first he had felt the anger; it was with him all the time, it ran through him in waves. Now it was sadness. He wondered if it would help if he could cry, but he hadn't cried since he was a child. As a child you think things like that will help. You get over that. Emotional tantrums don't get you anywhere. He forgot that still, sometimes, with anger. At best it would frighten people into doing what you wanted, but that wouldn't last. The minute the anger and fear went away the effect was over.

The good thing about anger was that it sustained you. It gave you a reason to live and act and hope. It became your center. He knew how dangerous this was, he saw it all the time. Anger fed off you, destroyed you, ate away at you from the inside out until there was nothing but a hollow shell filled with rage. Then sometimes it was uncontrollable; it could destroy everything in its path. Including you.

The emptiness at the center of him was unbearable. Sara was gone. He had tried to fill it up—this emptiness—with police work, basketball and coaching, volunteer work, even with God. It hadn't worked. Nothing had worked.

Except anger.

And sex. Sex filled him up too but it didn't last and it left him feeling emptier, cold. It made him feel bad too. Stevie. She was a nice person and he was using her. He had never treated women that way and he despised himself for it. He despised her too for allowing it.

Maybe if she refused to let him treat her like that he could love her. It was her fault. He could feel the rush of scorn and anger. That was how it worked. You let the anger take over, run away with you, let it fill up the emptiness and give you a direction. He felt better already, even though he knew it wasn't Stevie's fault. He knew he was a weak sonofabitch for using her and for blaming her.

Sara, Sara. Why hadn't he seen, known how important she was to him? She had always been there in the background while he had gone off and done whatever he had to do, whatever needed to be done. She hadn't seemed that important but now he was lost.

A loose cannon.

He couldn't stop thinking about her. Did he even know her now? he wondered. She had changed so much, in looks anyway. Maybe that meant she had changed inside, maybe not. He didn't know the most common things, like where she bought her clothes and groceries and if she still ate cold cereal for breakfast. He didn't know where she was working or what she was doing.

Things had changed in her life. Common sense would tell anyone that. He knew it not just by the clothes she wore but by the way she carried herself. There was a new look about her. He admired it even as he saw that, inevitably, it would take her away from him. The clothes weren't cheap either. Where did the money come from, a new lover, a job? He had never thought about these things before, never cared. He had just taken it all for granted—that she would always be involved, always be there.

Well, he was wrong. He was the first to admit that now. And he wanted another chance. He would not make those mistakes again. Why couldn't she see that? Why couldn't she come back? Why couldn't they try again?

The thought of her having sex with someone else tore him up. All the love, all the closeness and feeling that he had poured into her. He had wanted her to see that for what it was, love. Sex with Stevie was sex, with Sara it was love. The thought of her, naked, alive, flushed with desire and passion in the arms of someone else drove him crazy. He wanted to pour all of his love and tenderness and passion into her. He wanted to love her and please her. He wanted to keep her forever.

But it didn't matter what he wanted.

It was her choice. She could keep him out of her life forever. She could love someone else, give him her body.

It drove him crazy.

It drove him into the streets to watch her, to *know*.

He had no idea where she was during the day.

So there was no way to pick her up earlier. He couldn't be sure, either, that the tip he had gotten was reliable, but he thought it was. They had been in the past. You got to know your sources. Some were reliable, some weren't. All of them were scumbags. They weren't doing it out of the goodness of their hearts, they were doing it for the payoff. Usually money, but not always, not this time. His mouth twisted sardonically. You played on a weakness, you worked with it. You used it and made it work for you.

It was almost six, time to go home, kick back, have dinner. The thought of his empty house, cold stove, and colder bed was like a rabbit punch in the gut. He sucked in a breath, then made himself breathe easily, regularly.

He had to know. He told himself that was all. He told himself that she was free to make her own decisions, and that he knew it and would let her do so. He believed it when he told himself this. Why not? He had done harder things.

He had left work late—there were things he wanted to finish up—and then he had headed over here. To the bed-and-breakfast in midtown.

He wanted to know. He wanted to see. That was all.

He parked down the street, just close enough to keep the block and Cousin Annie's under surveillance, far away enough to be inconspicuous. He was good at that, at fading into the background. Six-thirty now. Plenty of light left. He needed that, he didn't know what she was driving. At night he couldn't see to identify her, not unless it was a familiar car. Unless she parked on the street and walked in. He would recognize her walk.

It was a wait. Forty-five minutes. But he was patient.

And then she arrived.

He was sure it was her. Almost sure. The light was starting to shift and the shadows were playing tricks with his eyes. A blue Ford Escort. He wrote the number down. The vehicle turned into the driveway next to Cousin Annie's and pulled all the way to the back. Then nothing. He was disappointed but not surprised. There would be a back door.

He would wait for a while, see if she went out again tonight. Then he would leave. He told himself that. Darkness crept down the block and swallowed him. Imagination was freer in the dark, he'd noticed that many times.

He would just walk around a little bit, down the block, maybe up to Cousin Annie's for a look-see. Then he would leave, he told himself that.

The curtains were lace and he could see through them into the lighted room. She came into the room, laughing and happy, gesturing and talking to an older woman as she walked over to the windows and started to pull down the shades. Plain as day he could see her and her happiness.

He knew he wasn't going to leave then.

He no longer told himself that.

CHAPTER 38

I was half a block away and running.

Jed was on the stairs, on his way to the front porch.

I'm a fast runner.

And I took the stairs two at a time.

"Yo, Jed."

To say that he was glad to see me would have been a pretty big exaggeration.

"Hello, Kat." Resigned and annoyed was more like it.

"We've got to stop meeting like this, don't you think?"

"I think you should mind your own business."

"This *is* my business. Believe it or not, I am paid to snoop on you, not to mention remind you to mind your manners." I spoke slowly and patiently. I mean, it's not as though we hadn't gone over this territory before. A couple of times to be exact.

Jed frowned and sort of snarled at me.

"*Nice* scowl." I'm all for handing out appreciation where appreciation is due. "Unfortunately, I'm not as easy to intimidate as a lawbreaking scumball on the street."

He sighed. "What do you want, Kat?"

"I want you to leave here now. I don't want you to make any effort to come back or to follow or see Sara at work, home, or any other place where she might be. I want you to leave her alone and get out of her life. You're a nice guy, Jed. You have a lot going for you. Let the past go and get on with your life," I added on an impulsive note.

"Fuck you."

I rolled my eyes. *When* am I going to learn that unsolicited personal advice is generally not greeted with joyous little cries?

"What do you want, Jed?" Forget friendly and impulsive, we were back to harsh and grim.

"I want to talk to Sara. That's all, just talk to her for a few minutes. Then I'll go."

Jeez. Imagine being a therapist and having to listen to the same old dysfunctional crap day after day.

"You can't. You may not talk to her or see her. Not now, not later, not anytime. Now get out of here."

"Just for a few minutes, then I'm out of here."

"Do you need a cop to explain this to you, Jed? Or maybe you're looking to put stalker on your résumé. Hey, that's a winner. You probably figured that one out all by yourself, huh?" Hard, mean, sarcastic—I stood there and stared at him and was all of those.

He gave it right back to me. Cops have the tough-guy routine down pretty well; it's not easy to beat them at it.

The front door opened and Sara stood there, framed in light and looking angelic. "What's going on?"

"Shut the door, Sara," I snapped as I made a dash for it.

Jed beat me, roughly shoving me aside. Belinda was making little worried bleating noises, like a truck that's backing up and doesn't want to hit someone. Except I thought the odds were rapidly increasing on the hitting someone angle.

"I want to talk to you for a few minutes, Sara."

"Oh. Well, I really don't want to talk to you, Jed." She spoke to him in a soft, soothing voice. Predictably, it had no effect on Jed.

"Let's go inside." Jed grabbed her firmly by the elbow and force-marched her in, Belinda trotting and bleating behind. Me too, but I was walking and looking for a phone. Cops get paid to deal with crazed yo-yos with guns, not me.

Belinda was now running around fussing and flapping her apron like someone shooing chickens. "All right now, everyone in the kitchen. As long as we're here we'll discuss this in a civilized manner over tea. Come now!" Her tone was crisp and authoritarian.

Okay by me, I thought. Over tea and with cops. I looked for the office.

"Don't, Kat. Don't call anyone. We're going to discuss this and then that will be that."

It was Sara. Go figure. I stared at her in silence.

"I'm giving Jed five minutes to say what he has to say. Then he'll leave. It'll all be fine."

I continued to stare at her in silence. I'm an upbeat, optimistic person who believes in the essential goodness of mankind, but this was taking things a bit too far.

"Please," she whispered as she leaned over and put her hand on my arm. "Please, I know what I'm doing."

I still said nothing. In the background Belinda was fussing around making tea and setting cookies on a plate.

"These are sugar cookies. Here are the date delights and the jam fills and, of course, the chocolate. Kat, sugar in your tea?"

"You have five minutes, Jed. What do you want?" I spoke brusquely.

He ignored me—that was a surprise—and focused totally on Sara. "I'd like to talk to you alone, Sara."

"No!" Me and Belinda. Even Sara shook her head.

He looked down at the delicate china cup that looked like a dollhouse toy in the large, strong, tanned hands. Hands that could squeeze the life out of Sara in a minute. Hands that could push someone into a flooded, out-of-control river. Hands that could steer a car over a body in the road. He put the cup down and gazed at Sara, seeing only her. Belinda and I could have been in a parallel universe for all he knew or cared.

"Sara, I'm worried about you. I know what you're doing. I know how it works. This is not for you. I *know* you. You're not that kind of person. This is *wrong*."

"I need to make my own decisions now, Jed."

"This is *not* about making your own decisions. This is about right and wrong. Black and white. It's that simple."

She started to respond.

"*Listen* to what I'm telling you." He pounded the table. "I *know* what

I'm talking about, who better than me? It's not right and you need to do what I say."

"Cookie?" Belinda was bleating again. "Try these coconut ones. Really, they're quite excellent. The chocolate too." She held the plate out to Jed.

Roughly he shoved it away. Cookies flew everywhere.

"This is not about cookies, *goddammit*, it's about right and wrong. It's about the way you live your life. *Listen* to me, *listen* to what I'm telling you." Jed had never taken his eyes off Sara. *"Listen!"* He pounded his fist on the table and a cup skittered off, tumbled onto the ground and smashed.

Belinda was white-faced, frightened and shaking. Sara was pale but apparently gutsy and stalwart. "I am listening, Jed, I really am, but it's time for me to make my own choices now. This is my life. I know what I want. I'll do a good job of—"

He roared.

I called the cops.

Jed never even noticed when I left the room. Or when I came back. He was still roaring. It was the same stuff: Right and wrong and he knew what was right and Sara didn't. She should listen to him and do what he said. Do what was right and not get into trouble. Not screw up everything *they* had worked so hard for for so long. (Somehow he got in there too. But why not? Ranting diatribes tend to be unfocused.) She should listen to him, *listen* to him, *goddammit*.

By then Sara and Belinda were both frightened. Belinda kept eyeing the carving knives. Sara looked like she was about ready to slide over the edge. I looked at the clock.

Someone pounded on the front door.

God, I love it when cops are prompt.

I let the cops in.

We were in the hall but we all heard the sound of the slap. In the kitchen Jed was standing over Sara, who was white-faced and crying. There was a large red mark on her cheek, the hothanded tattoo of violence.

It was something watching everyone's face. The cops knew Jed of course. And didn't look pleased—who can blame them? They were used to having Jed as part of the solution, not the problem. Jed made a huge effort to push his anger back. He wanted to hit someone, it was obvious. Not much of a choice there though: a woman or a cop. This is probably small of me but I enjoyed his struggle, *really* enjoyed it. He got it under control. It was equally obvious that he didn't want to spend the night in jail.

Then he tried to joke it off, buddy up to the cops, get them to take off leaving him there. No one bought into that.

"Everything's fine now, guys," Jed explained in a hearty voice.

Belinda, Sara, and I—in an impromptu but surprisingly well synchronized chorus—shook our heads, rolled our eyes (that was just me, actually), and made no-way-don't-believe-him sounds. Loud ones.

"Take him to jail. Let him cool off there," was my helpful suggestion.

"I'd like to press charges," was Belinda's helpful backup.

Jed made a growly sound and we all—including cops—turned to stare at him. So he changed that ugly sound into a smile (okay, grimace) and an apology, just like that.

I got the names of the officers; the three of us were pretty chatty, actually. "Hey, guys, could you swing by as often as possible tonight to check on things? You know what Jed drives, right? His personal vehicle is a new red Ford Ranger. His official vehicle is a recent-model baby-blue Cutlass. Imagine! He came by in an official police car to break the law." I shook my head in a sad, world-weary way.

Jed started with the if-looks-could-kill routine but dropped it pretty fast. Being on the bad-guy side was cramping his style, I could tell. He wasn't used to having cops look at him the way he looked at suspects.

The guys—good-guy cops and bad-boy cop—started to leave. Sara and Belinda had made themselves tiny, quiet, unobtrusive pieces of the background. I wasn't through yet.

"I know I don't need to explain the law to you, Jed. Or I shouldn't have to," I amended. "Sara's going to get a restraining order tomorrow. If you violate that it's not only a crime, but you lose your right to carry a gun. In your case, it's not just a right, it's your job."

In the total silence I could hear the solemn *tick tock* of the grandfather clock in the hall. A car backfired down the street.

There was hatred in Jed's eyes as he walked out flanked by cops who were his friends, but not right then and not first of all. Not anymore.

I locked the door after them, finished pulling down the shades, checked the back door—also unlocked. They were still unclear on the security concept here, I guess.

"Yes, please," I said to Belinda back in the kitchen.

"I beg your pardon," she stuttered out in a baffled fashion.

"One sugar in my tea, please."

Suddenly she smiled at me. I smiled back and began picking up cookies and putting them on the plate. "Mmmm, the coconut ones *are* yummy. If you tell me where the broom is, I'll sweep up, Belinda."

"Kat, for goodness' sakes." Sara sounded annoyed and exasperated, maybe even mad.

"I'll get to you in a minute." I said it pleasantly enough but there was a dangerous undertone there. "Ms. I've Got It Under Control and He'll Be Leaving in Five Minutes Don't Worry About a Thing." I snorted. Belinda pointed out the broom closet and I swept while she made tea. Then we all sat down.

"Let's start over, shall we?" Again, I was pleasant. "Let's start by stating what a stupid thing that was to do, Sara. You cannot reason with unreasonable and irrational people. I trust we can write this off to a learning experience, the I-have-learned-my-lesson-and-will-never-do-it-again kind."

She nodded. "Are you armed, Kat?"

Jeez. And just when I thought we were getting somewhere. "Remember in grade school, Sara, when they told us to settle our differences with words, not fists?"

She nodded.

"It applies to guns too. More so, in fact."

She nodded again. I had no confidence that she had really gotten the point.

"Tomorrow you get a restraining order."

"No."

"I really think it would be a good idea, dear," Belinda said firmly.

"No."

"Oh?" I asked conversationally. "Over your dead body, I suppose?" I helped myself to more tea and another cookie. "I'm speaking literally of course, not metaphorically." And I was taking a great deal of pleasure in the strained, white look on her face.

"Surely you must see this is something you can't handle by yourself, Sara?" Belinda said in a coaxing voice.

"Well, not that way," Sara agreed halfheartedly.

"What way?" I asked, always willing to be enlightened.

"I need to be better at this, to stay out of his way. I need to be more careful. If he doesn't know where I am, if he can't find me, then everything's okay."

"Theoretically that will work," I agreed.

"Theoretically?" She stumbled over the middle syllables.

I nodded.

"What do you mean?"

"If you could accomplish all that you would be safe. It is theoretically possible but practically speaking . . ." I shrugged. "I doubt it. You would have to change jobs frequently, move often, and use unknown vehicles. Or you could move to a different area, one where no one knows you or can recognize you.

"You will then have to drop all contact with friends and family and tell new associates nothing. You can't leave a paper trail of any kind, which means you'll need a new name, identity, Social Security number, medical history, financial history, driver's license, and so on. This can be done, although it is very difficult.

"Short of that, any decent private investigator will find you very quickly. And a cop will find you even faster. Jed has a lot more resources at his disposal than private investigators do."

"But that's illegal! He can't use police resources on a personal thing," she wailed at me.

"Ah," I said. "Well, silly, cynical me."

"Sara, this is your life, not a trip to Reno. You cannot play games and take foolish chances." Belinda's voice was shrill and unhappy. "Listen to Kat. Do what she says."

Sara shook her head stubbornly. "I admit it's a difficult situation but getting a restraining order won't help. Law enforcement is on Jed's side."

"I thought the cops handled things well tonight."

"They're on his side."

"Maybe. Maybe not. Without a restraining order they don't have much to work with."

"It's a piece of paper. It won't change anything."

"Oh yes it does. Violation of a restraining order is a crime. And not exactly the same league as disturbing the peace."

She shook her head miserably.

Jeez, it was like talking to a brick wall.

"How did Jed know where to find you, Sara?"

Her head snapped up. "I don't know. How did you? He followed you, I guess. Hardly anyone knows to find me here."

"He didn't follow me."

"You can't be sure."

"Yes. I can. Did you tell anyone you were here?"

She shook her head. "No. I didn't mention it to anyone. I . . ." Her voice trailed off.

"Who?"

"Joy. I told Joy." Her voice was miserable. "I went back there for something I'd left behind and I told her. But she wouldn't tell, would she? My own sister?"

I thought she would spill the beans in a heartbeat. Less. "Call. Ask her."

She hesitated, then picked up the phone on a nearby stand. I reached over her and punched the speaker phone button.

"Joy, it's me."

"Where are you? What are you doing?"

"Did you tell Jed where I am, Joy?"

"Why would I do that?" Her voice was defensive.

"Did you?"

"Yes, I did. He said he had something very important to say to you."

"I asked you not to tell and you promised me you wouldn't."

"And I wouldn't. Ordinarily, I mean. But he said it was important. *Very* important."

"Do you think my safety and life are important, Joy?" Her question was tinged with sadness.

"Oh, *please*, give me a break."

"*Do* you?"

"Of course I do but that's not what we're talking about here."

"Yes, it is. It's exactly what we're talking about. He's hit me, he's threatened to kill me. It's exactly what we're talking about."

"For godssakes, Sara, there you go again. You always need to make yourself *so* important. You always have to be the center of attention, the focus of everyone's concern. Life and death. Drama, drama, drama. Life is not a thriller movie or a romance novel. Grow up, will you, just *grow up*!" The phone slammed down.

Sara stared at us, speechless and shattered. Neither Belinda nor I said anything.

"I can't believe it," Sara whispered finally. "I just can't believe it, can you?"

Belinda and I both nodded. Joy hadn't scored high in either of our books. Not in understanding, compassion, or sisterly love. Or sharing. Okay, I was still a little bitter about the Oreos.

"What do I do now, Kat?"

"Exactly what I tell you."

"All right."

She didn't, of course. It was a lie. A mistaken promise on her part, to use her words. I didn't find out most of this until later.

What else was new?

CHAPTER 39

The book was an old one, the leather worn smooth by the passage of time and the hands that had held it and turned the pages. It was massive, so big that I could hardly hold it on my lap, the pages thick and stiff with more photographs than I could count.

I had started at the beginning, paging through sepia photos faded with age of people and a world that was now more than a hundred years gone. Pictures of solemn hard-eyed, unsmiling people in high collars and dark colors. Just married, then holding their first child in long lacy christening robes, later surrounded by children large and small, the parents still hard-eyed and unsmiling but their edges softened now, rounded and filled out with added years and pounds.

More weddings and christenings, the parents turning into grandparents and even great-grandparents, their eyes gone from hard to wise and their hair from dark to white. And still no smiles, no softness, no joy that was not hidden.

At first the little boys had worn dresses, then shorts and finally long pants, the girls dresses with petticoats and ribbons in their hair. Over the years they had started smiling, the children and the parents, the just-marrieds and the old ones. In summer and in winter. In the Great Depression, in war and in peacetime. In the country and in the city. All these people had lived their lives and left their mark on the generation to come.

I had seen Hank in some of the old pictures. In his grandmother and his father. In the eyes and the mouth, the set of shoulders and shape of jaw, the hair falling over a forehead. And then just Hank. Over and over. A baby, a toddler, a four-year-old dressed as a cowboy for Halloween and caught, laughing, in his lariat. An eight-year-old on his bike. A fifteen-year-old in a basketball uniform. His senior prom. His first car. Then college and a uniform, Army Reserve followed by the police department.

Wedding pictures. Hank and his wife and their house. Vacations and happiness. And then nothing for a long time. Emptiness and darkness after her death, nothing to fill the pages in his heart or in a scrapbook. And then I was there. Hank and Kat. Smiles and happiness. New hopes and dreams and lives, for each of us and both of us.

When I was a child we had told a stupid joke with many answers.

What's black and white and red all over?

A newspaper.

What's black and white and red all over?

A blushing zebra.

What's—

The day of the funeral it was sunny and lovely. I could feel the breeze in my hair, the warmth on my face. I could hear the birds sing and smell the flowers. There were so many flowers, their colors bright and beautiful. But in my mind now, in my memory, everything is black and white and gray.

I can see the photograph of the granite headstone, sharp-edged and cleanly chiseled. *HANK PARKER.*

Black and white.

And a drop, a single red drop. It could have been a tear. And then a smear and a splash and a wave until everything is a solid sheet of blood.

Red all over.

And after that the pages in the book are thin and empty. There is nothing written. No photographs. No newspaper clippings. No wedding or birth announcements. Nothing.

And now there never would be.

Davis?"

"Katy, how are you?"

"Fine." This was a lie. The book sat on my lap and I was not fine, I was a mess. "How are you and Maggie and Josie?"

"Wonderful. When are you coming to visit us?"

"Soon."

And that was it. I was exhausted, sad, and had no more social graces. I had nothing but tears and questions and a book with too many empty pages.

"Davis?"

"Nothing, Katy." He spoke gently. "Nothing. I would have called you if we had something. I hoped we would. And we will. It's a matter of time, that's all."

A matter of time. I thought of all the empty pages. Clean and white. And the blood started to fill them up too. Blood and tears and regret.

"Somebody must have seen or heard something. Someone must know something. It happened in daylight in a well-populated area. Davis—"

"I know, Katy. I know."

The reason we have funerals is that there is something so harsh and final about them that you have to accept the truth. Otherwise your mind keeps going, makes up things—possibilities—creates hope where there is none. This is true especially if the death is sudden. In one second all is well and in the next that life is over. Is memory.

There is no room for hope and possibility when you hear the dirt hit the coffin, when you walk away and leave them behind, there in the city of the dead.

"We have a couple of leads, Katy. We're working on it every day. All the time."

"Okay."

My voice sounded funny. I thought how little Josie, who was six weeks old, would grow up hearing about Hank but never know him. We were her godparents and he would never hear her first words, see her walk, or watch her play softball or kiss her at her wedding.

"Thanks, Davis." And it was the best I could do, honest.

"We love you, Katy."

I heard an echo of Hank in his voice, in his words.

"Buck up, buckaroo." I could hear the little hint of a smile in his voice, the same thing I had always heard in Hank's.

Hank had made me promise him two things. That I wouldn't die before him. He said he couldn't do it again. He couldn't lose me, not after losing his wife, Liz. And I had promised. I don't know how you can promise that, but I had. And he had made me promise that if something happened to him I would love again. I promised that too, but I didn't mean it. I didn't know how I could go on either.

The phone rang less than a minute after Davis and I hung up. I didn't answer.

"Katy, I know you're there, so pick up. It's important, I'm not kidding." Charity's voice on the answering machine. "If you don't I'm coming over."

Since she was as good as her word, I picked up.

"Hi!" she said cheerfully. "Want to go out and get drunk?"

"What's so important?"

"Do you?"

"Davis called you, didn't he?"

"Yes. Do you? I know it's not a sensible way to do things but sometimes you just have to. It helps. And here's the good part. Tomorrow, when you feel like shit and have the world's most gawd-awful hangover and wish you were dead?—it'll be for the right reason."

I laughed. I couldn't help it.

"I'm coming over to get you. We'll do Chinese take-out and drink margaritas. Can you drink margaritas with Chinese food?"

I thought about it. "We'll drink them first and have wine with dinner."

"Perfect."

So we sat on Charity's veranda in rocking chairs with Chinese food in the kitchen, nothing much on our minds and margaritas in our hands. The sun was starting its downhill slide, the birds were singing and the crickets warming up for the evening performance. The margaritas were cold and strong and good.

I was beginning to see the world in color again, not just in black and white and red all over.

The sun dipped beneath the tops of the cottonwood trees and bounced around on the shimmering surface of the pond, on the white splashes and the blue-black-green smears of ducks swimming placidly when Charity spoke in a light conversational tone.

"Read these." She pulled a handful of letters from behind the cushion of her chair.

Dear Charity,
I thought I couldn't have children and then I got pregnant. Wow, was *I* ever surprised! The doctor did a test and said that I was going to have two babies and that the babies had different fathers. I had an affair but it's all over and I wasn't planning on telling my husband. Now what do I do?
Pregnant, Puzzled, and Panicky

"Is honesty always the best policy in your business, Katy?"
"No, much as I wish it were."
"It's so difficult to know what to advise in a case like this."
"Especially when it's babies who'll pay the price."
She nodded. "Read the next one."

Dear Charity,
I never believed that I would wish for what I now pray will happen, the death of my beloved daughter. After an automobile accident, which was no fault of her own, she lies in an irreversible coma wasting slowly away. Not a vegetable, a fragile shell of a once vital being. Her soul is gone, yet they make it so hard for her body to leave. I hope people will open their minds and change the laws.
Broken Mom

"Is this your idea of cheering me up?"
She smiled. "What would you tell her?"
"To be true to her daughter's wishes, and to hers."
"And forget the law?"
"Yes."
I picked up the last letter.

Dear Charity,
Where the hell do you get off giving advice? It was your generation and the one before you that had it easy and that screwed up everything for us. I have a college degree and can't get a job. I'll never be able to afford a house. The rain forests are disappearing, and the ozone layer too. We have pollution and inflation and AIDS. And all of you who screwed it up for us? Still sucking up our money in Social Security and Medicare.
Young and Bitter

"How long did it take you to pick out these letters?"

"What do you mean?" Guileless, innocent blue eyes.

But she was right and I was glad that I had read them. And I knew that I had had, before I had lost, someone who loved me and didn't lie. And that there were fates worse than death. And that bitterness was a trap.

"Are you still angry, Katy?"

I nodded. "And sorry for myself. Because life isn't fair, because there aren't any guarantees."

The sun was sliding into the horizon now. I heard doves cooing and far away a dog howled. Jack (the Ripper), Charity's dog, stirred in his sleep at our feet and growled.

Life wasn't fair but it wasn't black and white either. Even in my sadness I knew that.

We had another margarita.

CHAPTER 40

She had always thought that Lorie sounded like such a fragile name. Like Laura in *The Glass Menagerie.* So easily shattered and broken. Other names were bendable and strong. Like Jennifer. Bendable, in names and people, was good. If you could bend, it was easier to survive.

Had anyone ever made a study of that, she wondered, of names and how they influenced your destiny? Did little boys called Butch and Spike grow up tougher and stronger? Elizabeth was a strong name—she had thought of changing her name to Elizabeth. Movie stars changed their names all the time. Who could imagine calling John Wayne Marion? Or Marilyn Monroe Norma Jean?

Was it too late for her? she wondered. If she changed her name right now, right this minute, could she change her personality? Her therapist didn't like her to talk like this. She said it was stupid. No she didn't. Therapists never talked that way. She sighed. Even if you said something that was dumber than dirt they wouldn't argue or give their opinion, they just shoved it back on you somehow.

She thought she would be an Elizabeth this morning. What would Elizabeth eat? Something robust and hearty. Bacon and eggs. She shuddered. Soft-boiled eggs and a roll? She could manage that, she could make up her mind to that.

Elizabeths were decisive. They made up their minds and then they did something. Maybe it wasn't always the right thing but it was something.

They didn't just sit on their hands and wonder what to do and if it was the right thing and the right time. They knew that you couldn't be absolutely, positively sure of anything, that you had to be willing to risk, to take a chance.

But that seemed so hard. Maybe she would just stay a Lorie after all, thinking about doing one thing and then another and then another. Weighing carefully all the possibilities and benefits and risks, deciding to decide only after more time and study and thought.

She would have a Lorie breakfast, she thought with relief. Not bacon and eggs, but juice and tea. Maybe a small piece of toast with a little butter and orange marmalade. Oh, she loved orange marmalade. It reminded her of the orange candies her grandmother used to make for her as a child. She never heard of anyone making candy now. Or ice cream. She could remember turning the handle on the ice cream maker and licking the beaters afterwards.

Her therapist said the past was over, the future wasn't here yet, and the present was all she had. She smiled. She did not think her therapist was very imaginative. She was an Elizabeth kind of person. Elizabeths didn't daydream.

But Lorie did. Lorie had a good imagination, could make up strong, beautiful, happy worlds. She wasn't stuck with this one and all its imperfections and uglinesses. Not really.

She hated ugly things. And messy things. She wished everything could be beautiful and neat and organized. The Sunflower Clinic was beautiful, she had agreed to come here because of that—the roses and flowers, the gardens and ponds. It was beautiful and restful. It was a place where she could dream.

When they would let her. And mostly they did.

"Who are you this morning?"

The voice was loud, bold and intrusive in the early-morning silence of the gardens.

"You're Lorie today, aren't you? I can tell by the way you're sitting with your hands folded in your lap, all proper and perfect. Elizabeth isn't like that." The young woman smiled, pleased with herself.

Lorie didn't smile back. She was annoyed that this loud person had intruded on her. And on her daydream. She was just thinking of going someplace wonderful in her mind.

The girl sat down on the bench across from Lorie. "I never used to pay much attention to time, you know. Getting through the day and getting high used it all up. Now it seems like there's so much time. What do you do with it?" She fidgeted in her seat, her feet jiggling, her hands twisting. "How do you fill all that time up? What do you *do* with yourself? You can't call up your friends because those are all the people you got high with, because now, like, they can't be your friends anymore. You can't have drinks or do a line. *Man . . .*" She flopped over on her stomach on the bench and stared at the ground.

"There's a lizard over there that's watching us. I bet they don't worry about how to fill up time. Eat a bug, eat another bug, sit on a warm rock, watch out for the cats. What a life, huh?" She rolled over and stared at the sky through the trees.

"What's your name again?" Lorie asked.

"I told you before." The girl's voice was resentful.

"I'm sorry. Will you tell me again?"

"Carrie. Like that stupid movie."

"Oh." Lorie had no idea what movie Carrie meant. She had heard of Stephen King but she would never read that kind of book, or bother to notice the titles.

"What do you do, Lorie? How do you fill up the time?"

"I think about things. And I read."

"What kind of things?"

Lorie shrugged. She didn't like to talk about her daydreams. She didn't think Carrie would understand either. "Just things."

"Weird." Carrie flopped back on her belly. "Lizards? Do you think about lizards?"

"No."

"Or getting out of here and what you'll do then?"

Lorie felt her heart beat faster, felt the panic inside her. "No."

She spoke a little too fast and Carrie looked at her curiously. "I do. I think about it a lot. I don't wanna do drugs again, I guess. I mean, it almost killed me."

"*It* didn't almost kill you." Lorie's voice was mean. She got that way when people asked about her dreams, about her world inside. "*You* almost killed you."

"Yeah. Well, that's what I mean, I guess." The curious look still. "But what am I going to do now? I didn't care about my job, that was just to buy drugs. And drugs were to kill time and—"

"And maybe you." Meanness again.

"And maybe me," Carrie agreed. "So what's left, I ask you? Nothin'. No friends, no job, no highs, no life, nothin' but a bunch of time to fill up. Eating bugs is looking better all the time, huh? I wonder which are best, the little fat juicy ones, or the leggy, sticklike crunchy ones? Here comes that new girl. You met her yet?"

"No." Her voice was nice now, her meanness all ready to be turned against the new person if it had to be. Old against new. Us against them. "Is she nice?"

Carrie shrugged.

"What's her problem?"

"She's a fatty." She was mean now too. She didn't like it when people were mean to her and the way to stop it was to give it back, right?

"She's not a girl," Lorie said in her stickler-for-truth voice.

"Whatever." Carrie shrugged again. "She's fat though."

"She could lose some weight." Lorie was cautious again. No point in getting too close to people who talked about eating bugs.

"Hello." A soft voice greeted them. "May I join you? I'm new here."

"We know." Carrie's voice was sullen.

"You're welcome to." Lorie thought she saw something she might like in this new person. "What's your name?"

"Patsy."

"Do you like bugs, Patsy?"

Patsy looked at Carrie in puzzlement. "Some, I guess. I like butterflies and ladybugs and even praying mantises. Not ants though, or termites. Why?"

"Why are you here?" Lorie jumped in quickly before Carrie could answer. She'd had about enough of bugs.

"I eat too much. I guess you could tell that though." She smiled but she looked a little ashamed, and she looked away, didn't meet their eyes.

"Oh." Lorie smiled. Fat people made her feel superior. Imagine stuffing all that gross food in your face! Patsy. That was a perfect name for a fat person too, wasn't it? Fatsy Patsy. She let her smile widen.

And then Carrie popped her bubble. "Look at you, Miss High-and-

Mighty. Don't you go copping an attitude now." Carrie's voice was rough and threatening.

She was right, Lorie thought, not to trust her. She made her face a mask, tried to make her whole body into a protective shell.

"She's a nutcase. She makes up stuff and then she believes it. Good, huh? And I do drugs. Did, I guess. I dunno yet."

"Are you always this mean to each other?" Patsy sounded both curious and as though she was ready to run.

"I guess. Why?" Carrie was back to shrugging.

"Well, we're all here because we have some kind of problem that we couldn't fix on our own but that doesn't make you a bad person, does it? It's the problem that's bad and problems can be fixed. People can change."

"She's in bad shape, she's a nutcase." Carrie jerked a thumb in Lorie's direction.

"She eats bugs." Lorie's swift and vicious retaliation.

"You're doing it again," Patsy said.

In the silence a bird called and the lizard skittered away.

"Are you ever mean, Patsy?" Carrie asked in a nice way; she was genuinely curious now.

"I try not to be. People have been mean to me all my life and it really hurts. I know."

"Why?" Lorie asked, pretending to believe that she had forgotten why she was mean to Patsy.

"They think it's okay to be mean to fat people. You can't tell Polish jokes or Jewish jokes because ethnic humor is politically incorrect. You can't tell African-American jokes, that's racist. You can't make fun of women, that's sexual harassment. And gays, that's infringing on their civil rights. But everyone thinks it's okay to make fun of fat people."

There were, maybe, tears in her eyes. "Except for fat people—we don't think it's okay. We think it's mean. We hate fat jokes and, sometimes, it's really hard not to hate the people who tell them."

"I'm sorry." Lorie said it in a whisper.

"You guys have problems too, or you wouldn't be here." Patsy's glance included both of them. "And I promise I'll try never to make fun of you for that. You know where you're lucky?"

They shook their heads.

"Your problem is hidden. People can't look at you, make fun of you and feel superior. They don't hate you if you take up too much room on an airplane or a bus, or despise you if they see you buttering your bread or having dessert or putting cream in your coffee." Her voice wobbled.

"You don't have to go to special stores just to find clothes that fit you. And every time you pick up a magazine or turn on the television you don't see hundreds of people who don't look like you, never did, and never will."

"They don't look like anybody," Carrie said. "They're little twigs with plastic surgery scars. A lot of them have eating disorders or do drugs to stay that way. I knew girls like that. L.A.? Hah! L.A. is *full* of girls like that. They're not happy, you know."

"Well, I'm not happy either. And if I had a choice I'd rather be skinny and unhappy than fat and unhappy." She sniffed.

"There's a girl here who weighs eighty-four pounds," Carrie said.

Patsy stared. "How tall is she?"

"I don't know. Five five maybe. She's just skin and bones. She looks like the pictures you see of people in Africa after they've been starving for months, or like concentration camp pictures. It's really awful. She's getting better now, I think; she used to weigh even less. I lost a lot of weight when I was doing drugs. I looked pretty bad. Do you think you can do it, Patsy?"

"I hope so, I'm really going to try. Do you think you can—"

"Beat drugs?"

"Yes."

"I dunno. You came here because you wanted to, I came here because they made me. I guess I have to decide if I want to. I have to figure out what to do with my life; I need to find something besides drugs and I don't have a clue."

"Why are you here?" Patsy asked Lorie. "Did you want to come or did someone make you?"

Lorie flushed, turned away her head. She didn't like answering questions like that.

"They made her." Carrie answered Patsy's question for Lorie. "And don't try checking out either 'cause guess what? You can't. You have to have approval and who knows what kind of shit. It's easier to get in than get out, that's for sure."

Across the garden a bell rang. Patsy looked up in surprise.

"Breakfast. C'mon, walk over with us. We'll introduce you to people and stuff. You can sit with us if you want."

"*I'm* not sitting with anyone who eats bugs," Lorie announced loftily.

"Okay, you can sit with me if you want." Carrie grinned at Patsy. "I don't know about Her Highness."

"Thanks," Patsy assented shyly. They started off, Lorie trailing behind.

"Have you met Dr. Saunders yet?"

"Just briefly. What's he like?"

Carrie shrugged. "He's pretty cool, I guess, but be careful."

"He has a girlfriend." Lorie's voice behind them.

"Really? What's she like?" Carrie half turned around.

"It's hard to see her. She comes in late and leaves early. Pretty, I think. I've only seen her a couple of times when I was up real early."

"I'm starving," Carrie announced. "I hope we have waffles this morning. What will you eat, Patsy?"

"I don't know. Not waffles." She and Carrie laughed together. "A cornflake and a slice of apple maybe."

"Black coffee," Carrie added. "All diets have black coffee. Good thing you have a sense of humor, Patsy."

The bell rang again. There were a lot of people on the paths now. A lot of questions in the air.

CHAPTER 41

"It's not what it seems."
I laughed.
Jed glared at me.
We were not off to a great start.
"Oh, come on, Jed, lighten up. How many times have people you were interviewing said that and how many times have you laughed? A million?"
The glare intensified. "It's not the same thing."
"Right." I sighed. Not that Jed was the first person to lose his sense of humor when he got into trouble. "Let me recap here: Your soon-to-be-ex-wife is getting a divorce, says you've beaten her and threatened her, and holds you responsible for the death of a friend in what she claims was a murder attempt on her life. She also claims that you have followed her, harassed her, and generally made her life miserable.
"As a matter of record you have been seen watching her and following her. You were caught lurking in her apartment parking lot at night, were apprehended breaking into and searching her apartment, all the while making attempts through mutual friends and family members to find out where she was and what she was doing. You followed her to a friend's house, entered uninvited, refused to leave, got threatening, yelled at her, slapped her, and had to be escorted off the premises by officers as a result of a nine-one-one call." I paused and sucked in a breath. "And you say it's not what it seems?"

He nodded. "Exactly."

I howled with laughter this time. Finally, wiping the tears from my eyes and holding my sides—which were starting to ache—I looked at Jed. "I guess you're just going to have to explain it to me. I'm having a tough time seeing it that way." I snickered. I couldn't help it, honest.

By then Jed had replaced the glare with a look of long suffering. It wasn't bad, but I wasn't impressed.

I barely stifled a yawn.

The glare was back, just like that. "You don't find it odd that all my friends and associates vouch for my honesty, integrity, trustworthiness, and probity?"

"No."

He stared at me.

What? Was I supposed to say more? "Look, Jed, that's what friends do. They believe in you no matter what. That's one definition of a friend, steadfast in the face of facts."

"That's not how my friends are."

I didn't even stifle my next yawn. "Okay, it's not what it looks like and your friends are unbiased, expert witnesses. Put yourself in my shoes and—no, better yet, put yourself across from someone who is saying that in the face of the kind of evidence I have just enumerated. Hah. You'd be ready to read them their rights and slap the cuffs on."

Jed was starting to look pretty frosted. Good. I was baiting him, I admit it. I figured the more irritated, even pissed off he became, the more likely he was to spill his side in an intemperate, unrehearsed and unedited fashion. Actually, I agreed with some of what he said. And I wasn't surprised he had suspicions; I had quite a few myself.

I held my hands out a bit and studied my nails. *Whoops*, I needed a manicure. One every two and a half years just wasn't doing it. I studied them more carefully. A hangnail? Horrors! Then I yawned again. "You got something to say, say it. I don't have all day here."

Jed stood, kicking *my* office chair in the process.

"*Hey*, watch it, that's furniture, not firewood."

"Look, Kat."

He started pacing around my office.

I looked.

And saw a man pacing. Big deal. Been there, done that. I went back to staring at my nails. Got bored and stared out the window instead.

"I never thought I'd say this, Kat."

And he got my attention just like that. He wasn't angry, he wasn't raging. He was sad.

Jed sat down. "I don't know what my wife's doing, not exactly, but I don't like it. I never have. We had a good marriage, we really did. I know that's hard to believe with Sara acting the way she is, but it's true. We were happy. We talked about things all the time, we told each other everything. And then things started changing."

"A lot of possibilities there, Jed."

"Shit, I know that. You're thinking an affair or something, aren't you?"

That's what I was thinking. I said nothing.

"Well, that's what I thought at first too. Losing weight, new clothes, a change in hairstyle." He shrugged. "I mean, I'm not a fool. I know what that means in other people's marriages; I knew what it could mean in mine. But things weren't adding up that way. Maybe there's a guy, especially now that we're apart, I don't know, but there was a lot more too."

Outside a garbage truck inched its way down the street, roaring, clanking, and wheezing. I thought—and not for the first time—how nice it would be if we could just bundle up our emotional, intellectual, and psychological garbage, toss it in the can and wave goodbye. In my dreams. I waited for the "lot more."

"There had to have been extra money coming in, quite a bit of it, and it wasn't coming out of our budget, that's for damn sure. The clothes she was wearing, the jewelry? They were expensive. Sara couldn't, or wouldn't, account for them. Or she lied.

"She told me a friend had gained weight and given her the clothes, traded them for Sara's help with her computer." He snorted. "Those clothes were brand-new. I even found bags in the trash from Macy's and Nordstrom. And silk underwear? Who gives away used underwear? Do you?"

He looked the question over at me but I declined the distraction of underwear. "The jewelry?"

"Yeah. It was real, not costume. Silk scarves, fancy shoes and handbags. We're not talking Kmart here."

"Maybe they were gifts. Maybe not from a girlfriend."

"Maybe. I thought of that. I had to accept that as a possibility. Cash too?"

"Maybe," I said. I could hear the doubt in my voice.

"Maybe she wasn't a consultant or whatever, huh? Maybe she was a hooker?" His voice was harsh. "I thought about that too, wondering if I should be wearing condoms at home."

Another comment I had no answer for.

"I found a credit card and a bunch of cash in her purse. The card was in her name but the billing wasn't. I checked. And that card is nowhere on her personal credit record. The few receipts I found were from living high on the hog. Not just clothes and jewelry but fancy restaurants and hotels, that kind of thing."

"You confronted Sara with this?"

"Of course I did."

"And?"

"She denied it."

Anticlimactic answer. We both knew that.

"And then?"

"We fought."

"Verbally?"

"Yes." He looked disgusted, which I thought was uncalled for. "Sara lied, stonewalled me, and denied everything. So basically I stood there with my thumb up my ass."

"The credit card and wads of cash?"

"She denied that too, then dumped her wallet out on the table for my inspection."

"No credit card or extra cash?"

"You got it."

I listened to the garbage truck making its way down another street.

"By then things were going to shit fast. We were fighting all the time and she was accusing me of not trusting her, checking up on her and spying."

"All of which was true."

"Yeah. Goddammit. All of which was true. But I am not out to get my wife, Kat. I know I've said this before but I mean it every time. I love her, I really do. Even if she's divorcing me I still love her. Love doesn't stop just because of a stupid action or—"

"What stupid action?"

"What she's doing. I love my wife, Kat. I'm trying to protect her, not get her."

"Why are you here, Jed? I'm working for Sara. Why come to me?"

"Because I can't protect her. She won't let me. She won't let me help her in any way. She won't let me get close to her, even talk to her."

I reflected on the evening at Belinda's. "I haven't noticed you doing much talking. You were yelling the night I called the cops."

"Yeah. I lost it. There's no excuse for that. But it's hard. I'd never do that on a case but when it's something personal—" He shook his head. "It's hard. I yelled because I care, because I want her to do the right thing."

"And not just yelling—slapping."

He shook his head again. "I've never touched her. I didn't slap her that night either."

"I heard you, Jed."

"You heard a slap."

"I saw the mark on her cheek."

"You saw a mark on her cheek. You didn't see me slap her. She tried to hit me. I caught her wrist, held it, dropped it. Then she smiled at me and hit herself open-handed in the face. It must have hurt but she kept on smiling. And it made her story sound good, I'll give her that. I was the bad guy, I was the problem."

"And you just accused Sara of telling implausible stories."

"It's the truth."

"You didn't answer my question. Why are you here, Jed?"

"Because I care about Sara. Because I can't protect her. I'm putting all my cards on the table, Kat, telling you everything I know. Telling you the truth. That's all I know how to do. That's the only way I know how to help now." He stood, nodded at me, and walked out.

I sat and thought about truth. About how many faces it had. And voices and versions. And how truth is something different to each of us.

Sara's sounded better than Jed's though. A lot better. Jed's sounded like a cover-up. *She slapped herself.* Yeah. Right. *I followed her, snooped through her personal things and spied on her activities, but it was all for her own good.* Yeah. Right. *I only yelled because I care.* Yeah. Right. Too bad he forgot: *This hurts me more than it does her.*

Sara forgot a few things too. That it's harder to get away with things when you're married to a cop. That detectives are trained to dig up stuff you'd rather not see. That home sweet home is incompatible with lying, sneaking, and stonewalling. Not to mention cheating and sleeping around. Or any combination of the above.

I picked up the phone.

CHAPTER 42

I called Jill, Belinda, and Joy. Jill was out, Joy hung up on me, and Belinda didn't have a clue.

"I haven't seen her, Kat, not since the morning after the night you and Jed were here. We had breakfast together the next day and she seemed normal as pie, ate half a grapefruit, an omelet, and toast. She said she was going to make some calls about a temporary job, maybe try to get something in Fresno or the Bay Area. I went out to do the day's shopping and when I got back she was gone. We had plans for lunch and everything."

"What about her things?"

"Gone. Everything was gone."

"A note?"

"No, but she called later in the day and told me she was fine and not to worry. I asked where she was and she said the details weren't important. I asked how long she would be gone and she said she didn't know."

"Did the subject of a restraining order come up?"

"Yes. I asked about that too and she said she wouldn't need one, she was quite sure she'd be safe without it. That's just how she put it too—'quite sure.' "

"Did she give you a phone number, a friend's name, any way at all of getting in touch with her?"

"No."

I made an exasperated noise. "Or tell you when she would be in touch?"

"No, not really. She just said several times that I wasn't to worry, that she'd be fine. She's very hardheaded and stubborn, Kat."

No! Do tell, I thought to myself.

"She always has been, even as a little bit of a thing. I had to make myself not worry about her then. I'm trying to do just that now."

"Belinda, will you do something for me?"

"Oh yes, of course, anything."

"Call your long-distance carrier and ask if there were any long-distance calls made in the time Sara was staying with you—ones you can't account for."

"All right. I'll do that right now. Let me just jot down your number and I'll call you right back."

She was as good as her word. I had barely had time to finish my apple when the phone rang.

"Kat, there weren't any."

Okay, it had been a long shot. "Thanks for trying, Belinda."

"You're welcome. I'll be in touch the minute I hear something. Please call me if you do."

I agreed to that although by my estimate I had a snowball's chance in hell of hearing from Sara. The phone rang again almost immediately. Jill.

"Hi, Kat. What can I do for you?"

"Do you know where Sara is?"

"No."

"Or how to get in touch with her?"

"No."

"Neither does anyone else. She's disappeared again."

"What?"

"Flown the coop, blown this popstand, on the run, off in—"

"I get it, Kat."

"Sorry, I'm pissed."

"I don't blame you."

"And I quit."

"*Please* don't."

"Your office will shortly receive faxes of two letters, one to you and one to Sara, stating just that. Hard copy by registered mail will follow. Also to your office since I have no way of contacting Sara directly."

"Kat, *please*."

"If and when her body turns up I want no part in, or professional responsibility for, her safety, well-being, or situation."

"I know she's difficult, Kat, but—"

"No, not difficult, we're way past difficult. She has refused to follow any suggestions I have made for her safety. She will not obtain a restraining order against her husband. She does not take even minimal precautions to ensure her safety, nor will she—other than paying my suggestions lip service—do so. She does not take me into her confidence, even to the point of keeping me informed of her whereabouts.

"I am not Superwoman or God. I cannot keep her safe under these conditions."

"But—"

"And I will not continue in this charade any longer. I will not take money for a job I cannot do."

"Okay." Jill's voice was resigned. "I understand. Thank you for your efforts to date. Please send me your final bill."

"You got it."

I was feeling free as a bird, almost cheerful by the time I hung up.

I should have let it go, left it there, let sleeping dogs lie, as Alma would say. But I was pissed. And the trouble with being pissed is that it goads you into doing things you wouldn't ordinarily do. I am also—have I mentioned this before?—just the *tiniest* bit stubborn and hardheaded myself.

Forget *let sleeping dogs lie*. My guess anyway is that you can easily find a dog to suit your purposes. For instance, *like a dog worrying a bone*. Or *going after something doggedly*. Or *doggoned*. Or *hot dog*.

I was all of these.

And hot on the trail.

CHAPTER 43

The anger was almost overwhelming sometimes. He felt it in him, rising, filling him up. Taking over. Almost out of control. Almost. Almost it was the anger telling him what to do, not the other way around. Not him using the anger, sharpening it, honing it into a perfect weapon, a weapon he could control.

You had to control the weapon, you couldn't let it control you. The weapon might be a gun or a knife. Or anger. Pride. It could be a lot of things and the minute you let it go out of control it could be used against you. He saw that all the time. Any cop did.

He saw guys out on patrol—cops who should know better—get mad, lose it in a street situation. Some punk would mouth off at them and they would act like they'd been dissed. And the anger would take them out of control, make them as stupid as the gangbangers they were talking to.

You saw it in mob violence. People chose to give up themselves as individuals, as human beings with values and morals and standards, and instead embraced the ugliness, the baseness that is in us. A lot of guys beating up on one guy. Rape. Looting. Fire, destruction, anything those baser instincts shouted out. Gangbangers, soldiers, cops, citizens. Whites, blacks, Latinos, Jews, Asians. Anyone was capable of it.

Hate was easy to give into.

He had to go over this stuff, to remind himself, to get himself in line when he felt the anger filling him up. Because anger was hate. And hate was an ugly red spiral that twisted through your guts and took you down. And could take a lot of people down with you.

He tried to focus on more positive things, to remember what he'd been taught as a child or in church. *Do unto others. Love thy neighbor. The Ten Commandments. Condemn not the sinner, but the sin. Start each day with a smile.*

He would never think of those last words without remembering the sweetness of his mother's smile. And that he had never known a day she hadn't started out with a smile for him. She was a simple loving woman and life had been simpler then. No, that wasn't fair, to dismiss it—her—like that. His father, an angry and unhappy man, had started each day with a frown.

Everything in life is a choice.

He felt the anger within him still. Like hot metal. Burning. But he was in control now. The anger was his weapon, not the other way around. He could take that anger, forge it, shape it, hone it to a razor-sharp point and use it. It would be his then, a weapon, a power. And it would be dangerous.

Sara.

They say love and hate are very close together. He wasn't sure that was true. It might just be one of those things that people say because it seems to explain a lot and sounds good. A lot of what people called love was ego and power, control over another person. That feeling could easily turn to hate. It was easy to hate someone who slipped out of your control, your command. But real love? He didn't think that was close to hate. Maybe close to madness. If you lost what you loved and weren't careful it could push you to that edge. Even over.

Sara.

He tried to be careful. Very careful. He loved her, he knew that. For a long time he had thought she would come back. Then he hoped she would. He no longer thought that. Or hoped that. He knew she wasn't coming back. He needed to focus on getting on with his life, he knew that too. He needed to think about what the right thing to do was, and then do it. He needed to let things go—the past, her, the anger.

The anger. It was almost overwhelming sometimes.

CHAPTER 44

"I'm paying for this, right?"

Joe Crocker looked around Biba's, a wonderful Italian restaurant where the food is divine and the prices high.

"When have you *ever* paid for lunch, Joe? The only question here is whose account are you going to stick it on."

"Assuming that it's work-related," he said sternly, but there was a twinkle. "It's only because I've known you for a long time, know that you deliver."

I knew that about Joe too. I'd known him back when he worked for an insurance company, then quit to go out on his own specializing in insurance fraud. Joe is good, nobody better in town. And like me, he's willing to trust a gut feeling, an instinct, a hunch, whatever you want to call it. Joe and I have delivered a bunch of cases on that basis.

"I heard about Hank. I'm sorry. You doing okay?"

"No. Getting by."

He nodded. "I'm here, you need me."

"Thanks, Joe."

"You got a story for me?"

My turn to twinkle. "A good one. It gets convoluted so be patient."

"My kind of story."

The waiter showed up and Joe looked at me appraisingly. We hadn't even opened the menus.

"This one's too skinny." He gestured at me. "Bring us the specials: appetizer, soup, salad, main course. We'll be surprised."

The waiter nodded. No risk there. It is absolutely impossible to have a bad meal at Biba's.

"One each of the soup, salad, and appetizer. We'll share," I qualified.

"And a bottle of the Pinot Grigio." He winked at me. "Time to perk you up."

"Two glasses, not a bottle," I amended again.

The waiter retreated.

"What have you got, Kat?" He gave me his full attention.

"Three versions of a story. And not one of them is the truth."

He nodded. Our wine arrived.

"Version one. A woman comes to me claiming she's a victim of spousal abuse. She refuses to go the restraining order route because her husband is a cop and she claims the system won't work for her. She wants me to amass enough evidence to put a stop to it." I sipped.

"Joe, this is *very* good wine." The appetizer was melt-in-your-mouth gnocchi swimming in butter. Yum. It seemed like a long time since I had really tasted anything. Or anything had tasted good.

"Version two is the husband's. According to him, and everyone else I talk to, he's a straight shooter. He admits to keeping a close eye on her but says it's concern, not harassment. Later he updates the 'concern' to a focus on something that is possibly criminal but he doesn't know what. He does know that fairly large sums of money are going through her hands, money he *can't* account for and she *won't* account for."

The soup and salad, neatly portioned out, arrived. Joe ate steadily as I spoke.

"Version three is mine. I'm following him following her and I'm also following her. It turns out she has a night job as well as a day job. She leads motivational meetings in the evening—the very moving and inspiring kind. She's *good*, there's no question about it. I've only listened to a couple but they all run true to formula. Motivational blah blah blah. Then she always brings up insurance as the method of payment, and she always refers people to the same clinic, the one she credits with her 'turnaround.' I followed her to the clinic. The connection is there.

"The formula, the insurance tie-in, and the clinic lead me to believe that she is a recruiter. Her subterfuge and the unexplained cash lead me to believe that there is a scam of some kind going on."

Joe finished his wine and waved at the waiter. A bottle of wine appeared, along with our entrées, salmon with—maybe—cucumber dill something or other—I'm not that great at ingredients. I have met the slim and beautiful Biba. How anyone can stay that way, eating like this, is beyond me. Joe didn't say anything; he wouldn't until he was sure I was finished.

"And I haven't mentioned the death," I continued. "Two versions of that too. Murder and accident, the latter the current official one. There are unresolved questions there, I'm sure of it; it's all part of the same mess." I tasted my salmon, which, predictably, was yummy.

Joe skipped to the part that interested him. "What kind of a scam?"

"Don't know. Doubt that I'll find out from the outside."

"I'm beginning to see my part in this." He spoke wryly.

"Good. I'm sure you work with companies that do business with the Sunflower Clinic—"

"The Sunflower?" Joe whistled.

"Gosh, didn't I mention that before?" I asked innocently.

Joe snorted.

"Have you heard anything about the clinic?"

"Plenty. Nothing like this though."

"I want to go undercover there. For a few days at first, more if what I find warrants it. How about it?"

"I'm interested."

"If I uncover something, we split the credit and the fee or fees from the insurance companies. And I get to use what I need to finish up the case I'm working."

Joe nodded. "All right. Let's see if we can hammer this one out."

"You can set it up? Find an insurance company who will back me on this?"

"For a couple of days? No problem. And if you find something we'll not only have their support, we'll be raking in bonuses." He smiled.

Me too. Joe and I both get off on nailing bad guys, as well as on bonuses. He filled our glasses. And on wine. Good thing we could both walk back to work.

"I couldn't be happier to be involved, Katy. I've wanted to sink my teeth into a case like this for a long time."

A couple of state legislators that I recognized moved through the room taking up a lot of space and making a good deal of noise. God forbid that we not notice them or, even worse, not know that they were Important People.

"Oh look, Joe. Our tax dollars at work. Or maybe play." I said it in a very snippy voice.

Joe laughed. "Back to work. The biggest problem I see is that you know the recruiter. Getting popped the first day on the job is not going to get us anywhere."

"I've thought that one through pretty carefully. As far as I can tell she's rarely there and never on a regular basis. My guess is that she reports in but not necessarily in person. And I doubt that she would associate with the patients. Sooner or later someone might put two and two together and question how reliable her recommendation is. Being on the payroll is very different from being a former satisfied patient."

He nodded.

"I'm willing to take the risk. And if I get popped I'm on my own. It's a personal investigation having to do with a client, not insurance fraud. *Insurance fraud, what's that?* Moi, *a fraud investigator?* and so on. I figure the worst thing that can happen is that you have to send someone else in behind me. I don't anticipate that happening though."

"Okay, good enough for me. Obviously you can't go in as Kat Colorado."

"No. What I need from the insurance company is a name, a medical history and problem, evidence of insurance coverage, and a referral to this particular clinic."

"Piece of cake. Anything else?"

"A 'friend' or 'relative' to drop me off and a car not traceable to me stashed in a nearby safe place. I can't imagine I'll need it but—"

"Always good to know where the escape hatches are."

"Yes. We also need to find out what the patients are allowed to keep in the way of personal items."

"What's on your list?"

"A phone, maybe a gun. I'll have to come up with a way to conceal them."

"I'll take care of the phone, get you something about as big as a candy bar. You set on the gun?"

"A three eighty."

"Yeah, that'll work. I'll find out what's allowed, consider hiding places. You think you'll need a gun?"

I shrugged. "I never think I'll need a gun. Well, not unless I go to a Seven-Eleven at two A.M., which I am way too smart to do—*then* I think I need a gun."

"You got any preference in names or disorders?"

I shook my head. "No. Just keep it simple. Nothing wild, outlandish, or unbelievable. And something simple to sustain, a nice low-maintenance, not-much-acting-out kind of problem. Not something where I don't have a clue and will trip up either."

"You got it." He looked at me appraisingly. "Daphne. I always wanted to know a Daphne. It sounds so exotic, so mysterious, so—"

"So not me," I finished in a dampening tone of voice.

He was still laughing when the waiter dropped by to suggest dessert. I passed but Joe didn't.

"How quickly can you make this happen, Joe?"

"Won't take long at all. Couple of days at the most. Hot to trot, are you?"

I was, yes.

"Anytime okay for you, anything holding you back?"

"No, I just need to arrange for the animals and tell a few friends I'll be out of town. What do you think—a week on the outside? I'm hoping a couple of days will do it."

"That's optimistic. A week might be too. It takes a while to get a feel for a place, to learn your way around, figure out what's standard and what isn't—all the time maintaining your cover. A person with a problem is going to behave a lot differently than a hot dog investigator. Want a bite of this, Katy? It's really good."

"And only six billion calories." But I had a bite and it was worth every calorie.

"That's going to be the hardest part for you, Kat."

"What?"

"Staying in character. You ever do any acting in college? . . . Yo, Kat. Hell*ooo*. Earth calling Mars. Come in, please."

"Hmmmm?"

"Are you paying attention to me?"

"*Oh* for goodness' sakes. One of our elected officials just patted a woman on the butt. Don't they *ever* learn? How many more lawsuits are we going to have to settle before they get the picture? *Jeez.* I am tempted to go over there and give that jerk a piece of my mind. Look at that! Now he's taking a cigar out of his pocket and stroking it suggestively, as though it were a—"

"Katy." Joe sounded patient, the way you do when someone is trying your patience and you are making an extra effort, not the way you do when you are really patient.

"Hmmmm?" I was mesmerized. What *is* it with the handful of politicians and so-called religious leaders who can't keep their hands off women who have not invited their attentions? They must have a linked sex hormone and stupid gene. I watched as the cigar went back to his pocket and his hands dropped to his sides. The woman had a cold, hard fierce look as she spoke to him. *Hah!* Women and Taxpayers 1, Stupid Politicians 0.

"Yes, of course I'm paying attention. You asked if I wanted another bite of dessert." I glanced at his plate. Not even a crumb. *Oops.* "Sorry, Joe, what *did* you say?"

"Staying in character, that'll be a tough one, won't it?"

"I don't think so," I said, a trifle complacently. "I'm a quick study."

Joe made a snorting sound. "That's good coming from someone who just dropped Investigator at Work like a hot potato in favor of the role of Outraged Woman and Taxpayer."

I blushed. I *hate* it when I do that—it's like junior high all over again. "Okay, point taken."

"Be careful, Katy." His voice was gentle, even fond. "No one's got a scam going unless there's money in it. Big money, at least to them. Losing this kind of scam is not just losing money either, it's facing a loss of credibility, of patients, and of insurance approval, maybe even fines and legal charges. When people have a lot at stake and get cornered, they get vicious. They fight dirty. Killer instincts surface."

"I know, Joe. Thanks for reminding me." I was properly wary and chastened. "The minute you get the undercover profile to me I'll start rehearsing it."

"Not rehearsing it."

"Living it," I corrected.

We parted on the corner of Capitol and 28th and I walked back to my office in the spring sunshine, temporarily squished and out of breath from Joe's hug.

CHAPTER 45

Darby Sheffield?"

"Yeah. You like it?"

"Darby Sheffield? It sounds like a couple of English counties or a horse or God knows what, but not like someone from California."

"People in California come in all sorts, Kat, don't get yourself in a lather. You're a cocktail waitress and a part-time student who just broke up with her boyfriend. Pick your own hobbies and interests."

"Student in what?"

"Creative writing. How's that for wide open?"

"Good."

"You work at Harlow's, the club in midtown. They'll vouch for you in case anyone checks, though that seems unlikely. You might want to stop by the club and familiarize yourself with the layout just to be on the safe side. We gave you an address down there and a roommate. She'll vouch for you too. Ditto on the address and home familiarization."

"Will do. Why am I there?"

"At the clinic?"

"Yes."

"You have three choices. Eating disorder. They suggested a pattern of overeating followed by fasting. That should be fairly easy to simulate and would eliminate the need to induce vomiting et cetera."

I wondered what the et cetera was but decided not to inquire.

"A compulsive behavior disorder. Constantly washing your hands, checking things over and over, counting everything, something like that."

"That one would be a tough one to sustain, wouldn't it? It sounds like it would require a lot of acting out."

"Yeah, that's what I thought too. Okay, how about fantasizing? It's difficult for you to live in the real world so you make up fantasies that you like better. Sometimes you get confused between the fantasy and the reality. Well, not confused exactly, more that you'd prefer the fantasy, so you act like it is more real than reality. If you get my drift."

"Got it. I like that one best."

"Yeah, me too."

Not that it was much different from a bunch of my life, I reflected sadly. If I could—if I could convince myself—I would live in a happy fantasy with Hank at my side.

"That one should be easy to play however you want. And—if they're fantasies—you don't have to be consistent, right?"

"Right."

"Okay. You might want to work out a couple though, just to have them handy in the old back pocket."

"Will do. What did you find out about bringing in personal items?"

"Pretty much whatever you want in the small stuff. They suggested simple, casual clothing, toiletries and makeup, sports equipment as desired—they have tennis courts, a pool, and an exercise room. Also inexpensive entertainment items such as a portable CD player, Walkman, or radio, reading and writing materials, and so on. There are really no restrictions—"

I waited for the but.

"Except that they do 'review' everything that comes in with you."

"With me and on my person?"

"Yes."

"So we can safely assume that that lets out a gun and the phone?"

"Yes."

"Visitors?"

"Unrestricted access on visitor days and evenings."

"Search?"

"No, but no 'presents' that aren't inspected and cleared."

"Jeez. Why so authoritarian?"

"Apparently a significant number of friends and relatives will sabotage a treatment program by bringing in drugs, forbidden foods, alcohol, whatever."

"Oh. Yeah. I guess that was kind of a naive question."

"Hey kid, you're new to the disorder business, remember? Look, don't sweat it. The security there is reasonable but not tight. We'll figure out something."

"Fast?"

"You betcha Red Rider. We want bulletins and updates as soon as possible, with as much information as possible. And I want to be assured of your health and well-being at regular intervals. Got that?"

"Got that." I smiled at the tough-guy concern in Joe's voice. Even over the phone I knew what his expression was, hard and stern, with eyes that gave him away.

"We're still working on a 'relative' to drop you off. Everyone in my office is way too recognizable. I'm going to free up one of our cars though. It's leased—no trace back to you or us.

"You have a choice between a private room and a three- or four-bedder. You care?"

"Put me in with as many people as possible." I shivered inside. Not only am I an intensely private person but right now especially I found I needed quiet and space more than ever. "Might as well max out the informational possibilities. I won't be trying to call you from inside anyway, not with such extensive grounds available."

"Good girl, Katy. I know that is the hard way for you to go."

I shivered again.

"We should be able to get you in tomorrow or the next day. You ready?"

Ready or not, here I come. Long-ago echo from childhood. How often were we ready? Really? I was ready to learn how to ride a bike, to read, to work and live and love. Was I ready to fight the nightmares of being abandoned as a child? Or to shoot—and kill—the long-ago man who had tried to kill me? Was I ready to lose Hank?

"Katy?" Joe's voice was concerned.

I came back. "I'm ready. And Joe?"

"Yeah." Doubt in his voice.

"Call me Darby."

He chuckled. "Well, damn, I'll just do that, Darby. I'll call you tomorrow morning around ten with an update. Pack your bags, darlin'."

"Thanks, Joe."

"For what? I'm the one sitting on the sidelines. You're the one in the line of fire."

"For your backing. How often have you told me never to put a weak link in the field?" He started to answer me but I interrupted him. "A million and two times, I counted. And I know that right now I'm a weak link. Hank. Everything. So thanks, Joe, it means a lot to me."

"I'm behind you, Katy. Every time. My money's on your card."

"Darby. You meant Darby, right?" I said it in a cold, hard, mean voice.

We both laughed.

"Night, Darb. Talk to you in the morning."

The phone clicked softly in my ear and I wondered how people without friends got through life. I couldn't do it in the good times. And in the bad? Dead meat, buzzard bait—that would be me.

After I packed I called Charity.

"Can I trade you three animals for a tennis racket?"

"Sure. What's up, Katy?" A logical question since I didn't play tennis.

"I'm on my way over. Tell you when I get there."

"You'll stay for dinner?"

"Are you kidding? I waited all day to time this call. I'll bring dessert."

"What?" she asked, suspicion heavy and ugly in her voice. "Last time you said that, you brought low-fat frozen yogurt and Oreos. Yuck."

"Mmmmmmmmm," I murmured sensuously.

She snorted. "Forget it. Just bring yourselves. And *don't* forget Ranger's ball this time."

"Yes, ma'am." I half saluted the phone. Sheesh. Talk about a tyrant. She spoiled the animals terribly too.

I had to fake Kitten out by making lots of exciting "treat time" noises around the food and water bowls. Then I pounced, tossed him in the bedroom, and dug out the carrying cage. If he sees the cage first, he's into next week. Ranger? He's a car ride slut so he's easy. Phoenix was easy too. She's new, an unexpected gift from a man whom I would have sent to prison had he not chosen death.

And I picked some roses from the garden. The first roses of spring are so incredibly, breathtakingly beautiful. Red, yellow, pink, lavender, and fragrant. Oreos were nothing to them.

Katy, I have a question for you." Charity was a blur of motion, dicing, chopping, sautéing. The kitchen was warm and aromatic. The animals, hers and mine, were scattered around in strategic positions, hoping and praying for yummies to hit the floor.

"Sure." I was uncorking Charity's exquisitely delightful and expensive chardonnay.

"I met this really great guy and I thought of you. I was just wondering—"

She turned to look at me. Me standing stock-still with a bottle of wine in my hand and tears puddling.

"Oh God, Katy, I'm sorry! It's too soon, of course it is. I didn't mean a date or anything, just dinner or drinks."

I shook my head.

She flung her knife down—a really dangerous, really sharp one I might add—and hugged me, her hands warm and redolent with the smell of freshly chopped herbs. "I'm sorry sorry sorry."

I hugged her back, the wine cold in my hand. "If you let go of me I'll pour the wine," I pointed out at last and ever so reasonably. And she smiled and went back to chopping and mincing. I am sometimes amazed at the amounts of garlic or ginger or whatever she can put into a dish, but always pleased with the results.

"What are you up to now?" was her inevitable question.

I gave her the edited version and Joe's number. "Very safe," I added. "Nothing to worry about."

She glanced at me with suspicion. "Whenever you say that I know there's something to worry about."

I made my *Don't be silly!* face.

She didn't really buy it but she let it go. "I have a letter to show you. Do you want to see it now or later?"

"Now." Why not? All I was doing was sitting on a kitchen stool drinking wine and watching her cook.

"There." She waved a wooden spoon in a 260-degree arc that eliminated the living room furniture and the animals but not much else.

"Where?"

She pointed to the small desk in the kitchen. "The top one."

There were at least twenty-five or thirty Dear Charity letters in the pile. I pulled the top one and read.

> Dear Charity,
>
> What do you say to your children when you could lose your home? We have no money, almost no food, and very little hope. How do you help them believe and go on when you don't know how to do that yourself? What answer do you give to their questions when those are your questions and you have no answers?
>
> Devastated, Hopeless, and Tongue-tied

I looked at Charity.

"What do I say, Katy?"

"I don't know." I wasn't hungry and I wouldn't lose my home but I had the same questions: How to go on? How to believe things would get better? How to hope in the face of a reality that seemed only bleak, black, and hopeless?

"What have other people said?" Charity asked me.

I took a gulp of wine. "It ain't over till it's over." And I reminded myself to sip. Wine doesn't fill the emptiness.

"Hope springs eternal." Charity.

"It's not over until the fat lady sings." Me.

"Tomorrow is another day."

"Buy a lottery ticket."

Charity looked at me skeptically. "Who said *that*?"

I shrugged. "The commercials for the state lottery."

"Do we believe them?"

"Sure. After all, the odds are only one in fifty-nine gazillion."

"Is there an answer, Katy?"

"I don't know." And I didn't. "Maybe 'Don't give up.' "

We had Indian curry that night, spicy and hot. With cool and delicious mango chutney and more delicious white wine. I spent the night in Charity's guest room with two cats on my bed and a dog on the floor beside me.

In the morning, in the dawn, I looked for hope. And then for the Sunflower Clinic.

CHAPTER 46

We drove through the large wrought-iron arch that told us we were entering the Sunflower Health Spa and Clinic. Climbing red roses twined around the black iron of the arch. Once through the arch the drive opened out into a circular parking lot with flowers everywhere. The stately old wooden clinic building was serene and peaceful. Behind it small cottages dotted the landscape and everywhere there was grass, flowers, and shrubs. A stream meandered about the grounds with little bridges and stepping stones here and there.

Idyllic.

We had already dropped off my car in the prearranged spot and now "Aunt Abigail" was driving. I, presumably, was lost in fantasy. Aunt Abigail whistled and I glanced sideways at her. She had a mouth like a sailor, Joe told me, but was under strict orders to stay in character.

"Well, bless my soul, Darby, if this doesn't look like just the *nicest* place." There was a bit of an accent there—southern belle, perhaps—as she looked at me and twinkled. "They do say it costs an arm and a leg. But God bless that wonderful insurance company, that's what I always say. Don't you, dear?"

"Absolutely."

"Oh look, Darby dear, ducks! Aren't they the sweetest little things. Oh *la*. You lucky girl, you. Imagine walking over to that pond and feeding those dear little creatures. Such a thrill." Aunt Abigail pulled into a parking slot and bumped to a stop.

I got out of the car. Slowly. There's something much more appealing about enjoying the world around you as a free person rather than as an inmate.

Patient, Kat. I could hear Joe's voice in my mind. *Inmates are in prisons.*

But the minute you couldn't come and go as you pleased you were in prison, weren't you? There were no walls here. The sunshine and breeze was in my face and hair and I could smell the flowers and hear the ducks quacking and splashing. Except for Aunt Abigail's pitter-patter I heard no voices. No laughter.

This was a place where people brought their own walls. And paid the clinic to knock those walls down, to free them. I was here to find out if they lived up to their billing.

"Well, come along then." Abigail tugged at me, surprisingly strong for a little bit of a thing. I looked at her and caught the wink. "Chop chop." She gave me a friendly (strong) shove down the path to the front entrance and toddled along behind me.

The large, heavy wooden doors opened into a pleasant entry hall with a long countertop, like a hotel check-in. Plants, fresh flowers, and comfortable chairs were delicately scattered in random fashion. It looked like an elegant country hotel, not a disorder clinic.

No one was around. Abigail trotted over to the counter and banged the bell. My hands, I noticed, were sweaty. Deliberately, I let all expression slide off my face and slip out of my eyes.

A comfortable matronly-looking woman in her mid-forties bustled out. "Hello. Hello! You must be Miss Darby Sheffield. Welcome to the Sunflower Clinic. We have been expecting you and are so happy to see you."

I felt my eyes narrow. Was there the tiniest resemblance here to Nurse Ratched? My stomach did a two-and-a-half gainer backflip.

"Now, Darby, speak up, dear!"

So I said hello, but I couldn't make myself smile.

Aunt Abigail rattled on introducing herself, commenting on the weather and what a beautiful beautiful setting they had here. My stomach was still in the Olympic diving–trial mode. Jeez. Talk about being a big baby.

"Now, Miss Sheffield." The matron spoke very politely but there was a firmness in her voice, a tone that wasn't there when she spoke to Abigail. "If you will just be so kind as to show me what you have brought." She spoke as to a child.

My name is Kat Colorado and I am here on a job. I said it silently three times before I had myself under control enough to open my suitcase courteously.

She flipped through my things as expertly as a customs inspector. "My my, aren't you just the neatest packer! Look at that." Fake admiration oozed from her voice.

Aunt Abigail patted me on the shoulder and winked again. I took a deep breath.

"And your purse too, please?" She waited until I, reluctantly, put it on the counter and, reluctantly, let go of it. Matron deftly pawed through my purse removing all my money, paper and coin, and the one credit card Darby had.

"Would you like your aunt to keep your money and credit card, or would you like us to place it in the safe for you?"

Talk about out of left field? I hadn't foreseen this one.

"I'll take it." Abigail scooped it up briskly and tossed it into her bag.

"We've found it safer this way. Unfortunately some of our clients—not you of course, Darby!—cannot be trusted around the temptation of money. Such a shame!"

I was Darby now, not Miss Sheffield.

"Now then, do we have anything in our pockets or elsewhere?" The matron accompanied her jaunty little question with a quick frisk. Joe was wrong. We might be called clients but inmate was closer to it. And I was part of that hospital "we"—as in, *How are we feeling today?*—not me anymore. I took another deep breath.

Anytime you want to you can leave. Joe had spoken in a reassuring way. I had shrugged it off with a "Naw, I'll be fine." Would I? Another breath.

"You'll be saying goodbye to your aunt now," the matron/warden ordered me.

"What?" Aunt Abigail's eyes popped open in horrified surprise. "Oh my, no, I do *insist* on seeing my dear Darby's room and *everything*. I *must* see for myself where she is staying."

"Of course." The matron smoothly shifted gears. "This way if you please." And we followed her—me carrying my searched stuff—down a corridor and out into the grounds behind the building, taking a path that wound out for some distance.

There I saw other patients. A young woman smiled and said a shy hello to me. Others just stared in silence. We walked in the same silence, a short quiet parade out to one of the farthest cottages.

"Here we are!" That false hospital cheer.

A small white wooden cottage with dark green trim and climbing pink roses. *Home sweet home.* Matron marched up to the door, knocked, and entered without waiting for a response. We stepped into a tiny sitting room—four chairs, a table with a lace doily and a bowl of flowers—two bedrooms just big enough to hold the two single beds with simple cotton coverlets, and a small bathroom. There were a number of small prints and watercolors—all landscapes—scattered throughout.

"Well, this is just the *sweetest* little cottage," Abigail oozed. "Isn't it, Darby dear? Don't you just *love* it here already?" She reached up to pat me on the cheek. "Don't you, sweetie? Why, I do declare, flowers and lace and these pretty little pictures. It's just the *most* charming little place I've ever seen. Isn't it, dear?"

"Oh, *yes*." Darby tried to match Abigail's enthusiasm; Kat was less sure.

The matron pointed at a bed and I placed my suitcase and tennis racket there.

"Oh, look! What a sweet little bathroom." Abigail popped in for a look-see, then pushed me in as she exited. "Go on, dear, don't be shy. She always has to go after a car trip. I swear, she's just like a kid that way." Abigail bubbled at the matron who smiled back perfunctorily and glanced at her watch.

So I went to the bathroom. And retrieved the gun, the phone, the fifty in cash, and the credit card. The matron was no match for the likes of Aunt Abigail, dear sweet cunning little menace that she was.

"Why don't we just take a quick turn around the grounds?" Abigail suggested in her sickeningly sweet tone of voice.

The matron looked at her watch again.

"Oh, I do *insist*." Something in Abigail's tone.

The matron caved. "All right, but just a quick one. I'm afraid I have . . ." Her voice trailed off.

Aunt Abigail zoomed off into the grounds, nimble as a doe. I kept up with her. The matron trailed us, out of hearing but not sight.

"Got it?" she asked.

"Got it," I confirmed.

"The grounds are completely fenced."

I nodded. Eight-foot wrought iron with decorative spikes on top. It could be scaled but it wasn't like vaulting over a low wall.

"See the rock outcropping next to the fence over there?"

"Yes."

"Drop-off/pickup point."

"All right."

"You okay?"

"Yes."

"You don't seem very perky."

I flashed her a quick smile. "I'm in character."

She nodded. "All right. I'll take off then."

"Yes."

We finished the loop we had made of the grounds, then waited for the matron to catch up to us.

"Now you take good care of my precious little Darby, you hear?" Aunt Abigail managed to sound worried and emphatic both. "She's just the *sweetest* and *dearest* little thing in the *whole* world. And that's the truth!"

The matron looked from Abigail to me and back again, puzzled at the description, I guess. I gave her a sweet and dear little look. Aunt Abigail pinched my cheek. I struggled to maintain sweet and dear.

"Now I want you to write and call me all the time. She can do that, can't she?" Abigail was clutching me in a frantic but endearing way and directing an imploring look in the matron's direction.

"We don't encourage phone calls," the matron said in a dampening fashion. "It could impede our progress here. Letters are fine. We do reserve the right to just glance through them and be sure there would be nothing unsettling or upsetting to dear little Darby." She gave me a fake bright and friendly look.

I felt like I was ten. Tops.

"Oh." Abigail bobbed up and down nervously on the balls of her feet. "Well, I'll come see you often, Darby dear. When is the first visitor day?"

"This weekend. However, we do not encourage visitors for the first two weeks, sometimes longer. We have found it best for our patients to settle into the environment and routine here, to fully engage in the therapeutic process as it were." Same damp tone and fake bright, friendly look.

See, I thought darkly, *I was right. Prison. If it looks like a duck, waddles like a duck and quacks like a—*

"Oh my, my my my," Aunt Abigail murmured. "Well, there, it's all for the best, dearest." She wiped the concerned look off her face and replaced it with fake and bright. Just like the matron.

I was wrong, I thought, *there are walls here. Just very subtle ones and no barbed wire.*

"Give me a big hug and kiss, Darby dear. You work hard now, you hear, and get yourself all well and happy. I'll be thinking about you every day. And praying for you."

The matron was tapping her foot impatiently. Aunt Abigail pressed me to her skinny bosom and breathed peppermint on me as she kissed my cheek.

"I'll walk you out." Matron spoke firmly as she took Auntie's arm and quick-marched her off. She stopped for a moment, turned and addressed me. "You go back to your room. Wait for me there." Bright, happy, and friendly had bitten the dust and drill sergeant was here.

I stuck my tongue out at her back as she walked away. Treat people like ten-year-olds and guess what? Then I stood forlornly on the lawn and watched Abigail's small figure recede. Every five or six steps she stopped and turned, waved at me and blew me kisses. I waved and blew them back until finally the matron dragged her off.

"Piece of work, isn't she?"

I turned and looked at the young woman with pink hair and six hoop earrings in each ear.

"Everyone here hates her guts. She's sweet as pie and all kissy-face to the families, but to us? Hah. Big-time bitch. Who are you?"

"Darby Sheffield."

"My name's Carrie." She held out a small pretty hand with rings on every finger. Her wrists were badly scarred. I said nothing, just shook the offered hand.

"I was thinking about eating bugs, how about you?"

"No. I don't care for bugs. Or at least not for eating them." I made my face a mask. This was my reality now, this kind of conversation.

"I like to hurt myself sometimes. It hurts when you get your ears pierced, you know." She fingered her earlobes. "Maybe I'll get my tongue pierced. That *really* hurts. Look." She held out her wrists. "I did that."

"Is all this supposed to shock me?"

"I dunno. Maybe. Does it?"

"No. It makes me sad for you though."

Carrie stared at me for a long time, pink hair, earrings shining in the sun and no expression. "Why are you here?" she asked finally.

"I make up things and I live in my mind. If you do that too much it's not good." I shrugged. "That's what they say. I like it."

"You're like Lorie. She does that too, only she makes up whole other people to be, people with names and everything. Do you?"

"No. Who's Lorie?"

"One of the girls in my cottage. Where are you staying?"

I pointed out the white cottage.

Carrie clapped her hands. "Oh good, I was hoping you were. We had an empty bed. You're in my room, you know."

I smiled at her. I liked her, vulnerable and fragile underneath the pink and gold and bravado.

"When did you get here?"

"Just now. The matron told me to go to my room and wait."

Carrie nodded. "She likes to order people around at first, show 'em who's boss. After that she'll ignore you unless you do something wrong. I'll go with you, shall I? I could help you unpack." Without waiting for an answer she headed for the cottage, jabbering away.

"This doesn't look like a funny farm but it is. I never thought I'd be in a funny farm, did you, Darby?"

I shook my head. Darby was a patient here, not me, not Kat. It was the kind of place, I thought, where reality could easily slip around.

CHAPTER 47

"Two other women live here?" I asked Carrie.

"Well, yeah, if you can call it living."

"What do you call it?"

She shrugged. "I dunno. Passing time or something. I have a bad attitude, you know."

"Why?" I was unpacking my bag and putting clothes in the small chest of drawers that Carrie had pointed out as mine.

" 'Cause life sucks. God, your clothes are so boring. Blue jeans and T-shirts and stuff. Don't you wear any bright colors?"

"Not very much, I guess." And not right now. I wished I could ditch her just long enough to stash my gun in the concealed compartment in my suitcase. "Do you?"

"Well, yeah, duh. I mean, look at my hair." She pointed. "I wear a lot of black too. It fits my mood. Do you think life sucks?"

"I think life is what you make of it."

"You didn't answer the question."

"No, I don't. I think it's hard but I don't think it sucks."

"Do you have people who love you?"

I looked at the gamine in pink and turquoise, her head tilted to one side, her eyes questioning. "Yes. Do you?"

"No. No one gives a shit."

"They cared enough to send you here."

"Guilt. Embarrassment. Stuff like that. They don't care about me."

"Do people here care?"

"Some. It depends. Not that much really. They care if they make money or if you cause trouble, but I don't think they care if you get better."

"Do you care if you get better?"

"I don't know." She yawned, showing me almost perfect teeth. "Mostly I think that life's not worth living. There's nothing I want to do. Drugs are okay because they kill time, they make you feel better for a while and they make you forget. I'm going to get a Coke. You want one?"

"Sure. Thanks."

I watched as she drifted off, then stashed my contraband items and stowed the suitcase under the bed. Ten minutes later she drifted back, sodas in hand, vacant look in eyes. It made me sad to look at her.

"I think the Bitch is heading in your direction," she announced.

I sipped my Coke.

"Have you met Dr. Saunders yet?"

"No."

"That's probably it. He runs the place and he's the reason it's supposed to be good. He likes to talk to everyone when they first get here; you'll never see him after that. He'll decide on a course of care for you—that's what they call it. What bullshit." She sipped at her soda. "We all get the same care, you know."

"What?"

"You're supposed to do a sport and group activities, group therapy, and a couple of times a week you talk to your assigned counselor and report on your progress. Oh, and they like you to do the mud baths and mineral water soaks and shit like that. Healthy body, healthy mind." She sneered at the thought.

It all sounded sensible, if not therapeutic.

"Watch out for Saunders."

"Why?"

"He's a tricky bastard. They all pretend they like you but you don't know what's going on inside them. Wouldn't it be cool if people had windows in their heads? You could just open the window and see right into their thoughts. Look." She pointed out the window. "Here comes the Bitch. Okay, now here's what you do." Her face was solemn and earnest.

"Don't show any fear and make yourself look larger than you are. That's what animals and birds do. They fluff out their fur and feathers so they'll look more formidable and scary. Remember they can sense your fear, smell it and stuff, so watch out."

"I think you've watched too many *Wild Kingdoms*. Why do I have to do all this? They want to help me, don't they?"

"Well, yeah, that's what they *say*. You aren't dumb enough to believe *that*, are you?" She flopped down on her bed and rolled over on her side, her back to me.

"Darby."

The matron's cold voice cut into my thoughts. Carrie's back tensed and shifted.

"Yes." I sat on my bed, hands in my lap like a schoolgirl.

"Come with me."

No "Would you"? No "Could you"? No please, no politeness? I stood and walked with her.

"What is it?" I asked as we crossed an expanse of lawn.

"I'm taking you to meet Dr. Saunders."

"Why?"

"Enough. Be silent."

And I was silenced. Her shoes were loud on the paving stones. They were the kind with steel toes, I thought, for no particular reason. I took a deep breath to make myself look big.

"Aren't you supposed to be nice? How can people get better if they aren't in a warm and supportive atmosphere?"

She stared wordlessly at me as though I were a supremely grotesque and disturbing species of bug. From Mars. Or Franz Kafka's mind. I puffed my chest out some more but it had no noticeable effect on her. So much for *Wild Kingdom.* We reached the main building and she opened the door, giving me a vicious little jab that sent me tumbling and stumbling inside. So much for dignity.

A quick trip down the hall, a knock on a door, and I was ushered into Dr. Saunders's presence, the matron all smiles and affability now. "This is Darby Sheffield, doctor."

He rose to greet me and she melted from the room. "Won't you sit down and make yourself comfortable?"

He smiled as he walked around his desk to shake my hand and then indicate a chair. The office was elegant and solemn in mahogany paneling and brocaded chairs. In his expensive three-piece suit, professional demeanor and graying temples, he matched perfectly.

A tap on the door and a young woman in a starched white uniform entered.

"Would you care for coffee or tea, Ms. Sheffield? I am drinking tea."

"Thank you. Tea, please." I matched his graciousness, though in jeans and a T-shirt I was out of place in this elegant office. And at a subtle disadvantage.

We chatted about the weather, the gardens, and the theater—about which I know slightly less than nothing—until the tea came. Then it was down to business.

"We are pleased that you have joined us here. Please tell me how we may help."

"I don't know." I slid a look of confusion and despair on my face. "Isn't that your job? I have a problem and you fix it?"

"The only one who can change your life is you." He spoke gently. "But we are here to help. Tell me in your own words why you have come here."

"Because of the daydreams."

He nodded encouragingly.

"I know everyone has dreams and daydreams and that's okay but lots of times I like my dreams better than my life. I could spend all my time in my mind, in my dreams, if things would let me."

"Why do you prefer your dreams to your life?"

"They're better." Simple and stark. "I can make things just the way I want them. Perfect. You can't do that in real life."

"No," he agreed. "We can't."

"And it's more exciting. I can make things up. I can even pretend to live them. It's very exciting actually. Like if I was bored I could pretend to be someone like you, someone who helped other people get better. That's a nice thing to do. It's fun to think of being someone like that." I let my voice grow animated and tried to put a sparkle in my eyes.

Saunders smiled at me. "Do you often do that?"

"Sure, I pretend I'm someone else, or I'm me in their life, and then I try it out and see if I like it. It's like going to the store and trying on new clothes. Bright, pretty, exciting clothes." My voice was fast and excited now. "Not like *these*." I gestured at my clothing. "See how dull and boring my clothes are." Disdainful.

"They're very nice," he commented.

"Boring." I dismissed them with a wave of my hand.

"Is there anything in your life that you find exciting and interesting?"

"No." I dismissed Darby's life as easily as her clothes.

"Perhaps we could focus on that, on helping you make your life as interesting as your dreams?"

"Okay." Hope and doubt both crept into my voice. "How, exactly?"

"See if you can think of a way to start."

Oops. The ball was in my court again. So I sat looking numb and confused. He pressed a button and the woman dressed like a nurse returned to usher me out. His smile had faded before I even got out of the room.

I turned around to look.

Apparently I was on my own.

I headed back to the cottage to see if I could talk Carrie, or someone, into giving me the grand tour plus commentary. Carrie, outspoken and uninhibited, was my first choice.

She lay with her face to the wall still, her back tense and unreadable. One foot jiggled manically.

"Hey." I spoke softly. "Want to go for a walk or something?"

The foot stopped jiggling, her shoulders shifted. "Why do you ask me?" Her voice was apathetic.

"I like you. You're interesting."

"You mean weird."

"No I don't. I mean interesting."

She rolled over and stared at me, her eyes dark and sunk deep in the sockets. She'd been crying, I thought.

"You don't even know me."

"That's true, but I like you so far. Do you want to go on a walk or not?"

"All right." She pulled herself up as though she were coming out of a trance. "Where are we going?"

"Everywhere. I want to see what this place is like."

"Okay."

We walked out past the cottages to the gardens where a number of people were working.

"It's okay if you come down here and work. The tools are over there. These are the vegetable gardens and herb beds. Cutting flowers are over there. And fruit trees. Behind the trees are the grapes. Everything's organic." She squatted and pulled strawberries off their stems. "Mmmm, these are good. Have some. They're sweet, and warm from the sunshine."

We wandered over to the herb beds where Carrie picked sprigs of parsley, cilantro, and mint to chew. Occasionally I heard a voice or single comment, but no conversations, no laughter. We too spoke in low voices or were silent.

"What do you want to see now?" Carrie asked.

"The pool and tennis courts." I was trying to sound like a patient. Good, huh? And it was a better answer than corruption and scams. Though I would get to them. They were on my list.

The pool was Olympic-sized, natural thermal hot spring fed. The water was warm and inviting, smelling faintly of minerals I couldn't identify. There were outdoor showers and nearby were changing rooms, tennis courts, and even a basketball hoop. A woman was hitting tennis balls against a backboard with an intensity and viciousness that was almost frightening.

"The mud baths are in there. You can get herbal wraps and massages and stuff too." She shrugged. "I never go. I can't stand having people touch me like that."

"What about group therapy?"

"That's in the main building. Saunders and all the counselors have offices in there. They assign you to a counselor and to groups. You have to go but they're dumb."

"Why?"

"Why do you have to go or why are they dumb?"

"Why are they dumb?"

"They ask you about your feelings and stuff but people just blab on about anything. Hardly anyone tells the truth or even says anything important."

"What about the counselors?"

"It's stupid, they're just as bad. I mean, some of them are nice and all but they don't really know anything. Like they're not that trained or anything." She kicked a stone in the path. "I used to think things could change for me. It's not enough just not to do drugs, you know. You have to find something else. I used to get my hopes all up. You know, that they would help me find something, help me not be all empty and lonely." Her voice was despairing. "It's hard, getting your hopes up like that, and it really sucks when nothing happens.

"Hey." Her voice was raucous and loud. "See that pond. What do you bet I get way out there with this rock." She threw hard and it sailed through the air, hitting the far edge of the pond easily. "Life sucks," she said. "It's really pretty fucking simple. Pretty goddamn fucking simple. Hear the bell? It's lunchtime. The food is good here, I'll say that for them. C'mon, this way."

"What's the house on the other side of the pond?"

"Saunders lives there. Lorie says he has a girlfriend too, but I've never seen her."

She scampered off, pell-mell and awkward as a colt. I followed more slowly, caught up with her at the door to the dining area.

"You don't have a special meal, do you, health or weight or religious or anything?" Carrie asked.

"No."

"Then we just sit anywhere. I like to sit over there by the window, you can see all the ducks. Oh, never mind, there's Lorie and Patsy. We'll sit with them." She veered suddenly and plopped herself down at a middle table.

"This is Darby, she's my new roommate. This is Patsy and Lorie, they have the other room in our cottage."

I said hello to a small frightened, colorless woman and a vivacious, attractive overweight one. Patsy was picking at a small meal of things with hardly any calories. The rest of us began serving ourselves from the tureen of soup and the bowl of salad. There was freshly baked bread and chopped fresh herbs to sprinkle on your food. It looked delicious.

"So, what's your story, Darby?"

The well-rehearsed lines tripped off my tongue. "I'm a student, a cocktail waitress too."

They all looked at me in surprise. Lorie blinked and then started laughing. "You just got here, that's right, so you don't know. Here you're not a person, Darby, you're a problem. Like in a hospital people don't have names, they have conditions—the gallbladder, the heart attack in emergency, the kid with leukemia. So, when we ask that here, we don't mean Who are you? We mean What's your problem? For instance," Lorie added, "I have multiple personalities."

"She's a nutcase," Carrie corrected.

"And she's a drug addict, a thief, and a prostitute," Lorie retorted meanly about Carrie.

Carrie's face went white and still. "A druggie by choice, a thief and prostitute by default." She tried to speak with an air of nonchalance but didn't pull it off.

"They're mean to each other all the time," Patsy said to me.

"Why?"

"I don't know."

"Patsy is a . . . Patsy has an eating disorder." Carrie spoke carefully. "Tell us about you, Darby."

"I like my dreams better than my life."

"Who doesn't?"

Lorie spoke but neither Patsy nor Carrie disagreed with her.

"Pass the soup, please."

CHAPTER 48

What's the matter with Marianne?" Carrie asked.

"Who's Marianne?" Lorie didn't bother to look up. Picking at her salad was apparently absorbing her full attention.

"The blond girl, the one who's sitting over there all by herself crying. I'm going over."

Carrie shoved her chair back and wended her way through the tables. Almost everyone pretended not to notice either Marianne or Carrie. I watched as Carrie spoke to the crying woman, then picked up her plate, grabbed her hand, and led her over to our table.

"Hey guys, this is Marianne. She's having a bad day so I told her she should come over here and maybe we would cheer her up and maybe we would cry with her. Or tell her all our horrible stuff."

Lorie wrinkled her nose in disgust. Carrie put Marianne's plate down and pushed her gently into a chair.

"What happened?" I asked.

"Would you care for bread and butter?" Prim little Lorie enunciated her words carefully.

"They won't let me go." Marianne rubbed her hand across her nose and snuffled loudly.

Another look of disgust crossed Lorie's face.

"Go where?" Patsy's question this time.

"Home. I thought I could go anytime I wanted to but now they won't let me."

I looked at the diamond and the gold wedding band. "Why don't you call your husband or your family?"

"They won't let me do that either."

"Who is they?"

"*Any*body. *Every*body." She spoke dramatically.

"Well, *they* can't watch you every single minute, can they?" I asked.

"Right. Call when they're not around," Patsy agreed.

The conversation died, dropped dead just like that. Lorie, Marianne, and Carrie stared at us.

Lorie laughed. "There you go again, Darby. They just got here," she spoke in explanation to Marianne. "They don't know."

"What don't we know?" Patsy asked.

"There aren't any pay phones. Cell phones aren't allowed. Neither are fax machines, computers and E-mail, or carrier pigeons," Carrie chanted.

"Well, go someplace else and call," Patsy countered in a stubborn voice.

"They won't let us leave the clinic grounds. They won't let us talk to strangers. They won't let our letters go out uncensored."

Patsy's mouth dropped open. "Holy shit," she whispered.

"But on visitors day," I asked, "then you can talk directly to your family, can't you, Marianne?"

She shook her head, looking fogged and numbed.

"They've got it all wrapped up," Carrie explained. "If they decide it's not in your 'best therapeutic interest' to have visitors or 'outside contact,' then you don't and that is that."

Patsy was starting to sputter. "But they *can't* do that."

"They can and they do," Lorie said. "Pass the butter, please."

"Why are you here?" I asked Marianne.

"Shopping."

"Huh?" Patsy spoke it. I thought it.

"I love to shop. I *live* to shop. I shop all the time and I even buy stuff I don't need. And we can't afford." More tears. "Basically I'm out of control and it's starting to really mess up our lives. It almost got to where we had to put a second mortgage on our house. Isn't that awful? I was doing something that hurt my family. So when I heard about this place, and that they could help me, I couldn't wait to come."

"So why do you want to leave?" Patsy asked. "Are you over it?"

"No. I'm not, but I'm never going to be, staying here. My counselor doesn't know anything about it and she won't find me someone who does. And in group—nobody cares, nobody's interested. Shopping doesn't count as a problem, I guess. So I want to go home." The tears rivuleted down her cheeks.

Patsy reached over to help herself to the salad and bread.

"Should you be doing that, Patsy? If you want to lose weight, I mean. I think you're only supposed to eat what's on your plate." Carrie's voice was helpful and concerned.

"Mind your own beeswax," Patsy said crossly.

"How did you find out about the clinic?" I asked Marianne, one-track mind Darby.

"I went to this meeting at church with my girlfriend. The speaker made it sound so wonderful. She said they helped her lose weight and change her life. She said they could help me too and I believed her. She made it sound magical, wonderful—and it's *not*." She ended on a wail.

"What was her name?" Dogged Darby.

"I don't remember. She was blond and slim and wore really bright colors, and she showed us the clothes she used to wear. They were dark and huge and ugly. It was so exciting."

Sara.

"And then I got *really* excited when she said that if we had insurance it would probably pay for everything. Excited for nothing," Marianne said bitterly.

"See, Darby, I told you so." Carrie was smug.

"What?"

"Nothing much happens and you don't get better here."

Patsy helped herself to more salad and bread. Butter this time too.

"How did *you* find out about the clinic, Carrie?"

She shrugged. "I dunno, my mom did. She's pretty lame though. She'll believe anything. And if she heard it at church she couldn't sign on fast enough. She'd never research it or anything and she didn't come here and look around. She just read a brochure."

"Insurance?"

Carrie nodded. "We don't have this kind of money. I guess it costs like thousands and thousands a month if you pay for it yourself."

We stopped talking as they cleared our table of soup and salad and put out platters of baked chicken and broccoli. Patsy helped herself to some of both, even though Carrie glared at her.

"*What?* It's *only* broccoli and I'm not going to eat the chicken skin. Everyone knows all the calories are in the skin."

"I was thinking of you," Carrie said. "You can't stop until you want to, you know. That's the way it is with drugs too. You have to admit you have a problem and want to change it and—"

"Oh hush up, will you, and let me eat my dinner in peace." Patsy sounded cross again.

"How did *you* find out about the clinic?" I asked Lorie.

"What's it to you, Miss Nosy Face?"

"Just curious," I said innocently. "Why? Is it a big deal?"

She flushed. "I heard about it at a therapy group and I went to a meeting too. It wasn't the same person that Marianne heard though. She was older, very sincere and, well, comforting. She made it sound like no problem was too big or too small for them to help."

"And?" I asked.

"Well, no problem is too big or too small for them to take your money. I don't know about the help. I'm not getting much. None, to be exact."

Patsy had more chicken and broccoli. She was eating feverishly, apparently without enjoyment, and there were beads of sweat on her upper lip.

"Insurance?"

"Yes," Lorie answered.

"You're starting to get boring, aren't you, Darby?" Carrie drawled at me.

"Just one more," I said brightly. "Patsy—"

"A meeting. The bright pretty blond one. Insurance." There was grease on her chin and chicken in her hand. "I came because she said it was a really good program and I would lose weight fast."

Nobody said anything. What was there to say?

"What am I going to do?" Marianne whimpered.

"Wait until your insurance runs out. They'll kick you out then, that's for sure." Carrie, now in a practical and soothing tone.

"That won't be for a while. It's pretty good insurance."

We didn't have anything to say to that either.

CHAPTER 49

After lunch Carrie walked me around the rest of the grounds and accommodations, fifteen cottages with four beds each and a new building housing forty, for a hundred-patient capacity.

"Sometimes more even. They'll cram two beds in the single rooms if they have the people."

"Do they have sufficient counselors and staff to handle that?"

Carrie shrugged. "Like they care. They want the place full, that's top priority. I heard two counselors talking one day. One of them—she's nice, I kinda like her—said she thought she was going to be leading exercise programs and walks and stuff—she was a PE teacher before—but they asked her to be a counselor instead when someone else they hired didn't show.

"And the other one said he took a year of psychology before he dropped out of school. And the first one said she didn't feel right about being a counselor, not having any training or anything. And the other one said that since they paid counselors better than exercise leaders, she might just as well take the money and be happy. And—"

"They said this in *front* of you?" My voice was as surprised as I was.

Carrie snickered. "Oh *sure*. No." She shook her head. "They were talking out in the gardens and I was eavesdropping. I know a lot about what goes on around here but not because anyone tells me or it's in the brochures." She laughed at that thought. "Those brochures are just packs of lies. Where to now?"

We were in front of the main building in the parking lot. The front gates under the archway, the only way in or out, were closed.

"Are these gates always closed? They were open when I arrived. I thought maybe they were open during the day."

Carrie shook her head. "Oh no." She spoke serenely. "What! And risk losing a patient long before their insurance runs out? I think not. They only open them if they expect someone or it's visiting hours. They have a little gatehouse too—see, there behind the trees?—where they can post someone."

"Is that what they do, keep people here until their insurance runs out?" I stared at the gatehouse. It seemed somehow sinister to me.

"I can't prove anything, if that's what you mean." Carrie spiked her fingers through her hair. "It's just that when you see the same thing over and over you think that maybe it's not a coincidence, it's a policy. I guess they figure insurance companies expect you to stay as long as you can while they're paying, so they won't question it. You could stay longer if you wanted and pay for it yourself, but I don't think anyone ever has. I mean, why pay for help you aren't getting? Who's gonna be that dumb with their own money? Want to go inside the main building?"

"Doesn't anyone ever complain?"

"Sure." Cheerful as ever. "And Saunders gets all serious and thoughtful and says oh yes, they are getting help but they are in denial or rebellion, and that is very common and not to worry. So—"

"So?"

"So nobody does; nobody believes the patients; nothing changes. C'mon." She started for the main building. "You saw this already." Carrie waved at the entry area. A central corridor led out from the front lobby to the rear of the building. She headed in that direction and I followed, passing closed doors all along the length of the hall.

"This is Dr. Saunders's office and these are two sitting or 'interview' rooms. The housekeeper has an office here and the staff nurse and the facility coordinator."

"What is a facility coordinator?"

"Don't have a clue. We hardly ever see her anyway."

By now we had reached the far side of the building. Here the hall turned left; there was also an exit from the building, the door that I had used when I came for the interview with Saunders. We turned left and walked down the hall of the new wing, the outer wall of the building on one side, office doors on the other.

"The counselors have offices along here."

The doors had metal brackets and cards with handwritten names were slotted into the brackets. Except for a discreet murmur behind one door all was silence. Carrie started up a stairway at the end of the wing.

"This whole upstairs area is group meetings. There are eight rooms that hold ten or twelve people. Add in the two interview rooms downstairs and theoretically you could have everyone in a group at the same time." Her voice was quiet, almost respectful.

I assumed the circumspection had to do with being in the administration building rather than with a demeanor and attitude that came naturally to her. As far as I could tell none of these rooms was in use either. Carrie pushed open a door and we looked into a pleasant room painted in pale yellow with a cream ceiling and woodwork. Sofas and chairs were grouped around a glass table on an Oriental rug. A small refrigerator and a counter with a coffeepot and mugs were against one wall. There were landscapes on the walls and plants scattered about.

"They're all like this."

"When are the group meetings?"

"Midmorning, midafternoon, and evening. The number depends on how many people sign up."

"You decide if you're going to go?"

"Yeah. Pretty much. You're supposed to go to two a week but they don't check up on that carefully."

"And anyone can go to any meeting?"

"Yeah."

"Do they have specific meetings for drug dependency or alcohol or food or—"

"No. Not for anything. That's why Marianne was so upset. I told you, the meetings are just about people blabbing on and on about their feelings, it's about passing time." She shivered. "I'm going outside. I like it better in the sunshine and fresh air. Coming?"

I followed, watching as she practically threw herself down the stairs and out the door. She was standing on the lawn and taking deep breaths when I caught up to her.

"I guess everything's locked up at night," I said casually.

"What do you mean?"

"The cottages, the building, everything?" The building was my focus. I'd already checked for locks on the cottage doors. There were none, not even in the bathroom.

"Oh no, they're not big on privacy here, at least not for us. Our cottages don't lock, nothing does. Not the bathrooms or anything. And they don't lock the main building either. I mean, who cares? What's to steal? No one's around at night but you can go to the nurse's if you need to."

"She's there at night?"

"Oh please, of course not. Like they care. Her office is the one place that's locked, I guess she's got drugs and stuff, but at night she puts out a basket and a notebook. The basket has little packages, you know, like two aspirin or Pepto-Bismol or a Band-Aid. You're supposed to sign the notebook for what you take."

"Are there curfews? Do you have to go to bed or get up at a certain time?"

"You have to get up by nine if you want breakfast."

"That's it?"

She nodded. "They leave coffee, tea, and fruit juice out until ten P.M. in the Main Hall. You can go there and sit and visit or read, whatever you want until ten."

"Does Saunders design a therapy program for you?"

She shrugged. "That's not what I'd call it. You'll be assigned a counselor who will at least learn your name and maybe occasionally talk to you. They like you to play sports and stuff but no one checks on you. And they *really* encourage you to have mud baths, herbal wraps, massages, and all that kind of stuff. You can even get your hair and nails done. And facials, facial peels, all kinds of shit."

"Let me guess," I said dryly. "Separate billing on those items?"

She grinned. "You got it. They say it's to assist in the 'reevaluation and rebuilding of patient esteem' but really it's to make them a ton of money. Supposedly Dr. Saunders 'evaluates each case and prescribes as necessary' but really it's wide open. You can get your hair or nails done every day if you want, though I guess you can't have facial peels too often or your skin comes off or something. So, I saw your racket. Wanna play tennis?"

"Sure. I'm really lousy though."

She laughed happily.

"That's the truth, not modesty."

"Good. Wanna play for money? Like for a million dollars?"

So we played for a million dollars and I lost. I lost at double or nothing too. Twice. And then we had a lemonade and a shower and put on clean shorts for dinner. It was almost like resort life. Except for the closed gates and iron bars and the odd, sometimes unhappy, assortment of people.

The crickets sang in wild summer abandon and I swore under my breath as I swatted, swung, flailed at, and smashed mosquitoes. And thought longingly of the mosquito repellent in the medicine cabinet at home. I was moving quickly but it was taking me longer than I thought to make my way around the far side of the lake. The dusk was deep and heavy now, like an opaque curtain around me. I hoped to reach Saunders's house before darkness fell completely and I into it.

My earlier plan had been to walk around the pond during daylight hours, check out the house at a near but discreet distance, then come back at night. Then I had seen the car—Sara's?—winding down the narrow road that led to his home. The driver was a woman. At that distance and in the fading light it was impossible to say more. I changed my mind. You know what they say about the best-laid plans.

On to Plan B. I swatted at a mosquito. So far the score was Darby—3, Mosquitoes—49. The annoying thing was that I hadn't quite gotten around to a Plan B. So it was pretty much like a lot of my plans, I guess. Wing it. I pulled away from the pond near a narrow path that led up to the house, hoping desperately that the mosquito population would thin out as I got away from the water.

You know what they say about hope.

The late-spring air was pleasantly cool with a temperamental breeze that came and went and changed directions. Lights flickered on in Saunders's house and my pulse and interest quickened. Nothing like an evening of spring spying to perk your spirits up. I moved around the house quickly and heard nothing. The windows, alas, were closed. What was the matter with them, anyway? It was spring, too early to shut the house up and turn the a/c on. I paused in the back, under the kitchen windows I thought, and heard a trill of laughter. Nothing more, though I lurked for a while.

And around again to the front and the screened-in porch. The porch was about three foot off the ground and large bushes had been planted there to hide the latticework. I snuggled in amongst them and made myself as small and cozy as possible. The mosquitoes, I noted, had not abated. I was everyone's favorite dish.

As I waited I mentally relandscaped my yard with things like holly and pyracantha close to the house so that lurkers and prowlers like me couldn't snuggle up to the porch on lovely spring evenings. I felt better about my landscaping when I finished but not about the mosquitoes. Score now: Darby—12, Mosquitoes—104. Of course the home team always has the edge. I heard a door slam inside and a trill of laughter that sounded very close.

Did Sara trill when she laughed? Maybe with Saunders. I tried to isolate voices and words. Nothing. Well, nothing except the coos of doves, the chirping of crickets, and the whining drone of mosquitoes. The big ones licked their bloodstained lips and drooled too, I'm almost positive.

"Walker, it's beautiful out here. Let's sit on the porch for a while. I love watching the stars come out."

Dulcet tones. Sweet voice. Enchanting, lilting, persuasive. And definitely Sara. I hunkered down, trying to ignore the rock poking me in the butt. Even the blood loss was worth it now. I tell myself this kind of thing to keep my spirits up.

"What's your pleasure, my dear, here in the heart of wine country—a sauvignon blanc, chardonnay, champagne?"

"Oh, champagne! Let's celebrate our good fortune and our business, an evening together and—"

"And the sweetness of love." Saunders sounded kind of dopey and besotted.

I heard the soft pop of a cork and then the tinkle and clink of glasses. I licked my lips, immediately thirsty, parched, desperate for a cool sip of something. God, I hate it that I'm so suggestible. I licked up a mosquito.

Eeewww.

It took all I had not to gag and spit it out. And now I was even more desperate for a drink. I fought back the urge to throw up and thought of the lovely tall glasses of homemade lemonade at lunch. And of the mosquito flapping its frantic little wings inside me and— I opened my mouth slightly and made pushing movements with my tongue. It didn't help. In the background I could hear voices. (I didn't get an A+ in Snooping 101.) I forced myself to stop being such a big baby and pay attention.

"And your success this week?" Saunders's voice.

"Wonderful! Better than ever I imagined. People are so gullible, Walker. Promise them pie in the sky, tell them they don't have to pay for it—their insurance company will—and they can't wait to pull their chairs up to the table and stuff their greedy little faces full. If all the other recruiters are doing as well as I, then I think we can definitely open another clinic as soon as this fall. Wouldn't that be wonderful!"

"One step at a time." His voice was measured and slow. Glasses clinked again. "The others are good but not like you. But we *are* moving forward, I am looking at yet another site."

Sara laughed. I had never heard her sound so happy, so abandoned.

"This business with your husband worries me."

"Jed?" Her voice was scornful. "He is nothing, an irritation, no more. And I find him quite useful. It gives me a reason to disappear, to travel, to be secretive." Her statement had started out strongly but ended on a doubtful note. Saunders picked up on it too.

"What is it, Sara?"

"Hmmm. Oh. Nothing, nothing, I'm sure."

"Tell me." Almost a command.

"Sometimes I wonder if he suspects or knows what is going on, what I am doing. Lately . . . some things he said . . . the way he acted . . . I'm not sure. But it doesn't matter, I have planned for that too."

"I wish you would get a divorce and be done with him."

"All in good time. It's not that simple, you see. Jed's a cop and he has the tenacity and focus of a bloodhound. If he suspects something, he won't leave it alone until he finds out. If he finds out, he won't let it go until he stops it. Not it, me. I have more control over him married than I would divorced."

"At least get rid of the private investigator."

Sara laughed. "Why? She is harmless. That stupid girl believes everything I say. She thinks Jed is dangerous to me, that he is a threat to my life. She and the cops both." Sara made an insolent, dismissing sound. "She is the perfect witness, a disinterested third party who can testify to my abusive situation and husband. She is part of my plan."

I tried not to let it get to me, but it did. Okay, briefly my rage drowned out the sounds of the doves, the crickets, even the mosquitoes. *Harmless. That stupid girl. Believes everything I say.* And then it fell into place with a breathtaking beauty and simplicity.

"Sara—"

"Don't worry, Walker. I can control Jed and the investigator both. Leave it to me. More champagne, please!"

Clinking sounds. Rustling sounds. Sighing sounds.

"Walker!" A giggle. "*Stop* that. Suppose someone sees."

"Who? How? Come here, my dear. You have too many clothes on."

No! Talk about adding insult to injury. They were going to make love on the porch? With me as an unwilling and captive audience! *Jeez. Spare me.*

"Oww!" The small sound of a slap. "That damned mosquito got me. Let's go inside."

Chairs scraped back. Glasses and a bottle clinked together. Another giggle. And a chuckle. The door opened and closed. I heard the dead bolt shoot home.

The stars would have to come up without Sara tonight. I crawled out from under the bushes and struggled into an upright position. Cramped and grumpy—that was me. *Damn.* My foot was asleep. The lights in the front of the house went off. Good. It was bedtime and the bedrooms were in the back. I hobbled off in the direction of the driveway. Jogged away from the house when my foot finally woke up.

But not back to the cottage. To the main building. *No rest for the weary.* Saunders was very much occupied.

And "the harmless, stupid girl" was on the prowl.

CHAPTER 50

Saunders's office was not only locked, it was securely dead-bolted. I reviewed the layout in my mind—the adjoining interview room. It was locked as well but with a cheap lock, the kind you can easily pop—which I did, then closed and locked it behind me, slipped across the room to the interoffice door. Open. People are too trusting.

I thought of Sara and Saunders. Not that trusting was an adjective that sprang to my mind for them. The office was very dark, shades and curtains both. I looked longingly at the light but didn't risk it. A small desk light would have to do. A quick sweep revealed several desks, file cabinets, and a computer. Also phone machine, fax, and copier. All interesting items.

It was going to be a long night.

I started with the desks.

It took me three hours. I could have gotten more but I didn't dare push my luck much longer. It was well after midnight. Pumpkin time. And I had a lot. I had copied computer files and paper files, even photographs. I yawned and stretched and looked around, making sure everything was off, was as I had found it. Looking good, I thought, as I stuffed another yawn. I dragged my eyes away from the fax machine. It would be so quick and easy to fax this. Maybe they never looked at their fax log? By the time they got their phone bill I would be long gone, so why not?

I could see Joe's frown, hear the admonition in his voice. *Play it safe, Kat. Don't take stupid chances.* So I didn't. I checked the room one more time and then slipped out the way I had come in, out into the welcoming darkness. The cottages were lit by small lights over the doors. I headed not for the cottage I now called home but for the forested spot on the back edge of the property abutting the road.

And I wondered if bugs could drive a person mad and thought they probably could. It was cooler under the trees and damper. I felt the breeze on my face and was grateful. It seemed to push the mosquitoes away. Carrie had said there was no security on the grounds and I had seen none. Nor had I seen people—patients or staff. I was, apparently, the only one with a late-night/early-morning agenda. I put a call through to Joe's report-in number and left a quick but thorough overview of what I had seen, heard, and found. I requested an immediate pickup and checked for messages. There were none. I left the loot and, yawning again, headed back to the cottage. To bed. To a mosquito-free environment.

Carrie was snoring slightly, peacefully, as I pulled off my clothes, slid into bed, and closed my eyes. They popped right open again. Sleep was around the corner, across the block, and down the road a piece, as Alma would say. All the information I had discovered marched across my mind, spewed out and around like uncontrolled ticker tape.

The Sunflower Clinic was a for-profit business venture. The brochures presented one picture, an idyllic environment for optimal health and recovery. Patients were promised an environment of caring, compassion, and trust; a special assessment of individual problems and needs; a treatment team consisting of a physician, a psychologist, a nurse, counselors, a dietician, clergy, a physical therapist, and a recreational activities counselor; organized treatment and a schedule including work, group therapy, individual counseling, peer interaction, study/meditation/journal-writing time, and lectures. That was the promise.

What had I found so far?

I wondered if Saunders was a medical doctor—I had seen no diplomas on his wall, had I? I squinted my eyes together in recollection. There was one wall with photographs, pictures, something—I couldn't tell in the poor light. So I wasn't sure about the doctor. Solid assessment of patient needs? I guess that was the ten-minute interview and cup of tea with Saunders. Psychologist, nurse, trained counselors, dietician, clergy, and physical therapist? I had yet to hear of them, never mind meet them. Organized treatment? Ditto.

"Why . . . balloon . . . ice cream . . . circus leaving town. No! No!"

Carrie was talking in her sleep. Her arms and legs thrashed around, her voice was anxious. She half started to get up, then fell back into bed with a sigh and quieted. I listened to the sounds of her uneven breathing, the sighs. I remembered her lying with her back to me, tense and unhappy when the person she called the Bitch came to fetch me, her talking of eating bugs and losing hope and heart.

People are so greedy and gullible. Sara had laughed when she said that. Greedy for health, for peace, for an end to the destruction and disorder in a life. Greedy, I thought, was the wrong word. Gullible, maybe. Wishful and hopeful, definitely.

Greedy was the word for the clinic. And for the recruiters; all were paid and paid well. Fees had ranged from five hundred to twenty-five hundred dollars. Per head. That was how patients were designated. Patients were recruited solely on the basis of insurance coverage, not need or condition. They were diagnosed on the same basis, not medical assessment but an evaluation of maximum insurance coverage and payment. And they were not discharged until that coverage was exhausted, no matter what the patient desired, requested, or demanded.

Carrie tossed about in her bed and muttered again but I couldn't understand the words. Her voice was dead and toneless. Unhappy? Without hope?

I had copied the list of recruiters, the plans for the next two clinics. And the applications of two dozen of the staff, where the lack of professional qualifications and degrees was breathtaking. The hiring policy? *Can you walk? Talk? Can you follow orders and keep your mouth shut when we tell you to? You're hired.*

Not that I'm cynical, I thought as I moved restlessly in my narrow bed. God, it was small. I hadn't slept in a single bed since I was a child. All the people who were here came because they needed help and were committed to change. But how much hope and determination did they have? How much discouragement would keep them where they were? Or make it worse.

Hope was not a bottomless well.

"No!" Carrie cried out. "Not that, not *that*."

The morning sunshine woke me up. And then there was Carrie's voice.

"Hey, sleepyhead, you getting up? What time did you go to bed anyway? And where were you?"

"I went for a walk."

"*No*. Really? Why?"

"I like to look at the stars."

She looked at me dubiously.

I took a deep breath. "I'm not really used to being around people so much. I had to get away, to be by myself and think about things. To be alone."

"Oh." Carrie smiled and nodded. "Oh sure. I get that. How was it?"

"Okay." I sat up and looked at my bare arms. "Except for the mosquitoes."

She laughed. "You want me to wait for you or just go on over to breakfast? Ten minutes? Can you be ready in ten minutes? C'mon."

"Did you know you talk in your sleep?" I asked as I pulled on clean clothes after my quick shower.

"Yeah. Do I say anything interesting?"

"I couldn't understand what you said."

"No? Well, why should that be any different?" She hit the wall with her fist.

"Why are you mad?"

"If I can't understand myself, how am I going to get anywhere? You need a map, don't you?"

A map? I tried to think how to answer that.

"What are you going to have for breakfast?" Mad was gone, her voice sunshiny and light.

Maps, breakfast—what was going on here?

"Anything baked is really good. Mmmmm. There's a cook and a baker and you know what's funny? They're both really skinny. Isn't that odd? Maybe it's no fun to eat what you cook. Do you think I should change my hair color to orange or purple? I'm pretty tired of turquoise."

"I'm the wrong person to ask. Wasn't it pink yesterday? . . . What did you mean about a map?"

"Why are you wrong?"

"I would like your natural color best. This way it's as though you're trying to shock people, not just be beautiful. The map?"

"Beautiful? What do you mean? Do you think I'm beautiful?"

"I don't *think* so, no. I *know* you are. About the map?"

She swallowed hard and then shook herself like a puppy. "Well, duh," she said, flashing me a bored and superior look as we walked out the door and over to the Main Hall. "A map shows you where you are and then you pick out where you want to go and it shows you how to get there. There might be lots of stuff you need to know but wouldn't unless you read the map. Like, you know—icy when wet, road closed in winter, watch out for falling rocks, winding road, one-way street, unimproved surface. This is stuff you need to know."

I nodded.

"So I know where I am—Fucked-Up City—and I know where I want to go—Happy Valley—but I don't know how to get there because I don't have a map. Got it?" She sounded mad again.

"Got it."

"*Finally.*"

"And you're mad because you thought they'd give you a map here?"

She nodded. "Marianne thought so too. And Lorie. Patsy. That's why we all came. Maybe not everyone wants to get to Happy Valley but we all want to get somewhere. Somewhere real different from where we are."

Lorie wandered over in our direction, her mouth slightly tipped up at the edges—which I took to be a smile.

"Look." Carrie spat her words out rapidly as Lorie approached. "I'm sorry if I sounded mad at you. I'm not, not at all. You seem nice, really nice. I'm just mad and sometimes—"

"Hi," Lorie said in a depressed tone.

"Hi," we chorused back.

"Breakfast is buffet unless you're on a special diet," Carrie explained. We walked past Patsy, who was eating waffles and looking guilty.

"See." Carrie's voice was sad. "It's not her fault, she needs a map."

"What *are* you talking about?" Lorie asked.

We neither of us answered. I helped myself to a muffin and a slice of melon. There was coffee and juice on the tables, I noticed. I sat at a table with two other people.

"Hi, my name is Darby," I said.

"We know," a woman responded without interest.

"I'm new here."

"We know." She played with the jelly on her toast, making patterns and destroying them.

"What do you do here all day?" I asked.

"I'm going to get my hair and nails done."

"Tennis."

"Read and sleep."

"What about therapy and lectures and learning stuff and getting better?"

"Good luck." The woman stood. "You're on your own here. No one else cares."

Outside a horn sounded in a long, strident blast. And then shouts. The Main Hall emptied in a heartbeat, a clatter of dishes, and a stampede of feet. I followed. Ambulance chasing? Had it come to that?

A crowd had gathered on the lawn next to the drive. A panel truck was stopped there and the commotion was in the center of the crowd. I ran too.

Marianne.

"You can't do this, you can't. I want to go home. You can't keep me here against my will. It's against the law. It's not fair, you can't . . . you can't . . . you can't . . ."

Nurse, the bitch one, held grimly on to one arm and two of the counselors were attached like limpets to the other. They were trying to pull her away from the truck and she was fighting them hard. There was little movement in either direction. The Bitch started to twist Marianne's arm back, to hurt her. Marianne stepped forward to ease the pressure and the Bitch twisted again.

The dance continued.

Dr. Saunders walked calmly across the lawn toward Marianne. Silence fell around him as he approached until only the sounds of Marianne's sobs could be heard.

"What is the matter, my dear?"

"I . . . want . . . to . . . go . . . home." Her hair was wild and tears and snot dribbled down her face.

"Well, then." He smiled at her. "You shall. Come, let us arrange it." He held out his hand.

She stared at it, at him for a long time. "Really? You promise?"

"Really." He smiled at her. "I promise." He reached out for her hand, tucked it under his elbow—as though they were at the opera or ballet—and escorted her into the main house.

The small crowd moved nervously. A man in white materialized suddenly and began throwing bags in the panel truck. *SWEDISH LAUNDRY,* the faded lettering on the truck informed us. Swedish laundry? I'd heard of French and Chinese but Swedish? Doors slammed, the truck started, spurted off leaving us choking in exhaust.

"What happened?" I asked anybody.

"She tried to run off."

"Almost made it too."

"How'd they catch her?" someone asked. But no one answered.

"Will they let her go home now?"

My question. No one answered that one either. We watched as Marianne and Saunders disappeared into the clinic.

CHAPTER 51

G*reen light! Go! Accelerate! Fly!*

That's how she felt all the time now. *Lift off! Soar!* It exasperated her that Walker wanted to move so slowly, be so cautious. She had tried to move slowly, be careful. She had tried to see his point of view. Build slowly. Be sure of what you have before you move on. Center. Anchor. She sighed inwardly. Her common sense told her he was right, that that was the correct approach. Caution. Yellow light.

Oh, but she had been doing that her whole life. Now she wanted to forget caution, to speed, to go full-tilt boogie for the brass ring and success. But Walker knew what he was doing. He had more experience here than she did—she reminded herself of that.

And she saw how much they had already achieved. One clinic, soon two, even three—who knew where the end was, how far they could go? Who knew?

There were wild cards though, and they made her nervous. She had no one to talk to about this. Not even Walker. Jed? What was going on there? He had seemed so predictable once. She had always known what he would do even before he did it. Always—except in sex. She shivered. Then she had never known. Then he was unpredictable. It had made her wild with excitement, not knowing, not expecting . . .

She felt a tingling in her fingertips, in her skin. It still made her wild. Just the thought of it, of him. She wished they could be in an absolutely dark room. Naked. She didn't want to see his face or talk to him. She didn't want a relationship, just the purity of sex and passion, of visiting the unknown and finding your way back. Maybe that was part of the excitement, that little sliver of fear that warned you that the unknown was dangerous territory, that not everyone came back.

Naked. Bodies, minds, and emotions naked, that's how she felt about Jed still. But she didn't love him. It was a freedom, she thought. Loving tied you down. Passion left you free—as long as you didn't become a slave to it. Jed loved her still. That's why she couldn't get rid of him.

That's why he was dangerous.

She wondered if he knew he was dangerous. Probably not. Of course, dangerous people often didn't know, which made them even more dangerous and sometimes reckless. Funny that love should be a danger. You would think that it would be the other way around. Love should protect you, not endanger you. But love made you vulnerable, made you afraid of loss. Love even led people to destroy what they couldn't have and desperately wanted.

Jed was very dangerous.

She shivered again. She hadn't seen this coming, not this, she thought. Odd. She probably should have. And she wondered if she could have planned better if she'd understood and foreseen, if . . . Too many ifs. Life always had ifs, there was no way of getting around that. All you could do was deal with what you had, what was before you.

With Jed.

With Walker.

With the investigator.

She was annoyed with that. Very much so. She had thought she had that one all sewn up. At least the woman wasn't dangerous, not like Jed. The investigator wanted people to play the game her way but if they didn't? She left, she quit. Not like Jed, who got mad, who stayed around and interfered, who was a fucking cop twenty-four hours a day and thought everyone should be a twenty-four-hour-a-day do-gooder and—

She caught herself, made herself stop, breathe deeply. She tried to empty her mind of Jed. Her body couldn't have him, her mind didn't want him. How ironic. Her smile twisted. Too bad she couldn't turn it around. Okay, forget Jed. For now. She was dealing with it, with things. It would be all right.

The private investigator—was she a problem? Sara took a deep breath and in her mind she played out all the scenarios. A victimized woman hiring someone to help. A dead friend and a murder attempt. Jed following her. No, not following, stalking. The break-in at her place. The incident at Belinda's. The physical abuse. She smiled. That was so perfect. Now everyone could see and would believe. Everyone. Belinda, the cops, the investigator. She was set. The stage was set.

No. The investigator wasn't a problem. She would have preferred to keep her around, doing a few things here and there. Available. On call. She would have preferred it if she hadn't quit, but it was all right. No matter. She could work with things this way. It would be fine.

No, she wasn't a problem. She certainly wasn't dangerous.

Just Jed. Jed was the danger. How she wished you could cleanly sever one part of your life from the rest. She and Jed had had no children, only a house. It should have been so simple. She would go her way and Jed would go his. Maybe they would even smile and shake hands. That was a nice touch. And say a few polite and meaningless words. *Good luck. Best wishes.* That kind of thing. That was perfect.

If only Jed would do that, would let go. If he would just accept that the past was over. But he wouldn't . . . In her mind she visualized a beautiful shining, gleaming knife with an edge made sharp and deadly. She saw the knife flash down, slash through everything that Jed had used to bind her to him. No, not just a knife, a machete. Something strong. And wicked. Something beautiful. It could be used for good or evil. It could be used to cut away the past. To free you.

She sighed, feeling the tingling in her fingers again. The machete, yes. And then her beautiful new life.

CHAPTER 52

Day three . . . or four.

It was starting to blur, which was frightening to me. I called Joe at least once a day, talked to him whenever possible, and sent out reports. Still, I felt I had lost touch with the outside world. Reality had become what I lived every day. The Sunshine Clinic. Before, it had been a job. This was also frightening to me.

There were no newspapers or magazines though you could read all the junk you wanted. Romances were very popular. And bad mysteries. Happy endings play well in an institution. Television news, reporting or analysis, was also banned but you could watch a steady diet of talk shows, soap operas, and sitcoms if you chose. And movies. So this became reality too.

And the fear settled in deeper.

Joe tried to talk me out of it, out of there. "We have enough to move, Kat. Bag it. Give me a time, I'm there. We're gone."

"Soon," I told him. "Very soon." Marianne was on my mind.

She was not in her cottage and we had seen no one come for her. Theoretically it was possible that someone had picked her up in the dead of night and no one noticed but it seemed highly improbable.

No one spoke about her. It was eerie.

Well, no one but me. "Did they send her home?"

Carrie shrugged.

"Well, would they, do you think?"

"They don't usually, not if she still has insurance."

"If she's here, where would she be?"

The shrug again.

The staff had two versions: they didn't know or she had gone home. This was supposed to be a twentieth-century health clinic but it was feeling more and more like a nineteenth-century Gothic novel.

I had kept my eyes open and seen nothing. Not even after the fuss died down, which had taken a day or two. My reports to Joe were similar reports of nothing. No counseling, no therapy program, no physical therapy or dietary program. No nothing. My counselor, a balding, paunchy, ineffectual little man, had introduced himself to me and said I could talk to him whenever I wanted. "My door is always open, Derby," were his exact words.

I didn't knock on it. Or bother to tell him my name. Or go to group therapy beyond what I needed to report back. Nobody cared. I got a little better at tennis and a lot more in million-dollar debt to Carrie. Sara left and hadn't returned. Saunders was completely out of sight.

I was worried about Marianne. And about Carrie. And me. I felt like I was going nuts, only it wasn't just an expression.

Bad news.

How much more is a trillion than a billion?"

"I don't know."

"Isn't that the kind of thing we're supposed to learn in school?"

"Mmmm."

"Darby?"

"I guess. It's the kind of thing that didn't stay with me. Ask someone in the Defense Department. They spend that kind of money."

"I think you owe me a trillion dollars now. What are you staring at?" She swung the tennis racket vigorously, nearly taking out a hapless bee.

"The Annex. Does it have three floors?"

"I don't think so."

"Patients live on the first and second floors?"

"Yeah. Why?"

"Let's go visit someone. Who do we know in the Annex?"

"What's with you, Darby? Hey, wait up."

"Pick up your feet." I turned and grinned at Carrie. "C'mon, let's check out the view from the second floor. Who knows? Maybe we'd rather live there than a cottage."

"No way."

We entered at the front. A long corridor ran the length of the building with rooms off either side and a central lobby. There were elevators in the lobby and stairways at either end of the building. I took the stairs two at a time. The main staircase funneled you out into the light, airy living quarters of the second floor. A small, dark staircase continued up to the third floor or attic.

I walked down the second-floor hall to the lobby area and out onto the balcony. "Look, you can see the vineyards and gardens and hills. Hey, great view of the geyser."

"You can see all that from the ground. What's the matter with you, Darby, you nuts?" She looked at me sideways, biting her tongue.

"News flash!" I said.

We both laughed.

"Do you want to take the elevator down?" I asked. And we rode it down.

"What was that all about?"

I shrugged. "Just curious."

We walked outside in the general direction of the cottage. "You're just curious a lot, aren't you? You're always looking around and walking at night and poking your nose into stuff."

I smiled. "Aren't you curious?"

"You didn't answer my question."

"I get bored easily, I guess. I don't like TV and there's not a lot to do. Want to go swimming?"

"You keep changing the subject."

"Fine." I sighed. "I am an undercover agent for the IRS. To be frank, there were a few too many 'corporate lunches' deducted last year. So here I am, daring Darby, the darling of the IRS, making *your* tax dollars work."

She giggled.

I frowned. "Uh-oh, now that I told you, I should kill you."

She giggled again.

"Still, if you promise not to tell?"

"I promise." She held up her hand like a little kid. "Cross my heart and hope to die."

"Okay, want to go swimming?"

I had, I figured, a few hours to innocently kill. Then it was time to sneak and snoop. People around here didn't like to miss meals—the bell rang and they flocked in in a Pavlovian way—so I figured I'd sneak and snoop at lunchtime.

The bell rang and I was in a locked stall in a bathroom of the Annex waiting for quiet, empty sounds in the building around me. I made myself count to fifty five times and then I slid out the door, through the lobby, and up the staircase to the second floor and then to the third. I held my breath, hoping the door was unlocked. As it was. I slid through that too, letting it shut quietly behind me.

It was much hotter up here, no air-conditioning, and it had certainly not been built as living quarters. The small, cramped rooms were used for storage—furniture, pictures, blankets, pillows, and linens. Nothing was locked. Of course, nothing was out of the way either.

I noticed the sound first. Voices, but not live ones. Television? I turned the knob gently and pushed open the door. A twin bed with a person, a small bedside table, a television on a stand—that was it.

The woman lay half propped up on pillows, eyes on the TV screen. Her face was as vacant as a parking lot on Christmas Day, her eyes empty mud puddles.

"Hello." I spoke softly.

Her lips moved but no sound came out. Her eyes never left the television. I placed myself between the TV and her and tried another hello, this time a little louder, more lively in tone. Her eyes stared for the longest time at my midsection, where the TV should have been, and then traveled up to my face. Her lips moved soundlessly again. She was drugged to the eyeballs, out in the ozone, and definitely under control.

I moved across the room, holding her eyes with mine, and sat down on the bed. "Hello, Marianne, how are you?" I touched her hand.

Her eyes seemed to move around in the vacant lot of her face like small, wild, trapped things. Afraid. "You're . . . not . . . the . . . nurse."

"No, I'm a friend from outside."

It took her a long time to process the words, untangle the concepts. "Outside?"

"Yes."

She blinked her eyes, dark, muddy ugly puddles without life or spark. "I . . . want . . . to . . . go . . . home."

"I know, I'm trying."

"Cotton . . . candy . . . no . . . more." She spoke, not as though it was difficult to say the words but as though she could barely locate them, then barely decide which were the best ones, the most useful ones, and pull them out.

And, after all that effort, I couldn't understand. "Cotton candy?"

"In . . . my . . . mind . . . no . . . more." Fingers gripped mine. Strong and sure and frantic.

"Drugs? No more drugs?"

"No . . . more."

My hand hurt in her grip. I didn't know how to answer her and I wouldn't make promises I couldn't keep.

"Did you know that Jamie was having an affair?"

"Jamie?"

"Not really an affair. Two or three. He has a girl in every city, I understand. He promised at least one of them marriage. And yet you say I have no right to interfere and tell Tory the truth?"

"I can't believe it. Jamie? He's such a nice guy."

"Guys who are jerks often are. Real charmers."

"No. Jamie would never do this, not to Tory. He loves her."

The grip on my fingers slackened. The eyes got muddier. Marianne blinked at me, then tried to struggle into a sitting position. "Go . . . home . . ."

"And she would never believe this about Jamie. It would kill her."

Marianne struggled to push the covers back, moving as though she were imprisoned in Jell-O, frozen in aspic.

"Help . . . me . . ."

I reached for her.

"These are all lies. You're jealous and—"

"Well, well."

The ugly stridency of the voice cut through the semihysterical slosh of the soap opera. I whirled around.

Nurse—the Bitch—stared at me with her tight-lipped, ugly little smile. "And what would you be doing here?" she asked conversationally.

I took a deep breath and stood, dignified and solemn. "I am visiting Marianne, my client."

"Client?" The sarcasm was as thick and gooey as fudge.

"Client, yes. I am her new counselor and I have come to visit her and see how I can help." Another deep breath. "Help comes in many ways, you know, not just physical attention for the body but—"

"Put a sock in it!" she snarled, and stepped toward me.

I staggered under the sudden weight of Marianne who had somehow pulled herself out of bed and then fallen on me trying to stand on her own, or perhaps propel herself forward.

Nurse refocused her attention and viciousness, making Marianne the new target. We shuffled forward, Marianne and I, I now a pawn in a game that I had started but could not control.

Nurse lunged for Marianne and gave her a cruel shove that sent her sprawling across the bed. The mewling sounds of a baby or a kitten or something nonhuman filled my ears. Nurse reached into her pocket and pulled out a case. I stepped protectively in front of Marianne.

Someone screamed on TV and then started sobbing. A hypodermic needle advanced on me. And suddenly all I could see was the evil eyes of the woman and the metallic gleam of the needle. It was like being caught in a low-budget horror movie.

"Move," she snarled at me.

"Oh God, Jamie, how could you do this to me?" Tory cried out in agony. "How, how, how?"

I moved, watched in dull horror as she whipped up Marianne's nightgown and viciously plunged the needle into her buttock. The mewling sounds turned into a kind of high keening, then died off in moans and finally silence. I felt like a traitor. I could not have helped Marianne by acting in any other way, but still . . .

The nurse looked from me to Marianne's half-exposed body and laughed in a short ugly burst.

"So you're a counselor? You like to help people, do you? There are many ways to help someone, are there?" The words and tone were brutal. "Well, then, help me with her."

I made no move until the hypodermic needle was put away.

Roughly she picked up Marianne's legs and, twisting her body, tossed her legs down again. Gently I straightened the unconscious woman, pulled the nightclothes down and the covers up. I pushed the hair off her face and stroked her cheek. I had brought her hope and failed; it was now worse than before.

The nurse laughed in short, spitting coughs. "You're coming with me."

And of course I was.

My, my." Dr. Saunders smiled at me.

I started to relax, to open like a flower in the sun until I remembered. It was the same smile that I had seen when Saunders walked across the lawn to Marianne, took her hand, tucked it under his arm and escorted her off.

And look what had happened to her.

My smile froze. I tucked my hands in my pockets. Better there than under his elbow.

"I caught her in—" An ugly stream of vituperation started spewing out of the nurse.

"Yes. Thank you, nurse, that will do."

"But doctor—"

"Thank you." He nodded curtly and in clear dismissal.

"Please sit down." He indicated a chair as he sat, not behind his desk but in a chair not far from me. "And tell me what happened."

It was phrased courteously, as a request not as a demand, and he waited politely for me to gather my thoughts and begin.

Which I did, but with my guard up. It was too easy to forget around here, to be lulled, to assume that what seemed to be, was. Too easy, even for one who knew better. And way too dangerous.

"It started in my mind." I spoke tentatively.

He nodded his encouragement.

"At first it was just general thoughts about how nice it would be to help people. You know, the way you do, the way the counselors do. I kept thinking about how much I would like to do that. I think about it a lot, I really do, how maybe I could change my major in school from creative writing to psychology or social work or something. But then it just seems like it would be so long and hard and I get discouraged."

I heaved a heavy world-weary sigh and he accorded me a short nod and a smile.

"But this time I was thinking that I had already done that, all the training and stuff, I mean, and I could help people get better and all. Help them not be hurt and sad and just fix their problems, you know. And then I happened to find Marianne. So of course I talked to her to see how I could help and I was doing really well, believe me, and then the nurse came and—well, I don't want to be too critical or anything but she spoiled it pretty much. She's a *very* bossy person."

"Yes, that's true." The smile and nod again. "How did you happen to find Marianne?"

"Gosh." I made my face open, honest, guileless. "I guess I'm just a very curious kind of person, always poking my nose into things. Do you remember Curious George?"

Saunders looked puzzled.

"He's a monkey in a children's book," I explained.

"Ah." The puzzlement lifted.

"Well, I'm like that, I guess."

He held his chin thoughtfully. "I'm going to share something with you, Darby."

I smiled in a sappy, sychophantic kind of way.

"Marianne is much sicker than we realized at first. She is a manic-depressive and was suffering attacks. We have stabilized her condition and will now slowly be able to adjust her medications appropriately. She is, of course, receiving the best medical and physical care."

The vicious jab of a hypodermic needle into the bare, pink flesh of Marianne's buttock. "Of course."

"Interference could jeopardize her care and her improvement."

"I understand." I nodded solemnly

"It was a daydream you indulged in. You are *not* a trained professional. I know your interference was kindly meant but you must now agree to leave Marianne's care to us."

"All right." More solemn looks and nods on my part.

He stood.

I was dismissed. Free to go.

And he gave me The Smile again.

I shivered as I walked outside into the sunshine.

CHAPTER 53

You don’t really have a problem, do you?”

I jumped, caught off guard, then turned and smiled at Carrie. “Sure I do. I’m just good at hiding things. I—”

“I’m not buying it. You think I don’t know the difference between hiding and nuts? Wrong. I’m messed up big time. You’re . . . I’m not sure what you are but it’s not messed up big time.”

“Look, Carrie, we all have problems. Don’t make fun of me just because—”

“Fuck you.” Carrie’s voice was ugly and bitter.

I had nothing to say. She had taken me by surprise. Again.

“And the horse you rode in on,” she finished. “I don’t think you’re with the IRS, that sounded pretty bogus, but I don’t think you’re just another dysfunctional either. You’re here for a reason, aren’t you?”

“Yes, I’m—”

“You’re always asking questions, sneaking around and spying. You listen to people and watch and disappear and stay out late at night. Something’s going on. I know it is. So you’re not really fucked like the rest of us, you’re here to do something and when you finish you’ll leave, right?”

“I don’t know what you’re talking about,” I said quietly.

“I don’t know what you’re talking about.” She mimicked me.

“I’m here because I’ve got a problem, just like you.”

“I’m here because I’ve got a problem, just like you.”

My sarcastic echo again.

"Carrie, stop it, please."

"Carrie, stop it, please."

I walked away.

She ran after me and grabbed my arm. "It's not fair. It's *not*. You come here and act like one of us—maybe someone even likes you or something—and then BAM!—you're outta here. Just like that. Leaving us behind and everything. Not thinking about us or anything. Just AMF."

"What's AMF?" Lorie materialized out of a stand of trees and shrubs, startling us both.

Nobody answered her question.

"*Well?*" She tapped her foot sharply. "Well, what is it?"

"Tell her, Darby, *tell* her," Carrie snapped at me. "Tell her."

"Adios, motherfucker." I spoke the words without emphasis.

Lorie wrinkled her nose in obvious and well-bred distaste. "Are you going somewhere then, Darby?"

"No," I said calmly. "Not until my insurance runs out."

"That's a lie, nobody's insurance runs out after a week. You're going, I can tell. People who are leaving have a look about them, don't they, Lorie?"

"Yes." Lorie looked at me speculatively. "Yes, they do. Are you going, Darby?"

"Not until my insurance runs out," I said evenly. "And I don't know when that is, I told you."

"You're lying," Carrie said. "It's AMF time." She turned sharply on her heel and walked away.

"When?" Lorie asked.

I walked away too.

I was lying. I did know. I was leaving and it was soon, as soon as possible, tomorrow I hoped. I had called Joe earlier and told him to pull the plug on my "insurance coverage." I had had enough, and after getting caught with Marianne, things were getting a little hot. I didn't really believe that Saunders had bought into my daydream/fantasy story. And I *knew* Nurse hadn't. Carrie was right: it was AMF time.

But why was she so mad at me? It's not like I was the only one who played bad tennis. Tennis partners like me are a dime a dozen. And roommates and— *Okay,* I was the only one Carrie talked to about anything real. (Anything fuckin' real, in her words.) Friends were not exactly an excess commodity in her life.

This is a job, I reminded myself sternly. *And your job is private investigator, not social worker. Bust up this operation, get Carrie—and Marianne and Lorie—out of here and see what you can do to help. First things first.*

Sometimes lectures to myself help, sometimes they don't. So it goes.

Carrie refused to sit with me at dinner. Or talk to me. After dinner I went for a walk and looked for Hank in the stars. It was a beautiful night, clear and cool with dark skies and sparkly stars. But stars are cold and remote and Hank was warm and loving. *Was.* I thought of all the times I had heard people talk about the ones they had loved and lost in the past tense. I had felt sorry for them but I hadn't understood. Now I did. The past tense was as cold and remote as the stars.

I stayed outside until I had goose bumps and shivers.

Carrie slept with her face to the wall, her back to me. I wanted to hug her, to tell her the truth, to promise her hope and new beginnings. It was all there, I wanted to say, she just couldn't see it. Yet. But she would. I could promise that, I really could. I gazed at the thin sharp bones in her shoulders and arms, the turquoise hair. Tomorrow, tomorrow I would tell her—not the truth exactly, but something.

I woke up knowing something was wrong and not knowing what it was. A bad dream, I thought at first, but I didn't feel sad or scared or empty, the way I do after dreaming about Hank. Maybe it was just a bad, and restless, night. I had come in late; sometime even later I heard Carrie get up and quietly fuss around in the bathroom for what seemed like ages.

The first streaks of dawn were ripping through the sky, clawing their way into daylight and early consciousness. A few birds weighed in with isolated chirps, cheeps, and short trills, sounding lonesome and forlorn in the still-dark beginnings of the day. Carrie's breathing was labored and heavy.

Breathing.

I scrambled out of bed, rolled her over and shook her. Nothing. Her head lolled to one side like a goofy rag doll. A torn piece of paper that had maybe been in her hand before her fingers relaxed floated briefly and settled. "AMF." That was all it said. And more than enough. I raced for the bathroom and found a crumpled-up envelope with a lone pill and a half-empty glass of water. Overdose. I didn't recognize the pill but that meant nothing. I couldn't tell a sleeping pill from a vitamin.

I grabbed my phone and ran outside, punched in 911, called in an emergency drug overdose at the Sunflower Clinic in one of the cottages, victim comatose and breathing with difficulty. I hung up as the emergency operator started bleating frantic questions at me.

Get the front gate open and the EMTs in: that was first priority. There was an emergency bell in the infirmary. That was my next run. I punched it, held it for a minute at least. Nothing seemed to happen. Next stop the outdoor bell in front of the Main Hall that was sounded at mealtimes, lecture and movie times, and "in emergency." It cracked the early-morning quiet wide open. Wounded.

The kitchen crew was the first to respond, spilling out on the lawn in white coats and startled eyes. "Medical emergency," I hollered. "Call nine-one-one. Get someone to open the front gate *immediately*! Dr. Saunders's orders." The crew scattered every which way. I saw one of the cooks talking to a pajama-clad maintenance man who ran for the front gate. I started to breathe more easily.

And kept on ringing.

Carrie desperately needed anyone with medical training. Even the Bitch. She showed up minutes later (minutes!) in a bathrobe, a bad mood, and a vicious expression. I could hear sirens now.

"What in blazes do you think you're doing?" she shrieked at me as she grabbed for my bell-ringing arm.

I stopped. "It's Carrie in my cottage. She's having trouble breathing."

"Oh *right*. Sure she is," she muttered.

I glared at her and grabbed her arm. "Hurry *up*!" I tried to haul her along, tried to pick up the pace to a dead run.

She shook me loose and snarled, then ambled along the path, Sunday-at-the-park speed, her loose bedroom slippers slapping against the soles of her feet.

I ran ahead and opened the cottage door, then ran back and forth between her and the cottage trying to speed her up. Three guesses how successful that was. And I hated her more than I thought possible. Carrie didn't sound any better. Maybe worse. The sirens were very close now.

Nurse leaned over Carrie, listened to her breathing and poked her. "You stupid little slut." She spoke contemptuously. "I oughta smack you into tomorrow." She raised her hand.

"That wouldn't be such a good idea." I said it quietly, but with menace. She startled, apparently having forgotten I was there.

I walked out and started waving my arms and hollering at the EMT response vehicle which had hesitated in the driveway. Sirens going, lights flashing, it headed across the lawn toward me.

They were very professional. Everyone was cleared out of the cottage in a nanosecond and they had Carrie on a stretcher and hooked up to an IV in minutes. People were everywhere now, half dressed, wide-eyed and fearful. Whispers ran rampant. Nurse stood with her arms folded and glared at anyone unwise enough to meet her gaze. Not me. The minute they loaded Carrie into the van I faded into the background.

Fast. And made my way to the front gate. Fast. I wanted to be out of here. Faster than fast. Yesterday. I especially wanted to be out of here before the shit hit the fan. Maybe someone besides me had called 911 and no one would figure out that there had been two emergency calls and that one of them was me (someone presumably without access to a phone). Maybe no one would notice that I had been the one ringing the bell and issuing orders this morning, and that I had claimed Saunders's authority.

Maybe. But it was a stretch.

I was running again. The plan was to slip out through the gate just before the EMT van exited. The theory was no one would notice in all the excitement. Or that if they did, I would be long gone before anyone could do anything about it.

Plans and theories are fine—as far as they go. Fine, not flawless. There was a man stationed at the gate waiting to open it for the emergency vehicle. He was burly and buffed. And I didn't think I could take him. Not without a few more wild cards than I had in my hand.

My heart sank, my throat stopped up, my stomach tied itself in knots. AMF. I was back to that again.

I walked back to the cottage dragging my feet like an eight-year-old on the way to detention, my mind a sleek engine racing in overdrive dual-exhaust power-surge superwhammy-blastoff mode. *Wait for the cottage to clear out, pick up my gun, clamber over the back fence and hit the trail.* I slid into a little thicket and briefly scrunched up in the bushes, reported in the latest—including my almost certainly blown cover—to Joe.

It was a perfect morning, cloudless blue skies, happy frolicsome birds. Good guys and bad guys. Okay, almost perfect. I could see Saunders not far from my cottage. My feet slowed even more. I was sure he wanted to talk to me and, for obvious reasons, it wasn't mutual. Nurse stood next to him pretending she was a concrete pillar. I thought how nice it would be if a bird flew over and pooped on her. I thought too how nice it would have been if I'd been able to get Marianne out as well as Carrie. Soon, I promised myself.

Meanwhile I was drifting, camouflaging myself with a small group of people, close but not amongst them, my eye on them and Saunders both.

Which is why I overlooked Sara.

CHAPTER 54

Her eyes widened, her eyebrows shot up, and her mouth dropped. I pretended I didn't notice. She was fifteen feet away. I speeded up, lengthened the distance.

"Kat?" The voice was tentative and with an edge of doubt. "Kat?"

And persistent.

I picked up the pace again, joined a small knot of people in front of the Main Hall—who were traveling at the speed of snails—and drifted into the dining room where coffee, juice, and gossip was in full swing.

I slipped from group to group, apparently headed for the coffee, then glanced around quickly and peeled off into the kitchen. They were drinking coffee and gossiping there too. What a place. No friendship and support, no work ethic. What a deal.

I frowned at the cook who was frowning at me. "Isn't there any decaf?"

"Who are you?"

"And fresh juice?"

"Huh?"

I frowned again, walked through the kitchen and out the back door. No Sara. The cottage was empty. Lorie and Patsy had joined the gossipers somewhere, I assumed. I changed quickly into jeans, collected my gun, and put the money and credit card in the bottom of my shoe.

AMF time.

I could only play Sara for stupid for so long. Ten minutes was my guess, and that had come and gone. She would be looking for me. I gazed out the window and saw no sign of her—not that the coast was exactly clear but this was no time to be picky. I sauntered out the door and down a back path.

"Darby!"

Patsy. I sucked in my breath and tucked my head down in instinctive ostrich reflex. Guess what? It worked about as well for me as it did for ostriches.

"Darby, did you hear what happened? Where are you going?" She had trotted over to join me and now struggled to keep up. "Slow down, okay?"

I eased up slightly, resigned to her company. And Sara would probably be looking for one, not two. "What happened?"

"It was Carrie. I heard a lot of different things, I guess no one exactly knows. It was a heart attack or convulsions, a diabetic coma or even a drug overdose. But how would she get drugs in here? I saw her, she just looked *awful*." Her face was lit with a ghoulish interest and satisfaction. "Where are you going?"

"Into the woods. I like to sit at a beautiful little waterfall. Do you want me to show you?"

"Okay. Where were you? Didn't you notice anything about Carrie, hear her being sick or anything?"

I shook my head.

"I've never known anyone who tried to commit suicide, have you? I wonder what goes through a person's head. Do they imagine themselves dead? Do they think about how people will stare and talk and how it will be an unexplained death and the coroner will chop them up into little pieces and—"

"She is my friend, Patsy. Stop it."

Her eyes were animated, her face flushed and excited. "And then it will make the newspaper and everyone will talk—"

We reached the woods and I spoke. "Go away. I don't care to show you the waterfall after all."

She pouted prettily. "Don't be mad. It's all so interesting. I've just never known anyone who tried to kill themselves before, have you?"

"Yes."

Avid, greedy eyes. "How do they do it?"

"Some do it quickly with pills, in a moment of despair. Others kill themselves slowly, stuffing, gorging themselves on food over many years." I spoke in a flat toneless voice.

She stared at me and then turned. In the distance I heard the bell for breakfast ring. I scrambled through the woods headed for the back fence. It took me two tries. Not because of the height and difficulty but because the iron spikes on top were sharp. And then I was down, walking fast, heading for my getaway car. Free as a breeze.

I would have made it too except for the dogs. A Doberman and a rottweiler, both black. Like the dogs of hell. They were young animals, fast and strong, with pink mouths, white teeth, and strings of drool hanging from their jaws. They loped languidly up beside me and cut me off, smiling demonically, I thought, through the trails of drool.

Until I tried to move forward. And then they snarled and growled and their eyes got red-rimmed, their mouths opened and the sunlight flashed off their white, sharp teeth. I hate Dobies and rottweilers. And I'm not just saying this because of them.

The burly guy who had been at the gate was with the dogs. There was a surprise.

The jig's up."

The jig's up? "Nobody says that anymore, Sara. Talk about passé." I made no effort to hide the contempt in my voice.

Sara laughed.

Saunders stared. First at her, then at me, looking bewildered.

"I underestimated you, Kat. That was a mistake."

"You've made a lot of mistakes, Sara, and they're all catching up with you now."

"I think not." She smiled gently, serenely. "I know how you like to bluff, Kat."

"What's going on?" Saunders sounded as puzzled as he looked. "Why did you call her 'cat'? Her name is Darby. Darby Sheffield."

Sara tossed back her head and laughed. I imagined the Dobie and rottweiler sinking their teeth into her slim white beautiful neck. A pleasant thought.

"Her name is Kat Colorado. She is the private investigator I hired."

Saunders looked at me. It would be fair to say that it was not a friendly look. "Not Darby," he stated.

"Not Darby," Sara agreed. "Let me hazard a guess, Walker. Whenever there's been trouble, a disturbance, anything out of the ordinary, she's been around. Did she know the young woman who attempted suicide?"

He nodded. "They shared the same room."

I smiled brightly. "A coincidence."

"And who reported it, made it public by calling nine-one-one?"

"We don't know, Sara."

"Tank found a phone on her, remember?"

Tank was the name of the guy with the dogs, one of those rare instances of truth in advertising.

Saunders frowned. "She is the one we found in the attic with Marianne."

Sara nodded. "Exactly."

"Another coincidence," I said brightly.

"Nurse says she's a troublemaker."

"Me?" I put a stunned and surprised look on my face. "*Me?* You're *kidding*."

"Oh shut up." Sara spoke wearily. "At least I'm not paying you anymore."

"No. You're not. Insurance companies are."

The expression "you could have heard a pin drop"? I always thought it was a cliché without factual foundation. I was wrong.

"Insurance companies?" Saunders's voice broke the silence.

"She's bluffing." Sara, with scorn and disgust in her voice.

They both looked at me.

"No. I'm not."

And I was through playing games. I would not make the mistake Sara had, of underestimating an opponent or the danger in a situation. I was in trouble—Tank and the dogs were nothing to this—and I was on my own. I played my cards carefully.

"What are you doing for them?" Saunders.

"Go to hell." Sara.

I went with Saunders. "By the time I quit working for Sara I had a pretty good idea what was going on. I knew about the clinic and that Sara was a top recruiter as well as in a business and a personal relationship with you.

"I had reason to suspect that treatment at the clinic was virtually nonexistent but of course I couldn't prove that without more detail. I am working for Consolidated Insurance Investigations. They contract out on jobs to a number of insurance companies, and they do a lot of undercover fraud work. To say that they and their clients were interested in my story and willing to back me in an undercover investigation is putting it mildly."

Saunders was white-faced and silent, a picture of dignified and wronged innocence. It didn't work on me but maybe it would on a jury. Professionals always act so surprised when they get caught with their hands in the till.

I smiled at him.

Sara glared at both of us, then spoke fiercely. "She's making this up, faking it. Don't say a thing. She can't prove anything. It's a bluff, *all* of it."

"Shall I tell you what I know?" I queried.

Saunders nodded and Sara stared blankly at me.

"All right. Prove it, just fucking prove it," she snarled.

And I smiled again. I was on solid ground here. "Oriental rugs, antiques, fresh flowers." I gazed around Saunders's office. "You've got a nice thing going here. How about tea and cookies?"

Sara snarled again. I took that for a no. Her company manners needed work, that was for sure.

"I know how you recruit, and the names and salaries of your recruiters. I know about the expansion plans, another clinic this fall, perhaps one in the spring. I know patients are admitted on the basis of their insurance coverage, not their problem and that they are not discharged until that coverage is exhausted. I have personal knowledge of the setup here and the complete lack of treatment, counseling, therapy, and all the other things touted so highly in your glossy brochure."

I was on a roll, no question about it. And I had a captive audience.

"I have copies of paperwork on all of that, as well as of the job applications of your staff. These applications provide ample evidence of the total lack of training and competence of your staff for the positions for which they were hired. I have evidence not just of a lack of care but of abuse. Marianne comes to mind, Carrie as well."

"That's impossible. There's no way you could know, never mind have copies of all that." Saunders spoke briskly.

"She's a snoop, Walker. She's gone through your office and files and everything she can get her hands on." Sara was furious.

"Is that true?" Saunders sounded outraged.

I agreed to it.

"We need to kill her."

Sara spoke softly, almost sweetly. The anger, the fear, the sarcasm, were gone; she spoke as one who was sure, decided, and content.

Saunders frowned. "Sara, please. This is serious."

"Yes. We need to kill her."

He shook his head petulantly, as though a fly were annoying him. "I thought you said she was bluffing."

"I was wrong, she's not."

"Are you bluffing?" Saunders was slugging his way through this much more slowly than Sara.

"No. Consolidated Insurance Investigations has copies of everything I cited above, including my daily reports." I turned to Sara. "Killing me won't help. Your problem is a lot bigger than me now."

"That's a bluff." Sara's voice was confident. "Killing her will help. It will end the whole sorry mess and we can go on as we have been. Worst-case scenario, we have to start over someplace else, but maybe not. Probably not." She bestowed a sunny, almost beatific smile on Saunders and then on me.

"Dead meat, that's you, Kat," she announced cheerily.

"Sara," Saunders demurred.

"Think of it as war, Walker. You were in Vietnam, you understand. Sometimes people get in your way. They become your enemy and then you have to remove them."

Get in your way. Remove. We were back to dead meat.

"Like Lorraine," I said.

The sunshine faded from Sara's face.

"Who is Lorraine?" Saunders asked.

"She was a friend of Sara's, the first person Sara killed."

"She fought so hard." Sara spoke dreamily. "I thought I'd never get her in the river. And then she tried to climb out. I had to hit her over the head with a stick, make her go under and drown."

Walker Saunders stared at Sara in horror.

"Sara tried to frame Jed for that murder but it didn't work."

"Jed?" Saunders asked.

"He was the next one she was going to kill. He hadn't figured out all of it, not nearly as much as I have but—"

"But he would have." Sara still spoke dreamily.

"Yes. And he was a cop. He wouldn't have let it go, so—"

"Dead meat." Sara smiled.

"You killed Jed?" Saunders asked.

"Not yet. My guess is that Sara would have gotten around to him soon and very openly. She had used me as an independent witness to establish a pattern of stalking and abuse. The stalking was true, he was trying to figure out what she was up to; the abuse was not. Sara would have killed him and then claimed self-defense. She had me, other witnesses, even cops to back her up."

"I did a nice job with that one." Her voice was sunny and complacent. "I would have gotten away with it too. I still will. And with killing you, Kat. I'll get away with that too."

"You tried once already and failed."

"The guy who roughed you up and stole your car? I told him just to scare you. Of course, if I'd known then what I know now, I would have had him finish you off."

She paused and a meditative look crossed her face.

"I could shoot her, Walker, like I'm going to shoot Jed but it would be better if it was something else. Maybe drugs? Or a drowning? What do you think? Something that looks like an accident and won't bother anyone. Well . . ." That beatific smile again. "Except *her* of course." She laughed a sweet little laugh that was only slightly sinister.

Saunders smiled, tight-lipped and hard. Vietnam was one thing; business was another, and killing was not the way he dealt with business problems.

So it bothered him too. Was he a wild card now?

Maybe the odds here were improving.

CHAPTER 55

Dear Charity,

Because of a minor disagreement with my host—I wanted to leave the party early—I have been locked up in the basement. Surely this is a bit extreme, not to mention rude? Although I don't like losing my temper, I would really like to punch them in the nose. What do you think?

Irate

Dear Irate,

Punching people in the nose is correctly interpreted as losing your temper. And why not in such a case?

Charity

I finished constructing that letter in my mind and thought about making up another, but frankly, my heart wasn't in it. I examined the dark basement room again, cobwebs, spiders, and dust everywhere. Yuck.

As it turned out, I had been overly optimistic about the odds improving.

Saunders and Tank had escorted me down here at least an hour, maybe two ago. I had no watch and it was hard to keep track of time. No one had brought me tea and cookies either. And I had asked so nicely too. I got up, and out of boredom, made the rounds again. Twelve-by-fifteen-foot room with no closets, a cubbyhole with a filthy toilet, no sink, a number of old filing cabinets, a broken-down brocade easy chair, and a small window nailed shut and with a metal grate over it. The closest thing to a weapon was the toilet plunger. Not promising.

Where the hell was Joe? It was time for the cavalry to arrive.

Not that he was supposed to arrive, but still—if he hadn't heard from me the least he could do was check up on me. No?

So where the hell was he?

The devil makes mischief with idle hands. I could hear the echo of Alma's words as I had heard them so many times as a child. I hadn't been there two minutes, bored and restless, before I decided to make trouble. Using the toilet plunger I knocked out the glass in the window. And bent the grate, which turned out to be old and rusted. The window was too small for me to get out of, but not by much. I surveyed my handiwork with satisfaction. Very suspicious.

Okay, I was ready.

It was a long time before anything happened. I heard a lock turn in the door and got into place, only to be startled by who entered. Nurse. But why was I surprised? She did a lot of the dirty work. And she was tough.

She exclaimed when she saw the window, walked over and peered out. And let her guard down. Big mistake. I whacked her on the back of the knees with the toilet plunger. Not exactly King Arthur and his jousting knights but it took her down. Gracelessly, on her knees, and with a loud crash. A packet scuttled across the floor. I shoved it away with my foot and closed the door.

"Hi!" I gave her a cheery little greeting. Nothing like adding insult to injury.

She glared at me with malevolent eyes.

"You say or do anything except what I tell you and you'll get hurt."

"You and what army?" she snarled as she started to get up.

I took the gun out of my pocket. It had, until recently, been in the ankle holster. Tank had been a little careless about searching me. Tsk tsk.

"You are going to lie on your stomach, quietly, while I tape your hands and feet. One wrong move and I whack you. Go ahead." I smiled. "Give me a reason, even a feeble little excuse. Please," I begged her. "Make my day." Yeah, I know it's overdone, but I couldn't resist.

She lay on her stomach. God, I love duct tape. Someone had tossed the end of a roll in the bathroom—just for me. I taped her hands behind her back and her ankles. Then I rolled her over with my foot. It took all I had not to kick her. I ripped off another piece of tape and put it over her mouth. And looked at the fear in her eyes.

"Be a good girl, nurse." I said it in an evil voice. "I'll be back." The fear in her eyes deepened. I picked up the case—the same one I had seen in Marianne's room—expecting to find a syringe. And I did. "Is this what you used on Marianne? Nod or shake your head." Nothing. I leaned down and ripped the tape off her face. She cried out. "Shall we try that again?" I inquired pleasantly.

"Yes," she whispered.

"What is it?"

"Thorazine."

I checked the labeling to be sure she was telling me the truth. Yes on both the loaded syringe and a backup vial. And put another piece of tape on her mouth. "No noise, is that clear?" Nothing. I reached down for the tape and she started nodding vigorously, tears in her eyes. Bullies never like it when the shoe is on the other foot. I stuck the hypodermic packet in my back pocket and headed for the door. I had thought of asking Nurse what was happening upstairs but I wasn't up to wearing her down, and I couldn't stomach abuse. Threats, sure—but not abuse. I closed the door behind me.

I had a gun and a needle. Armed and dangerous—that's what I hoped.

It's not that I wasn't a brave little go-getter with plenty of guts and grit. I was. I am. It's that I was realistic. I was armed, I was dangerous, and I was also badly outnumbered. And that wasn't even counting the dogs, not to mention Tank, who more than made up for the temporary elimination and sidelining of Nurse. My plan was simple: Run like hell. Choke 'em in my dust.

Anything in the front of the building was out, that was Tank's territory. So I was headed for the back forty again, and another fun climb over the spiked iron fence. By my estimate I didn't have much time. Once Nurse was discovered Tank and the dogs would be back out on perimeter patrol.

Déjà vu all over again.

The only way out of the basement was the way I had come in, a short staircase lit by a feeble bulb. I counted the steps, cut the light, and up I went, listened at the door for noise and bad guys. Fun. I've had *almost* as much fun at an amusement park on a death-defying ride with a failed safety bar. The lock was an old-fashioned bolt on the staircase side, the kind that could be set by releasing a catch. I released it as I came through the door. Anything to slow down the discovery of the trussed-up nurse.

I slipped out into the hallway, blinking in the bright light. Here's where a disguise in my back pocket, or at least a reversible jacket and a baseball cap, would have come in real handy. I zipped down the hall wearing my oh-so-nonchalant-unfurtive-and-perfect-patient demeanor. It seemed to work really well but that was pretty much because I hadn't run into anyone yet. I curbed my complacency as I was still in the bad-news stretch of the building, with Saunders's office and the interview rooms to go.

Past the first one.

The second.

The third.

Almost to the door leading out to the back lawn, almost home free.

"Walker! She's out. Get Tank and the dogs."

Almost isn't there.

I dropped nonchalant and started running, swerved and took a left down the corridor. The back forty was out, or rather was now Tank and the dogs. *Been there, done that.*

Hot damn!

I stopped for the red box, grabbed the little hammer, smashed the glass and pulled the switch. And all hell broke loose. It was just as much fun as I thought it might be, although I felt a little guilty about the fact that there was no fire. I wondered if it was a felony to falsely report a fire. Not that felony false alarms were my number one problem now; felony murder was. Felony murder of me. I raced out the side door and headed for the Main Hall and the bell.

Yeah, I know, it was the same trick I'd pulled earlier, but *you* try to be creative and do your best thinking when any second there will be a Dobie and a rottweiler on your heels, not to mention people who think killing you is a good idea.

I started whacking the clapper off that bell the minute I reached it.

"Fire! Evacuate the premises at once. Proceed to the front gate. Fire! Evacuate the premises at once. Proceed to the front gate. Fire! Evacuate the premises at once. Proceed to the front gate. Fire!" I had a sudden glimpse of what Paul Revere must have felt like—although I am the first to admit that it would have been more exciting if I had been on a horse.

People were everywhere, disoriented, confused, running around in random patterns like headless chickens. I dropped the bell rope to join the chickens.

"The front gate!" I hollered, grabbing people and aiming them in the right direction with a friendly little shove. I wanted to keep the momentum up before someone noticed that there was no smoke. And that I had been the one ringing the bell and sounding the alarm. By that point a lot of people were tearing toward the front gate, jumpy and excited. Just like me.

I allowed myself a touch of complacency, a little smugness. This was working out well. Nothing about me stood out, I was just one more in the hysterical crowd. Hot damn. I hoped the fire trucks were as fast as the EMT van.

Someone bumped into me, stumbled and almost fell. I grabbed for her, set her on her feet and her way again.

"Thank you," she gasped. "Oh God, it's you, Darby."

"Lorie, watch out or you'll get run over."

I tweaked her out of the way of a guy in the kitchen crew who was streaking by in his whites. The phrase "women and children first" clearly meant nothing to him. "Here. Scoot." I propelled her along in front of me. "Pick up your feet!" I caught her as she stumbled again.

Where the hell were the fire trucks?

I moved away from Lorie into a knot of people I didn't know. It didn't matter. The trucks would be here. The gates would be open. And I would be out of here. *Sayonara, Sunflower!*

You'd think I would know by now, would remember the bit about famous last words. And *it ain't over till it's over*. And not *until the fat lady sings*.

Someone grabbed me by the elbow and yanked me out of the parade. A fairly strong someone. I didn't go willingly. And I was off balance and off guard or I wouldn't have gone at all. By the time I rallied I was staring down the barrel of a small gun. Not that it mattered—small, medium, or large, a gun was a gun.

"Nice try." Sara smiled. "Too bad it didn't work."

I shrugged, playing for time. *Where the hell were the fire trucks?*

"Walker called in a false alarm." Her smile widened. "There aren't going to be any handsome firemen in pretty red trucks to rescue you."

It was a blow, I admit it. Not that I planned to give Sara the satisfaction of seeing my disappointment. "Fire*fighters*," I corrected, assuming what nonchalance—not much—I could. "Firemen is outdated."

She laughed in my face, sounding happy and cheerful. *Jeez.* That was really adding insult to injury. And waved the gun at me, which by now she had slipped mostly up her sleeve.

"We are going back into the main building. We will walk closely together and I will have this cute little gun aimed at your spine. You know what that means, right? You will never walk again, maybe not even sit up, if I shoot. I'm a pretty good shot, did I mention that? And please, do not make the mistake of thinking I won't use this."

That was not a mistake I would make, not while I could feel the gun nudging my waist. Theoretically I could have ignored her threat. Who cared about a shot or two since she planned to kill me? But that was her theory, not mine, and naturally, a great deal more appealing to her than to me.

We started off in our own little two-man parade, me dillydallying as much as I could, Sara shoving me in the back with her gun. Behind us I could hear the bell ringing again and people shouting "All clear!"

It was tough giving up on the fire trucks, let me tell you.

"Darby, wait up."

I waited; Sara jabbed; Lorie scampered up and joined us. My mind swung into high gear frantically trying to figure out a way to use this to my advantage.

"What are you doing? Want to get a lemonade?"

"Yes." She was in front of me, Sara behind. I silently mouthed the words *fire alarm* and made a slight pulling motion with my hand.

"You'll excuse us, I know." Sara spoke in frigid tones. "We have business to take care of."

I mouthed and motioned again. Lorie stared at me, her jaw a little droopy, her eyes confused. Just a guess here, but I'm betting mime was never a favorite entertainment of hers. I mouthed a silent *Help!* as Sara marched me off, up the front stairs and into Saunders's office where he was pacing the floor, hands behind his back, frown on his face. The frown deepened as we entered but he didn't break stride. Sara marched me across the room and over to an elegant wing chair.

"Sit," she ordered, as though I were a dog.

I sat. As did she in the wing chair facing me, the gun pointing squarely at my midriff.

"Where is Mrs. Riley?" Saunders stopped pacing and fired the abrupt question in my direction.

"Who?" I was genuinely puzzled.

"The nurse," Sara explained.

"Oh. She seems so inhuman, I never thought about her having a name. *Mrs.* Someone *married* her? Does she have a first name too?"

"Answer the question," Sara snapped.

"I don't know."

"What happened?"

"What do you mean?" I did puzzled and waited hopefully for the fire alarm.

No one went for puzzled. Big surprise. I was afraid Lorie hadn't bought into the fire alarm concept.

"What happened when she came down to the basement?"

"Came down? To the basement?" I did incredulity in spite of my lack of success with puzzled. "I never saw her."

Saunders frowned. "The door was locked. How did you get out?"

"Through the window."

"It's not big enough."

I shrugged. "You'd be surprised. I'm a good squirmer."

"Walker, let it *go*. We have business to do."

Her tone was ugly. Uh-oh. And I was probably the business too.

"We need to take care of her."

"Take care of"—was that the same as "remove"? I looked from Sara to Saunders.

His expression was adamant. "For twenty-four hours only. That will give us enough time to get everything together and get out of here."

"I don't want to leave. We don't have to leave. We have a great setup here. All we have to do is eliminate Kat and we're fine."

"Not a pretty picture is it, Walker?" I assumed the informal mode of address. All this bandying about of my life had made me reckless with manners. "The woman you love is turning out to be a charming, well-dressed, bloodthirsty, innocents-slaughtering psychopath."

"You *shut* up," Sara hissed.

Saunders looked at me.

"I know it would give me pause, being in a business relationship with her. Never mind a personal one. Remember Samson? First she kills me, then—who knows?—maybe you?"

Sara shot out of her seat like a rabid dog on amphetamines and advanced with her gun in a swell position for pistol-whipping the tar out of me. Talk about resting my case. I stuck my tongue out at her—she wasn't the only one who could add insult to injury, and there is nothing I enjoy more than seeing bad guys lose control.

"Sara!" Saunders moved quickly, grabbing her arm and swinging her around, pulling her away.

I moved just as quickly, jerking the box out of my back pocket, yanking the syringe out of the box. I pulled the plunger out, rammed the syringe into Sara's butt, right through her clothing, slammed the plunger home. *This one's for you, Marianne.*

And yeah, sure, I know what you're going to say—I should have used a cotton ball and rubbing alcohol first.

Ask me if I cared.

Ask me if I enjoyed Sara's shriek.

She sagged into Saunders and he grabbed for her, trying, no doubt, to figure out what the hell was going on. He had missed the needle fun while he was struggling with Sara. I grabbed for her gun while he was wrestling with her dead weight—not much of a delay factor in Thorazine—stuck it in my pocket and pulled my .380 out of the ankle holster—*Never trust a gun you don't know*—then tossed the syringe on the chair.

"Put the woman down." Cold, hard, loud voice.

Saunders stared at me. Sara was almost out now. I had never seen Thorazine at work before and it was impressive. My gun was trained on him.

He laid her on the rug, half held his hands up as if to say, *No problem.* "There's absolutely no need for violence. You heard me. I never wanted to deal with things that way."

"Lie on the floor facedown. Do it!" I snarled as he hesitated. "Or there will be violence."

He did it.

"Turn your face to the wall."

He did that too.

"Don't move."

I backed up, placed my gun on the chair within easy reach, grabbed the syringe and the extra vial of Thorazine, loaded up, and nailed Saunders in the butt. *Another one for you, Marianne.* He groaned and rolled, grabbing for me.

Not a chance. I saw that coming and was way too fast.

He tried to get up but he knew he wasn't going to make it, I could see it in his eyes. Hatred and violence too. It was a good bet that he had changed his relatively friendly attitude toward me. Not that I cared. I didn't plan to be there when he came to.

He could tell it to the cops; they got paid to listen to bad guys whine. I picked up the phone and punched out 911. I had no idea how long Thorazine lasted and I wanted cops here—lots of them—before I found out.

CHAPTER 56

"Jesus Christ."

It looked bad—I would be the first to admit that—bodies littering up the floor every which way. The cops looked at me like I was, say, Lizzie Borden meets Attila the Hun in today's pale flesh and cold blood.

"They're not dead, they're drugged. And there's another one tied up in the basement."

"*Jesus* Christ," the cop said again.

"The whole place has to be searched to be sure that there are no patients locked up and drugged. I know of at least one."

"*Jesus* Christ."

It was a limited repertoire, true, but he said it with feeling.

The fire alarm went off.

Hey, better late than never. That Lorie, what a little trouper.

I didn't make a quick getaway. Neither did Joe, who came to lay out the situation from the insurance company perspective. The whole thing was a long, involved process. What kept me going was the thought that all the information we provided fattened the legal file in the case against Saunders and Sara.

By then the place was swarming with people. Social workers to explain things to the patients and notify their families, ambulances to pick up Marianne and a young woman by the name of Claudia Jansen. She was, the cops told me, a world-famous pianist. She had attempted suicide at the Sunflower and, although stable, was unconscious and heavily sedated.

To say that we were all horrified doesn't really cover it.

The file got fatter.

Joe finally checked us into the Calistoga Hotel. That night we ate in the little restaurant across the street from the hotel and drank Napa Valley wine. I couldn't get all the people at the Sunflower, hungry for help and direction, out of my mind, not even with Joe's quiet sensible words and the wine.

In the morning I went to the hospital to visit Carrie. It took me a moment to recognize her—they'd washed the turquoise out of her hair and she looked pale and pretty.

She was surprised but pleased. "How did you get out?" Her first words.

"I busted the place."

"Busted it?"

"Wide open." I grinned. "Cops, ambulances, county social workers, the DA's office, fire trucks—thanks to Lorie as well as me, the EMT van . . ." I paused and took a deep breath. "Insurance investigators, irate patient families, the dogcatcher, and a partridge in a pear tree," I finished on a musical note.

She stared at me for a long time, wide-eyed and openmouthed. "Wow. You're my idol. You did all that and you look so harmless, so . . . so normal."

"I am pretty much, until I get riled."

"What do you mean?"

"I never would have gotten involved with the Sunflower if a client of mine hadn't tried to use me. I dropped the case, but by then I was pissed off enough to follow up on it, and on her."

"And bring her down?"

"Yes."

She thought things over. "So you're okay, you're not fucked up?"

"I'm fucked up, I'm just handling it on my own this time; and this time you need help. Both happen. Both are hard."

She thought that one through too. "How are you fucked up?"

"The man I was going to marry was killed."

"Did you love him a lot?"

"Yes."

"And you didn't get to say goodbye or anything?"

"No."

"That's hard."

"Yes. Are you getting help that makes sense to you here?"

"Yeah. I guess. So now I'll never see you again?"

"You wish."

She giggled.

"I'll be back. And I'll give you my phone number."

"Is Darby your real name?"

I laughed. I'd forgotten Darby already. "No, it's Kat Colorado. I'm a private investigator."

She nodded. "Yeah, that fits you and it's better than Darby."

"Want to hear about the bust? I nailed the nurse."

"No!" She laughed. "The Bitch?"

I didn't leave until they kicked me out. Carrie told me she was dyeing her hair pink and orange and gave me a hug.

Do you know a good criminal lawyer?"

Jill gave me a noncommittal lawyer stare. "What is this in reference to?"

"Sara is in jail."

"A driving accident?"

"In her dreams."

"Jed. Oh my God, was it Jed? Did he attack her and—" Her imagination gave out.

"It wasn't Jed, not in that way. Jed turned out to be pretty much an innocent pawn in all this. She used him as she used me."

"Pawn? Used him, used you? Katy, what are you talking about? No, never mind that for now. What is Sara charged with?"

"Murder, attempted murder, kidnapping, fraud, extortion, parking on the wrong side of a one-way street, tying her shoes sloppily, chewing stale gum—they pretty much threw the book at her. And her partner."

"Partner?"

"Dr. Walker Saunders. The two of them had a nice little racket going at a place called the Sunflower Health Spa and Clinic." It took me a long time to tell it, to fill in all the details. And, periodically, to wait for Jill to catch up. She was still having a hard time thinking of Sara as a murderer and a con artist rather than an innocent victim of spousal abuse.

We came full circle, ending where we started, talking about criminal lawyers. I asked Jill to call Belinda. I couldn't face two more interminable conversations with people who thought that Sara was as innocent as the day was long and as pure as the driven snow.

In the *slammer*?" Jed was dumbfounded.

I had meant to do a better job, really I had, to be reasoned and logical and all that, but I hadn't, I had just blurted it out.

"In the slammer," I agreed. "It was criminal, you were right. And there was a man involved, you were right about that too." I threw the details at him as quickly as possible. I was tired of this story. And of Sara and Saunders and greed. Murder too.

"She killed Lorraine," I went on, still struggling against the tide.

"No. Impossible. You're wrong about that, I know you are."

"She confessed to it."

He put his head in his hands. "Why?"

"To make you look bad, to make the situation look serious, to interest me. I don't know, Jed. All of those are possibilities. I don't think she cares much about anyone but herself. She planned to kill me. And you. I think she would have eliminated—that's the kind of word she used, not killed—her business partner and lover if he got in her way."

"She loved me." He ignored my comment about Sara planning to kill him.

I said nothing. His marriage was over, his wife was in jail, who was I to shatter an illusion?

"I know she did." His voice was fierce. "I know it. What did she tell you?" He was urgent, demanding.

"She spoke about sex, not love, about how great the sex was with you."

"*And* about how much she loved me."

"No. Let it go, Jed."

But he didn't. He couldn't.

I thought about the classical pianist whose hands had lain still and white on the coverlet at the Sunflower. Would she play again? And about Carrie with pink and orange hair, chasing dreams instead of bugs.

Illusions, nightmares, and drugs are everywhere. And the answers? Maybe somewhere in love and music and dreams. I hope so.

Jed clenched his hands into fists as though he could pound reality into the shape he wished. As though he were willing to try as often as it took. As though reality were something that could be pounded.

His love was dead to him and he was fighting it.

Just as I was, just as everyone did.

I had seen too many old movies not to know how it should end. The bad guys are brought to justice and pay dearly. The good guys and the lovers live happily ever after and the hero rides off into the sunset.

There was no news from Davis. No answers. No bad guys brought to justice and paying. No triumphant ride into the sunset and no happily ever after.

The movies are not what they are cracked up to be and life is never black and white.

One cool shimmering spring morning, tears in my eyes, the air heavy with the scent of honeysuckle, roses, and gardenias, the bird songs and insect noises a wild, passionate cacophony, I said goodbye to Hank.

When the fat lady sings, is it a happy song?